The Wrong Witch
THE COMPLETE SERIES

ANNIE ANDERSON

SPELLS & SLIP-UPS, MAGIC & MAYHEM, and ERRORS & EXORCISMS
Arcane Souls World
The Wrong Witch Complete Series

International Bestselling Author
Annie Anderson

All rights reserved
Copyright © 2022 Annie Anderson
Paperback ISBN: 978-1-960315-19-9
Hardcover ISBN: 978-1-960315-06-9

No part of this book may be reproduced, distributed, transmitted in any form or by any means, or stored in a database retrieval system without the prior written permission from the author. You must not circulate this book in any format. Thank you for respecting the rights of the author.

This is a work of fiction. Names, characters, businesses, organizations, places, events, and incidents are either the products of the author's imagination or used in a fictitious manner. Any resemblance to actual persons, living or dead, or actual events is purely coincidental.

Edited by Angela Sanders
Cover Design by Tattered Quill Designs

www.annieande.com

Books by Annie Anderson

The Arcane Souls World

Grave Talker Series

Dead to Me

Dead & Gone

Dead Calm

Dead Shift

Dead Ahead

Dead Wrong

Dead & Buried

Soul Reader Series

Night Watch

Death Watch

Grave Watch

The Wrong Witch Series

Spells & Slip-ups

Magic & Mayhem

Errors & Exorcisms

The Lost Witch Series

Curses & Chaos

Hexes & Hijinx

THE ETHEREAL WORLD

PHOENIX RISING SERIES

(Formerly the Ashes to Ashes Series)

Flame Kissed

Death Kissed

Fate Kissed

Shade Kissed

Sight Kissed

ROGUE ETHEREAL SERIES

Woman of Blood & Bone

Daughter of Souls & Silence

Lady of Madness & Moonlight

Sister of Embers & Echoes

Priestess of Storms & Stone

Queen of Fate & Fire

IMMORTAL VICES & VIRTUES

HER MONSTROUS MATES

Bury Me

SPELLS AND SLIP-UPS

ARCANE SOULS WORLD: THE WRONG WITCH BOOK 1
ANNIE ANDERSON

Don't tell me the moon is shining; show me the glint of light on broken glass.

— ANTON CHEKHOV

CHAPTER 1

WREN

If fucking up were a superpower, I'd be considered a god by now.

This fact was no truer than right that second as I picked my way over the cobblestones on Factor's Walk, nearly turning my ankle in the process. Trying to right myself, I stumbled, knocking my shoulder into the brick façade, and nearly falling ass over tea kettle on the uneven stone.

It was as if the universe itself was waving a huge flashing neon sign that said I should turn around and never come back. Considering *who* I was and *where* I was, the universe was probably right, but I couldn't listen to the wisdom then.

Not with a life on the line.

The arcane side of Savannah was not a good spot for someone like me. As the designated degenerate fuckup of the

Bannister witch line, me stepping one toe into the hidden magical world was like slapping a bull's-eye on my ass.

Rubbing the now-sore spot on my skin, I gave myself a little pep talk.

Get it together, Wren. Ellie needs you right now.

As far as pep talks went, it was lame, but there wasn't much to be done about it now. Staring at my feet, I minced down the crooked lane, desperately trying not to fall again. Every tourist and their brother took a stroll down Factor's Walk at least once, the signs reminding them to watch their step. But if you stared too long at the walls, at the rows of historic buildings, at The Walk itself, even human eyes would pick up on the oddities.

Those nearly three-hundred-year-old bricks that had historians creaming all over themselves? Yeah, well, they were made of arcaner bones from the vampire wars in 1723.

That lane that should be straight, but wasn't? It followed a ley line—the former bloody battleground where so many lost their lives before the witches and wolves beat the vamps back.

Those little pockets of green in the middle of asphalt-laden streets? Those were portals just waiting to be used—put there by Fae and witches alike as a way to circumvent the bloody attacks that left so many of our kind turned or dead or worse.

Every part of the city I'd grown up in was practically built for arcaners—leaving me mostly stuck on the outside. But this particular section of town? Well, it had been off-limits to me since I was about ten.

No pity parties, Wren. You have shit to do.

Yanking up my big girl panties, I headed for the one place that might help me. Considering I'd already lowered myself to asking my mother—only to have her deny me—this was my last resort. Granted, what I was asking for broke about four arcane laws that I knew of—and probably a few I didn't—but I was desperate.

Ellie Whitlock was my best friend in the whole world, and she needed me. I'd relied on Ellie my entire life. She'd been my only friend in school, my only lifeline to a stable upbringing, and my only confidant in twenty years. We'd been BFFs since Pre-K—my mother making me go to school on the human side of town after an unfortunate incident at an arcane school when I was three. My fucked-up magic—or lack thereof—didn't affect Ellie or her family.

Hell, there were times I'd wished her family would have adopted me.

And now her mom was in the hospital and might not make it. The thought of losing Mrs. Whitlock made me want to scream. If Ellie had been my only friend, Alice had been my only mom. My parents hadn't ever been what one would call attentive. Hell, most of the time, I was pretty sure having me had been an accident—the pair of them too busy with their own love affair to actually parent their only child.

You'd think my mother would want to keep the woman who'd raised me alive, right? *Wrong.*

We can't interfere in human business, Wren. You know better than to ask me.

Rolling my eyes, I plodded ahead, my goal in sight. The Azalea Apothecary was the oldest witch shop in Savannah, but it was also the most rundown. The faded sign was a single storm away from falling off the building, the rusted bolts hanging on by a thread. But word on the street was that

Carmichael Jones was who you went to if you needed something off the books.

From what I'd heard—which was limited since I didn't exactly run in witch circles—Mr. Jones wasn't exactly a crook, but he wasn't exactly an upstanding gentleman, either. What he was for sure was a top-notch warlock who specialized in healings.

Whether or not he'd help me heal a human, though, was a whole other matter.

A shiver of unease raced down my spine as I clamped onto the rickety latch, and I had the strongest urge to not go in. Honestly, if I wasn't absolutely positive any spell I tried to do would backfire miserably, I would have turned tail and run. My gaze darted up and down Factor's Walk, the sensation of eyes on me nearly making me lose my nerve.

Ellie and Alice need you. Get it together.

Gritting my teeth, I snatched the door open and marched inside. Azalea Apothecary was no better on the inside than it was on the out. Dusty tables filled with odd trinkets and half-full jars gave way to bookcases stuffed with worn tomes and mounds of junk. Piles of random objects occupied the corners of the room hoarder-style, while bundles of dried herbs hung from every square inch of the ceiling. A grizzled gray man stood near the back of the crowded room near an ancient cash register, an unlit cigar hanging from the corner of his mouth.

"Get out," he barked, crossing his beefy arms over his substantial belly. "Ain't no way I'm gonna let a Bannister tromp all over my shop. Who knows what you'll break?"

Not that half the shit in this hovel wasn't broken already, but still, tears prickled at my eyes. Gritting my teeth against the sting, I managed to stand my ground. This wasn't the first time I'd been kicked out of a witch shop, and given my history, it wouldn't be the last.

"Please," I begged, reaching inside my bag for the wad of cash. Ellie and I had planned on moving in together after college, but here we were two years post-graduation, with no apartment in sight. Unearthing the fistful of bills, I held them in front of me to ward off my ousting. "I can pay."

His gaze snagged on the money in my hand, and he licked his chops. By the looks of this place, Mr. Jones hadn't seen a paying customer in longer than I'd been alive. "What? You stub your toe or somethin'? I ain't wasting my time on no silly girl with a hangnail."

Don't back talk the healer, Wren. Don't do it.

"It's not for me, you judgmental ass. It's for my best friend's mom. Do you really think I'd be tromping through here looking for you if it was something I could fix with a nail clipper and a manicurist? I'm liable to get tetanus in this heap." Gnashing my teeth, I took a deep breath, doing my damnedest to not start screaming. "It's systemic organ failure. Can you fix that?"

Carmichael narrowed his eyes. "Your *friend's* mom. Not *your* mom?" A slow smile pulled across his lips, exposing yellowed teeth and a fair amount of tooth decay. "You have my interest. What class is your friend's mother? She a witch like you or..."

This was the sticking point. If I couldn't get him to agree, Alice had no hope. It wasn't like I could bribe my way into my mother's good graces or beg my father.

"Human," I breathed, praying he wouldn't make a fuss.

He simply blinked at me for a solid thirty seconds. "I'm sorry—what was that?"

Stomping through the piles of junk, I slapped the money on the counter before reaching into my bag for the second roll of bills. It was my entire savings. Everything I'd squirreled away to set myself up. It wasn't just an apartment I was getting. It was a chance.

But it meant nothing if Alice wasn't breathing.

"She's human," I hissed. "Are you gonna help me or not?" The bank teller had audibly squawked when I'd pulled every dime from my account, her face purpling when I'd asked for it in cash.

Carmichael reached for the bills, but I slapped his hand before he could get within an inch. "Are you helping, or am I going to have to go down to the River Walk and deal with them?"

The "them" in question were the Fae, and I had no intention of dealing with that sort at all. Ever. Making deals with the Fae was tantamount to jumping off a cliff with piranhas, sharks, and razor-sharp rocks at the bottom. Anyone who had ever made a Fae deal regretted it, and I wouldn't be making the same mistake.

Luckily, my poker face was top-notch—otherwise Carmichael would have seen right through my bluff.

"What you're asking for is illegal, you know." He pretended to contemplate the legalities while pulling at his long, grizzled beard. "Healing humans ain't rightly my business, but I do love a challenge."

Raising a single eyebrow, I waited for him to continue. Hemming and hawing wasn't a promise he'd do the spell, and until I got that, I wasn't letting him anywhere near this money. I'd learned this the hard way at least twice—more if you counted how many times I'd begged my mom for things, only for her to tell me she hadn't agreed to anything.

"Fine," he barked, crossing his arms over his big belly. "At least your mama taught you that much, though, I'll be asking for my payment upfront before I get started."

"Shake on it," I insisted, one hand still on the money and the other outstretched. "In exchange for ten thousand dollars, you will perform one healing spell on Alice Marchand Whitlock. *Today*."

Carmichael coughed, sputtered, and nearly fell over. "*Ten thousand dollars?*" he croaked, turning a little red as he pinned his gaze on the pile of bills I was protecting. "Hell, girl, for that much I'll do it right now."

He stood straighter, hitching up his pants a little. Then he waved his hands in a complicated set of movements, which had me backing away from the counter, money be damned.

"No," I shouted, waving my own hands in the universal sign to "Stop." "You can't do it while I'm he—"

The ground pitched, sending the piles of junk toppling to the floor. I quickly followed, landing on my ass as a nearby cauldron sparked to life. The contents of said cauldron bubbled over, hissing like acid as it dripped onto the dirty floor.

"What the hell is goin' on? You did th—"

But Carmichael never got a chance to finish that damning sentence. All at once, the windows of his apothecary blew in as the caustic brew caught fire. Dodging glass and the heat of the flames, I scrambled to my feet, racing for the shop owner.

"You have to get out of here," I yelled over the now-roaring fire. "*Now.*" It didn't matter whose fault it was—and if anyone asked, I'd say it was *his*—this whole place was going up faster than a damned tinderbox.

Carmichael swiped his meaty arm across the counter, scooping up the money in one greasy, grizzled paw. Then the bastard took off, the heavy man moving far faster than I gave him credit for. He weaved around junk toward the back of the shop almost faster than I could track, leaving me behind. Almost as soon as he was out of sight, the path he'd taken was blocked by flames.

Maybe it was the smoke inhalation from the now-burning junk, herbs, and tinctures, but it took me a second to realize I should *also* be getting the hell out of there.

Coughing, I stumbled through the room, tripping over something or other. I fell, landing on my hands and knees, my palms cut to shit from the broken glass littering the floor. Then, I wasn't on the ground anymore, I was hanging upside down over a man's shoulder, the light of the early spring sunshine blinding me.

Unceremoniously, I was tossed off said shoulder, my ass taking the full brunt of the landing as I was dumped onto a patch of grass. Struggling for breath, I hacked and coughed up the caustic smoke, the fresh air slowly but surely filtering into my lungs.

Eyes tearing, nose running, I was so busy trying to breathe that I barely noticed the man who'd saved my life until he was already turning away. I wanted to say thank you to whomever kept me from frying like a red-haired shish kebab, but before I could get out a word, he was down The Walk, weaving through the stream of lookie-loos.

"There she is, Agent." Carmichael's booming Southern drawl echoed off the high brick walls.

Turning my head, I spied the beefy shop owner pulling a harried man through the gathering crowd. Where he'd fetched an Arcane Bureau of Investigation agent from, I hadn't a clue, but it didn't really matter.

Before now, I'd managed to stay off of the ABI's radar, but as the agent barreled toward me, I knew those days were over.

Once again, I'd fucked up.

Only this time?

I might just be in deep shit.

CHAPTER 2

NICO

"*Less do another shot.*"

It was official. I was in Hell.

Staring at the redhead slamming back another shot of tequila, I contemplated exactly what I'd done in my past lives to warrant this punishment. Being stuck watching this walking fantasy of a woman swallow down the amber liquid was the highest form of torture. She was stunning—with legs I could see wrapped around my body, hair designed to be twisted around my fist.

And those eyes?

It was harder *not* to stare at her than it would be to simply take her. Not that I knew what I'd do with her once I had her. She was trouble, with every single letter capitalized and underlined.

Wren Bannister was the definition of a hot mess, and I'd

never even spoken to her. Everyone in the arcane world knew about the black sheep of the Bannister family. The one who'd been responsible for more than her fair share of catastrophes.

Fucking with *that* witch would only destroy me.

Yet, the second I pulled her from the flames of that damned apothecary, her wretched curse became mine. Her touch, her scent, they burned their way through my very being until there was nothing left but the ashes of where my soul used to be.

But she wasn't my mate. *No.*

When a wolf found their mate, it was a link between two souls—one that could never be broken. Not even by death.

What she did to me—what her *touch* did to me—was the darkest of magics. It was lust and obsession and desire and a near-mindless need to keep her safe. It was her jasmine and honey perfume in my nose, and imagining what her gasp sounded like, and... I shook my head, trying to clear it.

There had to be a way to break her spell—*had* to be.

How was I supposed to find my true mate with her scent in my nose? How was I supposed to come into my full power as an Acosta Alpha if I was stuck being a spelled lapdog to an absolute train wreck of a witch?

With only a week until my thirtieth birthday, I had to get her out of my head. If I didn't... I didn't even want to think about what would happen if I was still obsessed with her by then. She had to have spelled me.

Right?

That's why I hadn't stopped following her since the explosion—or at least that's the lie I would tell anyone who asked. Hell, that's the lie I was still trying to convince myself was true. The near-constant fantasies I'd been having would remain a secret, too. Just like everything else I'd learned about the obnoxiously drunken witch across the bar.

"Iss no' fair," Wren slurred, making my eye twitch. This was her third time loudly complaining about her fate to the human friend at her side—a sentence she was damn lucky to get in the first place. "They said jail or ABI, and I said jail. At least in jail I can't fuck up. Thisss is *sooooo* bad." She dramatically thumped her head onto her folded arms.

After what she'd done, most people would count themselves fortunate to end up with a prison sentence—especially since the alternative was death.

But not one of the "blessed" Bannisters.

Her family name bought Wren more than a few favors from the ABI. It sure as hell hadn't been her parents responsible for getting her out of the mess she'd made. They'd left that girl high and dry after her arrest, cutting off any and all ties to their daughter. Still, her choice had been prison or a ten-year service commitment to the ABI—*if* she survived the selection process.

Funnily enough, even though she'd chosen prison, the tribunal shoved her into selection school so fast it made her little red head spin.

Hooking a finger around the neck of my beer bottle, I shook my head. It was bad enough that she was sloppy as fuck in a bar at damn near midnight on a weekday. But being surrounded by humans—humans I couldn't snap at or maul to death or pluck the eyes from their skulls for staring at her rack?

Yep. I was officially in the deepest pits of Hell, with Satan himself roasting me over a spit. And it was one of my own making, since I was the idiot who'd followed her to this backwoods human bar in the first fucking place.

Though, considering the last time Wren had waltzed into the arcane side of town, she'd blown up an apothecary, I supposed it could be worse. The place could be on fire. Maybe tequila shots weren't so bad—even if the bartender's eyes *were* glued to her tits.

My wolf paced at the back of my mind, aching for me to yank her off that stool and toss her over my shoulder. Jaw twitching, I took a gulp of my beer. It was either that or give into my animal. My wolf wanted to do far more than just toss her over my shoulder. He wanted his mark on her and…

Sitting back in the booth, I ripped my attention off Wren and focused on her human friend. While my obsession was downing tequila like someone was going to stop making it soon, her friend was smartly imbibing water. A frown puckered the human's brow as the scent of guilt wafted toward me.

It was rare that a human felt that much guilt unless they had something to feel guilty about.

"Iss fine," Wren slurred, propping her chin sloppily on her fist. "As long as it worked and she's fine, I don' care. I'd do it again if I had to. It coul' be worse, yanno." The redhead shrugged so hard she almost fell off her stool. My ass left my seat, and I nearly raced to save her, when she managed to catch herself at the last second.

Jesus Christ, she's going to give me an ulcer.

Reeling the upper half of her body to rights, Wren smartly took the large glass of water her friend offered.

She didn't actually drink it, though.

Instead, she waved the glass—half of the liquid sloshing over the rim. "To Alice," Wren shouted, startling most of the other bar patrons. "The bess bonus mom on the planet. May she live to a thousand."

Wren had been charged with setting the shop on fire after she'd failed to procure a healing spell from Carmichael Jones. Something told me Jones had been lying through his yellowed teeth when he'd spewed his testimony to the tribunal.

"Thanks to you," her friend murmured, tears filling her dark eyes. "I can't believe you did it, Wren. I can't than—"

Wren waved off her friend's thanks—once again nearly flopping off her stool. "Iss no prolem. She'da don the same for me."

Gnashing my teeth, my wolf continued his pacing. Sure, Wren might have screwed up, but the reasons may have been justified. It was so much easier to think of her as a fuckup instead of an accident-prone do-gooder.

Not that I'd be telling my superiors at the ABI that.

No one—and I did mean *no one*—knew I'd been at the scene, or that I'd been the one to yank her sexy ass out of the burning rattrap that was Azalea Apothecary. Hell, if I hadn't been tracking a spike in dark magic, I wouldn't have even been there.

It had been the same dark magic that trailed her delectable ass like a puppy all the way through Factor's Walk, though I hadn't scented it around her since. And just the thought of me not being there that day made my stomach pitch.

Yep. Definitely getting that ulcer.

A pair of boots clomped to a stop at the edge of my table. "Well, if it isn't my old pal Nico."

Shifting my gaze from the sloppy witch, I shot a glare up at the asshole who was dumb enough to follow me. "What do you want, Wyatt?"

Sure, I'd known him since we were pups, but right then, his presence was not welcome. Snickering, Wyatt slid into the booth across from me, his massive head nearly blocking my view.

"I needed a favor. You weren't at your usual haunts, so I followed your scent here. Considering I saved your ass in Canada—*twice*—I figure this is less a favor, and more me calling in one."

Of course Wyatt needed a favor, and of course he'd track me down to call one in. Though, it hadn't been him saving me in Canada from a den full of angry bears, rather it was me saving him, but whatever. He'd tell me whatever it was soon enough.

"What I wanna know is—why you're out here in the middle of bum-fuck nowhere in a human bar? Sure, beer is beer, but..." He sucked in a breath through his teeth, surveying the place, "this ain't your usual spot."

My eyes scanned the room before landing back on Wren. It was as if her ass was a magnet or something.

"Well"—He chuckled, taking a swig of his beer—"I take that back. *I* know why you're here. The real question is—if *you* know why you're here. Well, that, and if you've figured out why you're watching that woman like she's a nice, juicy steak?"

Scowling, I peeled my eyes off Wren's ass. "What's that supposed to mean?"

Wyatt snorted, scratching at his three-day scruff. "If you haven't figured it out yet, don't worry. You will."

Shaking my head, my eyes landed on Wren once more. Wyatt talked out of his ass more than his mouth most days. I wasn't going to be dragged into whatever bullshit he was spewing.

Wren lifted her heavy fall of hair off her neck, piling it on top of her head as she fanned her skin—the smooth pale column leading down to her shoulders, the curve of her waist. In my almost thirty years, I'd never wanted to sink my teeth into someone so bad.

That thought had me wanting to slap the shit out of myself to try and snap out of it. Again.

She had to have done something to me...

Wyatt whistled long and low, yanking my gaze back to him. "What?"

"Hoo-boy, you are in trouble. That's the Bannister witch, right? The one who blew up Carmichael's place?" He took a swig of his beer, seeming to hold in a snicker.

"Your point?" I demanded, raising an irritated eyebrow. "And didn't you want a favor?"

Wyatt's grin went wide. "No point, simply making an observation. Just like I observed every other man in this bar staring at those two."

Yeah, I'd clocked that about two seconds after sitting down. Wren and her little friend had garnered a lot of attention from the dick-swinging members of the population, and it was all I could do to not rip their throats out one by one.

And again, it made no damn sense.

She. Was not. My mate.

"I'm aware."

And by "aware," I meant that while I'd been watching Wren, I'd also spotted a pair of yokels circle the pool table like sharks, their eyes pinned on her. Out of every other group of men in this bar, they were the only ones who had the oily scent of menace to them. They smelled like predators.

My wolf scratched at the back of my brain, begging to be set free. He and I both knew what the score was with those two. If they didn't approach them here, they would elsewhere, and I doubted they'd be nice about it.

Wren slid off her stool as she slugged back the last bit of her water. I had to give her credit—at least it was water and not tequila.

"Time to go night-night," she slurred in a loud whisper— one that didn't take preternatural senses to hear all the way across the bar.

The plan was to make sure she got home safely, and then put my head in a bucket of ice or something to try and get her out of my mind. A plan that was quickly going off the rails as I watched the two men toss their pool cues on the table and chug the last of their beers.

Wren's human friend quickly settled the tab before slinging the drunk witch's arm over her shoulder and marching toward the exit. And just like I'd predicted, the two men hung back for less than thirty seconds before they followed the women right out the door.

Fuck.

I was up and out of the booth before the door closed, ready and willing to commit murder until an iron grip stopped me.

The growl that slipped past my lips had my best friend snatching his hand off my arm.

"You aren't planning on doing anything stupid, are you?"

Gritting my teeth, I fought off the urge to smash my bottle over Wyatt's skull and toss his ass out of my booth.

"You're the alpha's son, idiot. And we aren't exactly in the best place for whatever it is in that fool brain of yours."

Why did he have to go and bring that up? If we were on the arcane side of town, it wouldn't be a question, but so close to humans? I really hated it when Wyatt was right.

"They won't know I'm even there," I growled, amending the plan in my mind. Granted, the first one involved me ripping out their throats and dumping them in the river, so maybe the change was necessary.

Instead of following them out the front door, I strode to the back exit, careful to keep my speed within human limits. Though, once I was outside in the shadows, I stopped holding myself back. Rounding the greasy dumpsters, I caught Wren's scent—that jasmine and honey perfume that made me want to shove my head through a wall. Only it was tempered by the stink of stale beer and male body odor. The two humans had split up, circling the women in an almost choreographed move that told me they'd done this before.

If they were wolves, I could kill them without even so much as a slap on the wrist—pack law superseding ABI law on this one point. We didn't abide sexual predators of any kind, and murder was always a viable option for taking care of that problem. As their scent got stronger, my previous plan started looking better and better.

The world needed less men in it who'd hurt women. It

needed them broken and bloody. They were fit for nothing more than worm food.

Mate or not, wolf or not, I wasn't about to just sit here and let Wren get attacked.

Once again, though, I was stopped by a hand on my arm.

"They cannot see you. None of them. Got it?" Wyatt hissed. "I swear you're going to get us both killed if you can't keep ahold of your wolf." At my confused frown, he pressed on. "Your eyes are glowing, stupid. Keep a lid on your shit."

But they were getting closer and closer to Wren, a spike in desire cloying through the air as it made my stomach turn. Shoving Wyatt off of me, I snaked through the parked cars, keeping my body low. While hiding was something I was good at, I didn't want to right then.

Every instinct I had told me to run and bite and rend. They said to protect. To save. To make sure that threats were gone for good. Those instincts didn't give a shit about the law I'd agreed to uphold or the potential fallout. They didn't give that first fuck that this could all go sideways.

With my back against the grill of an enormous truck, I peered around the side. A wiry man was loosening his belt as he watched Wren's human friend struggle to get her nearly passed-out cargo into the back seat.

The likelihood that I would commit murder rose into the stratosphere.

"Ah, *fuck* no," Wyatt growled, finally echoing my thoughts. "Fuck what I said before. I don't give a shit if they do see us."

About fucking time. "Stay with this asshole. I'll get the other one."

In less than a second, I located the predator, his hand

nearly at the back door to the little car. Belt undone, fly down, he clamped his oily fingers on the door handle and tugged.

The growl that slipped from my throat had him freezing, his shoulders hunching as he slowly turned to look. But he never got a chance to see me before I shoved his head into the roof of the car, knocking him out.

I might have craved his blood on my hands and his flesh tearing under my claws, but I still needed to keep my ass out of the fire.

"What was that?" Wren mumbled sleepily from the back seat as I dragged the filthy human into the shadows, the pitiful parking lot lights giving far more hiding places than likely intended.

Instead of sticking around, I hauled the dead weight over my shoulder and headed toward the water. Killing this asshole wasn't on the docket for me, but that didn't mean I couldn't let a gator do my dirty work.

A moment later, Wyatt was behind me with his own unconscious cargo.

"Swamp?" he asked, and I nodded.

"Swamp."

Ten minutes later, the pair of us were up to our asses in marshland, but our load was a lot lighter. And if those screams that echoed through the cypress trees were any indication, there would be nothing left of those boys by morning.

"So, about that favor," Wyatt said, flicking a hunk of mud off his hand. "I need you to cover my next class coming through the pipeline. I have shit to handle that can't wait."

My boots squelched to a stop in the silty water as I shot him a glare. "What?"

Wyatt's grin made me want to knock the shit out of him. "I sai—"

"I know what you fucking said. Please tell me it's not—"

"The selection class that starts tomorrow? The one your little redhead is going to?" he finished for me, his smile only getting wider. "Why, yes. Yes, it is."

Wren going where I couldn't follow was my one chance to get her out of my head—my one chance to break whatever hold she had on me.

One of the screams abruptly cut off, a gator likely dragging a human under. Wyatt's eyebrows waggled as I realized there was only one answer I could give him.

Fuck.

Selection school here I come.

CHAPTER 3

WREN

I REALLY SHOULDN'T HAVE TAKEN THAT LAST SHOT.

Just the thought of all the tequila I'd drank last night made my gut do a flip-flop. Why did I think drinking away my troubles was actually going to help? It sure as shit wouldn't fix this bus ride, that was for sure.

The sun seared my eyeballs through my sunglasses as I rested my temple on the cool glass of the foggy window. The sway of the vehicle was doing a number on my stomach as the bitter churn of late-night tacos gurgled uneasily.

The bus was pointed north to Camp Blue Ridge, the ABI's selection school from Hell. I'd thought getting caught was the worst thing, but the sentence for my crime was far more dire than I'd originally thought.

Personally, I figured jail would have been an easier time.

Even though I'd heard horror stories of ABI prison, most of them centered around having one's powers stripped. Since I had no power to speak of—unless fucking up spells was one—jail would have been a cakewalk.

But *nooooo. Not a Bannister. Prison was beneath us.*

As soon as I uttered the word "jail," the portly man in the spiffy robes and giant staff turned purple, and two days later, I found myself on this godforsaken bus trying not to toss my cookies.

The only thing going for me nowadays was the fact that Carmichael had actually done the spell as promised. Alice's health turned around almost instantly, the doctors calling her recovery a "medical miracle."

As long as she lived, I didn't give a shit if I had to do ten years as an agent. But if I was being honest, the likelihood that I'd pass selection school was slim. What kind of agent would I be if no one could do magic around me?

I doubted I'd last a day.

Someone somewhere was going to do magic, and then there would be a fire or an earthquake or a fucking lightning strike, and then I'd get tossed out on my ass and thrown in jail.

The bus hit a pothole, launching my stomach into my throat.

Yeah, drinking last night was the dumbest shit I'd ever pulled, and going to that bar?

We were lucky we hadn't gotten eaten by an alligator or mauled by one of the patrons. But after receiving my bullshit sentence, I'd needed one last night of freedom. Paying for it now hadn't exactly been on my to-do list.

Two hours later, we started puttering up the mountain, the awful switchbacks having me wish puke bags were a thing on busses. By the time the monster vehicle rolled to a stop, I was sweating and ready to hurl my guts up.

"If you puke on my bus, cadet, I'll make you clean it up with a toothbrush," the sour driver barked, eyeing me from his seat. Nodding, I yanked my bag from the overhead bin and rushed down the aisle.

Soggy cedar-scented air slapped me in the face as I clambered down the steps, the humidity of the mountain a whole other animal than the warm caress of Savannah. A mosquito the size of a fucking barn owl buzzed in my ear, and I ducked, swatting at the thing, unsure if I actually wanted to make contact with a bug that big.

"Welcome to Camp Blue Ridge," a tall man called, and I straightened so fast, both my head *and* gut started swimming. His blond hair and light features blurred as I tried to get my shit together.

Alcohol. Bad. Tequila is the devil.

A small group of us loitered in front of the navy-blue bus as more people filed out. Another cadet bumped down the bus steps, her gait far more elegant than mine. Well, until she tripped over a rock I'd managed to miss in my flailing and nearly took a header. Me and another girl dove to help, and all three of us ended up knocking together and stumbling to the gravel drive. Sharp rocks dug into one of my palms, breaking the barely healed skin.

Perfect.

Me—totally used to biffing it—got up first, offering my

lone non-bloody hand to the closest victim of my magical fuckery, my cheeks burning. The laughs I got—when people fell down, it was usually comical—but the bitter stare from the man at the front made me want to crawl under the bus and let it take me out.

"Jesus Christ," he muttered, shaking his head at the lot of us. "When you're finished…"

Wincing, I gave him my full attention. *Off to a fabulous start, Wren.*

"Selection starts tomorrow and will run for three weeks," he barked, his face made of stone. "The rigors of the Arcane Bureau of Investigation are arduous. We expect the best and will not take anything less than that. Not all of you will make it."

And if he just so happened to be staring right at me as he said this, well, then, so be it.

"Once you pass through these gates, all magic will be nulled. This is for your safety, as well as to teach you how to survive without magic. In the ABI, you cannot rely on your abilities alone. You need wits and gumption and your training to survive in the world out there."

No magic? None?

A glimmer of hope bloomed in my chest. If there wasn't any magic, then I could just be a normal person for maybe the first time in forever. No backfires, no explosions. Shit, this was like Christmas.

"You are to surrender all weapons, charms, potion bottles, and electronic devices in one of our Amnesty boxes," he continued, his stance wide as he held his arms behind his back. What was that position called? Parade rest or something like that? "Phones, tablets, and allowed magical items will be returned to you upon graduation. However, if you are caught with anything I've listed, it is grounds for immediate expulsion from the program."

The woman beside me groaned as she unzipped her bag and unloaded a freaking mountain of magical shit. Necklaces with pretty baubles, bottles filled with glowing liquid, and a couple of athames were all dumped into a TSA-style bin with the name F. Jacobs on it. As someone who'd never worn a charm—let alone would try to test my shitty luck with a potion—the only thing I had to turn over was my cell phone.

The man—an instructor, maybe?—narrowed his eyes at me as he studied my nearly empty bin. "What else do you have on you? You won't get another chance to surrender your items without penalty."

Confused, I shook my head. I hadn't even brought my e-reader with me, since I knew all my shit would be rifled through. No one needed to know about my alien romance obsession. "That's it. You can go through my stuff if you want, but of the things you talked about, all I have is a phone."

I doubted tampons and toiletries were against the rules, but who knew in a place like this? I held out my duffle, the bright-purple canvas sticking out like a sore thumb. Yeah, it clashed with my copper hair, but the color was so pretty.

But the surly man didn't take it. Instead, he just clenched his jaw and jerked his head to the side to get me to move along. Reluctantly, I shouldered the bag and followed the other cadets through the giant gate. The thing had to be about twenty feet high, the hinges creaking as it opened wide.

As soon as my foot crossed the threshold, it was like a

weight had been yanked from my shoulders. Instantly, I felt lighter, freer, more in control.

Was this what no magic felt like? Was this what humans felt every day? Just breathing and living without a constant worry that they might explode something accidentally?

"Sweet mother of Christ on a saltine cracker," the blonde moaned, her knees practically buckling. "What the hell is that?"

"Whoa, there," I muttered, lunging to grab her before she fell, only this time I didn't trip us all. "You okay?"

She shook her head, her face pale and clammy. "I'll be fine. I thought... They told me it would be like this, but I figured they were exaggerating, you know?"

I actually didn't know, but I nodded, anyway.

Hooking an arm around hers, I kept her in line, marching toward what the angry instructor called our "barracks." In reality, they were four small cabins with pitched roofs and cute little gingerbread-style doors with numbers on them. Everything appeared clean and orderly—a task that would likely fall to us once we got settled.

"Males are in cabins one and four," the man yelled from behind us, making each of us turn to look at him. "Females in two and three. Pick a cabin and a bunk—that will be yours until you leave. Unpack your gear in your lockers. School starts tomorrow, so get some chow and rest. You're gonna need it." His tone was sinister enough—especially coupled with the dreaded up-down glare he gave me—that I figured he not only knew who I was, but he'd picked his punching bag for the duration of the course.

Lucky, lucky me.

After giving us a paper map of the grounds, which outlined the training areas, chow hall, latrines, and off-limits sections, he pivoted on a heel, making a hasty retreat. His instructions left a bit to be desired, but considering he was now gone, I supposed I shouldn't complain. I had a feeling he'd be in my shit far more than I wanted soon enough.

"Come on," I muttered to the girl I was still holding up. "Let's get settled. Maybe after some food you'll feel better?"

Shakily, she nodded, snagging the bag she'd dropped at her feet. "Pick a number."

Since the majority of the women had already chosen their cabin, I pointed us toward cabin three. Inside were four wrought-iron twin-sized beds, the linens stacked at the foot of each mattress. A pair of tall lockers separated the spaces, each one facing their respective bed, forming a giant metal wall for privacy.

I picked the bed farthest from the door, the dark corner of the cabin only boasting one small window. The walls were mostly wood planking with an open vaulted ceiling. Luckily there were ceiling fans situated over each bed since there didn't seem to be any air-conditioning to speak of. What was also missing was a shower—though the small bathroom did manage to have a single toilet and sink.

Unloading my duffle, I situated my clothes in the pristine wall locker, utilizing the hangers for my jeans and coat and folding the rest in the two large drawers at the bottom. I stacked my toiletries on the shelves at the side, stowed my shoes, and I was done.

My buddy, though, seemed confused at the lack of space. She sat on her naked bed, staring at the locker like it might jump up and bite her at any moment. I sort of figured she could still be feeling the effects of the no-magic wards.

"Hey, you okay?" I asked, startling her out of her horror-filled stupor.

Her smile was tremulous, but she seemed to rally. "Fine, fine," she said, waving away my concern. "Sorry. I just have never seen a wardrobe that small, and I was mentally trying to fit all my stuff in it." She held out a hand. "Fiona Ja—" She shook her head, cutting herself off as she took her hand back. "Never mind last names. Last thing we need is to get into a witch family pissing match. I'm Fiona. Just Fiona. What's your name?"

At this point I figured it was rude to tell her I'd already gleaned her last name from her bin. The Jacobs witch line was one of the oldest—save for the Bannister one, of course—their power and influence a force to be reckoned with—and not all of it good. Instead, I simply took her hand in mine and shook.

"Okay, Fiona, Just Fiona. My name is Wren." Honestly, it was better to not say my last name, anyway. When people found out, they either already knew about my degenerate status, or they wanted an "in" with my grams. Considering my grams didn't even like *me*, people usually got disappointed in a hurry.

The clomp of booted feet clambered into the cabin, accompanied by the screen door slapping against the outer wall. Fiona and I peeked around the wall locker to greet our cabinmates, the pair of them appearing tired and surly. One was green-haired and impossibly tall, ducking under the trim as she entered. I didn't know what class she was, but if I had to guess, I'd say ghoul.

Ghouls didn't typically join the ABI—or any other organization to speak of—mostly because their nest king or queen preferred keeping them in check. They were the tallest brand of arcaner—either born or made—and typically the crankiest, most destructive, and most whispered about, since they usually kept to themselves.

The woman following her was the ghoul's complete opposite. Her inky hair was pulled into a severe bun as she surveyed the cabin with disgust. Hell, if she'd have had a set of pearls at her neck, she would have been clutching them.

Fiona rounded the locker wall, approaching the two with a naivety that better suited a child. "Hi, I'm Fiona, and this is Wren. We chose beds already. Hope that's okay?"

The ghoul gently took Fiona's hand and slowly shook it. "Hannah. And that's cool. I like being by the door."

"Nice to meet you." Fiona's smile beamed as she moved to the uptight one, but she didn't take her hand.

"No offense," the uptight one said, her voice far kinder than I thought it would be, "but I don't shake hands."

Fiona's sunshine face fell. "Oh, well, that's okay. No worries. You got a name?"

The lady blinked at her for a second before shaking herself. "Malia. Sorry. I'm a..." Malia winced as she seemed to ponder the right word. "A psychic? Only I do psychometry. So, I try not to touch people or things with my hands if I can help it."

I couldn't hold in my wince. I'd read about psychometry oracles in one of my gram's books. Half the time they ended up batshit crazy or went to live in the woods alone, because they couldn't deal with learning every single thing about people from touching their stuff. I had a feeling those magic wards didn't help with a power like that.

Malia dumped her duffle onto her chosen bed, the sound of glass clinking making a damn racket. "Okay, unpack, food, and then we need to drink all the booze I brought before that chump decides that he meant to say we couldn't have alcohol, too."

Well, so much for first impressions, then. I'd sort of figured Malia would be an uptight goody-goody, and I'd never been so happy to be proven wrong.

An hour later, we were up the hill surrounding a decent-sized fire, a mix of arcaners on their semi-best behavior as they imbibed Malia's liquor. Her bag was filled to the brim with booze, but I was smartly drinking water, just happy to be invited. My red plastic cup rested on my knee as I listened to all the conversations.

People-watching was something of a hobby of mine. I liked trying to figure out what class everyone was and what powers they had. With no powers of my own, I loved learning about other people's magic.

To the right, a pair of mages lamented that they hadn't been able to produce so much as a spark from their fingers, resorting to starting the fire the old-fashioned way with a lighter someone had pilfered from the kitchens. A purple-haired guy was flirting hard with Hannah, even though he was clearly more than a foot shorter than her. Hannah didn't seem to care, though, so the flirting carried on, her cheeks as red as my damn hair.

Malia was talking animatedly with a pair of women that bunked in the other cabin, though she did it from a safe distance away to keep from touching anyone. She also didn't sit down, but she had donned a pair of elbow-length gloves. Fiona giggled with a few guys from cabin four, and I was sitting quietly on my log, trying not to smell the booze that permeated the air over the scent of burning wood.

Now that night had fallen, it was far cooler than I'd thought it would be, and I started rethinking my chosen outfit of short-shorts, an off-the-shoulder T-shirt, and combat boots. Okay, the combat boots were smart, but the shorts? Luckily, the mosquitos weren't so bad close to the fire.

Staring at the flickering flames, I let the conversations float over me. Well, until a man caught my eye through the fire. I probably should have noticed someone like him sooner, but with all the fuss and booze and buzzing banter, I had to have missed him.

Almost in the shadows, just outside the firelight, he stood with his feet planted in the leaves and his arms hanging loosely at his sides, his white T-shirt the only beacon, letting me know I wasn't dreaming. His hair was a dark tangle, sweeping back from his face like he'd ran his hands through it about a million times. But it was his jaw that really stole the show. Sharper than a blade and just as solid, even from here, I could tell he was in no mood.

Meeting his gaze across the flames, I nearly fell off my seat. It wasn't the fact that those eyes glowed in the firelight, either. No, it was the sheer heat in them that had me fiddling with my hair and adjusting my top. As dumb as it was—especially with a man seeming that pissed—I really, really wanted him to come over and talk to me. And if he happened to find me incredibly witty and blindingly attractive, well, then, all the better.

My breath hitched in my throat as my heart seemed to want to thump its way on out of my chest. There was no way he was that pretty, right? No way he was actually as fucking beautiful as I thought he was.

Right?

The best I could do was toss my hair, but when I tried resting my weight on my hand—for added cleavage building purposes—I missed the log completely and slipped right off my makeshift seat.

With my legs in the air and my hair snarled in the leaves, I seriously considered crawling away and burying myself in the woods somewhere. Add in the fact that my cup of water was now all over my shirt, I figured dying was my only option. Surviving this embarrassment didn't seem like a good idea.

The hottest man I'd ever seen in. My. Life. Just saw me biff it. Now was the perfect time to just expire.

But no. Instead of dying right there on the spot, I heard a deep, silky voice ask the most damning of questions. "Are you drunk?"

Glaring, I met his amber gaze over the fallen log, my embarrassment tempered by his rude question. Though considering everyone else was drinking, maybe it wasn't so rude.

"No. My beverage—that I am now wearing—was water. I'm just clumsy, but thanks for the assist."

Awkwardly, I tried to disengage myself from the brambles, but I wasn't having the best of luck. It was just my luck that I couldn't even die in peace.

"Here," he rumbled, kneeling next to me, "let me help."

His fingers made quick work of disentangling my hair from the bracken, offering me a hand up once I was free. I took it and he hauled me up with little effort. His hand was warm as it clasped over mine, his skin sending little jolts of adrenaline into my body. Up close, I noticed his five-day-old scruff of a beard that surrounded a pair of lips—

"You okay?" he asked, stepping closer, his voice doing very weird things to my middle as I stared at his mouth.

Stop staring at his mouth, Wren.

Shaking myself, I met his gaze and then lost my train of thought all over again when he gently pulled a leaf from my hair. Was I goo now? I had to be because there was no way I was acting like this. No, this was a dream—or a nightmare—and I would wake up anytime now.

But instead of extricating myself from the situation, I just. Kept. Staring at his fucking eyes. And those irises weren't only amber, either. No, they were the color of good whiskey, the firelight reflecting off them almost like a cat's.

Leave. Go. Dear sweet mother of all that is holy, get your shit together and walk. Away. Please.

"Fine," I croaked, my voice breaking like a teenage boy's. Cheeks burning, I cleared my throat. "Fine. Thanks for the help. I'm going to go back to my cabin and die now, if you don't mind." Reluctantly, I pulled my hand from his. "Tootles."

Tootles? Did I actually just say tootles? Someone kill me.

Nodding at the sheer embarrassment, I skirted around the hot man and marched double-time away from the fire. I heard my name being called, but I couldn't stop. Not even when I stumbled over a rock and nearly ate it. Again.

No, I practically ran, stumbling down the hill and praying no one followed me as I made my escape.

But escape was a stretch, wasn't it? Because I had three more weeks here, and I had a feeling I'd be seeing him again.

Whoever he was.

CHAPTER 4

NICO

Touching Wren was a mistake.

But what else was I supposed to do? Just stand there while she tangled herself in the brambles? Be an asshole and watch her squirm?

Though, as soon as my skin made contact with hers, that pull that had been tugging on me since I'd yanked her from the flames, crashed over me like a tidal wave once again. I was supposed to be distancing myself from her, not getting closer, but I couldn't seem to stop myself from seeking her out.

I couldn't keep myself from getting closer to her, making myself known. I needed her to see me for some stupid reason —needed her to know I was there. And as soon as I locked eyes with her, I was lost.

Again.

How was I supposed to loathe the woman when she was

that fucking beautiful? And the spark in those odd gold-and-green eyes—the way she blushed?

Gods, I was fucked.

The heat of her skin filtering into my palm was enough to make me want to sink my fangs into her neck and brand her with my mark.

She's not your mate, you idiot. This is just her spell—her power. Had to be... Right?

But when she practically ran from me with the scent of her desire on the air? Well, it had my wolf fighting against my hold, ready to race after her, even under these shitty null wards. It was bad enough I couldn't quite stop myself from following her through the forest toward her cabin. The lie I told myself this time was that I wanted to make sure she was safe.

There were predators in the woods, right? The magic and fences couldn't keep everything out.

And this was Wren, for fuck's sake. She needed a keeper.

But I'd been watching her all night, and it wasn't until I stepped into the firelight, did she start stumbling all over herself. Truth be told, that shit was fucking adorable. The flush to her cheeks, the way her heart fluttered like a hummingbird's, the way her pupils dilated.

And her scent nearly made me go out of my mind.

She slammed into her cabin, muttering to herself, not knowing I could hear every word. "How could you do that, Wren?" she grumbled, crashing against something metal. "The hottest man you've ever seen, and what do you do? Spill your stupid drink all over yourself. No wonder he thought you were drunk."

I pressed my lips together so I didn't laugh outright. It was tough to reconcile this version of Wren with the black magic witch who'd spelled me to obsession. And wouldn't a spell like that be dampened by the wards? Or was her magic like mine—unable to be controlled by nulling spells? Those spells didn't dull a single aspect of my wolf—my senses just as acute inside this facility as they were back home.

Which was why the shuffle of steps through the leaves had my eyes rolling. Sneaking up on a wolf was a ballsy move.

"So, you've picked your prey, then?" Ames taunted, likely trying to get under my skin. Chet Ames was an asshole of the highest order, and that assessment had been made before he'd ever even opened his mouth. His name was Chet for fuck's sake. It was as if his parents knew he was a blight on the arcane world before he ever left the womb.

As soon as I'd arrived, he'd taken it upon himself to show me the "ropes," as he liked to call it. Even though my clearance was higher than his, as was my rank. Plus, this wasn't my first rodeo at selection school or covering for Wyatt. It figured that his inferior ass would follow me, though, why anyone in their right mind would try to sneak up on a wolf was a damn mystery.

Unlike him, I still had all my powers.

Ignoring Ames seemed like my best option. We did this with snapping pups all the time. And that's exactly what he was, nothing more than a yipping puppy with no damn sense.

"She is hot, right?" Chet said through a chuckle and my eye involuntarily twitched. "Though, I wouldn't touch that ass with a ten-foot pole if you ask me. Fucking Bannisters, tossing their power around at every turn. I still can't believe she got out of jailtime after what she did. I can't wait to toss her ass out of here." He rubbed his hands together like he couldn't wait to enact his plan. "After I make her suffer, though. She needs someone to teach her a lesson."

Gritting my teeth, I tried not to snap, keeping my eyes trained on cabin three's door. This idiot had no idea what he was talking about. He knew nothing about Wren or her family, and he sure as shit wasn't going to touch her—not on my watch.

But it also wasn't my job to defend Wren's reputation.

Not that my tongue got that memo.

"She chose jail, actually. And that family you hate so much? They cut her off. She probably hates them just as much as you do. Maybe having an agent in our ranks with the Bannister name might be the way to keep those assholes in check." I finally broke my gaze from Wren's cabin and loosened the leash on my wolf a bit. "But it won't be *you* tossing her out anywhere. Or making her suffer."

Especially since tossing her out would be a death sentence for her. I'd perused her intake paperwork and it was all there in black and white.

Jail wasn't an option for Wren.

It never had been.

Chet stumbled back a step. "Dude. How are you doing that? Even Cassidy can't shift here."

But I hadn't shifted at all. I'd simply let a sliver of my wolf shine out of my eyes. And the reason was simple. "I'm an alpha. Wyatt is not. Now run along and collect the others. The party should be dying down soon enough."

And as soon as the cadets were tucked safe in their beds, Hell Night would begin.

There was a blissful simplicity to Hell Night from an instructor's point of view. It reminded me of stalking prey. All you had to do was wait until they felt safe and warm and relaxed, bide your time until they rested, and then rip it all out from underneath them.

The tough part was busting into a cabin in the middle of the night with a female ghoul right by the front door. It didn't matter what those null wards did, they didn't change the basic physical makeup of an arcaner. And a nearly seven-foot-tall ghoul was scary no matter whether she was hungry or not.

Naturally, I left that task to Chet, allowing his stupid ass to go in first and flip the mattress of Cadet Dumond. One of the last of her line, Dumond had likely fought plenty of arcaners just to stay alive. Chet was about to get his shit rocked.

Smartly, I stayed on the outside of the cabin, stepping to the side of the door once Dumond's growl rumbled from her chest. Two seconds later, Chet came flying out of that door, landing on the soft dirt in front of the cabin. He seemed dazed for a second before he peeled himself from the ground and marched right back into the line of fire.

"Everyone up," the idiot yelled, not realizing all four women were wide awake and already getting dressed. "Get your asses in formation. Let's *go*."

It took everything in me not to haul him from the women's cabin myself. There was no reason he should be in there in the first place. Regs dictated that only female instructors could enter their cabins after nightfall. But there weren't any female instructors here this iteration, so I had to go with it.

Squawks and distressed cries came from all four cabins, the clang of locker doors being opened, items being thrown to the ground, mattresses being flipped over.

Cadets spilled out of their cabins at the shouts of cadre, some scrambling barefoot to get in line, their ill-suited clothing choices likely about to bite them in the ass. The last cadet to leave was Wren, her red hair piled on top of her head as she hopped to finish tying her boot. She raced past me, trying to get into one of the two lines.

"It's marching time, ladies and gents," Girard announced, clapping his hands together. He was the oldest cadre member and likely the surliest. If I was stuck being the commandant of bootcamp from hell, I'd be pissed, too. But there wasn't much room in the ABI for agents that didn't follow orders—a fact I'd need to remember if I didn't rise to Alpha.

"Grab a ruck and a canteen and get back in line," Girard continued, his booming voice carrying through the trees. "Move."

The cadets raced for rucks, some testing the weight before attempting to choose lighter ones. Not Wren, though. She hoisted the first pack she grabbed onto her back before helping a smaller girl do the same, snatching up a canteen for her when the pack threatened to tip the poor girl over.

"No helping," Chet snarled, his gaze trained right on Wren. "Worry about yourself and your own pack and get your ass back in line."

Wren nodded and moved to obey him, stumbling around other cadets as she tried to return to the line.

"Get your ass in gear, cadet," Chet yelled, planting a hand in her rucksack, and shoved.

Wren stumbled, managing to catch herself before she fell, but her canteen went flying, landing with a *splat* in a puddle. She reached for it, but Chet was there again, shoving his soon-to-be dead hand against her bag. This time Wren did fall, landing on her hands and knees in the mud.

The growl that ripped up my throat was involuntary, the quiet snarl alerting every single arcaner with acute hearing of my displeasure. Wolves did not harm women—not *ever*. Warlocks, on the other hand, had a long history of doing unspeakable things, no matter the gender.

"I said move, cadet," Chet shouted, bending down so his wide-brimmed campaign hat was right in her face, *tap-tap-tapping* on her forehead as she struggled to get up with fifty pounds strapped to her back.

I figured it was high time for Ames to have a different job, or maybe it was about time for him to stop breathing altogether. My hand latched onto the back of his neck, hauling him to standing as I pulled him away from Wren. He was out of line, and it didn't matter who Wren was. Thick talons erupted from my fingers, pressing into the struggling man's flesh as I marched him over to Girard.

The death mage's eyes widened when he noticed us, but he kept his cool.

I... *did not*. "Either you teach him the right way to discipline cadets," I hissed under my breath, "or I will. You pick, but know this, he harms another student, and my lesson will be bloody."

No wonder Wyatt wanted me here. Covering for him had

only been part one of his favor. Part two was sniffing out what the fuck was going on that had all the female instructors requesting transfers left, right, and center.

Girard had let this fuck get away with too much for too long.

"Noted." He tilted his head to the side. "You gonna let him go now, or am I going to have to bury him out in the woods somewhere?"

Opening my hand, Chet dropped like a rock. Good. Maybe he learned something from this experience. Though, he was so damn stupid, the likelihood was slight.

Turning to survey the cadets, I purposely kept my gaze from the far-left line, preferring to keep the brim of my black ball cap low. I didn't wear the traditional cadre garb, nor did I don that ridiculous campaign hat. But the siren call of her eyes on me was more than I could bear.

My chin tilted up, my gaze locking on those odd gold-green eyes. They widened, her luscious mouth forming into a pretty "O" of surprise.

Yep, definitely shouldn't have touched her. This was going to be a long three weeks.

CHAPTER 5

WREN

Pretty please with sugar on top, someone, somewhere please tell me I didn't embarrass the fuck out of myself last night in front of one of my instructors.

An instructor that I would like to maul with my mouth at the first given opportunity.

Of course I did. It was bad enough when I'd assumed he was a student. But an instructor?

I most definitely should have crawled into the woods and just perished.

Shaking myself, I snapped my mouth shut, pointing my eyes at my feet so I didn't get lost in his gorgeous gold ones. My mother frequently got onto me for "catching flies," but if she were in my shoes, she'd be doing it, too. Here I was muddy, wet, and already sweaty at the ass crack of dawn while the hottest, most unattainable man I had ever seen in my freaking life just stood there looking like *that*.

A black T-shirt stretched across his pecs with "Cadre" printed across them in gold. Tight on his biceps, the cotton strained against his muscles like it was in danger of ripping. The other instructors were in weird fatigues while he was in climbing pants, hiking boots, and a ball cap, his scruff working that jaw for all it was worth.

And he'd pulled that blond guy off of me—the same one who'd been so rude when we'd arrived. I'd sort of expected selection school to suck, but I hadn't quite wrapped my head around getting shoved to the dirt on the first day. I also hadn't expected to get some weirdo's hand in my face, poking my forehead like he was trying to pop a zit.

It was humiliating to say the least, but he'd simply strode over and picked that guy up like he was no heavier than a feather, frog marching him right on over to the angry lead instructor—who seemed all the way over it—holding up the asshole by his scruff like he was a naughty puppy or something.

Yes, my heart was going all pitter-pat, trying to pump its way out of my chest. I'd have rolled my eyes at myself, but I didn't want one of the instructors to think I was doing it at them. I was in enough shit already.

"Turn to your left," the older instructor boomed, making all of us jump.

I did as told, my pack bumping into Fiona's as she turned right by accident. Jesus, it was like a damn clown show. She nearly fell over, the pack's weight too much for her, and *I* nearly fell trying to keep her up. Without a word, I planted my hands on her shoulders and steered her in the right direction.

"March, ladies and gents," he called, and it was the start of a very, very long day.

If I heard the word "march" one more time, I was going to smash my ruck into someone's face.

"Get your ass in gear, cadets. Let's move," the instructor, who'd finally introduced himself as Girard, called. And he'd done that announcement while we were all chin-deep in a trench, crawling under barbed wire with that godforsaken pack still on our backs.

The damn thing had to weigh at least fifty pounds, and the longer I wore it, the more I knew my back would never be the same after this. The blond instructor was Ames, and the hot guy with the impossibly gold eyes and the jaw from the angels? His name was Acosta.

It figured he'd have a cool last name to match his wide shoulders and fabulous ass.

That tight behind was the only thing keeping me going at this point. I focused on those rock-hard buns and marched my face off. I had blisters on my heels, enough bug bites to qualify for a malaria trial, and mud in some very unfortunate places, but I had a carrot marching in front of me and that was enough.

There were three other instructors: Haynes, October, and Pierce, but they mostly stayed on the periphery, herding us up this bullshit mountain.

Fun fact: the mountains in northern Georgia were a bitch.

The biggest bitch known to mankind. They were awful and just mean. Filled with limestone and sedimentary rocks, I slipped more than I thought possible, the mud caked on my boots making them damn near pointless. Also? Push-ups were the bane of my existence. Struggling to heave my body off the ground while wearing a pack that heavy should be against the Geneva Convention or something.

My only saving grace was that I hadn't drank last night, because Fiona, Hannah, and Malia? Well, they were dehydrated, puking, and desperately trying not to pass out. Since I'd avoided imbibing, I was only ahead in the "not puking" department.

"Time for a water break," Girard shouted, and the lot of us let out relieved groans. "Remove your packs, take a rest, and drink the water you have left."

The sun was high over our heads, the trees giving us plenty of cover but exciting the bugs something awful. There wasn't a salve in the world that would fix my itching skin, but weirdly enough, the mud had helped a bit.

Dumping my pack, I used it as a seat to keep my ass off the ground, and sipped my water. You couldn't pay me to chug anything right now, my stomach giving me fits. Everyone smelled like they'd rolled in manure—which we probably had—it was hot, and I was getting a headache.

Fiona and Hannah downed the last of their canteens, dropping their rucks as they wilted to the ground. Malia was still climbing up the hill, practically crawling the last few feet with a full pack on her back. She struggled out of it, rolling to her side as she caught her breath.

Out of curiosity, I opened the top flap of my ruck, finally

able to inspect the contents after hours of carrying it. Inside were four two-liter bottles of water, a laminated map, a compass, and a plethora of dive weights. No wonder. I probably had bruises on my back from the ill-padded bag. I pulled a water bottle from the pack and filled my canteen, using a handful of it to wash the burning salt, dirt, and who knew what else off my face.

My eyes drooped once my face was clean, that small bit of comfort making me want to sleep for days. Every part of me ached—from my mud-caked scalp all the way down to my toes. I also had a sneaking suspicion my feet were bleeding, but I didn't want to take my boots off to check. We were up the mountain in the middle of nowhere, and I worried I wouldn't be able to put them back on again.

Several of the male cadets complained, their stomachs making them far more irritable than the rest of us. I wished there were some kind of rations in my bag, but I was too tired to get off of it to get a better look. Ignoring the complaints, I sipped my newly procured water and waited, trying to keep myself awake.

Trusting people had never really been my strong suit, but after the last day? I figured my wariness of the instructors was warranted. No one had touched me since Acosta pulled that dude off me, but I wasn't going to fall down at his feet in thanks.

Okay, so if he crooked his finger at me, I totally would, but that was beside the point.

By the time I looked up, it was damn near dark, and the instructors were nowhere to be seen. Alarm and a fair amount of adrenaline lit my limbs on fire, and I jumped to my feet, the ache in them tempered by fear. I hadn't exactly been paying attention to my surroundings while I was struggling to breathe, so I had no idea where we were.

The faint thrum of an engine drew my gaze up and to the right, the gentle glow of what had to be taillights peeking through the trees. Girard stood near the driver-side door of a giant pickup truck and cupped his hands around his mouth.

"The lot of you have until sunup to get back to camp. Any stragglers who don't make it back before the deadline will be cut from the program. Any do-gooders caught helping other cadets will be punished. The first ones back will get a reward. Good luck, people."

Then Girard hopped into the bed of the truck, his seat a suspicious-looking lump as the truck rolled away. A faint flash of army-green canvas caught my eye, and a pit of dread opened up beneath me. I knelt, snatching up my pack, the slight bit of reassurance needed to make it so I didn't start crying.

A few minutes ago, I'd hated the damn thing, but as my gaze flitted over the ground nearby, I realized just how lucky it was that I still had that damn lump of heavy canvas. Frightened squawks of protest rose from the other cadets, and my hand tightened on the strap. Girard had made it sound like helping others wasn't allowed. The last thing I needed was someone to steal it right off my back.

"Gods, what are they trying to do to us?" Fiona moaned, her hands empty and canteen hanging open at her side.

Those bastards had told us to drink all our water, stole all the extra, and then bounced out with no way home.

"Break us down," Hannah muttered, cracking her neck.

"How are we supposed to be good little agents if we aren't obedient lapdogs first?"

Obedience had never really been my style, though. A few of the other cadets were already walking down the mountain, probably half-delirious from dehydration and would likely pass out after one rough stumble.

"Wait," I called to their backs, already regretting what was about to fall out of my mouth. "Does anyone else still have your ruck?"

Hitching the strap higher on my shoulder, I grimaced when most everyone shook their heads. Eight liters of water wasn't going to cut it for sixteen people. Plus, I couldn't remember the last time I'd eaten something. Or gone to the bathroom. Or slept.

"Thank the gods for that. At least they did us a solid and took them back with them," the purple-haired guy groused. "At least when I'm stumbling through the woods in the dark, I won't be carrying all that weight."

Jesus, Mary, and Joseph, they had no clue what was in those bags. "Those rucks had water in them. And a map, compass, and a bunch of other shit."

Those distressed sounds from before were nothing compared to the moaning I heard now. A few of the males' gazes laser-locked onto my ruck, a calculating gleam to their eyes as they stepped forward.

"Stop right there," Hannah growled, peeling herself from the ground to stand in front of me. "Take one more step and you'll regret it."

Peering around the ghoul, I met the purple-haired guy's eyes. "I plan on sharing so keep your panties on."

He frowned. "They told us not to help each oth—"

"No," I denied, cutting him off. "They said helping each other would get you punished. *You're* not helping anyone. I am. I'm the only one with a pack, map, or water. I say we get some light, some water, and figure out where the hell we're going."

Another guy stepped forward. "And what about the reward for getting there first?"

Rolling my eyes, I shook my head. I swear it was going to turn into *Lord of the Flies* soon if I didn't get these people some sleep and food. "I could have kept my mouth shut and left you all here, you know. Why don't you quit thinking with your lizard brain for two seconds and work the problem?"

Plus, I'd really like to see Ames' face when I got there long before sunup, and if I was being honest with myself, I'd like to see Acosta's, too. A teensy part of me wanted to know if he'd be proud that I made it back on time.

Ugh. Get it together, Wren. He is not going to give two shits whether you make it back or not, nor will he wave a banner in the air if you get everyone back safely.

But that didn't mean that wasn't exactly what I wanted to do.

CHAPTER 6

WREN

The class was getting restless, and if I didn't cough up some water soon, I was undoubtedly going to get shanked.

"Look," I grumbled, setting down my ruck, "you can give me your canteen and I can get everyone some water, or you can walk by yourself down the mountain without so much as an idea of where you're going. Those are your options. Take it or leave it."

"And if you start getting cute," Malia hissed, tossing a softball-sized rock in her hand, "I'll cave your stupid little skull in. Got me?"

Note to self: do not piss off Malia.

Purple-hair Guy and Jerk Face raised their hands in surrender.

"Okay, someone get some deadfall for a fire. We need light

to see this damn map," I suggested, glad I had at least a few people on my side. Jerk Face took off into the trees, hopefully going to collect some sticks big enough for a torch or something.

One by one everyone passed their canteens to me, and I distributed the water while Purple-hair Guy started a fire. Granted, he tried starting it with his magic first, but failed. When we had a bit of light, I pulled the laminated map from the bag, along with the compass, and a few other items from the dark recesses.

Unfortunately, other than far too many dive weights, there wasn't much more than what looked like water purifying drops and a pocketknife. Good to know if we found water, I could at least make it drinkable—in theory.

Unfolding the map, I tried to gauge where we were. Sure, I'd been camping roughly a zillion times with Ellie and her family, but I'd never been dropped out in the middle of nowhere and told to find my way back. My orienteering skills weren't exactly on point. Most witches knew the directions just by breathing. I didn't have that luxury, my wonky magic fucking even that up.

I latched onto the compass, trying to decipher the map.

"No," Fiona breathed, staring at the slick map, her eyes widening before narrowing to slits. "They did not have us march in fucking circles all damn day." She pointed at a spot on the paper, looked around, and then pointed at a spot very close to her other finger. "We're here," she said, her eyes lighting up with relief. "See that dip? It matches the terrain over there. Our camp is maybe a mile away."

An all-day hike only to go in circles? Yeah, that sounded about right.

But the sneaky part was that if we hadn't had that map, we'd be wandering in the woods until we *maybe* stumbled on the camp.

"Who wants to show these instructors they can't break us?" I asked, my grin just a touch evil. If Margot Bannister couldn't break me, I seriously doubted the ABI would be able to do the job.

Forty-five minutes later the camp finally came into view, cabin three's pitched roof never looking so good. Granted, I hadn't really inspected it before now, but damn, was it pretty.

In the back of my mind, I was already eating a fair-style turkey leg while I took the longest, hottest shower in the known universe. Though, as soon as the roofline registered to some people, they raced for the cabins like their life depended on it. I was at the back, Fiona's arm slung over my shoulder as she hobbled with renewed vigor. She'd turned her ankle a while back, the darkness most definitely not on her side.

It was clearly well before sunup, and since there was nary an instructor to greet us, I figured no one expected us to get back this fast. Relief hit me as soon as Fiona and I stepped onto the packed dirt of the camp, the flat terrain a blessing after trying not to fall down a hill for so long.

"Well, well, well," Ames called from somewhere, sending my gaze skittering around to try and locate him. "It figures *you'd* be the one to disobey orders."

But we hadn't been given an order not to help—not really.

He separated himself from the shadows as he stalked over to

us. This wasn't a man who seemed to be in charge of his mental faculties. Ducking under Fiona's arm, I moved in front of her. For some reason, she seemed to need more protecting than I did.

"You want to tell me why you disobeyed a direct order, cadet?" he snarled, looming over me, even though he was only a handful of inches taller. "You were told not to help your classmates."

Was I really going to get in trouble for doing the right thing? It looked like it.

"Technically," I began, making his rage-filled eyes widen, "there was no order. Commandant Girard said helping would earn punishment—not that we couldn't do it. I'm the one who helped after we were dropped in an unfamiliar terrain in the dark without supplies. If making sure everyone made it back safe and sound is a crime, you can go right ahead and punish me."

Was I daring a man who seemed to have no qualms about accosting someone he was supposed to teach? Maybe. But he wasn't getting the girl at my back.

No way, no how.

Ames' eyes narrowed, his shoulders bunching like he'd really enjoy punching me in the face, but a slow clap had his expression clearing in an instant. He took a step back, grinding his teeth as he straightened, his eyes promising vengeance.

A deep male laugh had shivers racing up my spine—the good kind this time. "Give it a rest, Ames. She beat us at our own game."

Turning the both of us to keep Fiona away from Ames, I spied Acosta stalking from the tree line behind us.

So I guess we were never really alone out there.

Oops?

"Hit the showers and then grab some grub," Acosta ordered, making everyone snap to. "Cadet Bannister here has just volunteered to put every cabin to rights so you all can get a good night's rest. We're starting early tomorrow, ladies and gentlemen, so get to it."

My stomach yowled in protest. I wanted a shower and food. But most of all I wanted sleep.

"Oh, no," Fiona whispered, her whole body trembling as Ames' gaze narrowed on the other instructor. She audibly gulped, and then she backed me up. "I helped, too. No one else could read the map. She shouldn't have to do it alone."

My lips pressed together so I wouldn't start bawling. Fiona could barely stand up on her own, and she wanted to help?

"Me too," the purple-haired guy—AKA, Benjamin—protested. "I gathered sticks for torches and helped people across streams."

"And me," Hannah called. "I provided security and passed out water. We all helped each other. Punishing only her is wrong."

Acosta's smile was feral and yet somehow warm. "Yes, but she was your leader. I watched every step you all made out there. Not a one of you would have made it back without her. I'd have been scooping you all up and shipping you back to your mommies."

As good as the praise felt, my stomach was still mad at me. If only those damn rucks had food in them.

"Get what you need for your showers and get some food," Acosta ordered, but no one moved, a solid mutiny working its way through the crowd.

"Now," he growled, that single word laced with enough power to make me want to kneel. Hell, if I weren't holding Fiona up, I probably would have.

Everyone moved—even Fiona—her pitiful hobble away making my heart lurch. Her ankle was the size of a grapefruit and most likely broken.

"Jacobs, go to the medic first. Dumond, you take her."

"On it," Hannah muttered, scooping up Fiona like she weighed nothing.

His gaze moved to me, the first time he'd looked directly at me since Ames had thrown his hissy fit—what felt like a week ago—before sliding right off to stare at the instructor in question. "I've got this, Ames. You can clock off, yeah?"

The asshole shook himself like he had no idea he was still standing there. He shot me a scathing glare before marching off as if he'd been the one to suggest it. I sort of wished I knew what his problem was, but it warred with the smart part of my brain that knew it was not my business.

If I had a guess, the name Bannister was the likely culprit.

Two decades ago, the Bannister name heralded a rich ancestry of powerful witches, deep pockets, and a boatload of influence. Today, my lovely fuckups tarnished our name so bad it was a wonder I made it here in the first place. Someone somewhere had to have pulled quite a few strings to keep me out of jail—something I was lamenting hardily at that particular moment.

At least in jail I wouldn't have to worry about sepsis from a muddy blister on my heel.

My gaze tracked Ames as he stomped off, his form blending

into the darkness as soon as he moved out of the dim light amassed from the cabin porch lanterns.

"You did good out there," Acosta murmured, pulling my gaze back to him. I was so tired, I'd almost forgotten I was standing there covered in sweat, dirt, and blood. Wiggling a toe, I nodded.

Yup, definitely bleeding.

"It was no big deal. I'm sure someone else would have done the same if they'd saved their pack." Or I was being incredibly naïve. That was a failing of mine. It was hard for me to think of only the worst in people. Maybe if I had thought about myself a little bit, I wouldn't be stuck here now.

He shifted, moving closer to me, and I had the very sudden realization that we were alone out here. "I don't hand out compliments, Wren. You acted like a leader out there because you are one. But that's going to paint a target on your back just as much as your name will."

The sound of him saying my name had my knees knocking together. Did he say something after that? Oh, that's right, I was in deep shit. Yeah, I knew that already.

"For giving a shit that people didn't fall off this bullshit mountain and die? I *guess*." I tried to shrug my shoulders, but every muscle felt like it was going to snap in half and slither off my body. "I was raised better than that."

Acosta snorted, the derision on his face curling his upper lip. "By Margot Bannister? Unlikely."

My gaze narrowed, my jaw clenching. What the hell did he know about my mother?

"Margot Bannister is a name on a birth certificate. Alice Whitlock raised me, and she taught me better than only looking out for myself. That a prize is nothing if I have to sacrifice my honor to get it." I met his gold gaze, those eyes for once not making me melt. "Letting people fall off a cliff because I wanted to win? That would be losing my honor. If that means I have to clean up wall lockers, well, then, so be it."

Pivoting on a heel, I tried to stalk off, but my poor feet had other plans. My stalk was more of a limp, the pitiful squish of my boot making my exit less than ideal. Plus, a warm hand caught my elbow, the gentle hold sending shivers down my spine.

"You know damn well everyone is trying to clean up their areas before you can get to them," he murmured, his breath close to my ear. The heat of his hand on my skin had my knees ready to give out. "You impressed them all out there. This was a task they were meant to fail, and they know it."

My eyes stayed glued to his hand on my arm. I wanted to look up into those eyes, but if I did, I knew I'd do something stupid. Like faint or kiss him or…

"Look at me," he growled, yanking my gaze up like all I needed was the order. His nostrils flared as his eyes narrowed, almost like he was mad at me for something—the change in his demeanor quick enough to give me whiplash. Leaning in closer, he growled, "You're bleeding. How long have you been bleeding, Wren?"

Why did my name on his lips make my insides go funny? But the best I could do was shrug.

Again.

"I was too scared to look. I worried if I took the boot off to check, I wouldn't be able to get it back on. Walking in the middle of nowhere without shoes on seemed like a bad plan."

Gently, I tugged on my arm, signaling him to let me go, but all it did was make his eyes start glowing as a growl rumbled from his chest.

No moving. Got it.

"You need a fucking keeper, you know that?" he murmured, the words harsh but his tone was something else. He readjusted his grip, pulling me closer, his nose barely an inch from mine as his gaze bore a hole into me. "When are you going to start looking out for yourself, huh?"

CHAPTER 7

NICO

The scent of her blood had my wolf howling inside my brain, cutting off any and all thought or reason. She was hurt—hurt because I couldn't protect her. Failure threatened to cave in my chest as her green-gold eyes widened at my question.

My failure.

It was true: Wren did need a keeper, and she sure as shit needed to think about herself for a change—no part of my words had been a lie. But they failed to convey just how fucking proud of her I was. No magic to be had, no food, no sleep, and she'd made it so every single one of those ungrateful fuckers made it back to camp.

It took everything I had in me to let her walk that long, to let her starve. And now she was bleeding?

My wolf wouldn't let me do it another second.

Without a word, I lifted the pack off her shoulders, the slight weight probably too much for her to carry that long. An angry red indention bloomed across her pale skin under her soiled tank top, making my eye twitch and my teeth grind.

The pragmatic part of my brain argued once again that she wasn't my mate, but my wolf stomped it down and told it to shut the fuck up. Either mate or spell or blind baser need, Wren needed to be taken care of, and I didn't trust her to do it herself.

In an instant, I had her pack on my shoulder and her lithe body in my arms, her scent powering through the dirt and grime and sweat of the last twenty-four hours. Ignoring her frightened squeak, I marched us toward the only place I wanted her to be.

"Where are you ta—"

"Hush," I barked, refusing to look at the woman. Looking down at that face would do me in. I was already half-insane. I didn't need one more temptation—not when I needed to see where she was bleeding and stop it. Not when I had to make sure she was okay.

Not stopping for a second, I kicked in the door of my cabin with about as much finesse as a battering ram. The instructors had private quarters, and I'd taken over Wyatt's cabin for this class. My wolf practically yipped inside my head, the idea that she was in my den, in my space, calming him and riling him up all in one go.

At least I had enough brain power to close the door behind us so no one else could see me completely unravel—except Wren. Her gaze hadn't left my face once, the burn of it racing down my spine all the way to my cock.

Fuck.

Continuing my trek, I strode to the private bath. Unlike the cadets, each instructor had a studio-style cabin outfitted with a full bath, kitchenette, microscopic living room, and bedroom. They were small and bare bones, but it got the job done. I didn't see any of it, my eyes on the prize of getting those damn boots of hers off so I could inspect her feet.

You could have gone to the medic instead. Why did you bring her here?

I knew the answer to that question, but avoided it like the plague, my wolf slashing his claws into my brain.

Reluctantly, I set Wren down on the closed toilet lid and flipped on the shower tap. She had been rucking through mud and dirt and who knew what else—she'd need to get cleaned up before I could dress her feet. Yes, that was the very good reason I had for stealing her away to my cabin without so much as a word.

Yep.

Totally logical.

"Umm... A-Acosta? I don—"

The sound of my last name passing her lips grated, making my jaw clench. "Nico," I growled, kneeling at her feet. "My name is Nico."

Eyes wide, she blinked at me as she digested the situation. "O-okay, Nico. I don't know what's going on, and I'd really like to."

While fair, I couldn't exactly give her an answer. I didn't know what was going on, either. "You're bleeding and covered in filth and about as sturdy as a cooked noodle."

All true, but not what she'd asked. Too bad, it was all I could give her.

Without further explanation, my gaze reluctantly left her face as I focused on the laces of her boots crusted with dried mud. Gently, I pulled one loose, working the lace so it was wide enough that I could pull her foot free.

As soon as I pulled on the ruined leather, she hissed and pressed a hand to her mouth as her face drained of all color. With nothing else for it, I yanked her foot free of the boot, barely managing to catch her before she went limp, passing out from shock or pain or worse. I didn't bother to look at her freed foot. Instead, I worked the other boot off while she was still passed out.

When I finally let myself move my gaze down, though, both my wolf and I nearly howled. Wren's feet were hamburger—blistered and swollen, completely covered in blood. Her socks were soaked, ripped in some places as the material had been worn thin by the sheer amount of walking. I'd never wanted to wring someone's neck as much as I did this woman's.

Why hadn't she said anything? Why didn't she tell me she was hurt?

She doesn't know you, stupid. And did you see every other instructor out there? Those kids would have been put through the wringer.

Cradling her to my chest, I tried to calm down as I waited, burying my nose in her hair in an attempt to appease my wolf. He wouldn't be satisfied until she was healed, until she was mine, until she was underneath me. But I could only help with one of those.

My eyes slid closed as I used the lone ability not given to me by my father.

The one I never used unless it was absolutely necessary.

The one I would not hesitate to use now.

Reaching inside the deepest parts of me, I called for my wolf, pulling at the thread of him until he reached back. I drew from him—drew on the healing that he so often gave to me, and clutched Wren closer, passing on that power.

Not all Alphas could perform this healing, the ability lost over the centuries as brute force and subjugation became far more revered.

It was as if I were a conduit, letting the energy flow from me to her in a steady pulse of heat, quietly drawing her pain away. I gritted my teeth against it, the sharp ache of the process leaving me cold and shaky.

How was she standing with pain like that? How was she breathing?

Pulling more from her, I sucked in a gasp. Her joints were on fire, her back aching, and her clawing hunger all slapped me at once, turning my stomach. But I could shoulder it. If it meant she wouldn't hurt anymore, if it meant my wolf would be soothed, if it meant this terrible throb in my chest would go away, I'd do it.

The heat of the water misted through the room as her scent filled my nose, and I slid my eyes open, inspecting her feet.

The damage was still substantial, but she wasn't actively bleeding anymore, nor did the flesh seem to be one wrong move away from infection. A tiny bit of pride suffused my chest, quelling that stupid ache I'd felt since the day I pulled her from the flames. It was always there, nagging, gnawing, picking at me until I saw her, until I scented her, until I held her.

Wren seemed to startle in my arms, yanking herself to consciousness by sheer force of will. Shuddering, she reached for her feet, even as my arms held her tight. Mesmerized, her hand shook as she gently prodded the wounds, her body stilling at the same moment her fingers did.

"How did you... You hea—"

"I didn't *do* anything," I lied through my teeth. For some reason, having her know was so much worse than her thinking she'd healed on her own. I had no idea why she shouldn't, I just knew it was bad.

No one but my mother knew what I could do—knew about the quiet alpha power that so few used.

And I didn't trust Wren.

Wanting her didn't equate to trust in my book.

"You should get cleaned up," I croaked, though I hoped it passed muster as a rumble.

Images of her stripping off her clothes filled my brain. Of the water sliding down her creamy skin. Of her flesh pebbling at the kiss of the water.

Nope. I needed to stop that thought right in its tracks.

But her scent in my nose, coupled with her short little pants, and the gallop of her heart were calling to every single instinct I had. My wolf howled, begging me to bury my face in her neck and take that scent for our own.

To make it ours.

"I'll leave you to it," I murmured, pulling us both up. I had to get out of this room before I looked at her face. One look and I would be done for.

Setting her away from me, I made for the door, only to be jerked to a stop by her voice.

"What do I do for clothes?" That voice was deep and husky and affected, and I desperately tried to ignore how her scent had changed.

Don't look. Do not look at her. You won't make it out of this room.

"I'll take care of it," I murmured, slipping out of the confined space before my wolf decided to do something stupid.

But as soon as the door closed behind me, a new dilemma dawned. The only clothes in this cabin were mine. Dancing in my head were the images of my shirt sliding over her shower-warmed skin. Of her bare ass barely hidden by the hem. Of her rosy nipples pebbling against the cotton. My name written across her back as my fingers fisted in her hair.

Nope. No. She needed her own clothes, and I needed to get the hell out of here.

Racing for the door, I breathed a shuddered sigh of relief once the fresh night air hit my nostrils, her scent diluted by the perfume of pine trees and fresh earth. Even under sweat and dirt and blood, her scent made me fucking crazy.

I kept to the shadows, picking through the camp as I made a beeline for her cabin.

She needed her own clothes. Her. Own. Clothes.

With a cursory check to make sure no one was inside, I followed that honey and jasmine scent to her bunk, dispassionately selecting underwear and soft garments to make sure she was comfortable, remembering the flip-flops by chance.

There was no way she would be able to put those boots on

again without pain—it didn't matter how much of the sting I'd been able to leech from her.

A few moments later, I was back at my cabin, desperately trying to quiet my wolf. He was so loud, I didn't even hear the water shut off. I'd had every intention of simply setting them on the toilet, but before I could, she opened the bathroom door.

Wrapped in the luckiest towel known to mankind, she stuttered to a stop as clouds of steam carrying her intoxicating scent surrounded me. Her warm, wet skin pebbled against the cool air just like I feared it would, the heat of it reaching me.

One pull and that towel could be gone.

One step and she'd be in my arms.

One kiss and she'd be in my bed.

Fuck.

I was doomed.

CHAPTER 8

WREN

WAS THIS WHAT PREY FELT LIKE?

Nico's golden eyes glowed with whatever power he kept hidden beneath his flesh. I wasn't quite certain what class of arcaner he was, but whatever it may have been, I was pretty sure it was some sort of predator.

His jaw clenched as he stared at me, the wadded bundle of fabric in his arms forgotten. Yes, I was acutely aware I was in a towel, still damp from the most blessed shower I had ever taken. Sure, the water pressure left something to be desired, but there was soap and shampoo and even a conditioner that smelled like Heaven.

But the crux of it was that I didn't have a stitch on me, and he did—specifically, he had what appeared to be my clothes in his hands.

"Are those for me?" I squeaked, my voice—along with my belly—doing very weird things at the moment. I couldn't feel my feet and the aches in my bones were long gone. And the way he was staring at me, like he'd really enjoy eating me up, well...

Nico took three long steps toward me, his gaze never leaving my face. He didn't say a word as his jaw clenched and unclenched, like any second, he'd stop holding himself back and kiss me or devour me or...

My whole body vibrated with the growing silence, or maybe that was Nico's growl. He seemed almost frozen, my near nakedness shorting out the rational part of his brain.

Hell, I was having a tough time not just reaching up and giving this little towel a tug. I didn't know the first thing about him, and the reckless section of my head didn't seem to give a shit.

My foot moved forward, not bothering to consult the rest of my mind, but as soon as my skin made contact with the floor, the pain came roaring back, making me wince. A hiss escaped my lips and that small sound seemed to break us both out of our haze.

"Here," he growled, handing me the bundle in his arms. "Get dressed, and I'll bandage your feet."

I was barely able to nod before he gently pushed me back in the bathroom and shut the door, the slap of the wood making contact with the frame the bucket of cold water I needed.

He's your instructor, Wren. You have enough problems trying to survive this stupid school without fucking your instructor on the second damn day.

As usual, my inner voice was right. A hint of shame made my heart ache as I hurriedly slipped into my clothes—or as hurried as one could be while trying not to aggravate their cut-up feet. He'd brought me a comfortable bra and underwear, a pair of lounge shorts, and a soft, oversized T-shirt that I frequently slept in.

That ache in my chest? Well, it doubled as his kindness hit me. He could have left me there or sent me to the medic.

Then why didn't he?

I didn't have an answer to that, and I doubted he did, either.

Without the desire to ransack Nico's bathroom for a brush, I messily piled my wet hair on top of my head and opened the door. Nico was in the small kitchen, bracing his hands against the counter as he hung his head.

"Everything okay?" I murmured, unwilling to step farther into the room. It wasn't the pain in my feet, either. There seemed to be a weight in the air between us in that unknown space that resided there.

"Fine."

Nico shoved back from the counter and strode over to me. Without a word, he lifted me up in his arms, carrying me to the kitchen. His scent enveloped me, the woodsy wild cologne surrounding me. He'd been out in those woods all damn day, and yet, he smelled like I wanted to lick his neck and reach my hand down his pants.

Where the fuck did that come from? Get it together, Wren.

The cool kiss of the counter against my ass had me shaking myself. My feet were still injured—not as much as before, I knew that much. Nico had to have done something, worked some kind of magic on me. But how?

Maybe it was the wards that protected us, maybe it was just him, but no one had ever been able to use magic around me without consequences.

Ever.

So how was he able to help me?

His hands left my skin, and he studiously ignored me while he readied his supplies, opening a jar of salve with a jerking twist.

Wincing, I stayed his hand before he could grab my foot. I'd have to warn him, and I really didn't want to. "That stuff is spell-free, right?"

Frowning, he jerked his gaze to mine. "Why?"

Screwing my mouth to the side, his shoulders hunched all on their own. "Magic goes wonky around me. Spells? They go haywire."

Nico's face blanked, shuttering completely before I could figure out what he was thinking. Not that I knew—ever—but before I could sort of guess.

Now his face was a mask of nothing, like maybe he didn't believe me and didn't want me to know it.

The tried-and-true sense of shame crawled out of its hidey-hole to slap me in the face. I couldn't expect him to understand something like that. The Bannisters were one of the oldest witch families in the States. We had been a legacy once upon a time.

Now because of me, we were a joke.

Or *I* was.

Dropping my gaze, I inspected the floor, counting rows of

hardwood planks rather than looking him in the eye anymore.

This was stupid. I was stupid. I never should have come here. They should have just sent me to prison and threw away the key. At least there I couldn't hurt anyone. At least there I could be where I belonged with all the other fuckups.

"Yes, it's free of magic," he murmured. "It's a regular salve for cuts and bruises. May I?"

Jerkily, I nodded, not bothering to look at him. His fingers found my ankle and he held my leg steady while he gently spread the ointment over the worst of the cuts.

Other witches could heal themselves up just fine. Me? I was stuck with human-grade healing and no way to speed up the process. Under the null wards, at least the rest of my class was in the same boat. Part of me wished for a way to synthesize those wards down to something smaller so I could walk down the street in peace.

It didn't have to be in Savannah, either.

I'd like to go anywhere where the Bannister name wasn't known. I'd like to go into a shop without worrying I would hurt someone. Or maybe simply live in the knowledge that my bullshit existence—such as it was—wasn't a blight on the butt of humanity.

Gritting my teeth against the sting of the ointment, I started counting the planks on the walls, avoiding the man who was so carefully tending to my wounds.

How do you keep getting into situations like this? Can't you keep your nose clean for one day, Wren?

My inner voice was sounding an awful lot like my mother these days.

In no time at all, Nico was done with the salve and on to

wrapping my battered feet in gauze. I wasn't sure how I was supposed to keep them clean and dry in an environment like this. If the coming weeks were anything like the last twenty-four hours, I was screwed.

I'd likely end up with gangrene and die. Wouldn't that just be a cherry on top of the shit sundae that was this week?

When he started taping the gauze down, I'd formulated a likely flawed plan. I could go to the kitchens and maybe pilfer their plastic baggie supply. That would at least keep mud and dirt out of my wounds—in theory.

I was in the middle of my baggie heist plans when Nico moved in my space, his face right in mine.

"You're going to take care of yourself, right?" It was less a question and more of a direct order.

The best I could do was shrug. Did it really matter? If I washed out, I'd go to jail where I'd always planned on going, anyway. What did it matter if I washed out medically or because of outright failure? Either way, I would still be the family fuckup.

"If another all-day hike is on the menu, I might fail on purpose. Jail is sounding better and better all the time."

His gold eyes started glowing again as his hands bracketed my hips on the counter. His body seemed to get bigger, wider, as he loomed over me.

"You do realize that jail is off the table for you, right? If you wash out of this course, jail isn't your fallback. Execution is."

A cold pit of dread yawned wide in my belly.

"But... it wasn't even my fault! I told him to stop. That he couldn't do the spell around me." Yes, I'd just admitted to bribing a warlock to do a spell for me in the first place, but the punishment for that wasn't *death*. Hell, neither was burning his shop down.

The punishment according to the witch covenant was reparations and jail time. Not...

"They don't care, Wren," he murmured, his warm breath skating over my skin. "You need to get your shit together. You need to succeed here. Because there is no fallback plan for you."

Gulping hard, the dread snaked its fingers through my entire chest, making the breaths in my lungs stutter. No fallback plan. No jail. No safety net.

I gritted my teeth against the urge to curl up into a ball and start screaming. This wasn't fair—none of it.

"Deep breaths," he commanded, cupping my chin in his hands. "Breathe in for the count of four and out for four."

When I didn't comply immediately, he tilted my chin up almost roughly, getting my attention.

"Breathe, Wren. In for four and out for four. Do it."

With nothing else for it, I did what he said, sucking in breaths as he counted. Still shaking, my breathing regulated.

"Good girl. Now what are you going to do?"

"Pass. Survive," I croaked, and a hint of a smile lifted the side of his mouth.

He took a short step closer, his slim hips fitting in between my knees. "Good. And you're going to take care of yourself, right?"

His scent enveloped me in a tight embrace, and even though he wasn't touching me anymore, I still felt him everywhere. My heart picked up speed once again, only this time it wasn't the threat of death or the pain.

It was him so close to me, his scent in my nose, and his mouth so close to mine. I wanted to fall into that mouth, lose myself for a second in those lips. Hypnotized, my torso drifted closer to his, my breasts brushing the wall of his chest.

I nodded in answer, brushing my nose against his with the movement. All I could see were his glowing gold eyes, as the rumble of a growl vibrated through us both. The heat in them made those eyes pools of molten metal as his lids drooped just a touch.

A shuddering gasp squeezed from my throat in anticipation, the almost-touch too much for me to bear.

And then all I felt was cool air as Nico's gaze narrowed to slits and he moved back.

"You should get some sleep," he practically growled, half-turning his body away from me.

Confused, the cold slap of rejection woke me from my trance.

Oh. *Oh.* I was so stupid. I'd misread him somewhere. He didn't...

Swallowing thickly, I gingerly hopped off the counter, gritting my teeth against the pain in my chest and the ache in my feet.

"Thanks for..." *Everything?* "Your help and advice. I appreciate it."

How I'd strung those words together without bawling was a fucking miracle, but I did it. I didn't meet his gaze the entire time, but I fucking did it.

And I could do this. I could make it back to my bunk and... and...

Stupid tears welled in my eyes as I looked for the flip-flops

Nico had brought with him in my bundle of clothes. I'd left them in the other room, along with my filthy clothes and ruined boots. Clenching my teeth against the pain, I minced to the bathroom and snatched everything up, sliding my poor feet into the scant shoes.

He'd been so kind and all I'd taken it as was a plea to fuck me. Gods, I was so fucking dumb.

I made a move to go out the front door, when he caught me by the arm. "It's not safe to go that way," he murmured, the sound of his voice making me want to crawl in a hole and just... "You need to use the back door."

Wetly, I chuckled, the shame and mirth of the double entendre warring in my chest. It wasn't the first time I'd been shoved out the back door so no one would see. And even though I had the mental maturity of a twelve-year-old boy, everything just hurt.

It *hurt*.

Pulling my arm from his grip, I let him lead me to the door that was hidden in a back nook of the cabin. I could do this. I could walk back to my cabin and shore myself up and pass this gods-forsaken course.

I could.

It didn't matter that my mother thought I was the worst mistake she'd ever made or that my grandmother wished I'd have never been born. I could be a halfway decent agent if I put my mind to it, right?

Maybe be an analyst or a researcher. No one in their right mind would let me out in the field, but I could be useful. I could matter.

Steeling my spine, I marched out the door, not looking back

at Nico. He'd helped me, healed me, and patched me up. He could have my thanks and that was it.

My march turned into a hobble after about a minute, the trek to the cadet cabins far longer than Nico had made it seem. By the time I made it to the porch, I was breathing funny, sweating, and so close to tears it was dumb. All I had to do was make sure the cabin was clean and I could go get some food.

My stomach howled in agreement. Food would make it better.

But before I could close my fingers around the handle, it was yanked out of my grip. Fiona stood in the open doorway, a relieved smile on her face. She was clean, walking on her own two feet, and seemed a lot better than when I'd left her. It made me wonder just how long I'd been gone.

"Get in here," she insisted, looping an arm around my middle, and helping me to my bunk. The cabin itself was also clean, Hannah's bed righted and made, and Malia's locker back to order.

Fiona was chittering about how the other cabins had cleaned up their own messes and how no one was going to let me lift a finger. A warmth built up under my ribs, easing the ache there a bit.

"Thanks," I whispered, squeezing her hand as she settled in next to me on my bed. "I really appreciate you guys."

She snorted, shaking her head. "You know damn well we would have all fallen off this damn rock without you. Even if no one else says it, you saved us. For some of us, the ABI is all we have left. It's our last option. I won't forget how you helped me, Wren. Not ever."

That was it. I was going to start crying any second now.

"Quit it before I start sobbing into my pillow," I grumbled, gently shoving her shoulder. "How's your ankle?"

She lifted the formerly offending appendage in the air to show me. "Good as new. The healer here is fabulous, plus it's the one place where the null wards aren't—except for the practical areas—so I got to actually breathe. I swear, these wards are for the birds."

The reality of what could have happened if I would have taken her to the healer sobered me. Gods, would there ever be a time where I could just be normal? Ever?

The cabin door opened, Hannah and Malia filing in, both their arms loaded down with plates.

"Look who's back," Hannah said, a wide smile blooming over her face as a knowing look filled her eyes. I didn't quite know what that was about, but I had a feeling I didn't *want* to know. "We picked you up some grub."

"More like she bribed the cook to heat up everything he could before she threatened to eat him, but whatever," Malia teased, a sly smile curling her lips.

"I didn't say I was going to eat him," Hannah protested. "I said I was hungry and growled a little, that's all. It's his fault if he assumed."

Hannah had informed us that ghouls only had to eat flesh every six months or so to stay healthy, and more often than not, they chose the freshly dead to consume. Most were morgue attendants or funeral home directors—fitting into polite society with ease.

She dropped a plate on my lap and handed me a fork. "Eat up. Tomorrow is going to be a doozy, and that Ames fucker has a bug up his ass about you."

I took the fork, and it was as if it unlocked my hunger. A moment later, I was drowning my sorrows in mashed potatoes. I'd eat, and sleep, and tomorrow I wouldn't look at Nico —*Acosta*—once.

And I'd make it.

Wouldn't I?

CHAPTER 9

NICO

Four.

Fucking.

Days.

That's how long it had been since Wren looked in my direction. Four days since I watched those green-gold eyes spark with heat, since I let her scent wrap around me like I was sinking into her body. Four days since she acknowledged me at all.

Four days since I fucked up.

But what else was I supposed to do? I had already been pushing it taking her back to my cabin—a solid idiot move, if I do say so myself. If I'd have kissed her, there would have been no stopping us. I would have fucked her right on that tiny kitchen counter, and then where would she be?

My bed.

Where would I?

My bed.

Because I sure as shit wouldn't be letting her out of it once I had her, that much was certain. The way she called to the wolf under my flesh made every single minute of the last four days its own version of hell on earth.

I didn't know if I believed her tale of not being able to do magic. Or that she hadn't set fire to Carmichael's shop. If she couldn't do magic like she said, then why the fuck was I so damn smitten with her? Why did my eyes follow her every movement?

Why did I still feel the heat of her body against mine four days later?

Gritting my teeth, I watched her grip the rifle with the moderate efficiency of someone who had handled a gun a time or two. She wasn't failing, but she wasn't a sharpshooter either, which was exactly where I wanted her to be.

She needed to keep her head down. She needed to survive.

But even though she hadn't looked at me once, she still did exactly what I'd told her to. So far, she'd passed every test, no matter how much Ames threw at her. But there was a cold look of determination behind her eyes that I hated—mostly because I'd been the one to put it there.

That coldness hurt, and it was all my fault.

"Get your shots on target, Bannister, or I'll take that rifle away and give you a fucking BB gun," Ames screamed six inches away from her ear.

I had to give it to him: he hadn't once touched another student since I "counseled" him on his methods, but that didn't stop him from singling Wren out. Unfortunately, there was only so much I could protect her from without waving a huge red flag that I was showing her favor.

My gaze shifted to her target. Out of the twenty shots she'd fired, she'd hit about fifteen center mass and four in the head. The lone shot she'd missed, was barely a centimeter off. And what was worse? The poor bastard next to Wren hadn't managed to hit the target more than a handful of times.

Wren's cheeks pinked as her eyes narrowed, not sparing Ames a glance. In quick succession, she fired off six shots, each one hitting the target right in the head. I had a feeling she'd been picturing Ames' face while she did it, too.

Then again, it could have been mine.

The scent of her sorrow was still in my nose, the rejection and sudden change in my attitude undoing every good thing I'd done since taking her to my stupid cabin. I'd hurt her. A lot.

"I guess I just need to yell at you every time you shoot, then, now, don't I? I mean how else are we going to get you ready for the real ABI?"

Gods, Ames was such a fucking idiot.

The instructor straightened, narrowing his eyes at me. Out of the two of us, my students were actually being taught by a competent instructor and doing fine. His eight students—save for Wren and a few others—were floundering.

Barnes was barely hitting the target, Faust was still trying to load his rifle after twenty minutes, and Ponda's weapon was in pieces on his lap.

Raising an eyebrow at him, I circled my finger, signaling for him to wrap it the fuck up. We needed to move this along and him not helping the others wasn't going to get us all to lunch on time. Ames' hands fisted at his sides, his anger getting the best of him as he stalked over.

"What?" he hissed, glaring at me. "You mad because I'm schooling your girl?"

And this was exactly what I'd been afraid of when he walked up to me that night before the course officially began. The last thing I needed was him figuring out just how much Wren meant to me. Irritated, I crooked my finger, walking back a few paces out of the null line where I knew no one could hear us.

"No, I'm mad, because despite the time you've spent 'schooling' a cadet that doesn't need it, Ponda's weapon has come apart, and Faust hasn't got a shot off. You have eight students. Not one. I cannot teach all sixteen by myself or... maybe I can, and you should go take a nap since you're acting like a fucking toddler."

But then I'd have to get closer to Wren, and I had a feeling she'd like to turn that gun on me.

"What do you mean?" Ames whipped his head to stare at the wonder twins who were fucking up royally. "Oh, for fuck's sake. Gods, those two are going to give me a fucking aneurysm. If it isn't arcane related, they act like it doesn't fucking exist."

Ames marched right back to the wonder twins and started his rant while I got Barnes in hand, putting me right next to Wren.

Fuck.

Her scent filled my nose again, and it was as if my wolf had been waiting for it. He whined in my head, begging me to get closer. But I'd been dealing with his complaints for four fucking days, so gritting my teeth against them was nothing new.

By the time Ames was done kicking Faust and Ponda off the range, I'd managed to get my wolf under control and fix the problem with Barnes' sights that had him aiming for the fucking moon.

Ames pressed the red range button that signaled everyone to put their weapons down. "Police your brass and stow your weapons. It's time to finally get to the fun part of this exercise."

Ames slapped the blue button, recalling the targets and replacing them with closer ones. He opened the closest locker, revealing rows upon rows of glowing orbs.

Wren stumbled back, trying to get as far away from Ames as she possibly could without drawing attention to herself. Her fiery braid practically trembled against her back as she seemed to search for an exit. Ames called a few cadets up to pass out the potion bombs, but I was more focused on Wren's face going white.

She was typically pale, but red splotches were forming on her chest as her breathing hitched in her throat. Wide-eyed, her panic permeated the air as she shuffled back. I'd figured she'd been lying to me when she said she couldn't do magic, but what had she said?

Magic goes wonky around me. Spells? They go haywire.

I didn't know how much of that was true. Sure, it seemed like it was true with her freaking out, but—

Wren's scared steps had her accidentally knocking into Barnes who had a blue orb in his hands. Barnes, the clumsy idiot with a shock of purple hair, fumbled the orb before dropping it. Wren dove for it, managing to catch the orb before it broke, her face white as a sheet.

Hell, she looked like she was ready to throw up.

Gently, she handed it back to Barnes before steeling her spine and marching over to Ames.

"Get back to your spot, Bannister," Ames barked, his hands full of potion crates.

Wren shook her head, her knees knocking together, even though her shoulders were back. "I can't," she insisted. "Someone is going to get hurt if I stay here."

Ames rolled his eyes as he passed off a crate to another student. "Yeah, yeah. We all know about your penchant for blowing things up. No one gives a shit. Get in line."

"You don—"

Ames advanced on her. "I said get back in line, or I'll make sure you're booted out of this school so fast it'll make your head spin." A cruel smile bloomed across his mouth. "Literally."

That little fuck. He was taunting her, baiting her.

Threatening her.

I clenched my teeth against my wolf's howl as I watched Wren shrink back.

What are you doing? You're just going to stand there while he threatens her? You aren't worthy of her as a mate, you selfish prick.

But she wasn't my mate, and even if she was, how could I defend her here? In front of all these cadets? No, I'd need something else, something lasting so Ames knew never to fuck with her again. Mate or not, I couldn't watch her all the time, and with this kind of escalation, it was only going to get worse.

"All right, people. Take a single potion bomb and aim for your target," Ames called loudly. "These are light arms, little more than colorful smoke bombs. They are often employed by agents to help clear a room, or based on the spell, incapacitate a perp. Since they are training rounds, they are mostly neutralized except for a tiny bit of magic."

The quickness with which Ames went from threatening Wren's life to following the lesson plan made my stomach turn.

Ames' face twisted into a scowl when Wren made no move to touch the potion crate. "What did I tell you, Bannister? Pick up a potion bomb."

I noticed the instant she was going to defy him and moved, getting right in her space, managing not to stare into those gorgeous eyes by sheer force of will.

"Maybe if Miss Bannister doesn't want to complete this iteration," I growled threateningly as I latched a hand around her bicep, "she'd be better served cleaning the dining facility." But my will crumbled in an instant, and my gaze found hers, anyway. "Maybe that'll teach you to bail on lessons."

Roughly, I jerked her away from the line as the first potion bomb was thrown. What was supposed to be a little smoke bomb turned into a ball of fire as soon as the glass smashed against the target. Green flames coated the grass beneath, blanketing the ground in an inferno.

Too late to stop the onslaught, the other potion bombs were already in the air, their landings detonating like the bombs they were, and then it wasn't me pulling Wren, it was *her* pulling *me*.

Flames exploded across the berm as the grass caught in an almost-wildfire. All the target stands were engulfed in mere moments as the flames reached farther, almost catching the stands on fire. Students shrieked as they raced for cover, but Wren yanked us toward the null wards, her red braid flying behind her as she dragged us both across it.

Breathing heavily, she stared at the empty firing line, tears pooling in her eyes. As soon as she crossed the line, the flames died, the grass smoldering where the fire had once been.

Shaking, she finally looked at me, something she hadn't done on purpose in four fucking days. Her face was gray as she gulped in air. Eyes wide and shocky, she put a trembling hand to her mouth.

"Did I... did I hurt anyone?" she whispered, a tear cresting her eyelid and falling down her cheek.

Gods, what I wouldn't give to be able to hold her right now. And what I wouldn't give to not have to look away.

But I did, scanning the crowd of students and Ames, trying to scent blood or pain over the pall of smoke and charred grass. I couldn't detect any, and the students seemed to be fine as they dusted themselves off and ventured closer to the stands, their voices buzzing in alarm.

Ames stood, his face white and voice cracking. "Everyone, calm down. Looks like we got the wrong batch from the apothecary. I'll test the next few potions to make sure, but we should be fine."

Wrong batch my ass.

Wren shook her head, the violent motion nearly bringing her to her knees. "They can't," she hissed. "Not while I'm here."

Giving her a quick jerk of my chin, I tightened my hold on her arm and resumed my march toward the dining hall, more to hold her up than anything else, but no one else needed to know that. Plus, I had to keep up the appearance of her "punishment" or Ames might catch on that Wren had most definitely caused that fire.

She'd also caused the Azalea Apothecary blaze, too.

Just not on purpose.

She hadn't been lying to me—she couldn't do magic. Wren couldn't so much as cast a single spell—not without severe consequences. And if she couldn't cast a spell, and all spells around her exploded, she'd never survive here.

They'd toss her out the first chance they got.

My wolf howled, clawing and slashing in my brain hard enough to make me wince. I had to figure something out—if only to give me more time to come to grips with my other realization.

Because if she didn't do magic, then what had she done to me?

"You've never cast a spell?" I asked under my breath—the answer vital if I was going to do this.

If I was going to put my life on the line to... to...

Wren shook her head. "Maybe when I was little, but not since I could remember. I didn't even go to arcane school—too dangerous."

Nodding, I breathed a sigh of relief as the empty dining hall came into view. "And the apothecary?"

"Has everyone heard about that damn thing?" she asked, her chuckle wet as she shook her head again. "I tried to stop Carmichael and then the whole damn place exploded."

And had I not been there she would have died in those flames.

Fuck, this was a mess.

And all of this meant she hadn't put a spell on me. She didn't make me act this way—at least not on purpose.

And it meant Wren wasn't a fuckup, not really. She had to be cursed or born under the wrong stars or worse. I'd never heard of a witch being born that way. Uninherits, sure, there were plenty of witches who didn't get magic, but to amplify it, to change the magic itself?

No. That was a first.

I couldn't stop the incessant nod or the way my wolf sucked in her scent. It was like she was leaving me, and I needed to keep her in my nose as long as possible.

I had to fix it.

Simply the thought of what could happen if Ames—or anyone—figured out Wren's little magic problem. They'd kill her.

And then I'd kill them.

Ushering her inside the building, I raced for the custodian's closet, dragging her behind me. There, I snatched the bucket and mop, some cleanser, and some rags. It had to look real. It had to look like I was punishing her for not participating, and then...

Then I'd make sure no one knew what she was. No one.

"Stay here and clean the place up. Pout. Make it look good. Lie if you need to. But stay the fuck here, got it?"

Wren stared at me with those gorgeous eyes and didn't say a word. Not until I grabbed her hand and gently shook it.

"A-Acosta—"

"No," I growled, advancing on her until she pressed her

back against the wall. "When we're together, when we're alone, you call me Nico. Understand?"

She gulped, tearing her gaze from mine as her shoulders curved in. "No," she croaked. "I don't understand."

Gods, I was a fucking idiot. Hooking a finger under her chin, I lifted her face to mine. Yes, we were in a damn broom closet. Yes, it was the wrong fucking time. Yes, I was being a first-rate asshole, complicating this *whatever* between us, but she needed to look at me.

I *needed* her to look at me. As soon as those gorgeous fucking eyes met mine, I couldn't stop myself from getting closer to her, boxing her in, surrounding her.

"I'm going to fix it," I growled, my voice barely above a whisper as I lowered my lips to hers. "I'll make it so you're safe here."

It was a promise.

An oath.

A vow.

Her gaze flared as my lips inched closer, and I watched those green-gold embers blaze bright until I was mere millimeters away from Heaven.

"Say my name, Wren," I ordered softly, my lips brushing hers as I spoke. Her breath hitched as her scent rose, her trembling fingers fisting in the fabric of my shirt. "Come on, my beautiful little bird. What's my name?"

"Nico," she breathed—like it was permission and a plea all at the same time.

Putting us both out of our misery, I pressed my lips to hers, sweeping my tongue into her mouth as she parted her lips on a gasp.

Gods.

If she smelled like Heaven, her taste was pure paradise, and the moan that vibrated up her throat? I was a goner with one fucking kiss. Helpless against its pull, I gripped the end of her copper braid and tugged, tilting her head back so I could devour her mouth.

Her scent perfumed the air around us, taking over all my senses as I crushed my mouth to hers. Her tongue stroked mine as her fingers fisted in my hair. Without a moment's hesitation I let go of her braid and found her hips, lifting her up and pressing her further into the wall. The friction of her center against the bulge in my jeans had a groan ripping up my throat.

I wanted her—more than I'd probably wanted anything or anyone else in my whole fucking life.

And I couldn't have her.

Not right now. Not while she wasn't safe.

Just as fiercely as it began, our kiss gentled, our heavy mingled breaths fanning the flames of our need.

Gods, I needed inside her. I needed her creamy skin against my sheets and her moans in my mouth.

"Four days, Wren. I've been wanting to do that for four fucking days."

Her brow furrowed as she took my bottom lip between her teeth, her tongue taunting me as she laved the sting. "Then why didn't you?"

That was a damn good question. "I was trying to keep you safe. I can't keep you safe if I'm distracted."

Her head tilted to the side as if my answer didn't quite make sense. "And I'm distracting?"

SPELLS AND SLIP-UPS 99

Wren's smile was tentative and knowing all at the same time, and I wanted to fuck her against this wall and...

This is not keeping her safe, you idiot. Get your head out of your dick for five seconds, will you?

My hand flexed on her hips as I forced myself to let her down. "You know damn well that you are."

Her expression was just as confused as it had been a moment before, but I couldn't explain—not if I was to get to Savannah and back before nightfall.

Not if I was going to keep her alive.

"Stay here. I'll find you when I get back."

With no time left, I pressed my lips to her forehead as I drew that honey and jasmine perfume into my nose, keeping it for myself. Then I forced myself to let her go, to leave that small piece of Heaven, to walk away from her.

To get in my car and leave her defenseless here while I went to Savannah.

But I needed witch help for a witch problem.

Unfortunately, I'd just have to settle for a warlock.

Too many hours later, my fingers fisted in the filthy fabric of Carmichael Jones' shirt. Knuckles bloody, I drew my arm back once more.

"Either you tell me the truth, or I end you right now, old man. What. Happened?" I growled through clenched teeth. "Don't make me ask again."

Carmichael spat blood on my boot, his eyes lolling in his head. "Fine, okay? I'll tell you. She offered me the money to heal the human, and I started the spell. Then all of a sudden, my whole damn shop is on fire, windows explodin' and everything. I don't know what else you want from me."

It had taken far too long to get this much out of him. I supposed he thought I'd get him in trouble or worse for lying his ass off to the ABI, hence why he was so cagey with the details. "Did she try to get you to stop?"

Carmichael shrugged. "Maybe? She yelled somethin', but then the whole place went up like a dang Roman candle."

"And then you ran off with the money and left her there to die? Is that it?"

"What's it to you?" The old man narrowed his gaze on me, a wide bloody smile on his crooked mouth. "Oh, this is good," he said on a chuckle. "The wolf prince and the Bannister fuckup. You sweet on her, wolf-boy?"

My smile must have been straight out of a nightmare because his fell as fast as mine rose. "And how would that make me any less dangerous to you? If I'm sweet on her like you say, and you left her to die, what's to stop me from ripping your throat out right here and right now?"

Carmichael lifted a shaky hand. "Now, hold on there. Maybe we can work something out. No need to do somethin' rash."

My grin widened. "As a matter of fact, I do think you can help me."

CHAPTER 10

WREN

There was no way that just happened.

No. Way.

Pressing my fingertips against my lips, I stifled a laugh. I'd spent the last four days pretending Nico Acosta didn't exist—the last four days pretending his gentle touches and caring words had meant nothing. That he hadn't destroyed me with a single rejection.

I'd gone over and over it in my head—trying to figure out where I'd gotten it wrong. And now I knew I *hadn't* gotten everything mixed up. He'd wanted me just as much as I'd wanted him.

He just wouldn't let himself have me.

And what did his "I'm going to fix it" mean? I'd been dealing with this horseshit my whole life, and he was going to breeze in and fix it?

How? Was he going to whip out some shells and beads and pray real hard that this curse I'd lived with my entire existence just *went away*?

But a single, solitary section of my brain asked if maybe he *could*.

I'd been cut off from the arcane side of Savannah for more years than I could remember—forever maybe. Even with parents like mine and a grandmother with as much power as she had, no one had even given a passing nod to an attempt at fixing this albatross around my neck.

I *wasn't* a blessed Bannister.

I was a blight. A black spot. A section of decay that they'd rather cut out or forget ever existed than fix whatever it was that had made me this way.

A shining bit of hope broke through the hedge of thorns in my chest—the one that was supposed to keep me safe from gruff arcaners with gorgeous shoulders and soft lips that promised the world. My belly dipped at the ghost of his lips on mine, at the memory of his body wrapped around me, his hands palming my ass, his rather impressive erection pressing against my center.

Come on, my beautiful little bird. What's my name?

Goose bumps tightened all over my body. His wild scent still filled the small room, and I had to get the hell out of there before I did something stupid. Like swoon or think I could be normal or plan for the future.

Shaking my head, I snatched the cleaning supplies and marched out of the closet. The dining hall wasn't the cleanest place in the world. The tables were always slightly sticky, the floor could use a good sweeping, and the chairs

SPELLS AND SLIP-UPS 103

had this film on them that made me shudder every time I sat down.

Gross.

Though, I had the feeling that Acosta—*Nico*—didn't give a shit if I cleaned anything at all as long as I was far, far away from all the other instructors while magic was in play. The cold fear of breaking one of those potion bottles slapped me in the face as I sprayed cleanser on the closest table.

If Nico hadn't gotten me out of there—if he hadn't believed me...

I could have really hurt someone. This fucked-up magic could have caused some real destruction. Not just an apothecary. Not just a fire.

I could have killed someone.

My vision blurred as the reality of the situation set in. If Nico couldn't find something to help—something to tamp down whatever horrible magic squirmed beneath my skin—I couldn't stay here.

For the first time in my life, I actually had more than Ellie as a friend. I had Fiona and Hannah and Malia.

What if the wards fell and they did magic around me? What if I hurt one of them?

Blinking away tears, I furiously scrubbed the table.

What the hell was I going to do?

Reality eclipsed the small bit of happiness I'd had in that closet. If Nico didn't come back with something that would help before tomorrow—not that I thought he would find one in such a scant bit of time—I was leaving.

I couldn't go back to Savannah, of course, but there had to be somewhere in the world with no magic, no arcaners, no way

I could hurt someone. Maybe not in Georgia, but there were places.

Right?

The small slice of hope I'd felt at Nico's promise crumbled to ash in my chest.

Because where the hell could I go with no money?

And no ride?

And no real place to go?

And the ABI looking to kill me the first chance they got?

Because that was what they did to arcaners who were a danger to every single person they came into contact with. That's what they did to the anomalies. The freaks. The ones they couldn't pin down or shove in a box or control.

So I sprayed cleanser and I scrubbed and I tried to come up with a plan that kept me alive and everyone safe. By the time I was done, I had the first leg of a shaky strategy. It was weak at best, but it was better than nothing.

"If you scrub that table any harder, you're going to wear the paint right off it," Fiona said right by my ear, scaring the absolute shit out of me.

Shaking and weak-kneed, I slid into the closest upright chair and fought off the urge to spray cleanser at her like a misbehaving cat. "You suck, Fi. You really, really do."

"I'm not the one who was off in la-la land for who knows how long. You've been here for hours, chickadee. We done had lunch and everything while you've been over here working your little tail off. What gives?"

Oh, how to answer that question. "Acosta sentenced me to cleaning this pigsty, so that's what I've been doing."

Yes, I paired that with a shrug and a nonchalant tone, and I was not nervous or obvious about the fact that I was lying my ass off at all.

Totally.

Fiona jutted out a hip and planted her dainty hand on it, her purple polished nails looking like she'd just come from a salon. I was lucky my shoes were on the right feet, and she had time to paint her nails?

"I know I'm blonde, but blind and stupid, I am not." She stepped forward, dropping her voice to a whisper. "The range? What happened?"

Finding my feet, I went back to my scrubbing, moving onto the next table. "I don't know what you mean."

"Don't you dare piss on my leg and tell me it's raining." She rested her hip against the table and snatched the dirty cloth right out of my hand. "One second, potion bottles are exploding and there's fire everywhere, and the next, you're over the null line with Instructor Smexy Pants and the fire is out."

"Instructor Smexy Pants?"

She pointed at her face. "Not. Blind. Have you *seen* those buns? They are juicy enough to take a bite out of. Alas, all he's been doing for the last four days is staring at *you*, so I figure I've already lost my shot." She flicked the rag at me. "And don't change the subject."

Wincing, I fought off the urge to spray her. At the beginning of this, she'd said she didn't want to talk about our families, but if I was going to explain, there was no other way around it. "Does the name Bannister mean anything to you?"

It was a stupid question. Ames had shouted my name for all the world to hear about a zillion times over the last four days. And by the way Fi's eyes widened, she'd already heard about my family, my crime, *and* my sentence. She schooled her features from out-and-out shock to something resembling nonchalance.

"No," she fibbed, "can't say as I have."

Snatching the rag back, I gave her a grateful glance and got back to scrubbing. "Liar."

Fiona sighed like I'd really caught her in the mother of all cover-ups. "Okay, fine. Everyone—*and I do mean everyone*— has heard about the Bannister who started the Azalea Apothecary fire. Though, word on the street is that it was an explosion that leveled half of Savannah, but you and I both know that's not true."

Leveled half of Savannah? Shit on a stick. I'm going to have to change my name now.

"It was *one* apothecary, *no one* died, and I *tried* to tell that dipshit not to cast around me, but..." Funny, I'd told that exact same story to the council that handed down my sentence, but they seemed rather reluctant to hear me out.

There were seven arcane councils in this country, one in Savannah, New Orleans, Knoxville, Sedona, Salem, Portland, and San Francisco. And I just so happened to get the one that was the least lenient, least tolerant of my oddities, and least willing to listen to a damn thing I had to say.

"Well, that's what happens when I'm around magic. One little smoke bomb turns into an inferno. One healing spell blows up an apothecary. You get the picture."

Fiona tapped on her lip with a shiny purple nail. "You know, I've never heard of anyone being born with magic that wonky. You think one of your parents pissed someone off and you got cursed or something? Because that would make a hell of a lot more sense. The Bannister name brings its fair share of hate."

Her theory had merit—however, I'd been this way all my life. Even before the usual puberty bitch-slap of arcane magic that most witches get, I was still causing a ruckus. If Fiona knew how many times I was told to go outside or to Ellie's so my family could have a "single moment of peace," well, she'd get that sad look on her face, and I just couldn't deal with that right now.

"I've always been this way. As long as I can remember." Blinking back frustrated tears, I moved to the next table.

Nico wasn't going to find a thing to help me. He couldn't. Because if he could, then what did that say about my family? With all their power and influence and clout that they'd rather me go on this way than get fixed?

That they'd let me suffer.

And for what?

No, Nico wasn't going to find anything because there wasn't anything to find. And because he wouldn't, I needed to leave. Just get gone before someone figured me out and killed me on the spot.

"But surely someone can help. Have you as—"

Whirling, I slapped the bottle of cleanser on the table. "Yes," I whispered. "I've asked my parents. And my grandmother. And my aunts. And anyone else I could possibly think of to help me. My family is either incapable or not interested in making me a functional member of their coven. And since they have cut off all contact and let my ass swing in the wind at my trial, I'm pretty sure they don't give a shit if I ever do. I can count on one hand the number of people in my life that care if I lived or died."

And as soon as I started causing problems, the number would whittle down to just Ellie and Alice. They were the only people who didn't make me feel like a monster or a leper or unwanted. And if I left, I'd be losing that, too.

But even if I didn't leave, how long could I use them as a crutch? How long would it be until I couldn't even have that?

Fuck. It shouldn't be this hard, right? To live?

"Wren," Fiona cooed. "There are far more people that care about you than you think. And hey, maybe I can ask somebody? I know we Jacobs's aren't as hoity-toity as ya'll Bannisters, but there must be something someone can do, right?"

Shrugging, I gave her my best smile—the same one I gave Ellie when she said thank you for saving her mother. The same one when she apologized over and over for what happened. Ellie shouldn't have felt guilty for what happened in that fire any more than Fiona should feel pity about the family I couldn't change.

And just like with Ellie, I told Fiona the same damn thing. "Don't worry about it. It'll be fine. It always is."

Fiona, however, was harder to shake. "Again, woman. It ain't raining. Let's get you some food, huh? Classes are over anyway, and this place never looked so good. What do you say?"

Frowning, I finally took a look around. I was on the last table, and it was sparkling. So was every chair and the stainless-steel buffet. The windows were free of dust and grime, and the floor was spotless. An ache settled in between my shoulder blades and a gentle throb made itself known in my hands.

"Ya'll ate lunch here? Without me noticing?" I spotted a yellow rolling bucket filled with filthy water. When had I mopped?

"Hell, no. Malia and Hannah made everyone eat outside after they caught Patrick and Roman handing you cleaning supplies. Evidently, you were preoccupied with *something*, because as soon as one of those yahoos handed you a broom, you started attacking the floor. Same with the mop. Then when you ran out of floor to clean, you went back to scrubbing tables."

So that super-secret planning session I'd had where I'd mapped out my escape and everything, hadn't been as private as I'd thought.

Super.

Hopefully, I'd at least done it silently.

"You were in the zone," Fiona continued, ushering me away from the table I'd been attacking. "I've never seen anyone but my mama do that right before she blasted my daddy for some dumb shit he'd said."

She snatched the mop handle and guided the rolling bucket toward the janitor's closet. Gods, I had to be a mess if she was treating me with kid gloves. She dumped the water into the giant tub sink, and in the quiet of the room where I'd kissed Nico all those hours ago, the real interrogation began.

"So, what's going on with you and Acosta? Does he know about... *everything*?"

Oh, how to answer her.

"He knows enough." Hell, he knew more than I did if he

could find a way to keep me from exploding the whole freaking camp. But what was going on with us?

Even I didn't know that.

Studying the shelf filled with cleaning products, I ignored her pointed stare.

"And?" Fiona's gaze was likely to burn a hole in my cheek.

"And nothing. He knows about my problem. He thinks he can fix it, but he can't. And when the other instructors find out that I'm a walking, talking time bomb, they'll kick me out so fast I'll likely leave chem trails upon my exit."

Or blood from my inevitable execution. That was a very real possibility, too. Why was I still here again?

She dropped the bucket back in the sink with a clatter, and attack-hugged me until I squeaked. "Then let's hope he's right. I just found my people, you know. Can't have ya'll hauling off and getting kicked out already."

My smile was brittle as I hugged her back. Because I couldn't get kicked out of here if I left, now, could I?

I think Fiona knew I was planning something, because a few hours later, I'd finally convinced her I was fine enough to be left alone. This was after she'd stuffed me full of food, I'd managed to take a tepid shower, and I'd "rested."

Trust me, there was no rest to be had in this cabin—not with the contingency plans that circled on loop in my brain.

As soon as I was sure Fiona, Hannah, and Malia were out of earshot, I opened my wall locker and started packing my duffle. I didn't have much—just some clothes and toiletries, a few first aid items—so the bag was no fuller than when I'd started. Smartly, I left all the ABI trainee uniforms, boots, and insignia right where they lay.

I wasn't going to need them, now, was I?

As fast as I could, I got dressed in jeans, two pairs of thick socks, and my now-clean boots. Then I shoved my arms in a tank, a thin, long-sleeved shirt, and threw on a jacket. I was tempted to stuff one of the itchy wool blankets in my pack, but I knew if it got wet, it would only weigh me down.

I foresaw a ton of walking in my future, and my only hope was that my feet could actually take it this time. Then I waited, pretending to sleep until the entire camp was quiet and I could make my escape. It took a while, but once Hannah's snores started, I figured I was in the clear.

Sliding out of my bed, I gently pulled my duffle from underneath and minced to the back door and took a final look around. Fiona laid in a sprawled heap on her bed, a perfectly pedicured foot hanging off the mattress. She was a tiny hurricane, her area always haphazard and half-undone.

Hannah's snores ramped up, and I took that as my cue to scoot before she woke herself up. Slipping from the cabin, I shouldered my duffle and gently pushed the door closed, careful not to make a noise. There were plenty of arcaners that could hear my very heartbeat even under the null wards, so silence was the name of the game here.

Picking my way into the tree line, I managed to remain unseen, keeping to the shadows. The night was just on the warm side of chilly, and I thanked the stars above I managed to remember a jacket. I needed to get as much distance from the camp as I could before my bed got discovered empty, but first I needed to make it down the stupid mountain in one piece.

The gentle rumble of a pair of male voices stopped me in my tracks. Caught in the middle of a cleared trail, I whipped my head this way and that to try and find a big enough tree to hide behind. And the voices were getting closer. Without much grace, I shuffled behind a large oak, slowly taking my pack off before the bright-purple canvas gave me away.

"I don't get what's the big deal. She's fair game as far as I'm concerned."

Ames. And, without a doubt, that fucker was talking about me.

"You need to back off," Girard replied, his tone sharp as a razor. "It's bad enough I have instructors coming in my office bitching about you, but I have students doing it, too. Do you know how bad you have to fuck up that students are risking their entire careers to tattle on an instructor?"

Their steps faltered, stuttering to a stop very close to my tree. Covering my mouth so I didn't make a sound, I tried to keep my breaths from coming in the frightened pants of a girl damn near caught.

One wrong move, and I was screwed. One sound and they'd find me.

"I don't know how she got those girls to follow her, but you have to—"

"It was an entire cabin. Of *male* students," Girard hissed, cutting Ames off.

"Then she's fucking them," Ames insisted, his petulant, scolded little boy tone grating my ears. "She has to be. She snared them just like she did Acosta. You've seen him watching her. You *know* there's something going on."

Shame and rage and a fair bit of revulsion shot through me at once. I fought off the urge to jump from my hiding place and punch Ames right in his stupid, bitch-ass mouth. Okay, so fighting off the urge was taking far more effort than I'd have liked. Digging my fingernails into the tree bark, I held myself there, barely breathing, barely moving.

And worse?

There were a pair of golden eyes staring at me through the trees. I froze, staring at the shining eyes, trying not to give myself away to the men on the other side of the tree, and praying whatever the fuck it was that had eyes that bright in the middle of this pitch blackness didn't eat me.

"Oh, give it a rest," Girard barked, making me flinch. "That girl barely has time to wipe her own ass let alone fuck an entire cabin. You've made sure of that. Back. Off. Or I'm going to have to report you to your collective and your superior. What strike are you on, Ames?"

Warlocks—what few there were of them—belonged to collectives. Like a witch's coven, they were filled with family and leaders, rules and regulations. Not that I'd ever actually belonged to any coven whatsoever, but I got the gist. To get reported to one's collective carried the same weight as getting charged by the ABI, and the punishments were severe.

And all that was going on in the back of my mind as I watched those fucking eyes get closer.

"Bu—" Ames began, only to be cut off with something that sounded an awful lot like a gurgle.

"Back. Off. Don't make me say it again."

Ames must have nodded or something, because the conversation ended, and their footsteps resumed.

And all the while, those golden eyes got closer and closer until the thing attached to them stepped into the faint light of the full moon filtering through the leaves. Peaked ears covered in gray fur led to a longish muzzle and a regal face—all awesome until I realized the very large apex predator stalking casually toward me.

It was a wolf.

A giant, gray killing machine with glowing golden eyes. My heart tripped inside my chest. There were wolves in Savannah, sure, but I'd never seen one, and I sure as hell didn't know how to not get killed by one, either. Stumbling, I moved, ready to scream my head off when that wolf wasn't thirty feet away anymore.

It was right next to me, a gray mist coating its fur as its body changed shape.

Then I was flat on my back in the dirt with Nico on top of me, his warm hand covering my mouth. And despite the fact that his body was on top of mine, and his arms were wrapped around me, the expression on his face was *not* happy.

No, I had a feeling I was in real deep shit.

CHAPTER 11

NICO

Wren's fear wrenched at the hold I had on my wolf, the animal so close to the surface, so recently in the driver's seat, it nearly stole all my control. Her wide green-gold eyes peered up at me as her scent filled my nose, and I fought off the urge to yell.

She was supposed to stay put. She was supposed to wait for me. I swore to her I was coming back with a solution to our —*her*—problem and here she was in the woods, nearly caught, nearly hurt, nearly...

"Going somewhere?" I growled through my teeth, forcing my hand off her mouth now that Ames and Girard were out of earshot. Wren's skin remained white for a moment until it flushed pink, the pressure of my hand on her too much, and that earned me a solid dose of shame until the guilt on her face finally registered.

The men's steps faded into the distance too far for them to hear anything we had to say. And if Wren was smart, she should start talking anytime now...

She sucked in a shuddering breath, likely unable to take a full one with my body on top of hers, but I was having a hard enough time not shifting as it was. Pinning her down was the last hold I had on my sanity at the moment.

"Yes," she breathed, her bottom lip trembling as tears pooled in her eyes. "I... I was leaving."

Just her admitting it had my gut falling to the ground and my chest caving in. Heat flashed over my skin as I gritted my teeth against the burn.

"Why?" I ground out, my jaw locked so I didn't toss my head back and howl. My wolf was too close, too in control, too powerful. With the moon full and my thirtieth birthday minutes away, not shifting seemed to be more and more impossible by the second.

Wren shook her head, shoving at my shoulders, and I fought off the urge to press into her more, to pin her down, to mark her with my teeth.

So no matter where she went or who she ran into, they would all know she was mine.

Mine.

But that was the wolf talking, not me.

Rolling off her, I found my feet, careful not to step into the moonlight. The last thing I needed was for that fucking moon to hit me again. Hell, I couldn't even look at her—couldn't stand the reminder that she was trying to run. And if I saw that gods-forsaken purple duffle again...

She was going to leave me.

"Because I didn't trust that you'd find anything to help," she finally answered, a kick in the gut if there ever was one. But then she continued, and the hits just kept on coming. "Because I don't want to hurt anyone. Because I don't want to die. You told me so yourself. They're going to kill me, Nico. And they will as soon as they find out what's wrong with me."

I swallowed thickly, the truth in her words as sharp as a razor, and I tilted my head back to stare at the forest canopy. The moon threatened to trickle through the leaves, and no matter how much we wolves said we weren't moon-called, the truth would come out eventually. Even then the moon beckoned me, begged me to let my wolf free, pleaded to let its silver beams fall on my skin.

Fisting my fingers, I shoved everything down—all the fear, the rage, the pain. "And what if I did find something? What if I commissioned someone to help? What if I risked everything to make sure you were safe, huh?"

Bitterness threatened to sink me. I'd done exactly what I'd said I'd do, and where was she? Not where she said she'd be—where I told her to be. I'd nearly woken up every girl in that cabin when I'd realized she was gone, only to find her in the fucking woods, not three paces away from Ames.

He could have caught her.
He could have killed her.
He could have...

Didn't she understand the danger?

Her gasp had me spinning to face her, lunging to catch her as she wilted to the earth. Her fingers found the threads of my shirt, yanking at it like she was trying to burrow into my skin.

The weight of the amulet in my pocket seemed like such a trivial thing to me.

It was inconsequential. Insignificant. But to Wren, it was everything.

"Yo-you did? You found something?" Pain ravaged her features, tempered only by the faint traces of relief. Tears spilled down her face, as the scent of agony burned my nose. With a shaking hand, she pressed it against the skin of my cheek. "Thank you. Thank you."

Her whole body trembled, and I couldn't have stopped myself from kissing her even if I tried.

My lips found hers, taking her mouth, her scent. It filled my nose, that jasmine and honeysuckle perfume that was all Wren as I tasted the sweetness on her tongue. My fingers found her braid, curling the red rope of her hair around my fist as I devoured her mouth, swallowing her moans like a man starved. She nipped at my bottom lip, the bite of the sting calling forth fangs of my own.

I wanted to sink them into her neck, marking her for all the world to see.

She's mine.

My wolf howled inside my head making me break the kiss, my breath mingling with hers. Unable to stop myself, I lifted my gaze to the canopy of trees, a single beam of moonlight falling to the forest floor. Finding my feet, I clasped her hand in mine as it called to me, beckoning me closer.

It was time—one I couldn't fight or say no to.

Normally, wolves were home on this night, knowing that once the moon hit us on our thirtieth birthday, our lives would change forever. If we were lucky, we knew our mate. If we were really lucky, we at least liked them. But there was always a chance that they'd died, or they were married to someone else, or they didn't want you back.

"Nico? What's happening?"

But I couldn't tell her. My wolf was driving this train and Wren and I were simply passengers. Pulling her behind me I strode toward that beam of light as if it were a siren call. Funny, because the woman behind me was the same, her song her scent, and exactly like those poor sailors, I would be crashing soon enough.

As soon as the light hit me, I knew I'd fucked up. I dropped Wren's hand as I fell to my knees, the searing heat of the light on my skin like the worst of burns. My wolf writhed under my flesh, aching to be set free, but I managed to keep him in check. What I could not do was stop his fangs from filling my mouth and his talons from erupting from my fingertips.

Shifting never felt like this. There was no pain, no agony. No bones breaking and reforming. But now? Now everything hurt, everything was on fire.

"Nico?" Wren called, her cool hands on my face as I tried not to howl.

Curling my arms around her legs, I clutched her to me as I tried to ride out the worst of it. But I didn't even know what this was. I had a vague idea of this being the mating and the rest of my alpha power coming to me, but no one had ever said it would be like this.

No one said it would hurt this bad.

No one said I would want to scrape my own skin off at the same time I wanted to bathe in her scent. And I did. I wanted the gentle perfume of Wren's skin all over me. I wanted her taste on my tongue, her moans in my mouth, her hair in my fist.

Burying my face in her belly, I soaked in her scent as I rode out the worst pain I'd ever felt. Another lash hit me, and I tightened my hold, earning me a gasp. She bent, curling herself around me as she held on, murmuring soft words and gentle shushes as she ran her fingers through my hair.

Somehow, she got on my level, her knees bumping against mine as I pulled her closer.

Mine. Mate. Mine. Mate. Mine, mine, mine.

That scent filled my nose, the one that was only Wren's—only hers and no one else's. Only she would do. Only she could quell this ache in my chest, this burn in my skin. Only she could soothe the beast in me.

I wanted to tell her what was happening—I did—but the words wouldn't come. The only thing I managed to get out was, "*Mine.*"

Those green-gold eyes widened, her perfect lips forming a small "O" of surprise, and I wanted to bite that plump bottom lip. Banding my arm around her back, I curled my other hand under her braid at the base of her skull. Wren's eyelids drooped as her scent sweetened, her gaze falling to my mouth before she closed the distance between us.

And now I understood why it hurt so bad.

I'd been holding myself back, making sure it was her choice—*I* was her choice. As soon as her lips brushed mine, the burn began to ease. Starving for her, the kiss went from a gentle brush to the pair of us doing our level best to devour each other. Wren wrapped her arms around my neck as my hands found their way to the back of her thighs. Yanking them up, she snaked those legs around my waist, and it was better than I dreamed it would be.

In less than a second, I found my feet, taking her with me, not once breaking the kiss. I pressed her back against the closest tree, missing the moonlight already. The heat of her sex filtered through our clothes and into my cock and I couldn't help my groan. She swallowed it with a gasp, her hips bucking at the contact.

Pressing into her further, I let my fingers explore, sneaking under the hem of her thin shirt to touch her soft skin. Even against the rough pads of my fingers, the curve of her waist was like the warmest silk. Her breath stuttered as I cupped her ribs and nearly stopped altogether when I flicked my thumb over her tight nipple.

Wren broke the kiss, gasping for breath and I took that opportunity to taste her neck, trailing nibbling kisses down the column of her throat. Her scent sweetened further, turned heady with her desire—her want—for me. Her pulse fluttered against my lips as her nails scraped my scalp, her hold tightening on my hair.

Mine.

I needed inside her, needed to sink into her softness, her heat. My wolf and I both craved it, near mindless from it. And as Wren writhed in my grip, her hips circling, pressing herself against the straining cock in my jeans, my control was slipping.

And fast.

Fumbling, I yanked at her jacket and somehow, we managed to get it off her arms, discarding it somewhere far away from her skin. Wren wiggled, pushing at my hold and somehow my brain got the message, and I relinquished my hold on her.

No. She's saying no.

My chest wanted to cave in on itself, but as soon as her feet found the forest floor, she tore off her shirt, revealing acres of pale skin for me to worship. In an instant, her bra was gone, the light-blue confection only in my way. My mouth found the peak of her nipple, the cinnamon bud just as sweet as the rest of her.

We fumbled together, unzipping jeans, shoving clothing aside, and before I knew it, I'd spun her in my arms, the curve of her luscious ass against my aching cock. One hand was full of her ample breast and the other cupped her jaw, tilting her head just so I could bury my nose in the crook of her neck. My fangs ached, ready to take her as mine before something told me to stop.

Ask. Don't just take. Ask her.

Through the mindlessness, through the lust and pheromones and just plain magic, I managed to grab hold of my sanity.

I tilted her head, making her look at me, watching her glorious green-gold eyes flare as they met mine. "Tell me you want this," I ordered, my voice rough with the ghost of my wolf. "Tell me you're mine. Tell me you want me."

As soon as she said yes—*if* she said yes—my mark would be on her forever.

She would be mine forever.

And I would be hers.

CHAPTER 12

WREN

Nico's eyes glowed with his wolf as he waited for my response, his whole body practically vibrating with need. I didn't know why he was so upset I'd tried to leave or what had made him feel so much pain in the moonlight.

Tell me you want this. Tell me you're mine. Tell me you want me.

His words seemed to mean something, resonating with a power I didn't understand. But I couldn't think with his lips so close—couldn't focus on anything but the heat of his skin against mine and his hand on my breast and the delicious way he made me look at him, forcing my chin up so there was no other option but to stare into those gorgeous golden eyes.

Maybe it was the way he said it, the desire to be wanted in return that sealed it for me, but my acceptance fell from my lips before my brain even had time to think of the consequences.

"Yes," I breathed against his mouth, and his hold tightened. "I want you. I want this. *Please.*"

His hand left my breast as he positioned his cock at my slick opening. He could breathe in my direction, and I'd be ready for him. His kisses, his hands on me? I was done for.

He hovered on the edge, the teasing pressure earning a whimper from me as he hesitated. I wanted him inside me, his groans in my ears, and his kiss on my tongue.

"Tell me you're mine," he growled, nipping at my bottom lip with his sharp teeth. "No one else gets you this way. No one else, Wren."

I knew next to nothing about Nico—other than his last name and the fact that he was a wolf, an ABI agent, and he had a keen interest in keeping me alive. But right then, I didn't care about what I didn't know or what my words might mean. I didn't care about anything other than letting him do whatever he wanted with me.

"Yes," I hissed, trying and failing to rock my hips back to take him in. His hard grip stopped me, and even that made me moan.

"Say it, my beautiful little bird. Tell me you're mine."

It felt like I was agreeing to something far more binding than I could comprehend, but I needed him inside me. I needed him to fill me up, to hold me, to bite me, to...

"I'm yours," I murmured, loving the way my lips brushed his as I spoke.

"That's my good girl." Nico wasted no time—as soon as those words passed my lips, he plunged inside, filling me full, with one long stroke. He swallowed my gasp as he pressed a searing kiss to my mouth, his tongue dancing with mine.

He pulled out, and I whimpered at the loss until he slammed back in, the force of it rocking me up on my toes. We fell forward against the thick oak tree, his forearm protecting my delicate skin from the roughness of the bark.

His hand left my hip, trailing down in between my legs to my sex. He played me like a well-tuned instrument, pressing on my clit with the perfect pressure. Pleasure seared through me as his strokes picked up speed. I was stretched to bursting with his searing hot moans in my ear, his beautiful fingers playing in the slick wetness at my center.

My legs began to tremble, my orgasm racing for me—too big, too much, too...

"Nico," I gasped, a warning, a plea. I needed more—more of him. "Please."

"You gonna come for me?" he growled in my ear, his voice deepening ever so slightly as it vibrated through my chest.

The best I could do was nod, but even that was feeble. I curled my arms behind me, clutching whatever I could reach, trying to hold on.

"Show me how pretty you come, beautiful. Show me."

As if on command, my release hit, slamming into me with enough force to weaken my legs, to make me scream. Fire raced over every inch of my skin, lighting up every nerve ending, every cell. Then Nico struck, his fangs burying into the delicate skin of my shoulder. It should have hurt, the skin breaking under the razor-sharp points of his teeth, but all I felt was a wave of bliss as he roared out his release.

His thrusts gentled and he found my lips, the taste of my

blood coppery on his mouth. I nipped at his bottom lip—hard—my teeth breaking the skin. Nico's blood mingled with mine, our kiss never once stopping, even as he pulled himself from me. Spinning in his arms, he pressed me against the tree, the rough bark against my skin making me moan.

Everything felt good—every cell in my body dialed toward pleasure. I'd just had the mother of all releases, and yet, I was starving for him, needing him again, even though I'd just had him. The heat of his bare chest against mine nearly killed me. It was as if I'd been drugged.

Nico broke the kiss, cupping my jaw in his hands as he stared down into my eyes. "I hope you were topped up on sleep. Because I don't think either of us are getting any tonight."

My sex clenched, aching for him again. "Promise?"

Leisurely, we righted our clothing, dropping kisses to all the skin in reach. After we'd found my jacket and bra, Nico shouldered my duffle, pulling me by the hand behind him as we headed back to camp. Only at the thought of going back, did the euphoria lift.

"I can't go back," I whispered, my feet stuttering to a stop. Nico had said he *might* have found something to help. I'd taken him at his word, but that was then, and this was now.

A scowl marred his perfect brow, and he let go of my hand to reach into his pocket. He pulled out a black velvet drawstring bag. "I went to Savannah. Talked to Carmichael. He admitted that you didn't start the fire." He pulled the bag open and dumped something into his palm. "In exchange for my silence, I had him make you this."

Nico pulled at the metal, drawing up the chain of a necklace, the yellow stone winking at me in the dark. "Your own personal null ward. It won't grant you any powers, but it will keep you from affecting everyone else's. It was the best I could do under the circumstances."

Shakily, I reached for the necklace. Something so simple, so easy. A null ward. Why hadn't I thought of that?

Tears filled my eyes as my fingers closed around the metal. All this time, every worry, every misstep, and it all could have been solved by a fucking necklace? Under the null wards already, I didn't feel any different when I held the metal, didn't feel any magic coming from the jewelry at all.

"How do we know it works on me?" All the bliss I'd felt moments ago was gone, now replaced with a lifetime of fear. Because things not working around me wasn't exactly new.

"Carmichael tested it himself, but we'll know for sure tomorrow. You'll have to retake the potion bomb iteration with Ames. And hey, if it doesn't work, I'll get you out of here, get you safe. Promise."

Nico plucked the chain from my hand and clasped it around my neck. "I won't let them hurt you, Wren. And I won't let you hurt anyone else."

The cool metal rested between my breasts, a gentle reminder that he'd gone all the way to Savannah and back for me. He'd hunted down Carmichael. He'd...

No one—not ever—had done something like that for me. Pursing my lips, I looked him over. "What—exactly—is your stance on blow jobs? Are they just okay, or are they like Christmas?"

Because if anyone in the history of ever deserved to be taken care of, it was Nico.

He banded an arm around my back, dipping his head to my ear. "I have a feeling anything you want to do to me will rock my fucking world, but if you want to suck my cock to show your gratitude, I won't stop you. I think you'll look fucking beautiful on your knees for me."

Forty minutes, a perilous trek through the camp, and a shower later, I found myself naked on my knees in Nico's bed. His back was propped against the headboard, his legs spread wide with me in between them. He'd already given me another mind-melting orgasm in the shower with his fingers, and I was eager to make him beg for me.

His fist was wrapped in my hair, not pushing, not guiding, simply there, letting me tease him with my mouth. I laved the underside of his cock with my tongue, running it over the sensitive spot just under the head. A growl erupted from his chest—not the fake kind men used when they were riled up but a real wolf one—animalistic and sexy as hell.

"Stop teasing me, beautiful," Nico snarled, and I figured fucking with him would earn me a glorious punishment.

Swirling my tongue around the tip, I bobbed my head, sucking him deep before popping off. "I don't know, teasing you is mighty fun."

I went back to work, taking him deep until he was a writhing mess ready to come at any second. Then like the absolute asshole I was, I drew off him, running my tongue up the underside in the softest of teases.

"What did you say in the woods? Oh, that's right," I

murmured, giving his cock a quick suck. "Tell me you're mine. That this is mine and no one else's."

Up until that moment, I hadn't quite comprehended just how fast Nico could move. Before I knew it, I was flat on my back in his bed with a very serious wolf in my face. Without an ounce of artifice, he answered me, "I thought this was implied, but I'll confirm it for you. I'm yours. My cock is yours—my body is yours and no one else's."

His rough palm ran over the skin of my thigh right before he spread me wide, fitting himself in between my legs. Slowly, he dipped his fingers into my folds, gently pressing against my clit. "Such a pretty pussy. I should taste it."

He worked his thick fingers inside me, hooking, pressing against the bundle of nerves just right to make me writhe. A moment later, he filled my mouth with those same fingers, making me taste myself as I sucked them clean. Then his mouth was on mine, his tongue sweeping inside to savor me. I only had his lips for a moment before he trailed them down my body, worshiping every inch of skin he came across, and then he was between my legs again.

Instantly, I regretted teasing him. If I was good at the game, Nico was a master. Before he was done, I was a babbling mess, pleading for him to just fuck me already.

And he did. Nico fucked me, made love to me, defiled me, and ravaged me in every position I could possibly think of and about twelve I had no idea existed. He wrapped me around his little finger, making me forget any lover before him and assuring there wouldn't be another after him.

As the sun threatened to crest the horizon, I'd confirmed two things. One: I was stupidly infatuated with a wolf shifter. Like falling all over myself, I didn't know how I was going to function around him, puppy-dog eyed and completely stupid, infatuated. Two: Keeping this under my hat was going to be the death of me.

But unlike in so many occasions before, I was pretty sure I was fucked in the good way this time.

CHAPTER 13

NICO

IF IT WEREN'T FOR THE SUN THREATENING TO CREST the horizon, I could have stayed in this bed for the foreseeable future. For the first time since Wren blazed into my life, my wolf was quiet. The scent of her all over me—in my nose, on my skin—soothed him in a way I'd never felt before. It was oddly peaceful to have him so docile, so calm.

It also scared the absolute shit out of me.

A week ago, I'd been lamenting that there was no way Wren could have been my mate—no way the universe could be that cruel. Now, I knew there was nothing I wouldn't do to protect her—nothing that I wouldn't sacrifice, no one I wouldn't kill. Hadn't I proved that already? Too bad protecting her right then came in the form of waking her up and getting her back to her cabin, preferably without my scent all over her.

My wolf roused at that thought, and I couldn't blame him.

Wren washing off my scent made my gut hurt, but that was the problem with this mixed bag of arcaners. Too many could smell me on her and confuse what it meant—think badly of her and I both, not realizing who she was to me.

If we were in a den, it would be different. If we were with my family, we'd be congratulated, the mate bond so powerful to my kind that it was deeper than any other vow we could have taken.

But Wren was a witch—an ousted one at that. And that made her a target here.

Dipping my head, I breathed her in, pressing my nose into her hair as she continued to use me as a body pillow. The copper strands were a tangled mess, scenting of her sweat, orgasms, and the traces of her desire. My arms tightened around her as if even they had no intention of letting her go. My mouth, however, had other plans.

"It's time to wake up, beautiful."

She snuffled, hiding her face against my chest as she moaned her dissent. I couldn't blame her. Other than a few cat naps here and there, neither of us had gotten anything close to a restful night.

"Okay," I conceded, settling in. "You can sleep in, but that's only if you don't mind every person within a mile radius knowing just how many times you came last night."

That did the trick. Wren shoved against my chest, spearing me with one bleary eye. "What?"

Tapping my nose, I murmured, "We smell of sex, my beautiful bird. And anyone else with a decent sense of smell will know exactly what we did last night, too."

Both of her eyes widened as she sat up, pulling the sheet

with her to cover her breasts. "I have a feeling sleeping with my instructor is not the best way to stay in this program, correct?"

My teasing smile fell. While that thought was always at the back of my mind, I didn't want Wren agonizing over her safety.

That was my job.

"No one is going to hurt you, Wren. I'll make sure of it," I murmured, cupping her cheek with my palm. "No one. But to stay on the safe side, let's shower and get you back to your cabin before anyone starts asking questions, yeah?"

Wren pressed her cheek against my hand, almost nuzzling it the way a wolf would, her body desperate for the contact that only a mate could give.

"You know, no one but Ellie and Alice have ever promised me anything... my family... they didn't..." She shook her head, her lips pressing together so hard they turned white at the edges. Sniffing, she shoved herself from the bed and marched to the bathroom, not looking at me again.

Clenching my teeth, I fought off the urge to howl.

Wren's.

Fucking.

Family.

Margot Bannister was a piece of work, and Wren's grandmother was a thousand times worse. And her aunts? There was a reason the Bannister name wasn't exactly liked in and around Savannah, even if it was feared. If Wren was the black sheep—and I had no doubt she was with a curse like hers—she'd have been demeaned and degraded, chastised and discarded more times than she could likely even remember.

Without the first clue of what to say, I followed her into the bathroom. She'd already flipped on the tap and was testing the water for temperature, not looking up once as I entered the room. She knew I was there—her skin pebbling as soon as I stepped across the threshold—but she didn't say a word.

Maybe now wasn't the right time to talk about this, but she needed to know she wasn't alone anymore. "I know this is rich coming from someone like me, with a pack like mine, but fuck your family, Wren." She straightened, a skeptical expression marring her gorgeous face. "Fuck every last one of them. It's okay to cut them out like a cancer. It's okay to ignore them like they ignored you. It's okay to let them go."

She lifted her shoulder in an indelicate shrug and stepped into the shower, letting the warm water darken her copper strands to auburn. She raised her face to the spray, cutting off any words that she could have replied with. With nothing else for it, I followed her in, wrapping an arm around her middle and kissing her wet hair.

She settled back into me, resting her head on my shoulder.

"You ever ached for the approval of someone you hated?" Wren asked, not turning, not moving, just resting against me like I was the lone person in the world holding her up.

I thought about the relationship I had with my father—the fights, the challenges—but I didn't hate the man. "Not really. My dad and I butt heads sometimes, but I still love him. I couldn't imagine not having a whole pack at my back and in my business." I dipped my head and pressed a kiss to her temple. "But I get it—the need to feel wanted. To require basic respect."

"To you, it's a stranger. Someone who shouldn't have a biological urge to give a shit. For me? It's my mom. You give a shit when you don't have to, and you did even *before* I blew you."

I'd never wanted to hug someone, while also dying to kiss them, while also doing my level best to not bust out laughing, while also needing to fuck every last bad thought out of their head before. "So, the bar is on the floor, then?"

Wren snorted, turning so her face was away from the spray. "The bar is on Satan's doorstep and even he thinks it's too fucking low."

Filtering my fingers through her hair, I cupped her head against my chest. "At least good old Satan and I agree about something."

We didn't have enough time for me to fuck all the bad thoughts away, but I still kissed her until she was smiling from ear to ear. By the time we got clean and dressed, the sun was really threatening to come up, and we had to race in the shadows to get her back to her cabin before anyone woke up.

It took everything in me not to kiss her again, to not mark my scent all over her. My wolf was not happy about it one bit but keeping her safe was far more important than my comfort. I'd just have to deal, and so would my wolf.

Mate.

Yeah, yeah, buddy. But keeping her safe is more important.

I so rarely talked to my wolf, but it sure as fuck was necessary now. Visions of dragging Wren back to my cabin and ripping the throats out of anyone who dared disturb us flashed in my brain.

Down, boy.

Before I forced myself to leave her, Wren grabbed my hand.

"Thank you," she murmured, her voice almost inaudible

even to my ears. "For helping me, for last night, for... everything."

I couldn't help it—just like I couldn't stop myself from kissing her that first time or the moon calling her to be my mate—I pulled her in and met her surprised lips with mine, tasting her one last time before letting her go. Backing away, I watched her shoulder her duffle and slip inside her cabin, fighting my damn wolf the whole time.

An hour and a half later, I was in the dining hall trying very hard not to notice just how fucking clean everything was. Sure, I'd told Wren to make it look good for her "punishment," but I hadn't expected her to take a toothbrush to the fucking grout for fuck's sake. It explained the aches in her body that I'd leached away while she'd slept.

Plus, the whole place was filled with her scent now, and it was driving my wolf crazy. Okay, so it was driving me absolutely batshit, too, but it was easier to blame the wild animal under my skin than deal with the fact that I was absolutely enamored by a woman I'd just met.

No wonder bonded men were so fucking protective over their mates. I hadn't understood until last night—hadn't even begun to comprehend just how far I'd go for her. I'd thought the swamp incident was bad. I was a damn fool.

"Excuse me?" a soft voice called, snapping me out of my Wren-induced craze. "Instructor Acosta?"

Turning, I found a short cadet with a severe expression, her dark hair pulled into an impossibly tight bun and her hands covered in gloves. Cadet Malia Nadir was in Wren's cabin, and the gloves were necessary so she herself didn't go absolutely insane in a group environment. A psychometry witch, Nadir was valuable to the ABI for so many reasons, but I cared more that she looked about ready to bolt.

"What's up, cadet?" If it weren't for the deep stench of abject fear coating the air around her, I probably would have told her to leave me alone, but something told me not to.

Her gaze shifted around before she moved closer. "I—*we*—have a huge problem. A girl is missing from my cabin. The other two girls went to go look for her, but I'm worried."

It was as if the bottom dropped out of my gut.

"Her bed is messed up as if she slept in it last night, and all her stuff is there—"

I didn't let the girl finish before I was off, racing for Wren's cabin as fast as my human legs would take me. I couldn't shift —not right then—but if what that girl said was true, I didn't know if I'd be able to hold onto this shape.

She left, anyway. I told her I would protect her, and she left. Sheleftsheleftsheleft.

My wolf was howling, and I gritted my teeth so I didn't follow suit, the burn in my stomach and ache in my chest almost too much to bear. Last night was too good to be true. Of course it was. No one found their mate before the turning. No one got them so soon. And she'd accepted me far too easily. I was a fucking idiot to think everything would work out.

Wren didn't want me—not really.

By the time I made it to her cabin, my wolf had wrenched control from me, falling into a scenting trance. Wren's was all over the place, but it was fresh, as if she'd just been here.

"Whoa, man. Are you okay?" Nadir asked, out of breath. "Your eyes are glowing, you know."

Unbidden, a growl rumbled from my throat. "Did she say

anything to you before she left? Any clue as to where she went?"

I'd find her. I would... I'd find her and... And what? Beg her to want me? Beg her to stay?

The cadet shook her head, her dark bun not budging an inch. "No. We went to bed and then she just wasn't here this morning. We checked the showers and the dining hall—hell, even the range." She marched past me, pointing to a bed that wasn't Wren's. "And it *looks* like she slept here..."

The confusion melted away as soon as the screen door slapped against the frame and Wren's scent mixed with the slightly dead one of a ghoul. I spun on a heel, staring down a distraught Wren who was huffing like she'd run a marathon.

"We ran the perimeter," Dumond announced. "I didn't smell her once."

Wren approached like I was a wild animal ready to strike. Fuck, I probably was one. Because all I could do was stare at her like I'd done the night before while she was pressed against that fucking tree, so close to being caught. My emotions were a mess—I was a mess—and I was probably scaring the shit out of these cadets.

"Ni—*Acosta*? Are you okay?" My last name on Wren's lips did nothing to calm me. In fact, it made it so much worse. I was Nico to her.

Blinking hard, I shook myself. I could *not* grab her and hide her away from everyone. I could *not* kiss the shit out of her. I could *not* let anyone know we were together.

Keep Wren safe, you fucking idiot. It's your one goddamn job.

"Fine," I ground out, amazed I could do that much. "Tell me what happened."

The screen door slapped again, with Ames strolling in like he had any right to be here. "Yeah, Bannister. Why don't you tell us all what happened?"

Don't kill him. Don't do it.

By some grace of the gods, Wren didn't even look at him, ignoring the antagonistic fuck-stick like he wasn't even there. "I don't know," she breathed, shaking her head. "We woke up, and she wasn't here. I figured she went to shower or something. We all got dressed for the day, but Fi still hadn't come back." She chewed on her bottom lip and began blinking like she was trying to stave off tears. "We checked the dining hall and the laundry and then we went to see if she was in the latrine. That's when we started getting worried. Malia came to find you, and Hannah and I ran the perimeter. It's like she's just gone."

Nodding, I tried not to wince. Hannah and Wren's scent could possibly mask Jacobs', making it that much harder to find her. First the female instructors leaving, and now this? Wyatt was right: there had to be something going on here.

"Bullshit." Ames scoffed. "What? She wanted to fuck her boyfriend in one of the other cabins and had you three make a big stink ab—"

Heat tingled down my spine as the urge to snap became almost too big to ignore. "Shut. The fuck. Up." It took everything in my power to keep my claws off that fucker. I heard every word he'd said about Wren last night, and him echoing those thoughts right now? Well, I was all out of patience. "Cadets? I need you to get to your next iteration. I'll look into this. We'll find her."

Wren was absolutely ashen, along with Nadir and

Dumond, staring at Ames like he was the damn devil. Well, Dumond seemed ready for an Ames-sized snack and Nadir seemed like she'd been hit by a truck, but the sentiment was still valid.

The cadets filed out with Wren taking the rear, her stricken face the last thing I saw before the door slapped once more against the frame. They left just in time for me to wrap a clawed hand around Ames' throat.

"What the fuck is wrong with you? A female cadet is missing, and you immediately think *slut*? Get your head out of your dick for about a millisecond, will ya?"

Squeezing his neck a little harder, I relished his face going purple before I let him go. Snapping it would have been so easy but killing him would be far too much paperwork. And no wonder he was on probation from his collective. With an attitude like that, it was a miracle they let him live.

"What's going on here?" Girard thundered from the doorway, likely wondering why Ames was gasping for air, and I was three steps past murderous.

Since Ames was incommunicado at the moment, I answered, "We have a missing student. The cadets all went to bed at the same time last night, but when they woke up this morning, one was missing. Her name is Fiona Jacobs, sir."

The Jacobs witch line was a big deal in the South, almost as big as the Bannister one. Not all of them had a squeaky-clean reputation, either.

Girard's jaw ticked. "And why is Ames on the ground?"

"In front of Jacobs' bunkmates, he suggested she was fraternizing with another student and not missing." I cleared my throat. "Only it was more colorful than that."

The older man's eye twitched. "I see." He looked down his nose at the warlock at our feet. "I believe we've had a discussion about your conduct, Ames. Is this something I'm going to need to report to your collective, or are you going to remove your head from your ass sometime this decade?"

Ames continued to gasp on the floor and Girard spared him another disgusted glance before returning his gaze to me. "I appreciate your quick action, Acosta, but Fiona Jacobs isn't missing. She left the program last night, electing to return to her family rather than continuing with us."

Interesting. A cadet—who was performing at the top end of her class—left without a word in the middle of the night, without her things. Not an explanation, not a goodbye. Nothing.

I smelled bullshit.

And that bullshit was coming right from the top.

CHAPTER 14

WREN

Worry churned in my gut as I shifted from foot to foot, staring at the target. Standing at the range podium, I clung to the wood, instead of doing what I really wanted to do, which was punch Ames right in the throat.

She wanted to fuck her boyfriend in one of the other cabins...

Fiona was missing. *Missing.* And he just wanted to brush it off?

Add that to the fact I hadn't exactly gotten to field-test the amulet at my neck, and well... I was a little out of sorts.

And it wasn't like I had any backup. It was only me and Ames out here, and it went without saying that the guy gave me the creeps.

Outside of the null line, I felt naked, and without my class or any other supervision other than this bumbling asshat? Not. Good.

"I can't believe you get to retake this test, Bannister," he grumbled, opening the armory cabinet that held all the potion bombs. "If it were up to me, I would have failed you. Though, it just goes to show that you and your family get all the special treatment, don't you?"

I'd sort of figured Ames hated me because of my name. Being a staunch misogynist and an all-around prick, it made sense that he'd hate me for something I couldn't control.

Roughly, he yanked out a flat of glowing orbs, smacking them onto the podium like he was trying to break them.

Shakily, I grabbed a bright-blue one, praying I didn't blow my hand off or explode the entire place as my fingers closed around the glass. Though, since it was just me and Ames, if the necklace was a dud, it was the perfect time for it to malfunction.

"Any fucking day now, Bannister. I do have other shit to do." Then he chuckled, a dark, creepy laugh that sent chills racing down my spine. "But you do, too, don't you? You're so busy fucking your classmates that I bet you've got plenty on your plate."

My fingers tightened around the glass. He'd made those same claims last night to Girard, sullying my name just because he was butt-hurt about whatever the fuck was stuck up his ass.

"You going to try and fuck me for a good grade, too?" He moved closer, in my space, and dropped his voice to a whisper. "Does Acosta know you're throwing your cat at everyone? I bet the big, dumb wolf can't even smell them on you. So much for him being an alpha, huh? But you can't fool me. And as soon as I have proof, I'm getting you kicked out of here."

But kicking me out of this school didn't mean jail anymore. It was a death sentence.

That fucker.

"Is that your go-to?" I said, a sneer firmly on my face as I backed up a step. "If a woman you don't like is doing better than *you* think she should, she's fucking everyone?"

Why that slipped out of my mouth, I didn't know, but I couldn't take one more stupid word. Right then, it didn't matter that he could get me kicked out. It didn't matter that he could use his power—both actual and perceived—against me. All that mattered was getting the absolute dumpster fire of a person to shut the fuck up.

Emboldened by the sheer rage churning in my gut—which seemed to overtake the fear at the moment—I tossed the potion bomb in the air, catching it and tossing it again.

"You and I *both* know I don't get jail if this doesn't work out. I know what my paperwork says." I tossed the bottle again, my rage reaching the boiling point. "So, every time you say you're going to kick me out, you're threatening my life. And if I'm fucking literally *everyone* like you say? Then what's to stop me from going to my classmates—to Acosta—and having them all make sure you don't wake up tomorrow?"

Was that a step too far? Maybe, but I was done with Ames' shit. He threatened my life? Well, I was threatening his. And I was loving the wide-eyed sputtering and abject fear on his face.

"I'm a big, *bad* Bannister, right? I've got ties and connections, without an ounce of a conscience or a lick of scruples, and my life is on the line. I'm capable of just about anything, aren't I?"

The temptation to rip off the necklace Nico had given me

and throw this fucking bomb at his feet—to watch him burn—would have scared the shit out of me if I were thinking clearly. But my mind was full of not finding Fiona, of racing around to try and find her. Of having Girard lie to my face and say she left of her own accord...

"I want you to think about that real hard before you open your mouth next time. Think about how good I am with a gun. Think about the potions exploding yesterday. Think about the apothecary that got me here." My smile was feral. "Soak it *all* in."

I tossed the potion again, practically giddy at Ames' gray face as he tracked the orb exactly like I had yesterday, praying it didn't explode.

It didn't matter that nearly everything I'd just said was complete bullshit—that fear, that worry, was priceless. It was about time he got back some of what he'd dished out.

"Or maybe you should do your fucking job and train me like you're supposed to without the sexual harassment and threats." Facing the target, I hauled my arm back and let the potion fly—not caring too much whether it actually exploded or not. "Just a thought."

The glass shattered on impact with the target, a gentle waft of smoke curled in the air before dissipating in the breeze just like it was supposed to. But I still saw Ames flinch out of the corner of my eye, and that was fabulous.

I wanted to feel the joy of the amulet working. Wanted to embrace the freedom it could bring me. But I couldn't focus on anything other than making Ames pay and Fiona.

Fiona.

What sucked? I now knew exactly how she would have felt

seeing my bed empty and me nowhere to be found. I knew exactly what it was like to worry, and to wonder, and to not have a single shred of explanation.

Ames snatched the tray of potion bottles off the podium, cradling them to his chest as he backed away from me. "We're good here. You passed this iteration. Go join your class."

Giving him my sweetest, "butter wouldn't melt in my mouth" smile, I said, "Thank you so much. I think this lesson has been *super* instructive. Don't you?" I tossed my braid off my shoulder and turned to leave. "You have a nice day now."

But as good as it felt to scare the shit out of Ames, I just couldn't enjoy it too much.

Two hours of lecture later, I was pretty sure I was one inane comment away from screaming. This particular iteration involved recognizing and concocting witch circles, sigils, antidotes, and sleeping potions. As someone who had researched all said items explicitly so I could *avoid* them, I was leaps and bounds ahead of my non-witch classmates.

"Take a break, everyone. Meet back here after lunch," Instructor Haynes announced. "Then we'll be performing practical applications of general antidotes and sleeping potions."

Haynes was a tall, gangly fellow with sunset-pink hair and dark-brown skin. A witch by nature, he seemed nice enough, but he was teaching a crowd of non-witches. The majority of the class were mages, ghouls, shifters, and psychics, and other than Malia, I was the only other sort-of witch here.

Fiona should be here, too, but she wasn't, and the sheer amount of rage at that fact, roiled in my gut.

"I don't know how I'm going to remember all of that," Hannah muttered, pinching her brow. "I feel like my brain is going to explode."

"Don't worry about it," Malia replied, stacking a paperback copy of the Proctor grimoire on top of her legal pad full of notes. "Your main concern is the sigils and circles. No one but a witch will be making potions, anyway, and those all have recipes."

I nodded. "If my two hundred- and fifty-year-old grandmother still needs to look at the book, no one is going to make you go without."

But I didn't give a shit about any of it. I wanted to know what they thought about Girard's pronouncement and if they believed him. And it wasn't until we heard Benjamin and Cole hissing back and forth outside of the dining hall did a spark of hope hit me.

"There's no way. Did you see how she was kicking ass yesterday? She had better grades than all of us, and then she up and quits? Bullshit, man." Benjamin ran a hand through his purple hair, tugging on the ends like he'd really enjoy ripping it out and starting over.

Hallelujah and a-fucking-men. At least someone was thinking the same as me.

"My brother's friend came through here two years ago, and they had something similar happen. A girl 'quit,'" Cole replied, using air quotes and everything. "But she left everything behind. Her clothes, her shoes, everything. They never saw her again. And where the fuck are all the female instructors? That seems a little off, man. Eight female candidates and *no* female instructors?"

My stomach gave an indelicate rumble as I diverted in their direction. But Fiona was more important than my hunger. "Thank the gods. I'm so glad someone else doesn't believe it, either."

Malia and Hannah nodded in agreement, just as worried as I was.

They knew just how determined Fiona was to do something on her own without her family involved. She wanted something for herself, and it was a common thread that we shared—the need to be something other than our last name.

"No way. Fi? Leave? She'd rather give up her entire shoe collection than pass up a way to stick it to her dad. And that girl has a fuck of a lot of shoes." Benjamin yanked on his hair again, his agitation making his fingers shake.

"Exactly," Hannah rumbled. "And she isn't the first girl to leave. Something funny is going on here."

Another girl from the other cabin joined our little group. Georgia? Gwendolyn? I couldn't remember her name. She didn't talk much and didn't seem to hang with the other girls in her cabin.

"Youse guys talkin' about Fiona?" she asked in a heavy Northern accent. New York or Boston, maybe? "I gotta tell ya, I'm worried. That girl is sweet as pie. No way she'd make us all worry about her like this. She woulda told someone she was leavin' this hellhole. No question about it."

I was ecstatic that I wasn't the only one to think something was up.

"Plus, my cousin gave me the skinny on that Ames jerkoff. She warned me about him. Said somethin' funny was goin' on that only started when he got here a coupla years ago. Female instructors started leavin' and students just up and went *poof.*" She looked right at me. "And he seems to have a beef with you, doll. Gotta say, I ain't feeling so warm and fuzzy about this place."

She wasn't the only one.

By the time we'd made it back to class, I'd actually learned the girl's name—Gianna—and now knew she was an Osprey shifter from Brooklyn. She also came from a big ABI family. Her parents, cousins, brothers, and her grandparents had been or were still agents. I'd never met a bird shifter before, but it did explain a decent number of her mannerisms and her bright-gold eyes that were more yellow than anything else.

"I want you to split into partners and work together to create the general poison antidote found on page forty-two," Haynes instructed, handing out metal cauldrons. "Once that is done, I want you to work together to find the ten sigils around the room."

With Fiona gone, there was an odd number of students. I supposed being by myself was probably safer, anyway. Trudging to the front, I was last in line for a cauldron. Haynes handed me one with a gentle smile, and I took it with a worried one of my own.

"This is just... These antidotes aren't meant to work, right? I know I'm the only witch here, but," I leaned in, whispering, "I don't really have any magic. I can mix the ingredients all day but the magic ain't there if you know what I mean."

Haynes' eyebrows shot up to his forehead. "You're an uninherit?"

Wincing, I contemplated his words. An uninherit was

exactly that—an arcaner that was born without any magic at all. Some lived to be ancient, some died a human's death. I was somewhere outside of that scope.

"Sure. We'll go with that."

Haynes' gaze narrowed. "A Bannister uninherit? Your grandmama must have had kittens when she found out. No wonder."

Shrugging, I nodded, not quite understanding what he meant. "I guess?"

Haynes rose from the side of his desk, flicking back his curl of pink hair. "Oh, honey, don't worry about a thing. I only want to make sure you can follow directions. Not all of us are like Ames, you know."

With that reassurance, I went back to my table and started the process. Antidotes required a hot cauldron, the right ingredients, and patience—or at least that was what I remembered my grandmother saying a very long time ago in one of my earliest memories.

The instructions called for a poultice to go over a poisoned wound and a tincture to activate the mixture. Quickly, I got to work, mixing the ingredients like it was damn cake and trying not to think about anything other than what I was doing.

Okay, that was a lie.

I was obsessing over the fact that I could mix the damn things together without blowing everything and every*one* to smithereens, Fiona, the delicious night with Nico, and wondering if I could poison Ames and not get in trouble. That was until I felt eyes on me. Looking up, my gaze went right to the window and a pair of golden eyes glowing in the distant tree line.

Last night when I noticed them staring at me in the forest, I'd been scared out of my mind. Now? I was doing my level best to not grin like an idiot while I stirred the poultice together in my mortar. For the first time since I'd left him, I felt semi-okay. Though, maybe he was just trying to keep me from burning the place to the ground, but I was sort of fine with that.

"That's perfect, Wren," Haynes murmured, staring at my mortar, and solidly breaking me out of my Nico spiral. "And the tincture?"

Shakily, I held out the glass vial filled with greenish liquid. Tinctures were usually alcohol-based and smelled to high heaven, but from what I heard, they worked. Haynes studied the bottle through a crystal monocle with sacred geometry etched into the glass.

He pulled the glass from his face. "You sure you're an uninherit?"

Wide-eyed, I stared at the tincture like it might explode. "I didn't say that. I said I couldn't do magic."

Haynes nodded, putting the monocle to his eye again. "Interesting. At first glance, the concoction seems completely without arcane residue, but... if you turn it to the light just like this and..."

Suddenly, Haynes' eyeglass cracked, as did the tincture bottle. He pulled it from his face, examining the crystal as if he'd never seen it before. "Interesting."

Cringing, I wrung my hands. "Did I fail?"

The instructor observed me with an enigmatic smile. "No, you did everything perfectly. Why don't you pick out the sigils hidden in the room, and I—"

"I already found them." I'd picked out the markings on my first visit to this room this afternoon after my foray with Ames. They were etched into the walls, hidden behind random objects, and even in the floor.

"All ten?" Haynes raised his eyebrows.

"There are twenty-three active ones and two inactive ones, but only if you count the etched circle under the desks that nullifies the no-magic wards. It's so weird a null on a null." It was why I'd given that particular circle a wide berth. The last thing I needed was to cross the damn thing while wearing this necklace.

Haynes' eyes went wide as his face paled. "Ah. Umm, anyone ever tell you you're a prodigy? Or call you blessed?"

My snort was indelicate but totally warranted. "No. I cannot recall any member of my family saying anything of the sort. The only person who calls me 'blessed' is Ames, and I don't think he means it in a good way."

Haynes seemed to take that in stride. "Fair enough. You have completed today's iteration and have passed with flying colors. You may go back to your cabin or..." He trailed off, staring through the window to the tree line. "Or maybe get dinner. Good work, Bannister."

I couldn't count how many times I'd been scolded or torn down in my life, but I could count the times I'd been complimented. Swallowing hard, I tried not to start bawling.

"Thanks," I croaked, proud for some reason. Okay, so I knew why. I'd stood up to Ames. I'd done a simple tincture and poultice without blowing up the room. I was on a roll.

Maybe I could really do this.

Gathering my things, I left the classroom, cringing a little when I saw Malia and Hannah's tincture. For one, it was bright purple, and two? The poultice was bubbling over the mortar. I was one thousand percent certain neither of those things should have happened.

The crisp mountain air hit my nose as the null ward closed in around me. But one thing stood out over the scent of oak and pine. Nico's scent was on the air—something I wouldn't have smelled before last night. He was in those woods somewhere, waiting. Watching. But it felt like a warm blanket, hugging me, protecting me against the cold.

But even though I felt his presence all around me, he never came out of the shadows, and I didn't see him as I went back to my empty cabin. The place was cold without Fiona, her bubbly nature livening the place. Without her, it was just a rickety cabin with metal wall lockers and a shabby exterior.

The last time I'd been in here, Nico had such an odd look on his face—like he'd expected me not to come walking in. It had been that same look on his face last night in the woods when I'd really been leaving.

And when he stopped waiting and finally came through that door, I didn't know who ran to who first.

CHAPTER 15

NICO

TWELVE HOURS.

Twelve fucking hours.

I'd counted them like years while I waited and watched and made sure Wren was safe. There was something going on here, and I'd been so stupid not to see it before. The worst part? If Wren hadn't been in my cabin last night, she could have been the one taken.

That thought always came back and bit me when I was least expecting it. As I roamed the woods trying to catch Jacobs' scent, as I tried to get a hint of that girl anywhere on the grounds. But it was if someone had erased her completely.

Because that was the rub, wasn't it? If Jacobs had gone of her own accord, she would have taken her things. She would have left a trail I could follow to the front gate. She would have said goodbye. Her situation was nothing like Wren's.

Jacobs didn't have to leave in the middle of the night without a word.

But she did.

She did, and there wasn't a single trace of her anywhere. The only place her scent remained was on a square of pillow. Not on her clothes, not in her obviously used bedsheets.

Nothing.

To me that meant spell work—high-level spell work at that. There were only a handful of arcaners I knew of who could cast under a null and live to tell the tale. And none of them I wanted anywhere near Wren. I had to get her the hell out of here. It wasn't safe for her anymore—if it had ever been.

A part of me hated myself for making her stay, for letting my wolf bind us when she was so vulnerable. What a fool I had been for keeping her here, but finding a way out now that wouldn't put her neck on the chopping block...

Well, I didn't know if there was one.

The sensation of her waiting was killing me. It was a weight, a living thing, and keeping away from her was so much worse now that I'd marked her that I wasn't sure if I was sane anymore. It had never made sense to me, the crazed need for one's mate, but now I knew.

I knew and it was awful.

My feet pointed themselves to Wren's door, moving faster and faster until I was no longer on four paws but two, racing for that damn cabin like I would die if I didn't. I'd meant to be smooth, to act like the adult I was, but twelve fucking hours of absence, one missing girl, and her scent so close?

I was done for.

In the back of my mind, I knew she was alone. I knew it

was safe to be there, and I was glad for that, because as soon as I opened that damn door that divided us, Wren was running, racing for me, too. I caught her on a jump, her arms and legs wrapping around me as mine closed around her in a gripping embrace. Then her mouth was on mine, the sweetness of her tongue dancing with my own, making the world fall away for a moment.

Naturally, her back found the closest wall, the press of her body against me, bringing a peace I thought was fleeting. Her finger scraped my scalp, and I fought the urge to rip her clothes right off here and sink into the blissful warmth between her thighs. Unfortunately, there was the matter of Wren's cabinmates and the fact I should not be in here at all.

Ghoul noses weren't easy to fool. If we gave into ripping off each other's clothes, our cover would be blown.

Somehow, I wrestled some blood back to the big brain and managed to break the kiss. Wren's breaths came in shuddering little pants, and that was nearly enough to drive me over the edge.

Mate.

Gritting my teeth, I set her down, but was unable to move away.

Her smile was half-lust and half complete innocence. "Good evening, Instructor Acosta. Is there something I can help you with?"

Why, that little shit.

Fitting my hand under her braid, I cupped the back of her neck as I bent down to whisper in her ear. "There are many things you can help me with, beautiful, but I do recall telling you to call me Nico when we were together. Maybe I'll tie you up and make you come over and over until you remember."

Her shiver was absolutely priceless, as was the scent of her arousal. If I could have that burned into my brain for the rest of my life, I'd live a very happy man.

"Is that supposed to be a threat?" she said breathlessly. "Because if it is, you should really work on your intimidation skills."

I wanted to stay right here—this banter, this bubble of happiness—but it wouldn't last. Not here.

"Grab what you need for the night. You're staying with me."

Frowning, Wren pushed at my belly. "No, I'm not." She gestured to Jacobs' empty bed. "Someone came into this cabin and took my friend, Nico. I don't know if you believe Girard or not, but I don't. No way am I going to leave Hannah and Malia to the same damn fate. What if…"

She grimaced, shaking her head. "What if I could have stopped it? What if I could have helped her? And now, I don't know where she is. I don't know if she's alive. Girard lied to my face. I know he did. And I—"

Gently, I put my hand over her mouth and a single finger to mine. "I believe you," I breathed, my voice barely audible to even my ears. "Pack a bag. A small one. You're coming back."

Yeah, she was going back, and I would be in wolf form, watching her cabin all night long and praying no one got by me. I'd already left five messages for Wyatt to get his ass back here. I needed backup—and yesterday.

Wren seemed to think about it for a minute, likely debating

her loyalty to her friends over finding out whatever it was I had to say. Her curiosity won.

"Fine," she mouthed, snatching her empty bright-purple duffle from under her bed, and stuffing a few things into it.

Shit she absolutely would not need. Like pajamas. And underwear.

In a matter of seconds, we were out of her cabin and picking through the trees to mine, sometimes filtering deeper into the forest to avoid the students returning from class. And all the while, my wolf was nearly silent because I had her hand in mine, bringing her back to my den.

Den? Gods, I'm going full-on wolf now.

As soon as I got us back to the safety of my space, I did what I'd wanted to do all fucking day. I wrapped my arms around her and breathed her in. I'd been on edge since I'd left her, and now? Now, I was almost okay.

Almost.

"Do you think she's dead?" Wren croaked, holding me tight to her as she buried her face in my chest.

I didn't know how to answer that. Could Jacobs be dead? Of course she could. But something told me she wasn't. Something told me none of the women gone were dead, and personally, I didn't think that was a good thing.

"No, beautiful. I think your friend is a fighter."

Wren lifted her head. "You think someone took her, too, right?"

Grimly, I nodded. Pivoting on a heel, I headed for the small kitchenette, needing a beer for this conversation. Popping the top off a bottle, I took a huge swig before offering Wren one of her own.

A little green, she shook her head. "No thank you. I'm swearing off booze until I can look at it without wanting to vomit."

I tried and failed not to smile at her aversion to alcohol. It was a shining spot in the absolute fuck-shit we needed to go over. Returning the beer, I selected a bottle of water and handed it over.

"A week ago, a good friend of mine asked me to come here to nose around. Over the last few years, female instructors have been consistently putting in for transfers or quitting the ABI altogether. So much so, there isn't a single one left at this post. Similarly, more than a handful of female students have also voided their contracts. Since the paperwork is fine, no one bats an eye, so it's tough to prove something is going on. I could easily brush this off, except…"

Wren jumped up on the counter, the same counter that I'd almost kissed her on what seemed like forever ago. "Except?"

"Except… I snooped around your friend's area, trying to catch a scent so I could follow her trail. Problem is? There isn't one. Not on her bedclothes or her shoes or her makeup bag. Not one scent."

She leaned forward, fitting her elbows onto her knees. "But you're a wolf. That's not possible. You would at least get the scent of the fabric or the products. You'd smell the leather of her shoes or the chemicals in her makeup. You'd get something. So that means someone spelled her things."

If there had ever been a doubt that Wren was a smart cookie, it was gone now.

"So, what do we do?" she asked, jumping off the counter. "Do we call in the cavalry? Get some agents here or—"

"We can't," I said, cutting her off. I hated to do it, but I didn't want her hope to grow. "We don't have a shred of evidence, other than me *not* smelling something. I can't exactly go to my supervisor with that."

Wren's face quickly changed from pale to pink to fire-engine red, her fists balling at her sides. "So, we do nothing?"

"I didn't say th—"

"No." She cut me off. "You said we can't call anyone. Even though there's enough rumors floating around that every single trainee is talking about girls going missing. That they see there aren't any female instructors, and they think it's weird as fuck. That people are scared they're going to be next. Sure, Nico. Now's not the time to call anyone. All because you don't have more. It's enough for an inquiry at the very least." Two steps and she was in my face, stabbing her index finger into my chest. "Bare minimum, call her family. Hell, call anyone's family. Call the agent's next duty station. Ask if they ever showed up. Ask if you can talk to them. Ask literally anything."

It was tough not to start smiling. My mate was smart and loyal and damn near rabid when it came to protecting those she held dear. I fucking loved it.

"Wyatt—my friend—already tried," I murmured, grabbing her hand, and kissing the back of it. "He couldn't get access to the files. I tried, too, when I got here. The only ones I had access to were current students. I looked a few hours ago—Fiona's file is gone."

Tears welled in her eyes as she clenched her teeth. "Shit. I'm sorry. I shouldn't have assumed."

It wasn't exactly a stretch to figure out why she wouldn't

want Fiona forgotten. Wren's family had done damn near everything they could to forget my lovely mate even existed. If the same fate had befallen her, I doubted they'd do more than shrug and say, "Good riddance."

They had no idea just how fucking phenomenal she was. How special.

"I won't forget her, Wren, but keeping you safe is a bigger priority to me."

Just admitting that out loud was risky. I'd grown to trust Wren, grown to feel something more for her. I'd accepted that she was my mate over all others, giving her my mark and...

But unlike me, she could leave. She could find someone else. She could choose another.

And I never would.

Wren's confusion made me want to walk up to her father one day and just knock his fucking head off. *How does a man stand idly by while their family shits on their little girl? How does he not fight for her every day?*

"Priority? But she's the one who's missing. I'm jus—"

"Really fucking important to me," I murmured, cutting her off. "What happened to her will not happen to you. You will be safe, and you will graduate this absolute farce of a course, and then we'll go back to Savannah where we fucking well belong."

Her confusion was sweeter this time. "You don't normally work here, do you?"

Clutching her to me, I shook my head. "Nope."

"You're from Savannah."

"Yep," I said, fitting my palms under her thighs and lifting her onto the counter. The last time she'd been up there, I'd wanted to spread her legs wide and taste her. "Born and raised."

Fitting myself between those glorious thighs, I cupped her cheeks in my hands, loving the flare of desire in her eyes as her lips parted.

"I wanted you to kiss me the last time I was up here," she whispered, staring at my lips.

"Funny, all I'd wanted to do was spread you on this counter and fuck that pretty pussy with my tongue." Bringing my mouth to hers, I devoured her moans as I kissed her senseless. "Consider this a do-over."

Dealing with the button on her jeans, we worked together to wiggle the denim down her hips. As more and more of her pale skin was exposed, I dropped wet, biting kisses to her flesh. She tasted fucking divine, that honey scent only getting stronger between her legs. It took work getting her naked, her boots an actual problem—especially with the limited blood flow heading to my brain.

Before I couldn't fight the urge to rip the damn things off her with my claws, I managed to get her naked from the waist down, her perfect pale ass kissing the counter. Needing her bare, we worked off her shirt and bra, and I got the pleasure of raking my fangs over one pert nipple, sucking it into my mouth as I yanked her ass to the edge.

Wren moaned, shaking with need as she clawed at my shirt. Kneeling, I fit my upper body between her knees, tossing her legs over my shoulders as I admired her slick wet sex with its tuft of auburn curls and perfect pink lips.

And her scent? Fuck, I was a goner.

Mine. Mate. Mine.

"Be a good girl and put your hands on the counter, sweetheart," I ordered, the command only making her wetter. She shuddered, her brilliant green-gold eyes practically lighting with challenge.

"What happens if I don't?" she asked, her hips betraying her by swiveling for a little friction.

My teeth found the inside of her thigh, and I raked my fangs against the sensitive flesh. She shuddered in answer, a moan slipping past her lips.

"So many things. I could spank that luscious ass of yours while I fuck it." She bit her lip at that one, and it gave me so many ideas, but I continued. "I could tease you until you beg me to come. I could tie them behind your back and make you." Another lip bite. Oh, I liked that. "Really, the options are limitless, but all of them delay my meal, beautiful, and I'm fucking starving."

Wren slapped her hands on the tile, and fuck, if that wasn't sexy, too.

Spreading her wide with my thumbs, I gave her sweet lips a long lick. It wasn't the first time I'd gotten my mouth on her pussy, but Wren was becoming my favorite treat. Before long I was devouring her, circling my tongue over her clit, pressing my fingers into her. Moans spilled from her throat, husky ones that made my cock harder than a rock and had my balls reaching up my throat.

"Shh, beautiful," I murmured before getting right back to work.

A shaking hand found my free wrist, pulling it from her folds. She then took those fingers and wrapped her lips around them, sucking on the digits like she had my cock last night.

Gods, this woman.

My cock—which had been harder than I thought possible—kicked against my zipper—making anything but taking her impossible. Finding my feet, I pulled my fingers from her mouth, unable to stop myself from kissing her. I wanted her taste on my tongue—all of it. And it just went on and on.

Together, our fingers worked my belt loose, and in far more time than either of us wanted, I was free of my pants. But as impatient as I was, I had nothing on Wren.

"Please," she begged, clawing at my shirt, only this time, the fabric tore under her ministrations. "I want you. *Please.*"

Far be it from me to deny my mate anything.

"Since you asked so nicely," I murmured against her lips, swallowing her moan as I pressed inside her wet heat.

Gods, she was Heaven. She was Heaven and Hell, the cosmos and everything in between. Her breath hitched as her eyes glowed with pleasure, her chest and cheeks flushed as her legs tightened around my back. Wren's release was coming fast, and I was right there with her. Lost in her passion, she bared her neck to me, unable to hold her head up a single second longer.

Her braid shifted, revealing the two crescents of my mark on her flesh, the sight making me feral. My thrusts got rougher, harder, her moans louder, and I struck, re-marking her as I had several times last night, ensuring my bite took, cementing us together again and again.

As soon as my fangs broke her skin, her sex tightened around me, her moans getting louder, more desperate. She was almost there. *Almost.* Fitting a hand between us, I circled her clit with my thumb, and she went off like a bomb, triggering a chain reaction of my own climax.

Heat raced up my spine as it overtook me, the last thread of control snapping as I pounded out my release.

I would never be able to look at this counter again without getting hard.

Never.

By the time the moon was high in the sky, we'd come together several more times, exhaustion pulling us into a deep sleep.

Maybe that was why I didn't hear the man's approach until he was already knocking on my door, until he was already too close for comfort. And I had a sleeping Wren in my bed.

A sleeping, naked Wren.

Who was most definitely not supposed to be here.

Fuck.

CHAPTER 16

WREN

THE SLEEP AFTER NICO FUCKED ME INTO A STUPOR WAS the absolute best. It didn't matter if it was five minutes or two hours, it was the most restful sleep I'd ever gotten in my life. Maybe I felt safe with him. And why wouldn't I? In the circle of his arms, nothing could happen to me. No one would get to me. I was special and whole and cared for. Or maybe he screwed me so good, I was incapable of thinking bad thoughts. Whatever it was, his penis should be classified as a deadly weapon.

One good dicking and I was down for the count until he found me again in the night, his hands urgent, needy, and I was fully awake, ready for the next round. There was no way this kind of pace was sustainable, but so far, I wasn't sore, I didn't have any regrets, and my lust wasn't going to die down anytime soon.

But this time when his hands shook me awake, I knew something was wrong. For one, his palm clamped hard over my mouth, pressing my lips against my teeth, and two? He led a finger to his own lips, begging for me to be quiet with his eyes. Unease filtered through my lethargic limbs, the sex-haze lifting as adrenaline kicked in. Then I heard it.

A knock. Someone was at the door. And I was naked in Nico's bed.

Shiiiiittttttt.

Wrapping me up in a sheet, he picked me up and lowered me to the floor, sliding me on the fabric until I was under the bed, the scant space tight, but I fit. Then he flicked the comforter over the side, hiding me from view.

Shuffling commenced, the rustle of clothes, I think, and then Nico opened his door.

"Girard?" Nico said, his voice the picture of surprise and innocence. "Is something wrong?"

"No, no, Acosta. Nothing's wrong, exactly. It's just... May I come in?"

My blood went cold. If there was a man I didn't trust, it was Girard. At least Ames was up front about his assholery. Girard was stealth about it, keeping his shit hidden until you were blindsided by it. I'd almost thought he was a good guy until he lied right to my face about Fiona. Thought he was better than the Ameses of the world.

But he was no different, except that he was the one wearing a mask.

"Sure," Nico answered, and I wanted to kick him.

Here I was lying naked, wrapped in a sheet on this dust-bunny hell of a floor, trying not to sneeze my head off, and he was inviting him in? Was he high?

The clomp of booted feet tramped into his cabin, and I tried not to pop out from under this bed and slap the shit out of the wolf.

"To what do I owe this pleasure?" Nico prompted, his feigned innocence on thick. The place probably smelled like sex, and I was one thousand percent positive we were going to get made.

A flutter of paper rustled, and Girard replied, "Apologies, I've been on the phone with Savannah for two hours trying to stop this, but you've been recalled."

Recalled? What the fuck did that mean?

"Now? In the middle of a class? I'm supposed to be covering for Cassidy until June. What gives?"

Nico plopped onto the bed, sending the mattress squeezing through the slats, closer to my face. The only thing that ensured it was him was the sliver of bare feet I could see past the comforter. The man even had pretty feet. How the hell was that possible, and oh, my gods, why was I thinking about his feet at a time like this?

Then it hit me. He was protecting me again, making sure Girard didn't come any closer. Still.

Recalled?

"That's what I said, but the brass isn't having it. They want you there first thing in the morning."

That cold pit of dread? Well, it was a certified iceberg now.

He was leaving? Now?

How were we going to find out what happened to Fiona? What about Ames? If Nico was gone, Ames would run roughshod over everyone. And I didn't trust Girard as far as I could throw him.

He was leaving. He was leaving me.

Me. Us. He could find anyone. Nico Acosta was a virile, hot-as-sin wolf with so much goodness in him it made my heart want to burst out of my chest. He didn't have to be stuck with someone like me, a fuckup who couldn't even do magic. A witch so messed up, even her own family didn't want her. Nico could have anyone he wanted. No doubt there were arcaners and humans alike, just throwing themselves at his feet while he walked down the street. It was a wonder he could get anything done at all.

He was leaving.

Tears welled in my stupid eyes as my chest wanted to cave in on itself. My throat hurt and my heart... This was just some fling. He could go back to his life and forget all about me—about this place. He could move on and not grasp at the straws of a mystery that no one had gotten anywhere on in years. He could be free.

A small place at the back of my mind wanted that for him. Happiness. Freedom. A life without worry, or a stupid girl clinging to him that was more trouble than she was worth.

Self-esteem needed on aisle three. We need some self-esteem over here.

Yeah, I was a self-deprecating, no-magic-having witch with abandonment issues, but that didn't change the facts. Nico would leave, and I would be here, and surviving would become a problem.

Fiona.

How was I going to find her now? By myself, I guessed. Because I wouldn't leave her behind.

I wouldn't.

Because the reality was, that if I had really left, no one but her would give a shit. She'd do whatever it was she had to do to find me. It was only fitting I do the same.

"Why didn't my supervisor contact me?" Nico countered, his tone conversational but probing. "This is pretty fucking irregular, man."

I wiped at my face, dashing the wetness from my cheeks, and swallowing down the rest of my tears. Tears never did help anybody, right? What good were they when I had shit to do?

Find Fiona. The rest of this shit doesn't matter. Your heart, your feelings? They mean shit.

"No idea. Check your phone. Maybe they tried."

Nico sighed. "I'll do that. Sorry to leave you in the lurch, Girard. Hopefully, Cassidy is already on his way back, so you don't have a hole in the schedule."

He was leaving.

Yes. He was. And as much as that shit hurt, as much as it frightened me with everything going on, as much as I would miss him, I had to get on with it. Get on with living without him. He'd be doing the same damn thing without me.

No pity parties. No moping. No crying myself to sleep. Nothing. I would be fine. I always was.

I always fucking am.

"Here's hoping," Girard replied, his booted feet plodding toward the door. "Sorry about the rush. Hope everything's okay in Savannah."

"Yeah," Nico said, rising from the bed. "Thanks, man."

The door opened and shut, and by the time Nico pulled the comforter back to tell me the coast was clear, I'd already dried my tears and concocted a plan. This one was slightly better than the one I'd come up with while cleaning the dining hall, but not by much.

You're fine. You always are. Just swallow it down and smile like the good girl you are and don't make a fuss. No one likes a fuss, Wren.

How many times had my mother said that?

No one likes a fuss, Wren.

Smile, girl. Gods, you got cotton for brains?

Can't you go over to your little friend's house so we can have some damn peace around here?

Don't make a fuss. Mama was right about that.

Nico held out a hand, and as much as it hurt, I took it, allowing him to pull me from the floor and into his arms, gritting my teeth all the while. His scent surrounded me, as did his heat—a warmth I'd only found right here against his chest. I never realized how cold I'd been for all these years—not until he held me.

He's leaving, and he's not coming back. This is goodbye.

His fingers burrowed into my hair, his blunted nails gently scratching at my scalp. It felt so good, and it hurt so bad all at the same time. Then he kissed my temple, my cheek, my neck, wrapping me up so tight, I almost believed he didn't want to go.

Almost.

I wanted to bawl. I wanted to rage. I wanted to tie him down and make sure he never left. But I didn't do any of those things. One by one, I closed every door and window into my heart, locking them up tight.

No more. I wouldn't give any more of me. Not one more bit.

I had to save something for myself. I had to make it so I could breathe, could live. I wasn't going to give more of myself than I could survive losing, and I would give him everything if I let myself.

As gently as I could, I pushed against his middle, aching for space, for an ounce of distance. He couldn't hug me and kiss me and make me think he wanted me—not when he was leaving me behind. Turning, I searched for my clothes and boots, my bag, anything, but the small cabin was cleared of my things. As if I'd never been here.

Nodding, that ache only got bigger. It was as it should be.

"Oh, here," he murmured, sensing my distress and went to a teeny closet. He pulled my bag and discarded clothes from the floor, handing them over.

I croaked out a quiet, "Thanks," before heading to the bathroom to shower and handle my business, the worst sense of déjà vu coming over me. Hadn't I done this yesterday? Hurt my own feelings and fled to the bathroom to shower off his scent? Hadn't I needed that space?

The water felt like needles against my skin, but I scrubbed him from me, every kiss, every scent, every hug—soaping them over and washing them down the drain. My skin was raw by the time I quit, but again, it didn't matter. None of it mattered.

Then I was out of the bathroom just in time to see Nico zip

a bag of his own. It was a little larger than mine, bright yellow, and it sat on top of our wadded-up sheets.

"Come on, beautiful. Let me get you back to your cabin safe, and I—"

"Don't worry about it. I can make it there on my own." I couldn't take one more kiss. Or hug. Or bullshit promise he knew he couldn't keep—that I knew he wouldn't keep. Giving him my best "I'm not broken" smile, I softened it with, "You need to go, right?"

Nico's gaze went gold, glowing with his wolf. "I don't want to go. You know that, right?"

Sure I did.

"Of course," I murmured, shouldering my bag. "I understand."

His fingers wrapped around my wrist, a gentle handcuff if there ever was one. "I don't think you do. I don't think you understand any of it."

But there wasn't anything for me not to get, and even though he was barely holding onto me, it hurt so fucking bad, I almost wished his grip was bruising.

"What's not to understand? You've been recalled, you need to go. I got it, Nico. Trust me."

Somehow, in the split second it took me to pivot away from him, he was in my space, my bag was gone, and he had backed me into a wall, my back flat to the planks.

"No," he growled, his chest rumbling against mine. "You don't. You couldn't possibly. Because if you did, you'd get that I would rather eat glass than leave you."

Hope bloomed in my heart. Stupid hope. What had hope ever done for anybody, huh? It broke you, that's what it did. It made you believe things were possible when they never were. It made you think if you just tried hard enough, if you just pushed a little more, if you were better, then people would love you. People would give a shit.

Hope made me a doormat.

But then he cupped my cheeks in his hands and stared at me with those gorgeous gold eyes, and I softened. Just a little.

"If you understood, you'd get that every time you leave my sight, I get twitchy. I get distracted. All I want to do is get back to you. If you understood, you'd know that I fucking hate that I have to leave. I *hate* it. You'd know that I'm scared out of my fucking mind something is going to happen to you. That I'm freaking the fuck out over here."

Goo. I was goo—puddled on the floor, certified liquid, goo.

"Problem is, if they're recalling me, things have gone sideways, and they need my help. They wouldn't do that—especially with this quick of a turnaround—if shit was copacetic. I need to get there, fix whatever the fuck it is that has them recalling me, and get back before the place explodes, or worse."

I thought about the cracked crystal in Haynes' hand. Blowing shit up was a very real possibility.

"So do you get it now? I don't want to leave, but I have to. I don't want you unprotected, but I don't know another way to keep you safe. And every single second I'm gone, it's going to feel like I cut out my fucking heart."

Rolling up on my tiptoes, I pressed a kiss to his full lips, tasting his words for the truth they were. When we were breathless and rumpled, I said, "Yeah. I was a little unclear, but I get it now. Thanks for the clarification."

"Good," he murmured, letting go of my face and grabbing my hand.

He led me much the same way he'd brought me here, through the forest, dipping through the trees when he heard something I couldn't. In no time we were back at my cabin, walking through the rear door. This time, though, the cabin wasn't empty.

Not at all.

CHAPTER 17

WREN

NICO FROZE AND THEN BACKED UP THREE STEPS, clutching me to his back as he moved, protecting me with his body. His entire form—save for his neck—was as still as a statue. That neck, though? It was tilted up by the point of a silver knife.

Hannah stood in the doorway, her giant ghoul frame of nearly seven feet blocking the entrance, the blade in her steady fist. And she was growling, a deep belly sound that rumbled from the depths of Hell.

Umm, Houston? We have a problem.

"Stand down, Dumond," Nico ordered, threading whatever power he had into the command. "She's right here. Look."

But the whispers around the camp were that Hannah had survived an almost extinction of her nest—the *only* survivor—and my green-haired ghoul friend had no intention of taking her eyes off Nico. Especially not when he was entering our cabin in the middle of the night right after Fiona had been taken.

But I'd be damned if Nico got hurt because of me. Hell no.

A film of red passed over my eyes for a moment before I barked, "Hannah Dumond, you get that knife away from his neck right now, or so help me, I will knock your fucking block off."

Could I knock her block off? Absolutely not.

The best I could do was kick her in the shin and run for my life, but that wasn't the point. That knife needed to be nowhere near Nico, and that was just the way it had to be.

Hannah finally flicked her gaze to me, her eyes going wide, shock and a fair amount of relief in those impossibly pale irises. In a millisecond, the knife was spirited away to who knew where and her hand was on my wrist, yanking me into the cabin with about as much finesse as a wrecking ball.

Nico seemed to take umbrage with her rough handling because the sound that came from his throat scared the shit out of even me. If Hannah's had been from Hell itself, then Satan or Hades or whoever ran the place was coming out of Nico.

"Lock your shit up, Dumond, you hear me? You don't touch her like that. Ever. Understand?"

It was more order than question, but she got it just fine, letting go of my wrist like it burned her.

"Got it, wolf. Crystal clear."

"Excuse the fuck out of us," Malia chimed in, elbowing Hannah out of the way, "but maybe don't leave your scent and impressions all over the place after one of our friends up and goes missing and then kidnap someone else in this cabin. You think you can do that, you fucking idiot?"

Then she took off her glove and smacked me with it. "And you. You think you can stave off spending the night with your boyfriend for one night maybe? What the fuck? We thought you'd been taken, too, until I touched your locker and found out otherwise. Dick. Move."

I shot Nico a withering glare. "Told you it was a bad idea to leave."

His answering smile told me he did not give that first shit about their discomfort. He did not regret a single second of our time alone.

Okay, I didn't either, but still. We'd been rude, worrying them like that.

"And if you could stop eye-fucking each other for five seconds, that would be great," Malia snapped, making my head whip to her.

Oops.

Nico tucked me under his arm, protecting me, even in this safe space. "How about you stop barking orders at us and agree to watch out for my girl here until I can get back? How'd that be?" His eyes flashed with his wolf, and I hated to say it, but it was really freaking hot. Nico's attention shifted to Hannah. "Not out of your sight for a second. It's going to be a while until I can get a buddy here. Do this favor for me and I'll owe you one."

Hannah crossed her arms over her chest, eyeballing him with derision. "A freebie favor from a wolf prince for doing something I was already going to do?" She shrugged like dropping that bomb was no big deal. "Sure, I'm game."

Wolf prince?

"Wolves don't have royalty like you ghouls, and you're one to talk, *Queen*."

"Don't fucking call me that," she growled, hers almost as scary as Nico's. "You're lucky she likes you, wolf."

"Yeah, yeah. I'm sufficiently scared," he deadpanned, his bored expression nearly making me giggle.

Giggling? What am I, twelve?

Nico grabbed my hand and lifted my knuckles to his lips. "Nowhere alone, beautiful. Not to the bathroom, no iterations, nothing. Got me? Don't make it harder for her to watch out for you or I'll never hear the end of it."

Rolling my eyes, I fit a hand on my hip. "I'm a girl, Nico. I haven't gone to the bathroom by myself since I got boobs."

He blinked hard at that one but nodded, anyway. "Fair enough."

Then his mouth was on mine, a searing kiss to tide me over for however long he would be gone.

"Be safe, Wren."

And then he really was gone, slipping out of the cabin as if he'd never been there. Already I felt cold, Nico taking all his warmth with him. Pouting, I plopped onto my bed, very aware of the two women staring at me like I had a second head.

"What?"

Hannah approached, leaning over my bed like a weirdo. "I don't care what soap you used or how much you scrubbed, I can still smell him on you. I would have given you shit about it this morning, but Fiona happened, so I skipped it." She tilted her head, her gaze flitting over the collar of my shirt. "So, you and the wolf, huh? Explain that to me."

Shrugging, I sat up and started unpacking my bag, unsure how to answer her.

"Wish I could, but I can't. It doesn't make a bit of sense to me, either. For some weird reason, he decided I was who he wanted, and..." I trailed off, shaking my head.

"So the sex is combustible. Got it." Hannah nodded like this was the best explanation. I wanted to argue, but she wasn't wrong.

"By the way," Malia chimed in, "everything you touch has Acosta's imprint all over it. Like literally everything. Question: Did he really do that thing with his fingers—"

"Whoa," I shouted, shooting to my feet. "That shit is private, ma'am."

But yes. Yes, he did do that thing with his fingers. And it was fucking divine.

Malia stuck out her tongue. "Don't touch my toothbrush, and I won't glean information I'm not supposed to have."

At that, I laughed—so hard it brought tears to my eyes, but then my mirth took a right turn back into depressed-land. Nico was gone. Fiona was gone. And somehow, we needed to pass this course and not get kidnapped, or killed, or worse.

Piece of cake.

Over the next few hours, we all got too little sleep, one of us waking up in the middle of the night, afraid of what could happen. At about two, we decided as a group to just leave all the lights on, foregoing sleep entirely.

Fiona had been taken right under all our noses. It could be any of us next.

After an uneasy breakfast, we were in the middle of a

necromancy lecture with Girard, going over all the ways the practice was regulated, what was allowed, and why you shouldn't raise the dead willy-nilly.

All while trying to stay awake. Sure, it was interesting stuff, but the lecture went on and on. Personally, I figured raising the dead was kind of a no-no on all fronts and any thought to the contrary was absolute insanity. But the arcane world probably didn't give two shits about my opinion on the subject.

And I got it—I did.

Savannah was home to hundreds of cemeteries. Our steps and walls and very foundations were made of arcaner bones. It wasn't like being surrounded by death was exactly new.

But making them come back to life? Full-on zombies?

No, thanks.

I was a criminal. Not an idiot.

After the lecture, there would be an exam—one I would pass, because the answer to everything was basically, "do not raise the dead, don't think about raising the dead, don't talk about raising the dead, and don't be friends with people who raise the dead." It was basically a no-brainer.

Sure enough, when the test was delivered, it was a poster lesson for "do not do the thing" and if you "do the thing," you would go to jail while you awaited your very swift execution.

So noted.

But as I was finishing my test, I dragged my feet a little, my original plan bubbling in my head. Girard was lying to all of us. Nico couldn't get a scent off of her things. Someone had to have enough juice to do magic under the null ward.

Who better to have that level of magic than the commandant of the damn course? All the fingers pointed to

Ames, but no way he was smart enough or had enough clout to fake the paperwork needed to keep this shit quiet.

But Girard did.

And if he was a creepy arcane serial killer, he'd have to keep trophies, right? I watched enough true crime shows to know all serial killers liked trophies. What if he had them? What if they were just sitting in his office? What if I could get the proof Nico needed to take this asshole down?

I looked it up. The ABI didn't require search warrants or Miranda rights. They didn't need permission—mostly because if they had a shred of proof you did something, they'd take your ass to jail posthaste.

So, any trial Girard had, it wouldn't get thrown out because I'd nicked some evidence.

And I wouldn't get a more perfect time to search, either. Girard was proctoring this test, and no one had finished yet. I had plenty of time to get in, search, and get out.

This is the dumbest idea you have ever had in your life, Wren, and that's saying something.

Okay, my inner voice—who still sounded like my mother—was accurate. This was stupid. But Nico was gone, and his friend was nowhere to be found, and who the fuck was going to look for Fiona while we sat here with our thumbs up our asses?

No one. That's who.

Shoring up my topsy-turvy nerves, I stood, taking my test right to the front and handing it in.

Girard's eyes sparkled, a warm smile on his face like he was a proud papa. It made me sick.

"Already, Bannister?" His gaze traced over the page as if he was mentally grading it on the spot. "Very good. You're free to enjoy some leisure time until your next iteration."

Pasting my best smile on my face, I shoved out a polite, "Thank you," before pivoting on a heel and marching through the aisle of desks to leave. But as I walked past Hannah's desk, she flung out a hand to stop me.

She didn't say anything. She didn't need to. Everything in her gaze said to go straight back to our cabin with no stops, and whatever it was that I was planning had better not happen.

I nodded, only to be answered by her narrowed eyes.

It was funny how well you could get to know someone so fast. Our silent conversation went a little like this:

Her: No funny business.

Me: I'm not doing anything.

Her: Bullshit. I'm watching you.

Me: Fine.

"Is there something wrong?" Girard asked, standing at his desk.

"No, sir," I called, pulling my wrist from Hannah's vise-grip of a hand. "Just leaving."

Then I was out the door, praying no one got wise for a little while.

The first problem I ran into was finding Girard's office. I vaguely remembered the map from the first day, which pointed out the medical cabin and surrounding offices. After Hell Night, I'd avoided the place like the plague, the lack of a null sort of a problem for someone like me.

But now I had a nulling necklace…

And even though Haynes' crystal had cracked, maybe the thing had enough juice to get me in and out of there without being detected. Directing my feet north, I stuck to the trees, skirting the buildings until I came to the medic cabin. Next to the cute cottage-style bungalow was another, recessed back into the trees as if it were hiding.

If I was a creepy whatever the fuck Girard was, I'd want an office tucked away, almost hidden from all the students.

Sure, and how are you getting in there? And what happens if this isn't the place? What if someone is in the building?

Okay, so my plan was "absolute flying by the seat of my pants, dumbest shit ever, why are you like this," bad. I should turn around and never come back, just keep my head down and get through the course and pray someone else got the balls to find Fiona.

Wren, there are far more people that care about you than you think.

Fiona's words hit me like a slap. She wouldn't chicken out on me. She would have found something. I was sure of it.

Gritting my teeth, I pressed forward. Smartly—one of the few smart moves I'd had all damn day—I circled the building, listening for voices or movement. With human-capable ears, I didn't get anything, and I prayed that was enough. Like most of the other cabins, there was a back door, and I tested the knob.

Much to my disbelief, the door was unlocked, and I walked inside, keeping an eye out for something or someone to jump out at me. The cabin was larger than Nico's, the main area divided into rooms instead of wide open. The back opened into a mud and laundry room with three pairs of soiled boots, all the same size. On the hooks were a few jackets in different weights and a stand-up washer-dryer combo.

From there, was a larger kitchen with new appliances and stone countertops that led into a decent living room, with a large television and standard bachelor-pad-style leather recliners. Across from the living room was a bedroom with a messy comforter and an office close to the front door.

This was Girard's home.

Somehow being in Girard's house seemed like way worse of an idea than his office ever was.

You should not be here, Wren.

Yeah, yeah, I knew that. But I was here already, and my time was running out.

Bolting for the office, I drew up short. For one, the place was an absolute mess. Papers were strewn all over the floor, the computer monitor on its side, the screen cracked. Blood dotted the white copy paper, blending into the black ink.

You should not be here, Wren.

Seeing the blood, the office, I finally decided my inner voice was right.

But before I could even turn to leave, a sharp pain tore through my skull, and everything went black.

CHAPTER 18

NICO

"Where the fuck have you been?" I barked, not taking my eyes off the road. There was little traffic this late at night, but not paying attention was a good way to ram right into a deer.

Wyatt was on the line, filtering through my truck's speakers, his chuckle dark. He was lucky he wasn't in this damn cab with me. I'd called that man no less than ten times, trying to get his ass back to the selection school, and now two hours into the drive down to Savannah, he was calling me back?

About fucking time.

"Cleaning up messes, man. Cleaning up a shit-ton of messes and making a few of my own. I got your messages. All ten of them. It's why I'm calling."

Pressing the accelerator, I ground my teeth, trying not to

yell. "Fabulous. We'll talk about your messes later. I need you back at the school. Now."

Wyatt sucked air between his teeth. "That's a tall order, my friend. I'm not exactly in a spot where I can just leave."

"She's unprotected, Wyatt. One girl has already been taken, and Wren is there without me. She is my mate, my *wife*. And because of my obligation to the ABI, I'm now driving away from her. So I need you to get to a spot where you can leave, and need you to do it now."

"Ho-ly shit. Really? I kinda figured she'd be the one, but... *really*? Do your parents know you mated with someone? Your mom is probably having a fit right about now. What did your dad say?"

Frowning at the slow-moving compact in front of me, I changed lanes and debated my answer. Might as well go with the truth. "I haven't told them yet."

Wyatt practically howled down the line, laughing his fucking head off. "You think you can keep this to yourself? You know they're going to know as soon as you walk in. You probably smell like her now. How is that honey and jasmine perfume she uses, by the way?"

At this rate, my teeth were going to be ground down to nubs. "I didn't plan on keeping it from them. It just happened so fast that I haven't had time to make a phone call. The girl that's missing? She was taken the same night of the mating, and then I was called away."

Honestly, based on Wren's reaction to me leaving, I wasn't certain she knew exactly what was happening between us. The scent of her pain was so bad, I thought I was going to keel over and die. She had to have thought I was leaving her forever to feel like that, and if that was the case...

Well, if that was the case, I was pretty sure I was screwed. But she was a Bannister witch. She was from Savannah. The Acostas and Bannisters did business from time to time—much to my mother's dismay. Most arcaners knew of wolf customs, right? They knew that the bite was as permanent as a marriage.

Didn't they?

"So that's why you're calling me instead of your family," Wyatt mused, probably petting the chia pet he called a beard as he did it, too.

"You *are* family, numb nuts. And you know damn well there is going to be an issue once they find out she's a witch. I'll be the first Acosta alpha in four hundred years not to mate another wolf. And a Bannister at that? You know damn well how fucked I am when I get home."

But I wouldn't trade it for anything—wouldn't trade *her* for anything. As much as I dragged my feet, as much as I tried to blind myself, I knew from the moment I put my hands on her that I was a goner.

"You know what I mean. I'm an Acosta wolf, but I'm not an Acosta. You have brothers. Sisters. Cousins. You could have called any one of them."

My chuckle was mirthless. "Sure, but then I'd have to explain why my entire family showed up at selection school to shadow a single Bannister witch. *You* are actually supposed to be there. You see the difference?"

"Well, you aren't wrong." Wyatt sighed like I was leeching his very soul. "Fine. I'll find a death mage to flit me over there or somethin', though you'll be responsible for the payment Simon will charge. You know how stingy he is."

That had the hair on the back of my neck prickling. "What are you doing in Tennessee?"

Simon Cartwright was the only good death mage I knew—including Girard—but his ties with the riffraff of Knoxville didn't sit so well with me. In the last year there had been a rabid shapeshifter on the loose, a whole wolf war, complete with Alpha challenge, and wolf zombies from a whacked-out death mage on a power trip.

I didn't want Wyatt anywhere near Tennessee. Plus, if Dad found out, Wyatt would be in deep shit.

"I'm not. But I do have Simon's number. He can pick me up."

Okay, one less thing to worry about.

"Good, good. Text me when you lay eyes on her." I thought about that for a second. "Please."

Wyatt's whistle rattled through my speakers. "Hoo, boy. You're going to be the worst, aren't you?"

Wincing, I shrugged, even though he couldn't see me. "Probably."

"Lucky me. Talk to you soon, man."

"Thank you, Wyatt. I mean it."

"I know you do, brother. Just try not to rip anyone's head off while you're apart. The last thing she needs is to be the one visiting you in prison."

And with that, I hung up on my best friend.

Two hours and Atlanta traffic later, I'd made it to Savannah. That was the problem with driving. I could have made it here in half the time, but even at two o'clock in the morning, Atlanta was still a fucking problem. Now it was four, I was exhausted, and I was about to run the gauntlet.

Half the lights were still on in the Acosta compound, a sprawling estate right next to Forsyth Park. The park afforded us access to a place to run, was solidly warded against humans paying us any mind, and had enough access to the historic district to make it worth it. Savannah had a small-town feel to it, without actually being a small town. I loved it and hated it in equal measure.

Parking in the drive, I snatched my bag from the back seat and tried to go inside without anyone making a scene.

I should have known better. I barely had the front door shut before my mother was on me.

"Nicholas," my mother whispered, opening her arms wide for a hug. "I've missed you."

I'd barely set my bag down before she had me wrapped up in her arms. I would deny it to my dying day, but my mother's hugs could cure any ailment. Or I thought that a week ago. But not even my mother's hugs could cure the deep pit I had in my belly at being away from Wren.

"I was away for less than a week, Mom."

At my mother's first sniff, I tensed. When her eyes went the amber of her wolf, I braced. And when she took a few steps back and pressed both palms flat against her chest as a look of pure joy bloomed across her face, I winced.

My mother was a classic Portuguese-American woman, fiery, slightly dramatic, and loud. As a young pup, I could hear her all the way from the other end of Forsyth. But she didn't yell like she was prone to do.

No, she frowned, her expression almost hurt.

"You found your mate so soon? Why didn't you call us?" She sniffed again, longer this time. "A young woman. A w—" She slapped a hand over her mouth, her eyes going wide.

Without another word, she snatched my hand in hers and dragged me up the stairs to my father's meeting room. It was one of the twelve sound-proof rooms in the house, and the closest from the entrance. Mom closed the doors as fast as she could while I waited for the bomb to drop.

"You mated a witch, Nicholas? Are you insane?" She sniffed again.

"Would you stop that? You realize I'll tell you everything. Quit sniffing me."

Both hands found their way to her hips. Uh-oh. I was in trouble.

"Don't you take that tone with me, son. I can still take you in a challenge, and don't you forget it."

Pinching the bridge of my nose, I sighed. "Sorry, Mom, but I want to tell you about her. Not you figure it out on your own by smell alone."

She waved my words away, perching on the edge of the table. "Fine, fine. Tell me why you mated a witch and didn't tell us. I'm all ears."

"You know it doesn't work like that. I didn't get a choice, but damn if I'd take it back now. I care about her. A lot. So I won't hear a single bad word about her, you hear me? Not one."

There were many things Catia Acosta could call herself, but "patient" hadn't ever been one of them. "Fine. I won't say a word about this witch mate you found. Can I at least get her name? What does she do? Is she from a good family? Details, son. I need the details."

"Her name is Wren, and she is from a good family. She's a probationary ABI agent going through the selection school." Vague. I would be as vague as possible, and maybe my mother would let something slide just this once.

Mom's eyebrows went up as she tapped her lip with her index finger. "Wren... I've heard that name before. What did you say her last name was again?"

No such luck. That woman did not miss a trick even at three hundred years old. She knew damn well I'd left her last name off on purpose.

"I didn't."

"Tell me her name, son."

Shaking my head, I backed away. "I'm not taking it back. It's permanent. Under the full moon of my birth, she agreed to be mine and me hers. She's my wife, Mom." Swallowing hard, I knew what she was going to say. "I'm not taking it back."

"What. Is. Her. Name."

But she already knew. I could see it in her eyes. My family didn't care for the Bannisters for several reasons, but my mother? Well, she hated Margot Bannister to the ends of the earth and maybe beyond. Not that I blamed her. Every time Wren got that broken look on her face, I wanted to rage.

"They shunned her—did you know that? They treated her like trash, like she was shit on their heel." I swallowed hard, remembering the scent of Wren's pain. Gods, it was like she was dying. Like her heart was shattering. I hated that fucking scent so much I couldn't breathe. "Do you know how much damage that woman has because of that family? How easily she believes I'll leave her? How every single kindness makes her light up with joy? You and I both know only whipped pups behave that way. You know, Mom."

I took another step back. "I'm not taking it back. She is my wife, my mate, and I'll challenge anyone who says otherwise."

A strange proudness wafted over my mother's expression. "Very good. And there is no taking it back. If you bound her as you say, then it doesn't matter what I think or who her parents are. We will welcome her as if she were one of us. Wolf or not."

I should have smelled the lie. Rookie mistake. "So, you were just fucking with me?"

My mother's laugh was an ounce of nostalgia from a happy childhood. "Sweetie, Wyatt called two hours ago to prepare me for the news. He also *may* have warned me a week ago after a human bar incident?"

Wyatt didn't have a mom. Abandoned with his father at birth, he looked to my mom a lot growing up. Hell, he was practically a member of the family. Of course he would call her.

"Really, son. Alligators?"

I still wasn't sorry about that. "They were going to rape her and who knew what else. Their pants were already unzipped, Mom."

Mom's face went green. "Wyatt seems to have left that part out. Does she know about it? Or about you hauling her out of that rattrap of an apothecary? The sheer fact the place didn't burn down twenty years ago is beyond me."

Wincing, I rubbed the back of my neck. "No. We haven't made it that far into the getting-to-know-you chats. We kind of got blindsided."

And that said nothing about the feeling in my gut when I thought about Wren's reaction to me leaving.

"Well, get some rest before you go into that infernal job of yours. Recalling you in the middle of the night?" She shook her head. "Taking you away from your mate? Disgraceful."

Opening my arms for a hug, she moved forward into them, squeezing me like she had when I was little. "Thanks, Ma. You'll prep Dad, right?"

She planted a gentle fist into my belly. "You know I will. Your father is far more excitable than I am." *Lies.* "It just makes sense to prepare him. But tomorrow. You need your rest."

With that, I let her go, snatching my duffle from the floor and turning right to head to the East wing. Almost every unmated pack member under the age of forty lived in this house, the rest living close by within walking distance. Only my older brother Santiago and my sister Mariella were left among all the other pack youngsters. I was the youngest Acosta to find their mate in two hundred years and the first to mate outside our species in four hundred.

As soon as I brought Wren home, we would be a spectacle. She would hate it. Hell, I would, too.

But she would be here. And safe. And with me. We would be surrounded by family. I could show her what that really meant—to have a big, huge, crazy family full of people who loved you and supported you. To have unruly holiday dinners full of mundane dramas and a comforting hug when shit went sideways.

Things weren't perfect here, but it was home.

I practically fell onto my bed, clothes and all, but as comfortable as it was, rest never really found me. More than a few hours later, I was back in my truck and headed for ABI headquarters, ready to face whatever it was that was keeping me from Wren.

The place was its usual quiet. No added buzz of activity. No extra people milling around. It was early, but if I was recalled, there would have been a reason. There would have been an emergency or something.

The dread had returned, that itchy feeling between my shoulder blades that spelled danger.

Taking out my phone, I called my supervisor, Erica. Serreno was a take-no-shit elemental mage with three centuries under her belt. As high as my clearance was, Serreno's was higher since she was the acting Deputy Director of the Savannah branch. Hell, she'd even deployed to Knoxville right after they lost their own director, trying to clean the place up until the new one had taken over.

The trill of her ringtone sounded behind me, and I whipped around, ending the call. I'd called her once and left a message, but it had been after midnight, so I didn't expect her to contact me—especially if she was in need of some shut-eye in the middle of a big case. But...

"What the hell are you doing here? I thought you were supposed to be up in Blue Ridge until June," Erica grumbled before sipping on her coffee, sweeping a long, dark twist of hair out of her eye.

My gut twisted as I plucked the folded recall orders from the folder in my hand. "I was given these at midnight. With your signature. Are you telling me I haven't been recalled back?"

Erica's frown intensified and she snatched the paper from

my fingers, studying it. "I didn't sign any orders for you to return now. I don't even need you since the spike in dark magic has died down." Her gaze speared the paper as if she'd like to light it on fire. "Where the fuck did you get this?"

Girard's faking the paperwork. He faked my orders. Wren. Wren, Wren, Wren.

"Victor Girard," I murmured, my entire body frozen for a second. "I have to go back. I have to go now."

I didn't wait for her reply. No, I ran as fast as I could on two legs, dialing Wyatt's number. He answered on the second ring. "Yeah?"

"Girard faked my orders," I growled. "Please tell me you have eyes on Wren."

"She was taking a test... that Girard was proctoring. I figured she was safe, and went to get coffee... You didn't tell me he was who you were looking out for." Wyatt paused before becoming all business. "I gotta go. I'll call you when I have eyes on our target."

Shit. Shit, fuck, cock-sucking motherfucker. Don't shift. Don't shift. Keep it together.

My truck came into view, and I jumped in, peeling out of the lot in a cloud of smoking rubber and squealing tires, steered toward the highway. I'd barely made it ten miles down the road before Wyatt called me back. I didn't even need to answer to know it was bad news, but I let him get it out, anyway.

"She's not here," he said, the regret and sorrow in his tone more than I could bear. "He's gone, too. His place is trashed. There's blood. Three kinds. Some of it's Wren's."

I couldn't even remember pulling off the side of the road. I wasn't even sure if I turned off my truck or hung up the phone. But as soon as I let the trees that lined the highway close over me, I was no longer running on two legs.

Answering my wolf's call, I landed on four, powering north as fast as they would carry me.

CHAPTER 19

WREN

Waking up shouldn't hurt this bad.

My shoulder pressed into a hard, freezing floor, the ache of it reaching its dreadful fingers up my neck and down my arm. The arm itself was asleep, so I had to have been here for a while. The shivering made my head throb, but I was so cold, I couldn't stop.

It felt like someone was driving an icepick into my brain.

"Wren?" a soft voice called. A familiar voice. "Wren, sweetie, you have to be quiet, or he'll know you're awake."

Quiet?

Then I heard it. The faint mewling of an injured animal. Only the animal in question was me. Swallowing hard, I tried to shut up, but I was only marginally successful.

"Fiona?" I croaked, happy as hell to know she was alive, and pissed as fuck I was in no place to offer her any assistance.

A frigid hand brushed hair from my face, and I chanced opening my eyes. The room swam as that icepick got a bit more aggressive in my noggin, but I was able to focus on her face. Fi's nose was puffy, a crust of dark red around both nostrils. One eye sported dark-purple bruising, the lid half-closed from the swelling.

He'd hit her hard. In his cabin, maybe? Had it been her blood on those papers? Had she fought back? Was that why he'd hit her?

"Found you," I whispered, trying to sit up. Only one arm worked, and it was weak, but I managed to slowly take the pressure off the aching shoulder. Pins and needles flooded the dead limb.

"Yeah, sweetheart. You found me. Though, I have to say I rather wished you would have brought the cavalry with you."

Yeah, me too.

"Well, the goal was to find out whether or not you were actually missing, so... Mission accomplished?"

Fiona's chuckle was mirthless and then her bottom lip wobbled. "It was Girard. You know that, right?"

I nodded and immediately regretted it. Nausea twisted my stomach and I prayed I wouldn't vomit. "Yeah," I croaked. "I kind of figured. He's the one who said you'd terminated your contract and left."

Fiona's good eye sparked with rage. "'Terminated' my contract?" she hissed, using air quotes and everything. But those air quotes made me realize why we were sitting on the floor. Fiona's wrist was cuffed, the manacle attached to a long chain that was secured to the floor by a solid-looking eye-ring.

And there was another chain, but unlike Fiona's, mine was attached to my very bare ankle.

Shit.

"More like he kidnapped me in the middle of the night, the bastard." She shook her head, an action I envied at the moment. "Though, he didn't mean to nab me. When you left, I sort of figured you were off to see Instructor Smexy Pants, so I stuffed pillows under my blankets and then went to sleep in your bed."

"What?" My stomach pitched, nearly making the contents revolt.

She shrugged. "I figured if Ames walked into our cabin or somethin' and he saw 'you' in bed, he'd leave, and no one would know you'd been gone."

Man, how I wished she wouldn't have done that. It was fucking sweet and probably one of the kinder things someone had done for me, but given our current predicament...

"Didn't that just come to bite me in the ass?"

"I'm so sorry, Fi."

She waved my apology away like she wouldn't hear of it. "*You* didn't take me from my nice, warm bed. *You* didn't spirit me off using some awful death magic, hopping through shadows like a wonky tilt-a-whirl. *You* didn't sock me in the nose and then blindfold my ass and try to sell me on the black fucking market."

The cabin tilted a little bit, the rough planked walls letting dim light and a bitter wind through. "What?"

There was a black market? A black market? For selling people?

And Girard had meant to sell *me*. My heart started beating

out of my chest, and a warm trickle of wetness seeped down the back of my head.

Please be sweat, please be sweat, please be sweat.

I reached for the wetness and my fingers came away red, and the room spun a bit more.

"Yeah. Only when Girard took me to his buyer, the guy said I wasn't who he asked for and wouldn't take me." Fi paused, letting out another mirthless laugh. "You know, I'm not sure if I should be grateful or offended. Obviously, I don't wanna be sold, but I'm from top-notch stock." She blew a raspberry, tossing her hair halfheartedly. "I'm a fucking delight, dammit."

"Right?" I agreed, trying not to nod as I chuckled. How Fiona could keep her head like this was a damn mystery, but I was all for it. But her tale had me wondering if all the women taken from the selection school had been sold like commodities by Girard.

It made me wish I would have known this place was so dangerous. It made me want better for us all.

And it made me fucking mad.

But all that anger, it fled my body as soon as footsteps clomped outside.

Fiona's gaze widened just like mine likely did. She mouthed a silent, "Pretend to be asleep," and I dropped to the floor, hurting my pins-and-needles arm and jostling my head. Closing my eyes, I caught one last glimpse of her frightened expression before darkness overtook me.

The door complained as it opened, the loud screeching nearly making me jump. Attempting to be as still as possible, I barely breathed while the boots plodded closer, each step adding to the dread in my chest.

Would Nico come looking after Hannah lost me? Would he blame her? And how would he find us? Girard likely covered his scent when he took me just like he'd done with Fiona. And where were we? By the state of this shack, we could be anywhere from northern Georgia to fucking Canada for all I knew.

Think, Wren.

But thinking was hard. My head hurt and I couldn't see anything, and Girard probably had a gazillion years on me. What the fuck was I going to do that he hadn't already thought of?

It turned out our deception was for nothing. After a few long moments of tense silence while I poorly attempted to feign unconsciousness, a hard grip found my shoulders and hauled my upper body off the floor, slamming me into the rickety wall. Even though said wall was no more than a foot away, my whole body revolted at the motion, nearly making me vomit.

Girard's steel-gray eyes glowed with his power, focusing right on me. Cupping my chin, he squeezed my cheeks with his long-fingered hand. But old Girard had seen better days. The long hair he usually kept in a bun or queue at his nape, was loose and wild like he'd run backward through a bush. His beard was bushy and unkempt, his nose bloody, and he had three thick scratches on one cheek as if someone had taken their nails to him.

Fiona maybe?

"Well, well, well. Aren't you the biggest fucking pain in the ass?"

Jerking my chin out of his hand made my head feel like it

was going to explode, but I didn't want his stale breath in my face or his slimy touch on my skin.

"I'm sorry," I said, sneering. "I didn't mean to get in the middle of your black-market trafficking racket. So sorry to inconvenience you. What was I thinking?"

This time Girard latched onto my throat, lifting me off the ground like I weighed nothing. "Does Acosta like that smart mouth of yours? Or does he shove his dick down your throat to keep you quiet?" He held me up off the floor, my toes scrabbling for purchase but finding nothing as I struggled to breathe. "What? No witty comeback?"

Then he dropped me, my ankle taking the brunt of the fall. That time, I did vomit, losing my meager breakfast on the rough wood floor.

Too bad I missed his boots. *The fucker.*

"Disgusting," he hissed, shuffling back to avoid my mess. "What they see in you, I'll never know. Maybe Ames was right about you."

"Fuck. You," I gasped, wiping my mouth of spittle and grossness.

Girard knelt, examining me like a side of beef. "No thanks. You belong to someone else. Bought and paid for already. Though, I should charge Desmond extra for as much trouble as you've been."

Desmond? Is that who he plans on selling me to?

"And you," he barked, giving Fiona a disgusted scowl. "What am I going to do with you? Desmond doesn't want you, you've seen too much already, and making you forget is tricky. It'd be easier to just kill you, but I'm not too keen on getting my hands dirty."

"Oh, poor you," I growled, repulsed after everything I'd been through, I was about to be bested by a man without an inch of sack. Fabulous. "It's not like you're being sold, so fuck everyone else, right? How many women have you pawned off to—Desmond, was it? How many? Ten? Fifty? A hundred?"

Girard whipped out a hand, slamming into my cheek with enough force to split my lip and nearly knock me unconscious. "Everything would have been a lot easier if Desmond would have just snagged you at that stupid apothecary. But *noooooo*. Pretty boy Acosta got in the way." He stood, pacing back and forth over the warped wooden planks. "He enlisted me to nab you, but lo and behold Acosta gets in the way again. Did you know your boyfriend has already killed for you? I bet you think it's real sweet."

Killed for me? Excuse me? "What?"

"Oh, he didn't tell you? That's rich. The wolf prince doesn't want his lady love to know about the blood on his hands, I bet. You went out drinking with your friend, and I paid two humans to bring you to me. They met a nasty end out in the swamp, but I had a backup. But every single time, he was with you or watching you or fucking you. Really. Does the man even let you pee by yourself?"

Wait. Girard said the apothecary. Nico was the man that got me out? He's known about me this whole time?

"It's cute how little you know. Maybe Desmond will make you his little pet. Put you on a leash and parade you around the Fae court. All that wide-eyed innocence will get stomped out in a week."

I thought about telling Girard to go fuck himself, but I

didn't have a whole lot of consciousness left under my belt, and I couldn't figure out our escape if I was knocked out.

"You got a lot of nerve," Fiona began, spearing him with her fiery blue gaze. "You know who I am, and you still want to kill me? Darlin', I don't know if you're brave or stupid." She clucked her tongue like a good Southern woman and shook her head. "Now, my daddy and I don't quite get along, but I'll bet every shoe I have in my closet he'll give a damn if some two-bit death mage takes out his only daughter."

Girard scoffed, standing so he could glare down at her. "They won't find out, but why would I give a damn about some backwoods witch coven?"

Fiona stared at him like he was two bushels shy of a full load. "I'm a *Jacobs*, you dumb bitch. Josiah Jacobs' only daughter." She raised her eyebrows, waiting for him to get it. Hell, even I got it, and I was so far removed from the arcane world it was silly.

Josiah Jacobs had been implicated in several high-profile murders, but no one could ever make the charges stick. Under his iron fist, the Jacobs coven had reached infamous status, with few willing to go against them. They weren't all bad. They took care of their own, and didn't make waves unless you got on their bad side. But oh, if you did…

Understanding dawned on Girard's face.

"There you go, Sugar Plum. Now you're getting it." She crossed her arms over her chest and leaned against the wall like she wasn't chained or bloody or freezing. "So that puts you between a rock and a hard place. You've got an Acosta on your ass for taking his girl, the whole of the Jacobs coven ready and willing to go to war at a moment's notice, and a Fae deal hanging in the balance. It *is* a Fae deal, right?"

At Girard's continued silence, she pressed forward. "So, breaking a Fae deal has consequences, and no one wants to do that, but is there a loophole? Why don't you think about it real hard, save your backside, and make me an offer?"

Girard's smile was snide, as a black ball of magic formed in his hand. It was putrid stuff, trailing down his arm and up his fingers. Oily and slick and made of death. "I think I'll just kill you instead."

Until that very moment, I'd forgotten about the amulet that hung around my neck. But as soon as I saw that magic, it reminded me of just how destructive I could be.

Just how deadly.

Because as soon as that ball formed in his hand, I knew our only option was the fucked-up magic that ran in my veins. The awful curse that made every spell backfire. That made every power fizzle and burn and explode.

Before he let loose that putrid orb of darkness, I fisted my hand over the chain and yanked, tossing the amulet as far away from me as the little cabin could provide.

Then everything seemed to happen at once. Fire bloomed in Girard's palm, the dark magic transforming on a dime. He screamed in pain as a force blew him backward into the shack's wall. And just like in that damn apothecary, the flames only grew, jumping from one plank to the next like a brushfire.

Fiona wasted no time, she stood, gripping both sides of the chain and ripping it up, yanking the eye hook out of the wood with her bare hands.

She held out a hand. "Come on."

Shakily, I got to my feet, and Fiona half-dragged, half-carried me out of there. She shouldered through the rickety door, hauling my ass behind her as we stepped out into the light. But what we found was little better than the cabin. As far as the eye could see there was nothing but trees. No buildings. No town.

Just more and more trees.

Fiona and I were both broken, both barefoot, and even in the back half of May, there was snow on the ground of this godforsaken forest. Still, Fi took off, dragging me along as she led us out of there. My ankle protested, my head throbbed, but I followed her down the slope like she knew where she was going.

All the while, we heard Girard's screams as he burned. Only... they seemed to be getting closer.

Then I knew.

I hadn't killed him.

Girard was alive.

And he was very, very pissed off.

CHAPTER 20

NICO

She's bleeding.

I stared at Wren's blood puddled on Girard's floor and made a decision. I was going to murder Victor Girard the first chance I got and there was not a damn thing anyone could do to stop me.

Two hours of straight running had landed me back at the selection school deep in the Blue Ridge Mountains, but even that scant bit of time had been far too late. Wyatt had corralled the students to search the woods for Wren, for Girard. All the shifters had been given her scent and a job to do. Even Ames was looking for her.

But Wren was still gone, and I needed more help than I had to find her.

She's bleeding. She's out there bleeding somewhere.

"I need you to get it together, Malia. That big puddle of

blood right there," I barked, pointing at the dark burgundy stain on Girard's wood floor, "is the best fucking clue I got in the middle of this shit. So, I'm going to need you to gather whatever gifts you have, and fucking find her."

Malia Nadir was a gifted psychometry witch. Unable to cast a single spell, but she was more than gifted when it came to gleaning information from objects. Nadir wasn't the first one I'd come across either, and oftentimes, it was possible for them to find someone in the future.

If they just fucking looked hard enough.

"And I told you five times already that I can't do it. I get all the past shit. Her life, what she was thinking when she lost the blood, whatever. But I can't get her future—not because I don't have the *ability*, but because something is *blocking* me. So throw your hissy fit somewhere else."

I didn't know what else to try. None of the psychics I knew could help with a witch they didn't know, and even if Wren had a few in her family, I doubted they would step up. What I needed was information, and I wasn't above doing shady shit to get it, either.

She's bleeding.

I had a feeling I knew exactly what was blocking Nadir's ability, too, and it was the same damn thing that made it so I couldn't find her, either.

That fucking necklace.

I'd been so proud of myself for getting Carmichael to make it for her, thinking it would be the perfect thing to keep her safe. Now she was alone with a death mage who had a history of taking women. She was hurt. And if she was still in these mountains, she had to be cold. A freak storm had been brewing over the last few hours, spitting snow even down here. The higher peaks were likely getting hammered or worse.

She's bleeding.

"Then I need someone—anyone—to think of something because I swear to everything I find holy, if something happens to her, I will rain down Hell itself," I warned through gritted teeth. "You hear me, Ames," I shouted through the door and the absolute moron who hadn't realized until an hour ago that Girard had been feeding rumors to the students to frame his idiot ass and keep himself out of the hotseat. "Work whatever magic you got before I lose my fucking patience."

"I've tried every locator spell on this planet, you prick," he fired back, kicking the door open. "I'm getting stonewalled. Maybe if you'd have told someone that she was a goddamned amplifier, you wouldn't have needed to slap a Band-Aid null ward around her neck that blocks us all."

I'd had to come clean about that, but I informed the warlock that if he told anyone, I would rip his balls off and shove them down his throat.

"Maybe if *anyone* would have said something, we could have gotten her the help she needed."

"Oh, that's rich," Malia hissed, staring at Ames like he was a steaming pile of dog shit. "This coming from the same guy who slandered her name every chance he got. Who threatened to kick her out at every turn. Who hounded her ass and asked if she was going to fuck you for a good grade. Eat shit, you prick. You never wanted to help her. Don't try to paint yourself as the good guy now that she's gone."

Asked if she was going to fuck you for a good grade.

Wyatt slapped a hand on my shoulder, keeping me from

killing the useless sack of shit. That was okay. As soon as I got Ames alone, it would be all over. But finding Wren mattered more.

"You do realize your days are numbered, right?" Wyatt said without a lick of anger or even so much as a frown. "You messed with an alpha's mate. I suggest you make right with whatever god you call holy before he rips you apart."

While that was most definitely true, I needed everyone to fucking focus. "What I need is for all of us to *think*. If Girard had to stash someone for a little while in the middle of this storm, where would he go? Does he have a house somewhere?" I growled, trying to stay on task. "Any friends with a property? Did he talk about needing to get away or having money trouble? Something?"

Wyatt snorted a laugh. "You don't know Girard very well. He doesn't talk to us if he can help it."

Fucking perfect.

If Wren were a wolf, she could have protected herself. If she were a wolf, I would know where she was because all wolves were connected. I would know if she was alive. I would...

After four hundred years of not a single wolf being mated outside of the species, and I was the one with the danger-prone mate who I couldn't fucking find.

Then in a single instant everything changed.

One second, I was fine—pissed, worried out of my mind, but fine—and the next, I could barely stand. It felt like an icepick had been rammed into my eye as my gut twisted, and I nearly fell to my knees. My ankle throbbed, and my lungs were on fire.

SPELLS AND SLIP-UPS 213

And I was scared—more scared than I'd ever been in my life.

But none of it felt like my pain, my fear, my exhaustion.

Gods, was this...

Was this Wren?

Mated wolves didn't work like this. Only our wolves were connected. This was—

Flashes of trees filtered into my mind, the pain of seeing them nearly splitting my skull. "Touch the blood," I gasped, trying not to keel over. "Do it."

Malia slammed her palm into the drying liquid, her amber eyes milking over as she searched for Wren once more. "She's running barefoot. With Fiona. Forest. There's snow on the ground. Not far. Past camp. Past the null line. Girard's chasing them." Malia paused, her breaths coming in pants like mine, likely feeling that same splitting agony in her skull. "She's hurt, Acosta."

But I didn't need Malia to tell me that. I knew it better than my own name at this point.

My mate was running barefoot in the snow to outrun her captor, and I was already turning, running, my feet taking me to her as I stumbled out of the cabin and up the hill. Wren was north in a place in the mountains where there was a decent amount of snow on the ground.

And then I was no longer on two feet, I was on four, racing up the mountain to find her. A moment later, Wyatt was at my flank. The screech of a bird up ahead called to me, almost begging me to follow it, and gods help me, I did.

My vision blurred as Wren's mind brought a cliff into view. I knew that outcropping. We'd been there during Hell Night, and I had to direct the cadets farther west so they wouldn't get past the null line.

Veering east, I picked up the pace, racing for Wren as if both our lives depended on it.

Because they did.

CHAPTER 21

WREN

Gasping, I landed on my hands and knees, trying to suck in a single full breath.

"Come on, Wren," Fi wheezed, her breathing no better than mine. "I need you to get up."

Fiona and I were chained together. No way could she carry us both. Not after a day with no food or water or sleep. But the world was swimming, and my lungs were burning, and my ankle wasn't going to hold my weight for much longer. And that snow on the ground? Well, with the storm clouds churning overhead, we were in for a fuck-ton more of it.

But living was more important than pain, so I stood up, ready to get moving again. Girard's screams had quieted but he was still stomping through the forest, the cracks of branches snapping beneath his feet made me jump every time. He was getting closer, and we didn't have time to fuck around.

Nodding, I took some of the chain's slack, wrapping it around my left arm so she didn't have to carry it all. We needed to keep moving.

Fiona took two steps right, and then it didn't matter if either of us were walking, because she was falling down a sharp decline. And since we were chained together, I was, too.

Rocks battered my skin as we skidded down the slope, a very real cliff rocketing toward us at breakneck speed. I scrabbled for purchase, grasping at anything that would keep us from sliding off this fucking, gods-forsaken mountain. My shoulder slammed into a rock, then my head, then it was sort of lights out for a second.

By some miracle, the chain itself caught on a boulder, yanking the both of us to a stop.

The metal cut into my arm and hand, and I immediately regretted trying to pick up the slack.

"Fi?" I called and instantly started coughing, the dirt and dust of our slide filling my lungs.

Her answering cough was music to my ears.

"I'm alive," she choked. "Maybe that rest was a better idea, yeah?"

Half-coughing, half-laughing, I assessed the beautiful, lovely, awesome rock that stopped us from tumbling off a fucking mountain.

"You got a hold on something?" I asked, really hoping she did. If I stayed here any longer, I was going to lose feeling in my arm, and that was most likely a very bad thing.

"Yeah, I got a root here, and the slope flattens out a bit before the drop. We can slide down slow and get our bearings."

And all we had to do was pray to the gods that Girard didn't look too close at this ridge or was temporarily deaf while we screamed down the side of a fucking mountain.

Sure. Totally plausible.

Groaning, I braced my feet and tried inching the chain off the rock bit by bit. But as much as I struggled, the chain just wouldn't budge, caught on something...

Then the unmistakable sound of heavy footfalls reached my ears, and I froze, trying to plaster myself to the side of the slope.

"You can't hide from me," Girard shouted from above. "I know you're down there."

Fiona scrambled up, trying to help me disengage the damn chain, but Girard was a fuck of a lot faster than either of us. In a swath of black smoke, he appeared right in front of us, wrapping his burned and weeping hands around our throats.

And then it felt as if my whole body was being turned inside out. The world spun at hyper speed as darkness cloaked me. I wanted to scream, cry, something, but all I could do was stand there while he seemed to yank me from space and time and deposit me somewhere else.

The "somewhere else" was nothing more than the outcropping where we fell, and Girard screamed in agony as all three of us dropped to the dirt.

"Didn't learn your lesson the first time, huh?" I croaked after spitting out a mouthful of dirt and blood. "You can't use magic on me, stupid."

"I sort of figured he'd learn the first time, but as my daddy always says, you can't fix stupid," Fiona rasped, cradling her cuffed arm against her chest.

Girard's charred face whipped to us. His beard was mostly

burned away as was a good chunk of his long hair. One eye was crusted shut, but the other gleamed with hatred. "I'm going to fucking kill you, you bitch. I'll kill you both."

"Go ahead and try, sport," I growled, staggering to my feet as I twisted the slack of the chain around my bloody hand. I wasn't quite sure what I was going to do with that chain other than wrap it around his fucking neck and pull, but I was damn sure I'd manage. "I fucking dare you."

Could he kick my ass? Absolutely. But I wouldn't cower, and I sure as *shit* wouldn't let him sell me to some Fae dickwad. Girard could eat this fucking chain and like it.

Then Girard's face went white as he took a big step back. And the best sound I'd ever heard in my entire life rumbled from right behind me. Not one, but two wolves growled, adding a level of backup I'd never had. Up above, a bird screeched, before diving for Girard. Its claws raked his face before flitting away, and he stumbled back a step, inching closer to that slippery fucking slope.

A cloud of gray smoke engulfed the bird, and then it wasn't a bird anymore. It was Gianna, with her odd yellow eyes, and a pair of daggers in her hands.

Before Girard could go over the side, Nico was on him, jumping from four feet to two in the span of a single blink. In human form, he vibrated with rage, his clawed hand digging into the skin of that asshole's neck. One flick of his fingers and Girard would be worm food.

Nico didn't say a word in threat—he didn't have to—his face said everything, but Girard would *not* shut up. "Yo-you can't kill me, Acosta. Think about the law."

Nico's smile was feral. "You broke the law already. No one

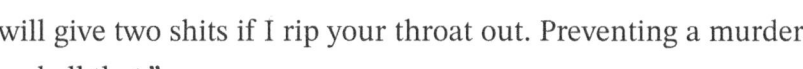

will give two shits if I rip your throat out. Preventing a murder and all that."

Girard's lone working eye widened. "Yo-you need me. I can give you Desmond. I can give you my buyer."

Nico flinched like Girard had struck him. "Buyer?"

"You think I killed all those girls? I'm not a murderer. I'm a businessman," Girard wheedled.

Like that would do him any favors.

"He's leaving a big part out," I rasped, my voice like I'd swallowed glass. "Desmond? His buyer? Is a Fae." And if Girard had made a deal with the Fae, there was no way he'd tell anyone anything about it.

Even I knew that.

Girard's eye went even wider. "I'll tell you everything I can. I *swear*."

Nico's lip curled as his fingers tightened on Girard's neck. "That's good to hear, Girard. But there's just one problem." He brought the death mage closer to his face and whispered, "I don't believe you."

Without hesitation, Nico slashed, ripping out Girard's throat as if it were a knife through butter. The older man fell, shock coloring his features before going slack, landing on the dirt like a sack of rotten potatoes.

It was bad that I wasn't sorry, right? That I witnessed that death and didn't even flinch, didn't gasp. That I was glad Girard was gone.

"Wren?" Nico murmured, and I blinked. Somehow, he was right in front of me. I was so busy staring at Girard bleeding out, that I didn't even notice when Nico had gotten there. "Beautiful?"

Then the shivers came flooding back as everything started crashing over me. The adrenaline, the fear, the rage... "Look, Fi. I brought the cavalry after all."

By the time Nico, his friend, Wyatt, and Gianna got Fiona and I down the mountain, the storm that had been swirling over our heads broke, dumping a mountain's worth of snow all over everything.

Currently stuffed under three blankets, a heating pad, and drinking a mug full of hot apple cider, I rested on Nico's—or rather *Wyatt's*—couch, answering questions from Deputy Director Serreno. Evidently, she had wasted no time following Nico up here after his abrupt departure, arriving along with a small contingent of agents just before the storm.

Nico had perched himself next to me, resting my legs on his lap as he rubbed my ankle and held my hand for all and sundry to see. Serreno was kind to me—to us both—telling me to call her Erica, but her questions made me want to burrow under the blankets and not come out for about a decade.

"Please tell me why you thought it was appropriate to break into Commandant Girard's home. Why did you feel that was necessary?"

Nico growled long and low, shooting me a look that promised we would talk about this later.

See? Definitely wanted to hide.

"I felt that if I could procure evidence that proved Girard fabricated Jacobs' paperwork, then an investigation could begin into the uncounted number of missing probationary and field agents. And according to Section 12.4.5908B, any concrete information brought to an agent must be investigated regardless of where it came from. Since I am not technically a member of the ABI until graduation, I could pass it off to an agent I trusted without breaking any laws." I swallowed hard, watching her eyebrows climb up her forehead.

"Other than breaking and entering, you mean," she murmured, poking a hole in my ABI law research. Luckily, I had a backup.

Swallowing, I continued, "And—"

"Oh, goodie," Nico groused. "There's more."

I shot him a glare. "*And* based off of Section 56.9.5732G, it is legal for any agent or civilian to enter the home of a suspected criminal uninvited if they fear an arcaner's life is in jeopardy. Since Commandant Girard threatened to murder Cadet Jacobs, I feel this qualifies under that statute. So..."

Nico twisted in his seat, his glare boring a hole in the side of my face. I sipped my cider and waited.

"You memorized the ABI statutes?" Serreno asked, her eyebrows not coming down anytime soon. "All of them?"

"Sort of," I mumbled into my mug. "I kind of thought we were supposed to know the law if we were going to enforce the law. And..." I shrugged, trying not to wince. "And I didn't want to get kicked out of here since it's a death sentence if I don't pass."

Serreno sat back in her seat. "What?"

Nico nodded. "According to her paperwork, she is recommended for execution if she cannot complete the course. I read it myself." He moved my feet off his lap and stood. "So if you plan on kicking her out, you're going to have to go through the entire Acosta pack. Just putting that out there."

Serreno blinked and then smiled huge. "So noted."

"Get out of my way right this instant," a shrill, and yet oh-so-familiar voice demanded right outside Nico's cabin before the formidable redhead burst through the door.

Eloise Bannister may have been a grandmother several times over, but her hair was as red as mine, her skin ageless, and her spine as straight as an arrow. And if the world could have let me melt through this couch and hide, that would have been awesome.

She took one look at my battered face, my blankets, and my cider, and her lip curled. "*Wren.*"

Just my name was a chastisement and a good one at that.

"Embarrassing the family name yet again, I see. Get up from that couch, girl. You're going home with me."

Nico squared off against my grandmother, and Serreno stood as well. But it was Nico who spoke first.

"The fuck she will. Wren isn't going anywhere near your family ever again. Not if I can help it."

Eloise startled, her disgust shifting to Nico. "You think that pelt of yours means something to me? Who do you think you are, wolf?"

Nico bristled, his eyes glowing, his fangs lengthening, his claws erupting from his fingertips. Long and low, he growled, before stating something that damn near knocked me off the couch.

"I'm her fucking husband. And you'll take her from me over my cold, dead body."

Umm, what?

I must have said that out loud because Nico turned, staring at me with all the truth and hope in his eyes.

We were married. His face said it all. In some weird wolfy way, he considered us married.

Holy.

Shit.

And if Nico's face was awash in hope, my grandmother's said she would greatly appreciate Nico's dead body on a silver platter.

And just like when he'd pulled me from those flames in that stupid apothecary, I was once again elbow-deep in shit.

What else was new?

MAGIC AND MAYHEM

ARCANE SOULS WORLD: THE WRONG WITCH BOOK 2

ANNIE ANDERSON

Everyone is a moon and has a dark side which he never shows to anybody.

— MARK TWAIN

CHAPTER 1

WREN

I WAS MARRIED TO A WEREWOLF.

Funny, I didn't recall saying "I do" anywhere in the last week, but there I was sitting on the tattered couch in Nico's cabin beneath a mound of blankets. A heating pad had been put under my back to combat the touch of cold I still had after tromping all over a mountain barefoot in a snowstorm, and while the apple cider someone had scrounged up was awesome, I was trying not to barf it all over the rough planked floor.

Concussions were a bitch.

All the while, I watched my wolfy husband and his boss square up against my grandmother.

Fun times.

And it wasn't like I could say anything about it right then—

not with Eloise Bannister staring down at me with wrath in her eyes.

My grandmother was one of the three people in the world I was afraid of. Okay, that was a total lie. I was scared of a lot of people, but my grams, my mom, and my aunt Judith were the three witches on the planet that put the fear of the gods into me. And old Eloise was in this cabin, trying to seal up my death sentence all nice and tight, and I was in enough trouble as it was all on my lonesome.

"I'm not going anywhere with you."

Did that sentence actually squeak out of my mouth? Why, yes. Yes, it did. I even sounded confident and everything. But she'd waltzed in here without so much as a "how do you do" and demanded I leave with her, fully expecting me to peel my broken body off this damn couch and follow along like an obedient pup.

There were several reasons why I wouldn't be going anywhere with her, the chief ones being my ankle was probably broken, I had a *mother* of a concussion, and if I tried getting off this couch, Nico's head might actually explode. Plus, there was a good chance I would be getting kicked out of ABI selection school and then summarily executed in the next five minutes or so.

She might as well save herself the trouble.

Deputy Director Serreno eyed my grandmother like she was a troublesome stain or a petulant child she needed to quiet down. Her dark eyes surveyed the Bannister matriarch with a calculated glint. Without a doubt, she knew exactly who my grandmother was, and was trying to figure out just the best way to get her to shut all the way up and vacate the cabin as soon as humanly possible.

Nico, however, had a low growl building in his belly, and pretty soon, it wouldn't matter if my grams could blow him to kingdom come or if Serreno could arrest us all. The thought of anymore bloodshed was turning my stomach.

I mean I'd already been kidnapped and nearly launched off a mountain while trying not to get sold off to some dark Fae—named *Desmond*, for fuck's sake—and then watched a guy get his throat ripped out. I was topped up on drama for the rest of the day.

And by the way, what the fuck kind of name was Desmond, anyway?

"Excuse me?" I called, breaking the intense stare down between Nico and my grams as they both turned their gazes to me. "Oh, good, you've realized I'm still in the room. I said I'm not going with you. I would like you to leave."

Look at me being all confident and shit.

I couldn't recall a single time in my life where I'd ever defied this woman, but today seemed to be the day for a lot of new shit.

Married? My gut churned. As far as I was concerned, marriage hadn't ever been on the table.

"And I would like to go a single week without one of your screw-ups, but here we are," she said, gesturing to the cabin itself. Eloise most likely found the place beneath her exacting standards. "Breaking into your instructor's home? Carrying on with this wolf? Sullying our name more than you already have? Really, Wren, are you trying to be this stupid or is it a honed skill?"

The sting of the insults sliced through my middle. She sure knew how to deliver a blow, my grandmother.

Nico's growl got louder, and he put himself further in between us, allowing me to school my features and wipe away the silent tear that tracked down my cheek. I could hug that man if I wasn't fighting off the urge to slap the shit out of him.

Married? Was he high?

"I wouldn't call it a screw-up," Serreno murmured, crossing her arms over her chest as she shifted her weight to her back foot. "Agent Bannister has displayed incredible fortitude and competency against a skilled and organized death mage, uncovered a black-market trafficking ring, and saved the life of one of her classmates in the process. I'm failing to see how you can find fault in any of those things."

Agent? For the second time in two minutes, I felt like bawling—only this time, it was happy tears.

Serreno tilted her head to the side. "I'm also failing to see how you were informed of any of your accusations at all. Especially without any of the actual facts. I'd love to know the name of your informant."

Oh, I had a guess, all right. Chet Ames was a bastard of the highest order. Since Girard was decomposing on top of this stupid mountain, there was only one instructor left that hated me. He'd been in my chili since day one, and if there was anyone who was going to tattle to Grams, it would be that asshole.

But... didn't he hate our family? Why would he willfully be in my grandmother's pocket?

Eloise adjusted the strap of her bag on her shoulder, the

clinks of potion bottles and spell ingredients whispering like wind chimes.

"How I got my information is of no concern of yours," she blustered, firming her jaw like she had a new adversary.

"Oh, I beg to differ," Serreno countered, a feral sort of smile widening her mouth. Nico had said she was a powerful elemental mage, but at that moment, she seemed like something else. "If information was leaked from this camp, not only is it my business, but I am also duty-bound to plug the leak."

Eloise sputtered, aghast that someone somewhere in this vast universe didn't give a flying fuck that her last name was Bannister. "You think you're going to throw your weight around with me?"

Serreno yanked a set of cuffs from her belt. "Not if you don't make me. But the way you're acting, I figure cuffing your ass will make my day."

Mashing my lips together, I did my best not to start cackling. Serreno was becoming one of my favorite people ever, and if she actually managed to cuff Grams? Well, it would make my whole year.

"Go ahead and try, mage. You have what? Maybe five years on me? That makes you practically a baby. You and your lapdog might as well be the ones cuffed."

Nico's growl rose on the air, and I figured we had about ten seconds before things got really dicey. Grams knew all about my predicament, but I couldn't remember if I'd explained to Serreno just how bad of an idea it was to use any sort of magic in my presence.

"You might as well give it up," I said, trying to defuse the situation. "I know who tattled, and you could get the phone records before she'd cough up a name. It was Ames. He's had it in for me since day one. It would have only taken a minor monetary contribution to make him rat me out."

I didn't bother looking at Serreno and I for damn sure wasn't going to look at Nico. Instead, I watched my grandmother's eyes narrow.

Yep, got it in one.

Granted, it wasn't much of a leap but still. It felt equally awesome to guess right and downright awful to know that my safety could be compromised so easily by a little money. Then again, I had almost been sold, so maybe that shouldn't have been such a shock.

"Do you care at all that I damn near died out there? That I ran for my life in the cold snow barefoot? That someone tried to sell me like I was property? Huh?" A flash of hurt and rage and... and I don't know what rippled through me so fast I thought I would explode.

Eloise's jaw hardened. *Yeah, I thought not.*

"So the only thing you care about is your silly little name and your bullshit reputation. What else is new?"

"A reputation you tarnish by the second, carrying on with this wolf. This is by far the stupidest thing you've ever done. And darlin' girl, that's saying something."

I could have been a stain on the floor for as low as I felt. But what had Nico said in the shower what felt like years ago?

Fuck your family, Wren. Fuck every last one of them.

As much as I wanted to smack him upside the head for his "husband" talk, he sure as shit had been right on this front.

Fuck every last one of them.

"No, the stupid thing was ever believing I had a family. Why don't you do yourself a favor and forget I exist. And if you can't do that, well, then just fuck all the way off, Grandma."

With as much grace as I could muster—which wasn't much since I was a broken freaking mess—I climbed off the couch and stood tall, firming my jaw and my fist. And I couldn't believe the shit that was about to fall out of my mouth.

Gods, give me strength.

"I don't want to see you again. I don't want to see *any* of you *ever* again. I'm a drain on you and your name? Fine. You heard Nico. You can keep your fucking name. I have a new one."

Out of the corner of my eye, Nico's shoulders relaxed in what seemed like relief as a sigh gusted from his lips. Instantly, my hand was in his and he held it tight, and that made me feel like the biggest pile of shit in the universe.

Eloise staggered back a step like I'd slapped her, complete with a fluttering hand on her chest as if she was fighting off angina or something. "You wouldn't dare. If you're smart, you won't do this, Wren."

With my free hand, I pulled my collar to the side, displaying the crescent-shaped mark where my shoulder and neck met. Nico had bitten me over and over as we'd come together, the bites healing almost instantly, darkening with each new nip.

Tell me you want this. Tell me you're mine. Tell me you want me.

I hadn't known what he'd meant at the time, but now I sure as shit did. Those marks meant something big—something likely permanent—and I had been oblivious. And even if I didn't have all the details, pissing off my grandmother had become my sole priority.

"It's already done."

Her eyes zeroed in on the scar as her lip curled, her distaste clear. "You think you've got a target on your back already? It will be a thousand times worse once people get wise you've left the coven." Eloise huffed out a mirthless laugh. "But I guess that's your new family's problem now."

With that, she adjusted the strap of her bag and swept from the room, her nose in the air as she went. I couldn't help it, I flinched at the screen door slamming against the frame and yanked my hand out of Nico's hold.

Staggering backward, I plopped onto the couch, the rough motion jarring my head. Why had I said that to her? Just to stick it to my family? My gut churned with the ache in my head and the bitter lie in my mouth.

Because I wasn't Nico's wife—no matter what weird shifter claim he thought he had on me—and he wasn't my husband. I didn't have a new family or a new name.

Gentle hands cupped my jaw, tilting my head as Nico's soft lips brushed mine. Stupidly, I jerked my face out of his hold, the rough motion sending a sharp bolt of pain through my skull.

Understanding dawned in his eyes as a wince pulled at his lips.

"Married, Nico? *Married*? Have you lost your fool mind?"

Nervously, he rubbed at the back of his neck as he speared me with that hopeful look again.

"Don't you puppy-dog eye me," I scolded, holding up my

left hand. "I don't see a ring on this finger or recall tiptoeing through the tulips wearing a white dress anytime in the last week. What. The. Fuck."

"Yeah..." Serreno broke in, "I'm going to step outside for a minute. Give you two some privacy."

Nico's boss hustled out of the room like her ass was on fire, that damn screen door making me jump once again as it slapped shut. If I had the power, I'd blow the stupid thing to smithereens.

But not once did my gaze leave Nico's nor did his leave me —a fact that was more and more uncomfortable now that his fists were stuffed into the very cushion under my ass, bracketing my hips, his eyes glowing with his animal.

Oh, but he wasn't going to Alpha his way out of this shit.

No way, no how.

"You have sixty seconds to explain," I threatened, holding up a hand with fingers ready to snap, "or we're going to see just how my magic reacts to null wards."

I was getting answers.

One way or another.

CHAPTER 2

NICO

My mate was certifiable.

The glint of challenge in her gaze equally scared the shit out of me and turned me on all at the same time. It was tough not to drop my lips to hers, to not wrap her in my arms and bathe in her scent.

She was alive. Hurt, concussed, and probably emotionally scarred from the attack, but alive. At that moment, I didn't care that she was pissed at me, didn't give a single shit that she was threatening to blow us to kingdom come. All I cared about was the breath in her lungs and the steady beat of her heart.

"I'm waiting, Acosta," Wren growled, her jaw practically granite. "And I've about had it with just about everything today, so cough it up."

It was a struggle to keep the grin off my lips. "Tell me what you know about wolf matings."

Her eyes narrowed. "Next to nothing, except that they mate for life." Her skin drained of color, bringing out the mottled bruises on her cheek and neck. "You're not telling me we're... that we're..."

Her breaths came in distressed pants, her eyes going so wide they showed white all around the irises.

With nothing for it, I dropped my lips to hers, gently brushing her mouth with mine before drawing back. "When a wolf is born, we're only given a fraction of our power. Some say it's so we don't mature too soon. Some say it's so we don't fuck around and kill ourselves before our frontal lobe develops. On a wolf's thirtieth birthday, we're gifted the remainder of our power, and with it, the call to our mate."

I kept my voice low, gentle. Wren needed gentleness right now.

"I got lucky," I murmured, cupping her face in my hands. "Most people search for their mate for years, decades, centuries. But I found mine before the turning, a freak chance that I happened to be at the right place at the right time."

Her gaze shifted from mine as chagrin twisted those beautiful lips. "The apothecary. Girard told me it was you who saved me."

Just his name had my blood boiling. Victor Girard was responsible for every mark on her beautiful skin, every cut, every drop of blood still crusted in her hair. His stink was on her even now, the cloying aroma of death magic and malice. And if I didn't have his blood under my nails, there would be no way I could stand it.

But he was dead, decomposing to ash somewhere up the mountain, and she was breathing.

And that's all that mattered.

Wren pitched her voice low as her gaze shifted to the window and then back to me. "He said yo-you killed two men—men he sent to kidnap me."

Oh, how my gut wrenched at the tremble in her voice. Wren had already witnessed just how brutal I could be. The absolute last thing I needed was her knowing everything.

Fucking Girard and his big, fucking mouth. It just figured he was the one to enlist those two fuckwads into snatching her.

"I did. Did he happen to mention that the men planned on raping you first before delivering you to him? You and your human friend."

Wren's face grayed out a little as she swayed in her seat. Maybe I should have kept that bit under my hat, but I couldn't take it back now.

"Wyatt and I took care of it."

Her jaw firmed as she pulled from my grip. "And while I'm grateful, that doesn't excuse what you did—not the killing part," she amended almost under her breath. "The mating shit. Why didn't you tell me what it meant? It's my *life* you're playing with here."

And wasn't that just a punch to the gut? Standing, I put a decent amount of space between us. "I thought you knew. It wasn't until I was called away, did I realize that maybe you didn't. But you're from Savannah. You belong to one of the biggest witch families on the planet, for fuck's sake. I thought—"

Wren shoved to her feet. "You didn't *ask*. You *assumed*. You know damn well what assuming does."

"Yeah, yeah," I said on a sigh. "Makes an ass out of you and me." It was one of my father's favorite sayings, and I'd heard it far too many times for the damn thing to not stick. "I know I fucked up."

But somehow, I just couldn't bring myself to tell her I was sorry—because as much as I regretted taking her choice away—I wouldn't trade what I had with her for anything or anyone. Maybe it was the mating bond, maybe it was just Wren, but to me, it didn't matter.

"That's it?" she barked. "An 'I fucked up' is all you're going to say?" Wren tried to march around the couch, but she stumbled on her second step, hopping on one foot as she cradled her ankle, hissing in pain.

In all the commotion, I hadn't gotten a chance to leach Wren's injuries from her. Plus, I hadn't exactly done it while she was conscious before, so...

"How about," I muttered, scooping her up before my brain ever registered the movement, "you stay on the couch and just throw something at me instead?"

The connection that had led me to her while she was in danger sent a spike of pain through my skull and that ankle? Well, it was so close to broken it made me want to steal every ounce of agony from her so she never felt like this again.

"My skull's thick. It can take it."

"Damn right it is," she muttered, her voice like ice.

As soon as I got her settled on the couch, a pillow slapped me upside the head. I supposed I deserved that.

Sighing, I plucked the pillow from her fisted hands. "I want to tell you I'm sorry, but I can't," I admitted, meeting those green-gold eyes. In them was a fair amount of hurt—too much of it my doing. "That would imply that I am not fucking ecstatic at the hand I've been dealt. That would say that I'm mad at the universe for choosing you for me. And that would be the lie."

Wren squeezed her eyes shut, shaking her head. "You took my choice away, Nico."

"And for that, I am truly sorry. I didn't know I was stealing it, but I can't change it. And if it meant losing you, I can't say I would ever want to."

Instead of the hope or joy or anything positive I'd anticipated she'd feel, all I got was a wave of pain. Not physical—no, it felt like my heart was getting ripped from my chest. I pressed my hand against my sternum to stave off the ache.

"Jesus, what is it?" I asked, trying not to run to her. The last thing she'd want was me coddling her again. "Why do you feel like that? Why are you in so much pain?"

Wren's face practically turned purple as a wave of rage nearly knocked me over. "What? My emotions aren't even private anymore?"

A full mug of still-warm apple cider came sailing at my head, drenching me in the sticky-sweet liquid. Luckily, I managed to catch the cup before it made contact with my skull, but that seemed to piss Wren off more.

"Is anything just mine?" she shouted, launching another pillow at me.

This one I caught, too, but at the expense of the mug. It fell to the floor, breaking into pieces, the sound making her jump. A fire burned in Wren's ribs—those fragile, bruised bones so close to broken it was a wonder she could breathe.

"Umm, guys?" Serreno called, poking her head in the door but smartly keeping her body on the other side of it. "I hate to interrupt this domestic you seem to be having here, but I'm going to need Wren."

"What now?" my mate growled under her breath, trying to school her features. Pasting a smile on her face, she turned to the door. "How can I help you, Director Serreno?"

Erica pressed her lips together in that way she did when she was about to ruin someone's day.

Ah, fuck. What now?

"Remember me calling you 'Agent' a few minutes ago? Well, I'm going to need to make that a reality. You're taking your ABI field exam. Today."

A wave of abject fear and a fair amount of nausea warred with acid churning in my gut. "How? She has four ribs bruised so bad they're damn near broken, a sprained ankle, a concussion, not to mention she nearly fell off a fucking mountain. You'd better have a good reason for this."

Another pillow bounced off my head, and I turned a glare at Wren.

"I can answer for myself, Agent Acosta," she hissed before shifting to face Erica. "Is there a reason why this needs to get rushed? I'm not through with the course ye—"

Erica leveled us both with a half-irritated, half-sympathetic expression. "The Bannister matriarch has made a few phone calls in the wake of her departure. How she got service in the middle of this storm, I have no clue, but she has already contacted the council. If we're going to make sure she doesn't sink us all, I need you to be an agent as soon as possible."

Erica winced in a way that told me even this was going to be a stretch. "As in today," she continued. "With the way you just puked up ABI statutes, you'll be fine."

"But..." Wren's eyes widened as she felt for the necklace that was no longer around her neck. "I can't do the practical. I'll—"

"She'll do it," I said, cutting Wren off. "Give us a few more minutes, will you?"

Wren whipped her head in my direction, but I was already at her side, covering her mouth with my hand.

"Sure," Erica muttered, slipping back out the door before Wren bit the shit out of me.

"What the fuck, Nico?" she hissed under her breath. "First of all, don't you ever put your hand over my mouth again. Second, you know damn well I can't take that exam. I'll kill someone and probably myself trying to do those spells. What the fu—"

Rubbing at the crescent ring of teeth marks, I let a growl rumble from my chest. "You bit me."

"Pot," she hissed, pointing at her own crescent mark, "meet kettle. I can't take that test, Nico."

Kneeling, I got right in her space. "Oh, so I'm Nico again, huh? What happened to Agent Acosta?"

A fair bit of desire tempered the rage in her scent, but I couldn't do anything about that right now. "I wonder if I bend you over my knee and spank that ass of yours, you'll remember to call me Nico."

The jasmine and honey perfume of hers deepened, telling me she liked the words, even if she was pissed as hell at me. Fair.

"Don't get cute. I can't take that test no matter how good you are at distracting me. You swore you wouldn't let me hurt anyone. Please tell me I can at least trust that."

Even if I don't trust you.

She didn't say it, but she may as well have, and that sobered me far more than Serreno's interruption.

You should have asked her.

"I'll take care of it," I murmured, fitting my fingers under her chin and tilting it up. "I made you a promise—that you would make it out of here alive, that you wouldn't hurt anyone—and I don't ever intend on breaking it."

Without warning, I drew on my wolf—on the healing ability he so often lent to me—and pulled on the aches and pains littering my mate's body. The coppery tang of blood filled my mouth, but I kept on, allowing her to breathe easy for the first time since we'd made it off the mountain.

Wren's eyes went wide as the bruises faded from her skin. "I knew it," she breathed. "I knew it was you."

She was likely referring to the time I'd drawn her pain from her feet after Hell Night. Her poor skin had been hamburger by the time she was done marching all over this mountain, and I'd been so pissed she hadn't said anything. Now that I could feel her pain, I realized Hell Night had nothing on this.

Wren held down her agony so well, it made me wonder how many times she had told someone she was hurting, only to get brushed off, to get told to shut up. It made me want to rip her parents apart with my teeth.

"This ability that I have? It's a secret. There is only one other person in the world who knows about it other than you." Gritting my teeth, I swallowed down more and more of her pain. "I'm trusting you with the knowledge—knowledge that could get me killed if the wrong person found out—just like you trusted me."

"Nico," she whispered, but I shook my head.

"I don't have to be your mate or your husband. You're not a wolf, so you have the freedom to choose your partner and the life you want to live. I don't. The universe made the incredibly wise decision of picking you for me. But if this isn't what you want—if *I'm* not who you want—you can choose to not be my mate. But I am—irrevocably—yours."

Gently, I pulled my fingers from under her chin, brushing her lips with mine before I drew away.

"And if you're on the fence, just think of how good the angry sex will be."

CHAPTER 3

WREN

DID THAT JUST HAPPEN?

Did Nico just turn me on, heal me up, and piss me off in one fell swoop?

Why, yes. Yes, he did.

Because instead of beaning him in the face with another pillow, I was imagining what angry sex would be like while also marveling at the fact that I could breathe easy for the first time in hours.

I'm trusting you...

I wanted to trust him—I did. I wanted to believe in kittens and rainbows and that today wouldn't take a solid turn into the shitter, but I'd already been kidnapped, beaten, and damn near fell off a mountain.

And it wasn't even dinnertime.

Now I needed to go take a test I was in no way prepared for, or else my grandmother was going to light the final match on my life.

But still, I was thinking about angry sex and Nico's growls in my ear and how good he could make me feel. Could anyone really blame me? Daydreaming about a hot shifter was far superior to impending doom.

"Thank you," I whispered, fighting off the urge to kiss him. He'd lied to me, he'd mated me or married me or whatever wolfy bullshit he'd done, and... Holding onto the rage was getting harder by the second—especially after he'd healed me.

"I'll get you a new null ward," he murmured, his eyes on my lips and his heat lowering my IQ points. "Keep my promise."

Shit. Had anyone ever kept their promises around me? Had anyone besides Ellie even made a promise at all? I was turning to goo again.

Get it together, girl.

But I flipped off my internal smart bitch and drifted closer to Nico, brushing his nose with mine. "I haven't forgiven you —not yet—but thank you. Again."

Then the day seemed to hit me all at once—being taken, running, falling, watching Girard get his throat ripped out— and shivers hit my whole body. I wanted to be strong—and I had been—but it was one thing too much. His kindness was too much. Even though he'd messed up, Nico still gave a shit. Warmth enveloped me as Nico wrapped me in his embrace, and with it, a level of safety I clung to like a drowning man.

"You've done so well, beautiful. You held yourself together so good," he murmured into my hair as he held me tight. "Most agents I know would have cracked by now. But I'm going to need you to be strong just a little while longer, okay? I'll even get you a new mug to throw at my head, yeah?"

Swallowing down the blind panic and fear at what my grandmother could be doing right now, I managed to chuckle wetly. "Good, but you should really shower. You're sticky and not in the good way."

Nico's irises flared gold with his wolf. "You're lucky I'm trying to be good right now." He leaned closer, his chest brushing mine as he whispered his threat. "Or else I'd turn you over my knee for teasing me. Play with your pretty pussy while I spank that ass of yours."

He drew back, and a rare smile pulled at the corners of his lips. "See? Told you angry sex would be fun. Just look at how flushed you are. Imagine how hot you'll be when I follow through?"

Jesus, Mary, and Joseph. Was it warm in here? And wasn't there something I was supposed to be doing? Staying mad at this man was going to be a challenge.

The man essentially married you under false pretenses, get your head on straight.

Oh, right. *Married.* That was the cold bucket of water I needed.

"How about you actually follow through with that null ward, and we'll just see who's getting spanked."

With that, I got up, steeling my spine as I marched past him. Nico wasn't the only one who needed a shower, and I would be damned if I was going to walk to the gallows with Girard's blood still on me.

"Where do you think you're going?"

Maybe it was the mild panic in his voice, but I stopped.

"I'm getting Girard's stink off me and putting on clothes that haven't been tossed down a mountain. Is that all right with you?"

"But all your things are here. Dumond packed your things up after you were taken so Girard couldn't steal his scent off your stuff—not that he ever put his scent there, but..." Gently, he hooked his hand around my elbow, pulling me back toward the bathroom. "Take your shower. Be mad at me. Just... can you not leave, please?"

Swallowing hard, I managed to nod, and his gentle touch left me.

"I'll get your bag."

My bright-purple duffle made an appearance, stuffed full of uniforms and toiletries. I picked through it, nabbing what I needed before carrying the armload to Nico's bathroom. It was so high-handed and so freaking nice all at the same time that I wanted to throw my shampoo bottle at him.

I'd need to get that urge under control at some point.

Probably.

Without a word, I shut the door and turned on the tap, not bothering to look in the mirror. I didn't need to see the remnants of Girard's handiwork. Yes, Nico had healed me, but I knew the blood was still there, the dirt, the fear. When he had healed me before, I hadn't believed it. I'd figured I was dreaming, or it hadn't been that bad, or whatever nonsense I used to gaslight myself. But Nico *had* healed me, funneled my pain into himself as he leached it from me. Mended bones and scrapes, put my tattered skin back together.

And it hurt him to do it. It was like he felt my pain as he took it from me, and that made my chest ache for some reason.

Hurriedly, I went through the motions of a shower without actually feeling any of it. Technically, I was clean, but that didn't take away everything that had happened or how sick I felt. As soon as Serreno could make it so, I'd be taking a final exam for a course I'd barely attended, all so my grandmother wouldn't have me locked up or executed or dragged back to Savannah by my damn hair.

Yippee.

A knock came at the bathroom door. "Wren, honey? You all right?"

I whipped that door open so fast an avalanche of steam billowed out of the bathroom to smack Fiona in the face. I hadn't seen her since Serreno hauled me to Nico's cabin for questioning. She appeared far better than the last time I'd seen her, all healed up by the med clinic and in fresh clothes.

Wrapping her in a hug, I was glad I'd managed to get dressed before her knock. "What are you doing here? Shouldn't you be resting?"

"And let you take that fool test by yourself? *Please.*"

Shoving her away, I gripped her shoulders with a little too much gusto. "What? No. Please don't tell me Serreno is making you test out, too."

Fiona frowned before giving me a winning smile. "If I want the charges against Girard to stick and a real investigation to be had into this place, then the both of us need to be agents, Wren. It just makes sense for us to do it now. Plus, it'll be a snap." She waved a hand as if it was so simple as she plopped onto the edge of the couch. "Hannah told me you blew them out of the water during your practical."

But Fiona was forgetting a particularly important facet of

that event—not that she was around for it, but whatever. Namely, the null ward I wore around my neck like my own personal good luck charm. It kept me from fucking up—kept everyone safe.

And to save us, I'd tossed it away. To save her.

How was Nico going to get me a new one? He didn't have time to trek down to Savannah and back. How was I going to pass this damn thing? Luck and blind optimism? I hadn't been lucky a day in my life.

"What about when Nico saved you?" Fiona replied to the thoughts I must have said aloud. "That seems pretty lucky to me. Of all the people to pull you from the burning wreckage of Azalea Apothecary, you got the super-hot shifter dreamboat with the giant dick and an unrelenting urge to keep you safe. If that ain't luck, I don't know what is."

"Whoa, who told you he had a giant dick?" Yes, that was what I latched onto, and yes, that sentence actually came out of my mouth.

Fi speared me with a sharp glare. "No one had to tell me that boy is packing a damn cannon in those pants. He just walks like he's got a monster in there. Like I told you before, I've got eyes, don't I?"

She wasn't wrong.

And now I was thinking of Nico's dick instead of how to escape this place before I blew it up. I really needed to sort out my priorities.

"Riddle me this, Obi Wan. How in the actual fuck am I supposed to do a practical exam without a null ward around my neck? You saw what happened on the range. That was unprotected. In case you missed it, I tossed the one I had so Girard didn't death magic you into oblivion."

Fiona winced. "Yes, that was unfortunate, but Instructor Smexy Pants is on the case. Though, you won't like who he had to bribe to get a new one."

Groaning, I skirted around her and plopped face-down onto the couch.

"It's that bastard, Ames, isn't it?" Yes, my voice was muffled in couch cushions, but Fiona heard me all the same.

"Got it in one," she said, smacking me hard on the ass. "Now get up, slap your hair in a bun, and let's get moving. Your grandmama is in a tizzy, stirring shit up so bad even my daddy has heard about it. The last thing I need is him moseying on over here before I have this shit handled."

That had me flying off the couch, wet hair smacking me in the face as I did so. "She told your dad?"

Josiah Jacobs was the Jacobs coven leader, and his method of rule was more like mob boss than President. If a Bannister had connections, he had *connections*, and all it would take is the right word, spell, or palm greased to get his nose all the way into our business. Though, considering a bunch of women were missing and there was a black-market ring selling them...

"Of course not." Fiona sighed, yanking me by the hand to the screen door. "Eloise Bannister giving my father a call? That would bruise her already-damaged ego. No, she got him word without *getting* him the word, if you know what I'm saying. He called a bit ago asking if I needed assistance."

Perfect. Just perfect.

Nico and his friend Wyatt sat in the two chairs on the cabin's front porch while a reluctant Ames stood several paces away. He held a golden necklace, brandishing it like it might ward off his impending doom.

Ames took a step forward but shuffled back three when Nico's snarl rumbled from his chest. "I told you to let her come to you. Don't think I've forgotten what you said to her, you fuck."

"And I told you that her grandmother filled my head with bullshit, man. How was I supposed to know she was lying through her teeth?" Ames flapped his hands, beaning himself in the head with the necklace as he went. "Everybody heard about her blowing up the apothecary. Shit, man, cut me some slack." He rubbed at the sore spot where the pendant smacked him, hissing in pain.

Ames had said some pretty shitty things to me in the week I'd been here—hounded me, humiliated me. And he wanted any of us to think it was just my grandmother's words that had done it.

Sure.

"What did she promise you?" I asked, pitying the poor bastard far more than I should. "I hope it was money and not respect. Eloise Bannister doesn't have respect for people she can manipulate, and you let her play your dumb ass like a fiddle. She doesn't give hand ups or handouts. She spins a web of words to make you do what she wants, and then hangs you out to dry." My laugh was mirthless. "Haven't you figured it out yet? The rumors are all true about her. *Duh.*"

If I'd been playing chess with the arcane world for two hundred and fifty years, a pissant warlock on the outs with his collective would be just the person I'd manipulate, too.

Grams was nothing if not consistent.

"But she said—"

"What? That I fucked around for grades? Or I was a menace to society and needed to be locked up? Or I was a vile little stain on the family name? I bet it wasn't that I got top marks in both high school and college. Or that I have a degree in chemistry and mathematics. Or that she hasn't been party to my life other than to tell me how big of a screw-up I am since I was a kid."

And all the while I was reading him the riot act, I was getting closer and closer. By the end, I'd snatched that damn amulet out of his hands, and had half a mind to beat him in the head with it.

Ames seemed both chastised and aghast. "Bu-but she promised she'd talk to my collective—get me reinstated. She said it would be a snap."

As if this joker needed to be near anyone with even a lick of power he could leach off of.

"She lied. It's what she's good at. If she does talk to them, it'll be to bury you. Loose ends and all that. Hopefully she's already forgotten you—that's the best-case scenario. Now, what does this thing do before I put it on? The last thing I need is another shitshow today."

The look on his face would have me pitying him if I didn't want to slap the shit out of him first. Ames shook himself. "It's a standard null. Nothing fancy. With the amplifying properties you have, you'll burn through it in a day. I'll make more. Send them with you."

"I'm sorry, what? Amplifying?"

"I mean, it makes sense why she'd want you back under her roof." Ames tapped his chin, a musing quality to his expression, which was a step up from the kicked puppy-dog one. "You probably fuel all their wards and spells. Who knows what'll happen if you leave for too long."

"What are you talking about? I'm not—" I shook my head, half-stumbling backward, the amulet swinging in my hand. "I'm not an amplifier. I'm a—" *Bane, albatross, perpetual fuck-up?* "—curse. Who told you that?"

"No one," Ames said, eyeing me like I was a special sort of stupid. "I saw the potion you made for Haynes. You cracked his seeing crystal even under two nulls. It's not rocket science. One plus one equals two. Totally makes sense why shit explodes around you. People are working with the wrong math, using the ambient magic like normal when you ramp it up to eleven."

He chuckled, shaking his head. "You're like a new moon, autumnal equinox, and a blood moon eclipse all wrapped into one. I'm amazed you've stayed under the radar as long as you have."

A pit of dread yawned wide in my belly. Hadn't that been what Eloise had said?

I had a target on my back.

Damn. I hated it when she was right.

CHAPTER 4

WREN

My breaths came in shuddering pants as I sprinted toward the berm that separated the testing area and the panel of judges that were grading my practical exam. Strapped to one thigh was a standard government-issue sidearm filled with sim rounds, and the other was a paintball gun filled with sleeping potion ampoules. Tied to my belt was a bag filled with witch tricks, potion bombs, smoke spells, and black salt—not that I'd be using any of that.

I was freezing, underdressed, and wildly unprepared for this shit.

My mission was to make it through a ramshackle warehouse building, clearing it before apprehending the bad guy. And this was after my abominable showing at the written exam—complete with five essay questions.

Five.

With a minimum word count of three hundred words.

Each.

My brain was fried already, and I hadn't even done the hard part yet.

Truth be told, I was probably going to fail this shit. I had done exactly one day of weapons and tactics. One. And they wanted me to clear this building? By myself? Armed with a paintball gun, sim rounds, and a hope and a prayer.

I didn't care what Nico said, I was doomed.

Peeking over the snow-covered berm, I scouted the area. The coast was clear, but that didn't mean anything. There could be sigils under the slush, activating a circle that could blow me up. I didn't exactly trust the amulet around my neck. Ames' motives were questionable at best—though, if anything happened to me, I had a feeling Nico would rip him limb from limb in my honor.

Still, I liked my limbs right where they were, thank you very much.

It didn't matter how big of a pep talk Nico had given me, I wasn't in the right frame of mind to be breaking into a building. But what were a few overused adrenal glands, right?

I supposed I could have stayed right there forever, commiserating my predicament, but a foghorn sounded, letting me know that the iteration had begun. I had to get through the warehouse, clear it, and apprehend the bad guy in under twenty minutes or I'd get dinged for each minute after the buzzer. With no time to waste, I crept over the berm, stalking toward the warehouse entrance like someone could come running out to kill me at any moment.

Which they totally could.

My mind raced with Ames' amplifier pronouncement. There was no way I was, right? No way I could be some kind of magical battery. He had to be yanking my chain because my grandmother screwed him over.

Though, his words made a sick sort of sense—especially since it meant that my whole family had been leeching off me my entire life. And wouldn't it make sense to keep me out of arcane spaces? Someone could find me out in a snap, right?

Shaking my head, I tried to focus on the problem at hand. Staying alive was the name of the game—not worrying about Ames' bullshit. Studying the entrance, I spied a sigil hidden in the graffiti plastered over the metal siding. It was a watching spell. Who needed digital cameras when all you needed was a spray paint can and enough power to fuel the mark?

Luckily, it appeared old, underpowered and fading—the first boon of the day. Still, I rummaged through the bag of witch tricks and yanked out the black salt. Salt was used for a lot of things, but black salt was for protection and breaking. I dumped a small pile of it in my hands and slapped it against the sigil, relishing the crackle as the marking faded into inert status.

One down, probably a million to go.

As an extra precaution, I dumped another little pile into my hands and blew it over the threshold before I breeched the building. Inside, it was a bevy of open space, rickety catwalks, and shoddy half-constructed rooms. And I'd have to clear them all. Aces.

After making sure the catwalks and obvious spaces were empty, I carefully opened the first room. Pitch black and full of debris, it took far too long to clear it. Maybe if they had put a flashlight in my pouch, it would have been different, but alas, I was stuck getting through the room by feel and the meager light from the open door. It took far too much of my allotted time, but I deemed the room clear and moved on.

The second room's entrance was around a rusty corner that had likely given someone tetanus at some point. A weathered nail protruded from the metal, covered in fresh blood.

Yep. Definitely tetanus.

As I skirted around the obstacle, a faint shuffling sound had me freezing to the spot, nearly snagging my shoulder on that damn nail. I drew my weapon, opting for the sleeping potion paintball gun rather than the Glock, and rounded the corner. I was met with a weapon of my own and a very familiar face behind it.

"What are you doing here?" I hissed at Malia, trying not to shout and give away our position.

She rolled her eyes at me, lowering her weapon. "Taking a test, silly, same as you."

"But—"

Malia shook her head. "We're running out of time. I'll fill you in later. Now, I've cleared those two rooms," she said, gesturing down the rusty, makeshift hall. "You?"

I pointed at the room behind me. "Just that one. Next hallway, you got my six?"

I'd always wanted to say that.

Malia's expression said she was having none of this, but she'd humor me, anyway. Weapons drawn, we crept down the next hallway, keeping our eyes peeled for sigils and circles. Granted, that was hard to do given the debris and just filth all over everything.

Things were going well until a faint crackle sizzled through the air. A hand fisted in the back of my shirt, yanking me backward, right as a blade whizzed past where my face used to be. Wind swirled through the hallway, kicking up the trash and dirt, and revealing the sigil hidden under three pounds of grit.

Sand blasted our skin as arrows crisscrossed the corridor, embedding into the rust-covered walls. I looked back at Malia in thanks, but it wasn't just Malia standing there. No, next to her was a very crouched, yet not alarmed Hannah.

"You got anything in that bag that'll help?" the ghoul shouted, covering Malia as best as she could. If I had a guess, she'd been the one to yank me back, and I wasn't quite sure how to thank her.

I felt like an asshole for slipping out to Girard's cabin while she'd been indisposed, and even worse, getting nabbed on her watch. But that didn't matter right now. Passing this test did.

"Yeah, I got something."

Yanking out the black salt, I managed to keep a small handful from blowing away in the maelstrom, but that wasn't the problem.

No, making it to the sigil without getting shot by an arrow with questionable origins was.

Just run, dive, and slap the salt on the sigil. Piece of cake.

Nodding, I'd managed to hype myself up enough to get moving when I was snatched back by Hannah again.

"What do you think you're doing?" she growled, her pale eyes glowing in the dim.

"I need to turn the spell off."

She let me go long enough to plant her hands on her hips and stare me down. "What's your plan on not getting shot?"

Other than running really fast, I didn't have one. But her hands were on her hips and not on my shirt, so I took that opportunity to haul ass. Three quick bounds and I dove, slapping the salt onto the very active sigil.

And hey, I'd only gotten one arrow graze for my trouble.

"Sweet mother of mercy, please tell me you did not just wade in here like a one-woman wrecking ball," a familiar voice hissed.

At this point, I wasn't even a little surprised to see Fiona emerge from one of the rooms, one hand holding her sidearm and the other gripping a potion bottle.

Considering she had approximately fifty arrows embedded in the door she'd just come out of, she should be thanking me, not griping, but whatever.

Getting up, I dusted myself off with a semi-bitter "You're welcome" and kept moving. I had no idea how much time this particular booby trap had wasted, but I didn't want to be on the other side of the timer—not if I could help it.

Between the four of us, we cleared the rest of the rooms in the hallway with little incident. Sure, the arm that had been grazed was hurting like a sonofabitch, but I'd power through. Personally, I'd have liked to rub black salt in the wound, but I didn't know if we needed to get through any more sigils.

Stop. You have a team now. You don't have to do shit by yourself.

"Hey, anyone have any black salt left?" I whispered, eyeing the next hallway from behind Hannah who had decided to take point.

I couldn't blame her. Out of all of us, she had the best hearing, sense of smell, and the most combat expertise. Fiona took the rear, watching out for any threats coming from behind.

Malia nudged the sore arm, and I fought off the urge to hiss. I took the still-full bottle from her and dumped a pile in one hand, slapping it against the open wound.

Yep, that stung like a motherfucker. Blistering-hot agony raced down my arm, and the oddest sensation of a spell breaking threaded through the limb. Oh, yeah, those arrows were tainted. I'd be willing to bet that rusty nail had been, too.

"Any of you cut?" I whispered through gritted teeth. *Shhhiiiitttt*, that salt burned.

I got negatives all around, so the fresh dripping blood on that rusty nail had to be from whoever we'd been sent in here to find. And they were already wounded.

With only one hallway left to search, we carefully went through it as a team. It wasn't until right before the last room did shit go utterly and completely sideways. At least this time, it wasn't my fault.

Oh, no. That honor was bestowed on Malia who crossed an active circle before either Fiona or I could stop her. The psychometry witch went flying, blown off her feet and into the closest wall by the force of it. In an instant, vines sprouted from the circle, latching onto Malia and drawing her in like she was a tasty snack to be gnawed upon.

Hannah and I dove for the small witch, keeping her from getting drawn in any further. Fiona kept her head, tossing a stunning potion bomb at the writhing vines. Unfortunately, all that did was make the spell defend itself.

Barbed spines shoved through the flesh of the vines,

turning the hungry plant into a mace as it whipped this way and that.

"Use the salt," I yelled, fighting alongside Hannah to keep Malia outside the circle. I had no idea what would happen to her if she crossed it again, and I sure as shit didn't want to find out.

"Are they tryin' to kill us?" Fiona grumbled, tossing half the contents of the salt onto the circle.

Acid spewed from the thorns as the plant seemed to scream, the vicious liquid hissing as it landed on the dirty floor. A bit dropped onto my pant leg, eating through the fabric all the way to my skin.

And that would be the cherry on top of the shit sandwich of my day, but the fire of a handgun echoed through the rickety warehouse making the lot of us hit the deck.

Looks like we found our bad guy.

Sim rounds hit the metal wall with a not-so-comforting *plink, plink, plink,* the rounds ricocheting off the tin walls like ping-pong balls. That's when I caught a glimpse of blond hair.

Ames.

Gritting my teeth, I covered Malia and Hannah, who were returning fire with gusto, guiding them to cover before snatching the paintball gun from the holster at my thigh. Ames hadn't been hit yet, unfortunately, but I had a feeling his luck was about to change. Fiona abandoned her witchy trick bag in favor of a spell of her own, using the desiccating vines as a base.

A moment later, Ames was screeching like a harpy as the vines crawled up his legs. Gun and purpose forgotten, he batted at the slithering ropes like they were actual snakes.

Then I gave into the urge I'd had since I stepped off the bus a week ago, firing round after round at the man until he fell.

I couldn't tell if the vines had tripped him or if the sleeping spell was taking effect, and really? I didn't give a shit. Every inch of exposed skin on the absolute worst instructor I'd ever met was doused in sleeping potion and the rest of him was trussed up like a Thanksgiving turkey.

"You know, I don't mind taking this test so much anymore," Malia said, her smile as vicious as her tone.

"Me either. Hannah, will you do the honors?" Fiona asked, staring at her watch. "We got two minutes before the buzzer sounds."

Hannah hoisted Ames up, tossing his vine-mummified body over her shoulder and hauling ass behind Fiona to the back entrance. The four of us piled out the building to the judges table, dropping the trussed-up instructor right at Serreno's feet.

A moment later the buzzer sounded, and the Deputy director's smile went wide.

Hope bloomed in my chest—well, that and Ames' amulet started burning my skin. Hissing, I pulled it from my chest without letting it go, praying no one noticed me as I moseyed on over to the null line and ripped the damn thing off before disarming myself.

Shit. Ames' amulet lasted less than an hour. There was no way I could rely on him to provide what I needed to stay safe.

"Congratulations, Agents. You have successfully completed the practical exam with flying colors. Each of you have passed the assessment and have been granted agent clearance. Because the four of you have worked so well together, I have decided to keep you all at the same duty location. I hope you like Savannah, ladies, it'll be your home for a while."

I passed.

I had half a mind to wilt to the ground and breathe the first sigh of relief I'd had since Nico had healed my ribs. Too bad the man in question had no intention of letting me wilt anywhere. A moment later I was swept up in warm arms, his shifter heat cutting through the chill of the night as he swung me around.

His lips found mine, his kiss warming me the rest of the way up.

"You did it, beautiful. You did so good," he said into my hair as he cupped the back of my neck.

Why was that a button for me? I swear he could get away with murder just kissing my hair and that little move.

"I watched you on the viewers. You took out the first one and we worried you'd take the rest out, too. You cleared every room, relied on your team. You got marks off for tripping the first trap, but you made up for it with the quick way you got out of it." Nico spun me in a circle. "Gods, babe, I'm so fucking proud of you."

Shit. Had anyone ever been proud of me like this? Ever? Maybe Alice. She'd been the only one to watch me graduate from college. She threw Ellie and I a joint party afterward. I wondered if she'd be proud of this, too.

"Thanks," I croaked, ducking my head to hide my face in Nico's shoulder, but his fingers found my chin, tilting it up to meet his gaze.

"Do you know how big of a badass you are? How well you did?" Gold shined bright in his eyes as he studied my face. "I know agents in the field right now who didn't come close to beating your score with years of tactical training."

I didn't know if I believed that. I'd messed up crossing a sigil and I should have seen the other watching spells. Plus, the null ward barely made it out of there. Twenty minutes of coverage? That wouldn't sustain me.

"I did okay. There are improvements I could make. Things to watch out for, bu—"

"Agent, you need to learn how to take a compliment," Serreno remarked, scaring the absolute shit out of me.

Smiling, I pushed out of Nico's arms. "Yes, ma'am."

I wouldn't say sorry because my mother and grams both hated it. *Don't say sorry, girl, get your head on straight.*

Yes, I was essentially three bags of trauma in a trench coat. So sue me.

She passed over a folded leather wallet with the ABI insignia embossed on the outside. I ran my fingers over the all-seeing eye bracketed by crescent moons. I'd thought this was impossible. Swallowing hard, I opened it, practically giddy at the gold shield and—

"What is this?" I whispered, staring at my college senior portrait over the name "Wren Acosta, Special Agent."

I didn't bother looking at Serreno. No, I stared at the culprit, ready to throw this badge right at his head.

Nico's face paled a little, but he swallowed hard and soldiered on. "You said you had a new name, didn't you? Well, now it's official."

The only thing that was official was that I was going to fucking murder him.

CHAPTER 5

NICO

IF I HAD A BRAIN IN MY HEAD, I WOULD HAVE TOLD Serreno no when she said she was putting "Acosta" as Wren's last name in the system. At the time, I'd thought it was clever. No one knew who Wren Acosta was. No one was looking for her—especially not a dark Fae dealing in the black market. And with my name came all the protections of the Acosta pack —enough to deter just about anyone.

Even Desmond.

Plus, it would make her grandmother think twice about starting shit, along with anyone else who happened to have a grudge against the Bannisters or Wren herself. The apothecary debacle hadn't been the first time Wren had caused havoc, and most people didn't care that none of it was her fault.

Plus, all it would take was Ames opening his big fucking

mouth, and the target on Wren's ass would double in size. Protection was a hot commodity right now.

But none of that seemed to make a difference as my gorgeous mate's eyes blazed with fury, her rage making it hard to swallow. It burned through my veins, a paltry echo of her own emotions.

"I said I had a new name—not that it was yours," Wren hissed, very aware of our boss standing two feet away, staring at us like we were adorable. "Of all the high-handed, patriarchal bullshit things for you to do right now."

Ouch.

Okay, she may have had a point on the patriarchal thing. Witches were inherently matriarchal. Male witches took the women's family name, foregoing their own, and gifts were usually passed through the mother's line. For Wren—or any witch—taking my name would be a legitimate sacrifice.

To throw my boss under the bus or to not throw my boss under the bus.

"It was my idea, actually," Erica announced, saving my ass. "The Acosta name offers certain protections within the Bureau that the Bannister name definitely does not. Your grandmother is doing her level best to start some shit, so the precaution is necessary. Plus, I can't station you two together if you're not registered as married in the system."

Aww, fuck. We were doing so well.

Wren pivoted on a heel to level me with the most scalding glare known to mankind before pasting a fake smile on her face and nodding, her voice the picture of a cultured Southern woman. "I appreciate your intervention then. If there's nothing else you need from me, I'll be heading to bed. Long day and all that."

Erica's smile was indulgent at best. "Of course. Congratulations, Wren. You really have done a phenomenal job. The ABI is lucky to have you."

Erica didn't hand out compliments—no matter if they were kind or not—so the praise was indeed genuine. Wren's head dipped in thanks before she spun, marching toward the cabins without a word. Yep, I was fucked and not in the good way—especially since she started heading for her old cabin instead of mine.

My fingers found themselves at her elbow before I could blink. "Where you going, Wren?"

The absolute last thing I could take was her not being safe. I needed that more than I needed air.

"Away," she growled, yanking her arm out of my grip.

I didn't touch her again, but I did step in front of her before she could take another step. "Please," I murmured, holding up my hands for her to stop, "don't take Erica's caution as another strike against your freedom. I know it stings, but I want you to see—"

Wren's badge smacked me in the face, the hard metal shield catching me in the forehead. "A strike against my freedom? A *strike* against my *freedom*? You don't know the first damn thing about me if you think I'm just going to let you railroad me into anything, Nico Acosta. I'm going to my cabin by myself, and I'm going to bed by myself, and I'm going to Savannah. By. My. Self."

There was a problem with all three statements, namely that none of those things were true.

I bent, snatching her badge from the ground, and in my distraction, Wren skirted around me, marching double-time to her cabin.

Welp, in for a penny, in for a pound.

Catching up to her in no time, I put a shoulder into her belly and lifted her over my back. Wren screeched as I adjusted course, heading for my—or rather, Wyatt's—cabin.

"You put me down right now," she ordered, but I was doing no such thing.

I'd tried sleeping without her last night, and that didn't work, and after the events of the previous twenty-four hours, there was no chance in hell I'd be trying it again tonight. Plus, the woman needed healing. Again. Already. The remnants of an acid burn and poison from a dart still coursed through her tired body.

We passed Wyatt on the trek to his cabin, the big man trying not to laugh at our antics as he polished a bright-green apple on his plaid jacket. "You're sleeping somewhere else tonight."

What had Wren called me? High-handed? Well, I was an Alpha, and I needed that cabin more than he did right now.

"I figured," Wyatt said before biting into the apple. "Good luck, buddy."

I'd fucking need it. Wren kneed me in the chest and elbowed me in the back. I'd need to teach her how to get out of this hold later, but for now, I needed her in a space—any space—with me. Preferably sans clothes, but I'd take what I could get.

In no time, I was back at the cabin and had Wren inside

and out of the cold. She'd gone into that broken-down building without a coat, minimal weapons, and thin body armor. Hell, if she weren't so mad, she'd actually feel it, too.

Reluctantly, I readied myself to set her down, knowing full well I might not get to touch her again for some time. Sliding her body against mine as I soaked in the last bit of her, Wren found her footing. My feet unwilling to move, only let me take one slight shuffle-step backward, her scent, her heat, her fire the only thing keeping me sane.

I held out her badge. "You worked hard for this. You earned it. I know you didn't want my name, but you have it and all the protection it provides. You have an entire pack at your back, Wren. Please understand what that means."

Her lip curled as she snatched it from me. "It's another bullshit yoke, is what it is. *Don't be stupid, Wren. Don't talk so much, Wren. Go somewhere else while the adults in the room talk, Wren. Mind your manners, Wren.* It's another family being disappointed in me and me failing to measure up. It's another leash. And I get it. I screw up all the time with this wonky shit in my veins. Get wild hairs up my ass about whatever, but this was something I could do that was just mine." She swallowed hard, the wounded child peeking out from behind the rage in her eyes. "Nothing is mine anymore."

Her words had me taking a step back. "Everything is yours. Everything. My pack is yours, my family is yours, my heart is yours. You earned that badge—not because of me, but in spite of me. Serreno doesn't give compliments. She sure as shit doesn't care if you've had a bad day. You impressed her and those judges. That badge is an honor, and you earned it all on your own with only a week of training. Don't you understand just how fucking rare that is?"

Unable to stay back another second, I crowded her, herding her to the closest wall so I could pin her in. "And my family is nothing like yours. We love each other. We care about each other. Just like every family, we have our problems, but not a single member would disrespect you the way your family has. Not one."

Wren's eyes blazed as she stared at my mouth.

"And my heart, my life, my soul, my happiness, my cock, my pleasure. All yours. You own it all, my beautiful bird. Don't you know that?"

Her head tilted as her gaze went heavy-lidded. "Prove it."

Her scent rose on the air, that honey and jasmine perfume of her desire. *Gods, I was doomed.*

"How would you like me to prove it? You want to tie me up while you make yourself come on my cock? You want me on my knees? Tell me, beautiful. How do you want me?"

A devious smile pulled at her lips as her heart picked up speed. Want flooded our connection, ramping up my own. I'd said something she liked, I knew that much, and I couldn't wait to sink into her now that there wasn't a null ward between us.

"Strip," she ordered, a lovely thread of power in her words. Wren didn't know it, but she was tapping into me just as much as I was her. "I want you naked."

At the command, I did exactly what she wanted, toeing out of my shoes as I peeled off my jacket and shirt, unbuckled my belt, and slid my pants off. Now only in boxer briefs, I stood before her, arms wide, loving the caress of her gaze skating over my flesh.

"Underwear, too. I want to see that beautiful cock of yours."

"Far be it for me to deny a lady," I replied, hooking my thumbs into the waistband and slipping out of them.

Her breaths quickened as she licked her lips. What I wouldn't give to have those lips on my cock right now.

"Tell me you have some rope in this place." A fire burned in her belly, blotting out reason and doubt, singing through the link we shared.

"Sorry, beautiful, I don't. I do have a few pairs of handcuffs, though."

Her eyes lit with joy as her smile turned sultry. "Perfect. Bring them to me."

Gods, Wren in charge was going to do me in, and we hadn't even gotten started yet. Like the obedient mate I was, I retrieved the cuffs and handed them over.

"You're doing so good, baby," she cooed. "Now lay down on the bed, arms wide."

So, tying me up, then. As long as I got her, I didn't give a shit what I had to do. Plus, Wren in charge was fucking phenomenal. Following her lead, I laid down, spread eagle, waiting for her to slap those cuffs on my wrists.

In a few twists of her wrist, I was secured to the headboard, the cuffs tight but not uncomfortable.

"You going to give me a show, beautiful?" I asked, watching as Wren peeled off her body armor and top.

"That depends," she replied, shimmying out of her jeans

and boots, "on if you can be patient. I need a shower, and you're going to stay right there and think about what you've done."

"Wren," I warned, pulling at the bonds.

"*Nico*," she responded, her words teasing. "I'll just be a minute."

Then she walked her sexy ass past me to the bathroom and shut. The. Door. Oh, I was spanking that perfectly plump ass just as soon as I got free.

Thirty minutes later—and yes, it was thirty because I watched every second of that clock—Wren emerged from the bathroom, her hair wet and piled on her head, her skin flushed with the heat. Her scent flowed through the cabin, greeting me before she did. Her sexy curves hidden by a towel, she stood next to me, a single eyebrow raised.

"You still want me?" she murmured, a seductive husk to her voice. Gods, this woman could do me in with a single question.

My gaze drifted down to my very proud, very erect cock and back to her face. "I think you know I'll always want you. But right now? I want you more than I want air."

Lust bloomed through our connection, nearly knocking me for a loop.

"That's good. You know, I almost touched myself in the shower without you," she admitted, opening her towel and showing me her perfect skin. "Almost made myself come all over my fingers just thinking about you tied up out here."

She threw a leg over mine, straddling me, my cock mere inches from Heaven. But did Wren even graze my aching, leaking head?

No. No, she did not.

Instead, she held herself from me as she grazed her own skin, palming her breasts, plucking her already-tight nipples.

"Fuuuuccccckkkkk," I groaned, shifting restlessly on the sheets, trying for just a brush of her sex against mine. The pleasure she was giving herself threaded through me—enough that I was ready to rip out of these cuffs and take her over my knee.

Her hands traveled down her stomach, her fingers threading through her auburn curls. "Just like this," she said. "But I thought you'd want to see me. And you want to, don't you? Watch me fuck myself?"

My mouth was as dry as the Sahara. "Yes," I croaked. "I want to see everything."

She whimpered as she grazed her clit with her thumb, fucking that sweet pussy with her fingers, her delicious heat so far out of reach.

"Let me taste you," I ordered, the thread of command thick in my voice.

Wren raised an eyebrow, not giving an inch. "Good boys say please, Nico. Everyone knows that."

"Please," I whispered, needing her taste on my tongue. Needing it, craving it. If she was going to torture me this way, I wanted something, anything of hers.

Wren's smile widened as she crawled up my body, grazing her luscious tits up my belly and chest. I tried capturing a nipple in my mouth, but she kept it just out of reach. She straddled my chest, her wet, slick heat so close and so far—all at the same time. I wanted her to sit on my face, wanted to lap her up, and drink her down.

Wanted her pleasure for my own.

But instead of letting me taste her, she went back to work, milking herself of pleasure just out of reach. Her scent filled my nose so much I could almost savor her sweetness, and as her pleasure ramped up, it got thicker in the air. She let her hair down, the wet strands curling over her gorgeous tits as she writhed. She plucked at her nipples, making herself hiss in desire.

"That's it, beautiful," I growled. "Make yourself come all over my chest. Fuck that gorgeous pussy."

My words must have done the trick because Wren went off like a bomb, her orgasm slamming into both of us, nearly taking me over with it.

But she didn't come to me, didn't press her body against mine, and that's when I decided I'd had about enough of this shit.

A flick of my wrists later, and Wren was on her back in my bed, her eyes wide. I nearly hissed at her warm skin against mine, but I was too preoccupied with her surprise. It was fucking adorable.

"Yo-you just broke out of... How did you... How strong are you?"

Like a pair of steel cuffs were a match for any shifter, let alone an Alpha. "Sweetheart, I'm an Acosta Alpha, next in line to take my father's place if he ever decides to step down. A shifter is strong. *I* am stronger. Now, you've had your fun. It's my turn."

Her wide green-gold eyes flared as her mouth parted, and even though she'd just had an orgasm, Wren's desire blazed through us. As reluctant as I was to move, I shifted the both of us, hauling her over my lap with her perfect, luscious ass presented to me like a present. As I ran my palms over her skin, she shivered—our connection, her recent orgasm, and her need making every inch of her skin something for me to play with.

And I was going to play.

Like a whip, my hand struck, spanking her perfect peach of an ass. Wren moaned as a bright-red palm print bloomed across her pale flesh.

"So fucking pretty," I growled, rubbing over the mark before striking again in a new spot. Her new moan was music to my ears. "I bet you're dripping now, aren't you, beautiful?

"Answer me." I struck again right where her ass and thigh met, so close to her exposed pussy I bet she could feel the displaced air before the hit. This time her moan was louder, needier. The orgasm she'd had was barely a memory now.

"Yes," she whispered. "I'm so wet. I need you."

Slipping my fingers through her folds, I pushed two inside her slick heat, relishing how she soaked my fingers.

"Tell me who I belong to, Wren," I ordered, grazing my thumb over her clit. "Who owns me?"

"I... I do," she moaned, shifting her weight to her knees.

With my other hand, I fisted it in her hair, arching her back as I fucked her with my fingers—or rather as Wren fucked herself on my fingers. Swiveling her hips, she stole her pleasure, rubbing her clit against my thigh for added stimulation.

"Who owns this cock?"

Oh, but my sweet mate wasn't going to steal another drop.

Pulling my fingers from her, I spanked the other thigh, her moan louder, longer, more desperate.

"Answer me," I growled, spanking her again.

She fisted her hands in the comforter, whimpering at the loss. "I-I do."

"Damn right you do." I sat back on my knees in the bed, moving her so she straddled my thighs again, her back to my front. Her warm skin kissed my chest, her trembling, needy breaths threading through me.

"You want my cock, beautiful?" I murmured, one hand plucking at her already-tight nipple and the other sliding through her slick folds.

"Yessss," she hissed, her hips bucking with need. "I want it."

Collaring her throat, I steered her face to mine, taking those lips for my own. Our tongues met, her desire ramping up with each second I denied her. But I couldn't hold back anymore. Abandoning her clit, I guided my cock to her opening, sliding into her with one slow stroke.

Wren moaned in my mouth, her hips bucking so hard, I had to hold her across her belly just not to lose her. She slammed herself back down onto my cock, finally taking her pleasure from me.

"That's it," I whispered against her lips. "Be a good girl and fuck me like you own me."

And she did, she slammed down on me, like any second now I'd take my cock away from her, and all the while, I took that sweet mouth, played with her clit, and relished the moans that vibrated from her throat.

"More," Wren whimpered. "I need more." Meaning, she needed me to take over.

"Good girls say please, Wren," I chided, parroting her earlier words as I pulled her off me, flipping her to her back. "Everyone knows that."

Her hips bucked in impatience, but I still got my "please."

Then I was inside her again, thrusting hard enough to make her whimper.

"Who do I belong to, Wren?" I asked once I felt her tighten around me, her orgasm so close it was like my dick was in a vise.

Her chest flushed, her eyes glowing with her pleasure—and a fair bit of magic—her lips wet with my kisses, she never looked so beautiful.

"Me," she whispered on a moan, her legs banding around my back so tight I could barely breathe.

"Who do you belong to?" I asked, slowing my rhythm, circling my hips to put pressure on her clit. "Tell me."

She bit down, those perfect white teeth indenting her plump bottom lip. "You."

I needed that whispered word more than anything. It was forgiveness and permission all at the same time. My fangs lengthened, the wolf under my flesh barely leashed, and I struck, burying them into her neck as my thrusts picked up speed. Wren's orgasm hit almost immediately, taking me down with her.

Heat raced up my spine, tying us together tighter than we had been before. Her emotions came through more, her heartbeat in my chest, her breaths in my lungs. I kissed her then, her blood still in my mouth, sharing the coppery nectar like it was ambrosia.

"There's no getting rid of you now, is there?" she teased, nipping at my bottom lip.

"Nope. You're stuck with me."

I had a feeling she didn't mind.

Not one bit.

CHAPTER 6

WREN

Waking up before the sun wouldn't be such a bummer if I always did it in Nico's arms. Warm and safe and delicious, we smelled of passion, a fair bit of sex, and blood. The coppery tang had never been so strong before, and I found it strange that with just a little bit spilt the night prior, I could still smell it now.

And if the shifters or ghouls got a whiff of me, they'd know exactly what we'd been doing all night—not that it mattered much anymore. I had a feeling word had gotten around about my and Nico's relationship, and if that didn't do it, the giant crescent bitemark on my shoulder would be a dead giveaway.

It had changed sometime in the night, too. Instead of the faint line it had been, the scar was thick, silvery, and nearly glowed in the dim light of the bathroom. I'd gotten out of bed to use the facilities and scrounge some breakfast, but stopped in my tracks at the reflection of the bite in the mirror. I'd remembered him sinking his fangs into my neck, sure, but it hadn't hurt enough to make this scar.

Had it?

The faint aftershock of the orgasm had my sex clenching. No, that bite hadn't hurt one bit. Smiling, I took a quick shower, and hopped out. I was under the impression we were leaving today to report to the Bureau, and we'd need to get a move on. I tossed on a pair of leggings and a tank, stealing a flannel from Nico's bag. Sure, I could wear something of mine, but I wanted something of his on me now that I'd washed off his scent.

Weird wolfy mating bullshit.

After tying my shoes and slapping a beanie on my sex-mussed hair, I was super bummed to find only beer, lunchmeat, bottled water, and—of all things holy—*pickled beets* in the fridge.

Coffee was required for a morning such as this. And *food*. I was hungry enough to eat my weight in bacon, but I'd settle for whatever was available. Quietly, I slipped out of the cabin, making sure the screen door didn't slam against the frame and cut through camp to the dining hall.

The place was mostly empty, only a few line cooks still behind the salad bar-style stations. I had no idea what time it was, but the containers were full of all the good stuff, so I snagged a tray and a couple of to-go boxes and started filling. By the time I was done, I had double the food I could usually eat, plus some. It might not be enough for a shifter, but it was the thought that counted, right?

I was in the middle of getting the coffee when the faint

trace of Fiona's perfume hit my nose and a hip bumped mine, making me bobble the empty coffee cup in my hand. Miraculously, I didn't drop it, snatching it out of the air before it hit the now-dirty floor. I'd cleaned this place good enough to eat off that floor not two days ago, and it was already trashed.

Ick.

"Oh, girly. You look positively rumpled," Fiona said, not scandalized in the slightest. "Nico's buddy Wyatt said he saw Instructor Smexy Pants toss you over his shoulder after the test. It looks like you got the *good* business last night."

It would be tougher to deny everything she just said if every bit of it weren't one hundred percent true. I shot her a conspiratorial smile and poured myself some coffee. I did get the good business and then some. The way Nico gave himself over to me, letting me know he was mine... I got the shivers just thinking about it.

"Good morning, Fi. How did you sleep last night?"

By the looks of her, Fiona hadn't slept a wink, though I couldn't say I blamed her. She didn't have her own personal wolf to keep the bad dreams and boogeyman away.

"I'll sleep better once we're out of here. You didn't stay for the briefing, but we're headed back to Savannah today. We have the rest of the week off, though, and report back next Thursday. Serreno gave us time to find a place, get settled."

That sure was nice of her. Though, I didn't know how settled I'd be with no money and no place to live. Carmichael Jones had taken every red cent I'd ever earned, and now I was on the outs with my family. I supposed I could stay with Ellie, but her house was so small, it really would be an imposition.

"Luckily, Dad already snagged me a place. When he heard

that all four of us passed and got stationed together, he snatched up a four-tier row house. Each of us get our own floor—that is, if you want to stay with us. I know you got a hot man who probably has a pack house on standby, but..."

Pack house? Hell, no. I couldn't imagine living in a house full of strangers, let alone meeting Nico's family. I knew it was coming with all the marriage and mate talk, but... The only mom who'd ever liked me was Ellie's and that was because Alice loved everyone. Any boyfriend I'd ever had in the arcane community—and the term "boyfriend" was a stretch—never wanted me to meet their parents. Never even wanted to be seen in public with me, and the human ones?

Ugh. I didn't even want to think about it.

There was no way I'd be walking into the Acosta pack house for Nico to tell his parents he got stuck with the Bannister albatross. *No, thank you.*

"I want the place," I answered, excited for the first time since forever. A place to live that wasn't anywhere near my parents. *Sign me up.* I wasn't sure how I'd pay for it yet, but I'd figure that out soon enough. "Where is it?"

I didn't have a car, so I hoped it was within walking distance of the ABI building.

"I think it's near something called Chatham Square? Here, I've got pictures," Fi said, handing over her phone. She must have gotten it back upon graduation.

Chatham Square was a block-sized greenspace, chock-full of Fae portals in the middle of wolf central and the witch territory. Granted, it wasn't far enough from my parents' house for my liking, but it was close to the ABI building. Scrolling through the pictures, though, I fell in love—especially with the ground-level apartment.

"Hannah and Malia picked their apartments, but I wanted to let you choose yours."

Blinking, I handed her phone back. "I couldn't. You pick, and I'll take what's left. And how much do you want for rent? Utilities? I don't have much right now, but I can get you money just as soon as we get paid."

That was a total lie. I didn't have two pennies to rub together, and I had no idea when we would be getting paid by the ABI. And just by the pictures alone, the place looked like it would cost in the millions. Even if I *could* pay rent, I might not be able to afford what she'd charge. Hell, knowing that, Fi might not want me as a roommate at all.

Fiona stared at me like I was two pickles shy of a full jar and snatched the cup from my loose fingers. "Girl, you put your ass on the line to save me. Hannah and Malia told me you were the one pushing to know more, to get Nico involved, to…"

She shook her head, her eyes welling up as she filled the cup with hot coffee, shifting her body so I couldn't see her face anymore. "I wouldn't be alive if it weren't for you." By the time she turned around again, her face was a calm mask. "Plus, I own the building," she said, offering a little shrug and handing over the full cup. "You don't pay rent. *Ever.*"

Blinking, I half-stumbled away from her in shock, nearly sloshing hot coffee over the rim. "But… I didn't… you shouldn't…"

Fiona rolled her eyes and waved her hand in mock defeat. "If you need to feel like you're contributing, you can chip in on utilities, but honey," she said, her eyes shifting around to make sure no one was in earshot, "I don't need the money. We'll get your apartment all warded up nice and tight, I just need to know which one. Hannah picked the street level, Malia the one above it. I was thinking of taking the top one because of the clawfoot tub, but I—"

"I'll take the ground," I said in a rush.

I absolutely adored the ground floor apartment. Sure, it had the most risk of flooding, and it was essentially a studio, but the walls were thick stacked stone, and it had the walkout to the courtyard. Plus, it had the best kitchen.

I'd always wanted a kitchen to myself where I could cook meals I wanted, without my mother's disapproval. Margot Bannister was rail thin and hadn't ever met a calorie she didn't despise—or chastise anyone else for enjoying. Hell, she didn't even season her food. All the flavor in Savannah, all the culture, and my mother couldn't be bothered to put anything spicier than pepper on her plate. Alice Whitlock, however, had taught me how to cook when I was eleven, and I'd always had a passion for it.

"Well, then that's settled. Oh, and you should check your bank. I've already gotten my signing bonus and my first check from the ABI and then some. Probably a bit of hush money for getting kidnapped by an instructor and everything, but I'll take it."

I shrugged. "I don't have my phone yet." I knew for a fact I didn't have a signing bonus and I was just lucky to get out of here without dying. "I'll check later. When are we leaving?"

Fiona checked her watch. "About an hour. Dad sent a car for us, so we don't have to ride that damn bus down the mountain. I don't know about you, but that was the worst ride of my life, and I don't intend on a repeat. Want to come with us, or is Instructor Smexy Pants going to toss you over his shoulder again?"

That brought me back to reality. I hadn't intended on being gone so long. "No idea. I'll come find you in a bit. And…" I enveloped her in a hug. "Thank you for everything."

After bidding our goodbyes, I finished pouring the coffees and headed back to the cabin. I'd need my phone at some point and to check my bank account. The apartments seemed to be furnished, but that could just be staging. I'd need to see how much I had in case I needed furniture.

Plus, all I had to my name was in my purple duffle. Just the thought of going back to the Bannister Manor and snatching my things sounded like a great way to get myself cursed or locked up or worse. If what Ames had said—and I still didn't know if I believed him—was true, then getting out would likely cause a shitstorm I didn't want to deal with.

I'd stacked the coffees one on top of the other, slightly bumbling the to-go boxes as I tried to open the screen door, when the damn thing popped wide, nearly knocking me on my ass. Somehow, I didn't drop anything but the top coffee—that was mostly empty—the remnants splattering across the porch planks.

I was met with a shirtless Nico, his jeans half-buttoned and slung low on his hips. His eyes glowed with his wolf, his breaths coming in distressed pants.

"Where have you been? I woke up and you were just gone."

My eyes narrowed. *Oh, no.* No, he did not just walk out of

that cabin half-dressed and have the audacity to ask where I've been. I was not a five-year-old who needed adult supervision. Gritting my teeth, I passed over his coffee and breakfast, which was all the answer he was going to get.

"We're leaving in an hour," I said, skirting around him with my own breakfast. "Do you think I could get my phone back from the amnesty box? I'd like to call Ellie and check my bank account."

"Wren," he called to my back as I rummaged through the drawers for a fork. "Answer me."

He even used that Alpha tone that made everyone within a mile radius want to fall to their knees. Funnily enough, it didn't work on me right then.

"I don't have to *answer you*, Nico." Rolling my eyes, I stuffed a pancake in my mouth, still irritated I was missing out on the rest of my coffee.

"The fuck you don't," he insisted, moving closer, his shoulders seeming to get wider, his body bigger. "You can't just—"

Swallowing, I cut him off. "You're holding hot coffee and breakfast. Where the fuck do you think I've been?"

This was not the start of the morning I wanted. I'd wanted to get us breakfast and continue the smoochy, lovey-dovey post-sex bliss we'd had all night. But *nooooooooo*. I got grumpy Nico who most definitely should not look that hot when being that big of a dumbass.

Nico blinked, finally staring down at the food in his hands. "Oh."

I swallowed another bite, this time bacon. "Yeah. *Oh*. I don't know who you think you are, but my daddy ain't it. I get it—with everything that happened—I'm a little on edge, too. But damn, man. You made me spill my coffee. That's just straight blasphemy."

He finally had the good sense to appear ashamed of himself. "Yo... you left the cabin without my wolf alerting me. You took a shower, and I had no idea. The only reason I woke up at all was because the bed was cold with you gone. I thought—"

But he didn't finish his sentence. Instead, he passed over his cup and kissed me on the forehead. "Thank you for breakfast."

His fingers drifted down to the neck of my—or rather, *his* —shirt. "I like this. A lot."

I just bet he did. "That I'm wearing your shirt or the giant glowing bitemark on my neck?"

"What?"

Nico hooked a finger in the collar to inspect the marking. Honestly, I was surprised Fiona hadn't said anything about it.

"It took," he breathed, marveling at what I'd already studied in the mirror. "I can't believe it. You really have an Acosta mark even though you aren't a wolf." Nico pressed a fevered kiss to my lips. "Do you know how fucking special this is? I'm the first wolf in four centuries to mate outside our class, and you took the mark beautifully."

I coughed, choking on my pancake. "What?"

Instead of answering, Nico kissed me again, but I pulled away, scrabbling to standing before either of us could blink. "So, you're telling me that not only am I a witch freak, but I brought your ass down with me?"

"No—"

Sure, I was still mad about the marriage bullshit but... "And you didn't think to mention that shit yesterday?"

Nico lifted his hands in surrender. "It's not a big deal. We'll go to the pack house. You'll meet my family. It'll be fine. They'll love you."

The laugh that came out of my mouth was pure hysteria. No family—save for Ellie's—had ever loved me, and there was no way a pack as big as the Acostas—with their proud lineage—wouldn't hate an Alpha mated to a witch. Especially this witch.

Not just hate it.

Despise it.

"The fuck we will. No. No way. Nuh-uh. Never. Not in a million years. Absolutely not."

I abandoned my breakfast and practically dove for my duffle. At this point, I figured fuck the phone, but a flash of light blue plastic caught my eye. Breathing a sigh of relief, I held onto the thing like my life depended on it.

"There is no way on this earth I'm meeting your parents, Nico. I have known you for a week. A week. And now you drop this bomb?" Shaking my head, I yanked the bag onto my shoulder and started heading for the door. *"It's not a big deal. It'll be fine,"* I mimicked, snatching up my badge from the counter.

"I'm going with Fiona, Malia, and Hannah. Fi has room for me."

"Wre—"

"No, sir. No. You had all the time in the world to drop that bomb and you chose to keep it under your hat. You can go to the pack house and tell them whatever the fuck you need to tell them, but your ass is going by yourself."

Nico latched onto my elbow, but a snarl ripped up my throat so fast it scared the both of us. I didn't snarl or growl or whatever noise wolves used. But I'd used it then.

Nope. No. I am putting that shit on the back burner, and we are thinking about that round about never.

By the time I made it to the cabin, I'd managed to paste a smile on my face. Twenty minutes later, I was in a luxury SUV tooling down the mountain. Six hours after that, I was stepping foot in the first home that hadn't been Ellie's or my family's in my life.

Ten minutes after that, I was staring at a very shirtless Nico who was sitting propped up against the pillows in my new bed.

Of course he was.

So much for getting the last word.

CHAPTER 7

NICO

My mate was doing my head in.

First, it was the perpetual clumsiness—which I found adorable, if not a little frightening. Then, it was the death sentence hanging over her head. We seemed to be on the other side of that at the moment, but the threats just kept on coming. There was something lurking in the shadows, just waiting to pounce, and I couldn't figure out how to let her know that we weren't out of the woods yet.

Plus, there was another problem—one I hadn't expected.

Namely, that she was exhibiting some brand-new wolf characteristics that I wasn't all too comfortable with.

My bite's effect on her had been unexpected. But the glowing eyes, the snarling, the aggression? Yeah, things were wonky. Which was why I hadn't let her out of my sight except for a few bathroom breaks in the last six hours. She might have thought she'd left me behind at that damn camp, but I'd been shadowing her ass the whole fucking time.

I supposed that I could have stayed hidden all night, staying out of her way and letting her calm down, but that just wouldn't be my style.

Wren's purple duffle smacked the ground, her green-gold eyes flaring with barely contained rage. I'd ruined her little storm-out and infiltrated her new home. What she didn't realize was—if this place was suitable—it would be our home, our den. We would be here together.

But only if she was safe.

Wren's whole body vibrated like a new pup's, ready to break free of her skin at any moment. But Wren wasn't a wolf. Wolves—like all shifters—had to be born. There was no such thing as turning into one, and I'd never heard of a witch—or anyone else for that matter—taking on the abilities of their mate.

Then again, how would I know? There hadn't been a wolf to mate outside the species in so long, I doubted anyone knew anymore.

A snarl once again ripped up Wren's throat, full of wolf challenge. Instead of letting it go this time, I met her challenge with one of my own, sliding from her sheets and stalking across the room to get in her space.

Her eyes popped wide at my own snarl—mine a fair sight louder, deeper, and full of every bit of Alpha power. A power I had a sneaking suspicion she was drawing on like I so often did with my wolf.

"See, beautiful, what we have here is a failure to communicate. I need you to listen to me without going off half-cocked. The only way we're going to be able to have a civil conversation is if you get out some of that rage."

I snagged my shirt and pants, donning them without breaking eye contact for more than a few seconds. I'd thought she'd have cooled off by now and we could cuddle in bed and talk it out.

Evidently, I'd been mistaken.

"Let's go."

"Go?" Wren challenged. "Go where? You want to have a knock-down drag-out in the living room?"

Wren hadn't explored her new apartment yet, but while she was getting her bag out of the car, I'd taken a cursory look around. There was a large courtyard just outside the French doors with enough room to let her really let herself rip.

Pointing, I drew her gaze to the doors. "Courtyard, Wren. *Now.*"

When she didn't move, I grabbed her hand and dragged her behind me to the open, ivy-covered space. The courtyard was large, nearly as big a footprint as the house itself, with foliage coating the back walls and along with the stone steps leading down from the street level.

At the center was a trio of concentric circles, most likely used in spell work. Like most homes on this side of town, it was retrofitted to include the arcane and hide it from prying eyes. The wards around this property pressed in on me like a physical thing, which was why I was still considering this being a good place for us.

Letting Wren's hand go, I strode away, leaving a fair bit of space between us before turning. "You learned enough in hand-to-hand combat training to do damage should you need to. I'll promise not to shift, if you promise to get your head in the game and take this seriously."

Plus, I needed to know just how much about Wren had changed in only twenty-four hours. The first time we came together, my bite hadn't done near as much as it was doing now. Maybe because she'd put on a null ward right after the first bite. Maybe because she hadn't known what she'd been agreeing to.

But now?

That bite had taken and then some.

Wren held her hands wide, not bothering to get into a fighting stance. "Why are we doing this? I get the whole 'getting out aggression' bullshit, but really? I'm not a wolf, Nico. And fist fighting my boyfriend in the backyard seems a little more toxic than I'm willing to go."

I am not her boyfriend. I'm her mate—her husband.

This time, I let my wolf shine out of my eyes as a growl rumbled from my chest. "You're mated to a wolf, Wren. Fighting out aggression is what we do. In our race it's healthy. Do you think you're going to hurt me, little bird?"

Wren's eyes narrowed, the green-gold orbs shining like diamonds even in the bright sunlight.

"Come on, then," I taunted, practically begging her to attack. "Show me what little birds can do."

In a flash of red hair, she'd come at me, but not where I'd expected her to. Most people usually came from the front or the back. Wren? She dodged to the left before coming at me from the side, her heel aimed right for my hip. It was a smart move, and as fast as she was moving, it would take out just about anyone—even another wolf. Too bad she was dealing with an Alpha.

I spun right as she extended the kick, making her stumble until I caught her by the back of the shirt, keeping her gorgeous face from meeting the pavement. Granted, I also spanked her luscious ass in the process, but that was neither here nor there.

"Good strategy, Bird. Smart. Try again."

Another snarl ripped up her throat as she turned on me, but instead of attacking as most would do when riled, she flitted away and back, nearly circling me before I had a chance to react. Just like a wolf would, she attacked just outside of my peripheral vision.

She was getting faster, but still, she wasn't fast enough.

Catching the fist she had aimed at my temple, I twisted us both, wrapping her arm around her middle. I'd planned on kissing her neck just so she could see how quickly I could bite her, but I hadn't planned on Wren outsmarting me. Instead of just standing there, she tossed her head back, catching me in the eye.

My grip loosened, and the little minx didn't waste a second. A moment later she'd swept my feet out from under me, and I was on my ass on the cobblestones. Her fist rocketed toward my sternum, but I rolled out of the way before it could land. Up and on my feet again, I watched as her fist powered through solid rock without her even flinching.

"Look at you, little bird," I taunted, loving how my flannel clung to her skin in the too-hot Savannah sunshine. "Look how strong you are. How fucking sexy."

She ripped at the fabric, pulling it from her shoulders with a strength she shouldn't have but turned me the fuck on all the same. Wren hadn't even broken the skin of her knuckles, and if my healing, my strength, my speed was being shared with her, fuck if I was going to complain.

"Fuck you, Nico," she growled, my compliments raising her ire.

"Sure, but later. We're busy." Then, instead of her waiting, I struck, attacking from her right side, my fangs and claws at the ready.

But it didn't catch my woman off guard. No, she caught me by the wrist and used my own momentum against me, flipping me over her hip just like I'd shown the student in her combat class. She expected me to go down, readying an elbow to strike, but midair, I snagged her other wrist, pulling her with me.

The pair of us landed on the stone—her on top of me—surprising my little mate.

She scrambled to her feet, ready to attack again, even though she'd had the wind knocked out of her.

"You're just playing with me," she hissed before coming at me from the side again. "Stop playing with me. It's bad enough you're stuck with me. Can't you ju—"

I caught her fist, holding it in my hand instead of letting her go. "*Stuck* with you? Who the fuck said I was *stuck* with you?"

She ripped her fist out of my hold, leveling me with a look so fierce it was as if she was touching my soul. "*You* did. You don't get to choose your mate, Nico. You got stuck with me. I was thinking about it on the drive down here. No one in your pack is going to want me there. Hell, you probably don't want me th—"

"That's enough," I growled, cutting her off as I crowded into her space. "I swear to everything holy, the next time I see your father, I'm ripping him limb from fucking limb. Him and anyone else who put that voice in your head that tells you you're not good enough. Not a damn one of them see what I do."

Wren's eyes misted over, the glowing green-gold dulling a bit. "What you see is blinded by sex and a mate bond." She shook her head, her gaze drifting off so she didn't have to look me in the eye. "You didn't even like me a week ago."

She didn't know just how wrong she was.

Cupping her chin in my hand, I walked her backward to the closest wall. "When are you going to get it? Huh? I was obsessed with you long before that bite took. Couldn't get you out of my head. Not a single waking minute of peace. Because if I wasn't thinking about your scent or your curves or the way I wanted you underneath me, it was just how fucking astounding you were."

"Is that a euphemism for stupid?"

My hand fisted in her hair, tilting her head back so she had to look at me. "You know it isn't. You know damn well that I have never—not once—thought you were stupid. A pain in my ass, maybe, but never stupid. Who told you that?"

"Nobody," she lied, not bothering to hide it. Her grandmother had called her stupid right in front of me, and what had I done about it?

Nothing, that's what. What I wouldn't give to go back in time and toss Eloise Bannister out on her ass.

"Do you know why I followed you that night at the bar?"

She rolled her eyes. "Mate bond bullshit, I'm guessing."

I pulled her closer—probably rougher than I should have—but I needed her attention. "No, mate bonds don't work like that. I wouldn't have been called to you until I turned thirty. But something about you made me follow your ass like a little puppy. I needed to figure you out. I needed to know why you were in that apothecary, needed to know why you'd risk yourself that way."

"I didn—"

"I'm not done," I barked, cutting her off. "You risked your life and your freedom to help your friend's mother. Then—shoved into a situation that your family could have *easily* gotten you out of—you stuck it out. You sacrificed your feet for fuck's sake, getting every single student off that mountain. You made sure no one forgot about Fiona. Everything you do is a testament to how lucky I am to have had the universe choose you for me."

I shook my head. "I'm not *stuck* with you. Because I was already half in love with you before that mate call ever came."

Wren didn't take that news like I'd thought she would. No, she looked at me like I was a little crazy. Maybe I was, but I'd be getting it through her thick skull at some point, and I didn't care what I needed to do to make that happen.

"Now, as much as I'd like to strip you naked and spank your ass for trying to leave me behind before fucking you until you finally grasp my point of view, I'm going to need you to maybe consider that the people who have put you down your entire life aren't the best people to judge your character. After that, I'm going to need you to get on board with the fact that if we don't go to the pack house—just to visit, calm down—then my crazy, loud, obnoxiously loving family will indeed break down your door and welcome you to the family, anyway."

Wren appeared positively distressed at the thought of my family railroading into her house.

"Plus, there's that whole 'displaying wolf characteristics while not a wolf' thing. That likely needs to get addressed ASAP—preferably *before* you go into work at ABI headquarters."

Her face paled as her fingers held onto me for dear life.

"So, to recap: I'm not stuck with you, you're not stupid, and yes, while our relationship is unconventional and rare, it is not fake, because of a mate bond, or whatever other bullshit you have in your head."

"You told your parents about me?" she asked on a whisper, her eyes shining with hopeful tears.

Chuckling, I pulled her in, kissing her forehead. "Out of all the shit I just said, that's what you're worried about?"

Not bothering to look at me, she nodded her head against my shoulder.

"For clarity's sake, I was not the one to tell my mother. Wyatt beat me to the punch about a week before we were actually mated. But I walked in there with your scent all over me, which is pretty much the same thing."

"A week?"

Sighing, I pulled her back to the apartment. "It was after the bar incident. And Wyatt has a big mouth. Now, if I know my family—and I do—we have less than an hour before someone will come knocking on your door. This house is nice and all, but I doubt everyone can fit in it."

Wren surveyed her place like she was trying to imagine

roughly fifty of my relatives crammed inside. Sure, the apartment was small, but the space had enough character to make up for it. Then she bit her lip as her gaze snagged on her purple duffle.

"I... I don't have anything nice enough to wear to meet your family, Nico."

Wren was wearing a black tank over black leggings, her red hair piled on her head, and because she'd been wearing my flannel all day, she was coated in my scent. She looked absolutely beautiful, and not a single person would care what she was wearing. Given that she was on the outs with her family—none of them would even bat an eye.

Plus, formal and Acosta had never really been synonymous.

"You are fucking stunning, but there is one thing..."

"Wha—"

Before she could react, I was rubbing my jaw against hers, scent marking her for the whole of my family—and Savannah itself. I kissed the silvery crescent scar on her shoulder, trailing them up before I nipped the lobe of her ear.

Instantly, her scent changed from worry to desire, which was the intended effect.

"There. Now you're ready."

I just hoped I was.

CHAPTER 8

WREN

IF THERE WAS EVER A TIME FOR A SINKHOLE TO POP UP and swallow me alive, now was the time. Sitting in the front seat of Nico's truck, I held onto the Lulu's box for dear life as I tried to make myself open the vehicle's door.

There was absolutely no way on this planet or any other that I'd go to meet Nico's mom without at least a treat of some kind. I hesitated going to Lulu's because it was a chocolate bar, but Nico assured me shifters—even wolf ones—were not allergic to chocolate. In fact, it was one of his mother's favorites.

"She's going to love you, Wren," Nico said for the fifth time since we'd parked, but I could not for the life of me unbuckle my seatbelt.

Before I knew it, the truck was off, and he was rounding the hood, opening my door long before I was ready. I mean, I was in leggings, for fuck's sake. *Leggings*. No hate to the most comfortable form of attire in the universe, but *leggings*?

I needed to be in a sundress with my hair done and enough foundation on to cover my sins, not in workout gear covered in flop sweat because I was meeting Nico's mom in a messy bun.

If my mother could see me now.

Then again, Nico's mama hated mine with a fiery passion—or so I'd heard—so maybe it wouldn't be so bad? The enemy of my enemy and all that?

Oh, who was I kidding? A bunch of sweets weren't going to make up for the fact that Catia Acosta absolutely, positively did not like my family. Not one bit.

"Come on, beautiful. I promise that no one will make you feel unwanted." He shot a look over his shoulder, almost like he was glaring at a window and then turned back to me. "Because if they do, I will tear out their spleen and shove it down their throat."

Swallowing hard, I held out a hand and let Nico pull me from the safety of the truck. "That was graphic."

Then again, I had watched him rip out Girard's throat, so it wasn't too far of a stretch.

"But honest," he replied, guiding me by the shoulders toward the carved front door with a distinct wolf baying at the moon etched into the wood.

The Acosta estate was a no-shit manor house straight out of *Architecture Digest* or something. Spanning two city blocks and butted right up to Forsyth Park, the sprawling home seemed so large and yet almost... warm? The Bannister family home was beyond cold. Sure, it had warm colors and pretty décor, but the life of the place was gone. This house—even as pretty and enormous as it was, already had so much life in it.

And I was still outside.

Instead of knocking, Nico opened the door and waltzed right on in like he owned the place, an act that sent me into a world of wonder and scandalized me all at the same time. I couldn't imagine just walking into my parents' house right now, and even when I lived there, it was more of a "sneak in and pray no one noticed I was home" kind of a situation.

"Nicholas," a woman breathed, descending the stairs like our coming was a surprise. She appeared barely older than Nico did, nary a line or wrinkle to show for what had to be centuries worth of years under her belt. Her glossy black hair was piled on her head into an elegant but messy bun—far classier than mine.

Dressed casually in jeans, a slouchy T-shirt and flats, the woman seemed so put together and so down to earth all at the same time. The signature of power coming off her was strong —strong enough that I hoped this was his mother, or else I was going to run screaming from the house.

Nico was enveloped in a bone-cracking hug, his mother's face the picture of joy at having her boy under her roof.

"Hi, Mom," he said, squeezing her back, a softness to his expression one I hadn't seen before. It was as if several layers had been lifted from him, easing an ache of worry somehow. "There's someone I want you to meet."

Oh, boy. Here we go.

"Mom, this is Wren Bannister, my mate," he said with a sort of pride that made my heart hurt and melt all at the same time. He was so proud of me—of us—and damn if I was going to disappoint him. "Wren, this is Catia Acosta, my mom."

Pasting a smile on my face, I brandished the Lulu's box like it could save me from impending doom. "So happy to meet you, Mrs. Acosta. Nico said you liked Lulu's. Sorry it's no—"

"Lulu's," she exclaimed, clapping like a little kid who just got a treat. "My favorite." But less than a second later, Catia had snatched the box out of my hand, passed it to Nico, and gave me my own bone-crushing hug full of wolf strength. "Oh, my goodness. I'm so happy to meet you. Nicholas has talked my ear off about you. How you did on your final exam and saving your cabin mate. What you must have gone through."

I would have replied, but Catia was cutting off all my air.

"And you brought me my favorite treats when you have gone through so much." Then she let me go, gripping my shoulders and inspecting me like Alice would while I sucked in a breath. "You need a good home-cooked meal and some wine. Yes?"

Wolf culture was brand new to me, but Southern culture dictated that if someone offered you a meal, you damn well took it, or else. "Oh, I wouldn't want to impose."

Nico's mom gave me a single raised eyebrow. "Sweetheart, I can hear your stomach growling." She directed her gaze at Nico. "And I instructed all your brothers and sisters and every pack member that they are to treat your mate with the utmost respect, or else they will eat their own spleen. That is what you wanted to ask, yes?"

She'd totally heard us in the truck.

Note to self: do not mutter anything under your breath at all —ever—around a wolf.

"Yes, Mom," Nico huffed. "Maybe also tell them to dial the crazy back just a little? I don't want to scare her off too early. We at least have to wait for her to meet Theo before this whole thing goes tits up and she runs screaming from the house."

Catia stopped dead in the hallway to fit her hand on her hip and stare her son down. "Nicholas Vincente Acosta, your brother is—"

But Nico was immune to her stare, smiling widely as he captured me under his arm again. "A wildly unhappy pain in my ass. That's not going to change anytime soon. He may be your firstborn, but he's also the reason Lara's husband refuses to sit too close to Dad, and Gustavo's wife nearly has a heart attack every time he gets too close to one of her pups. But sure," he remarked, walking us deeper into the house toward what I figured was a kitchen, "he's the picture of sweetness and light."

Oh, dear. I hadn't quite gotten the tea on Nico's family yet —probably so he wouldn't scare me any more than I already was—but *damn*. I sort of wished I had some popcorn. Honestly, Nico's brother sounded a bit like my aunt Judith... only a little less deadly.

"Don't worry," he rumbled in my ear. "I'll keep you safe."

Of that I had no doubt.

"Really, Nico. Airing out family drama so soon?" another female voice called from behind us. A young woman skipped down the stairs, her dark, wavy hair bouncing with her. Like me, she was in leggings and a top, but hers was slouchy and cute, hanging off one shoulder like she hadn't a care in the world. Devious green eyes sparked with mirth as she got closer.

"You should at least let her sit down at the table with some wine in her before she gets all the gory details."

As soon as she caught up with us, she enveloped me in a hug. "Hi, Wren. I'm Mariella, the youngest. You can call me Mari." She let me go and hooked an arm over my shoulder, pulling me from Nico and guiding me to a door. "Has Nico given you the family spiel yet?"

I shook my head as we shoved through to a robust, unpopulated kitchen where the rumble of about a zillion voices filled the air from what I could only assume was the dining room on the other side. There was a fully closed door in between that room and this one, and still, it was as if there was nothing. Eyes wide, I met Mari's gaze as I stuttered us both to a stop.

"Yeah," she said, nodding, "they're loud and you're going to forget everyone's names—even mine. We decided just the immediate family for the first meeting, so we wouldn't make you run for the hills and leave Nico all heartbroken."

They'd planned this? Shit, Nico wasn't lying. They really would have been to my house in an hour if we hadn't shown up.

Then again, if they showed up at my house, I at least would have had Fiona and Hannah and Malia as backup.

Mari dragged me by the hand to the next room, the voices only growing louder until the group at large noticed us standing in the doorway. Then you could have heard a pin drop. The dining room was probably the biggest room in the house—that I'd seen so far—and it was maybe half full of a boatload of people. Seriously, the number of people here could probably fill a large vessel.

"So, there's Theo, the oldest," Mari said, pointing at the

surly man with shoulder-length black hair at the end of the table that everyone seemed to give a wide berth. "Then Mateo, Gustavo and his wife, Zola, Lara and her husband, Logan, Dayana, the twins, Francisco and Ella, Santiago, Nico, then me, of course. Personally, I figure ten kids is too much, but Mom kept popping out babies until she got a grandkid to ease the baby ache, so here we are."

Sweet mother of all that is holy. I really hoped no one in their right mind expected me to start popping out babies anytime soon. I was lucky I was even here and semi-not running for the hills at the mate talk. I'd never been so happy to have an IUD in my freaking life.

"Everyone, this is Wren, Nico's mate."

Wide-eyed, I gave everyone a little wave.

No one seemed shocked or appalled that I was here or ready to kick me out because I was a witch. Sure, Nico had threatened spleen removal, but still.

Each of Nico's siblings got up and gave me a hug—well, all except Theo who stayed at the far end of the table like he wanted no part of this. Honestly, I didn't mind. Knowing who liked me and who didn't was good information to have. At least he was upfront about it.

Mari whispered to one of her other sisters—yes, I'd already forgotten everyone's name at this point. "She brought Mom Lulu's and didn't get all dressed up to meet us like she was going to some garden party. I like her already."

Smiling, I leaned over. "I totally would have dressed like I was going to a garden party, but I told my family to kick rocks yesterday and don't have access to my clothes. Just saying." I waved at my outfit like a gameshow host. "This is accidental."

Mari and her sister snickered, the latter snorting into her wine. "Fair enough. You can stay, but leggings fit in a lot more than dresses do. Have you ever ran at wolf-speed in heels? No thank you."

I blinked at her, wondering if I should say this next bit out loud. "Considering I'm not a wolf, no, but I get your point."

I mean, I had just run barefoot in the snow. It wasn't the same, but I got it.

Mari's sister frowned. "Wait, what?"

Yeah, I'd caught Mari leaving off the Bannister name on that introduction, too, but I figured everyone was going to find out, anyway, so...

"But the bite took," she said, pointing to the very large, totally unmistakable mating mark on my shoulder. "And your eyes are all glowy like a happy pup, and—"

"Her last name is Bannister, Dayana," Theo growled from behind his sister, staring at me like I was a particularly troublesome stain on his favorite shirt. "She's a witch. Can't you smell it on her under Nico's stink?"

When exactly he'd moseyed on over here, I didn't know, but his reception was awfully frosty.

Dayana, to her credit, didn't seem appalled per se, just confused. And what did *eau de witch* smell like exactly? And Nico didn't stink. He smelled like lust and man and... I shook myself as I attempted to not drool in front of Nico's family.

"Guilty," I said, shrugging. I couldn't help I was a witch any more than Nico could help that I was his mate. Speaking of... Searching through the sea of people, I finally located the man in question on the opposite side of the room, cornered by two brothers and a very pregnant sister.

And this is where they tell him he's crazy and to toss me off a cliff or something. Fabulous.

Nico met my gaze, seeming to feel it across the room. His eyes glowed with his wolf as a slow, seductive smile spread over his lips. Okay, so maybe I was overreacting.

"Don't you care that you're hurting his chances of becoming Alpha one day?" Theo demanded, spearing me with a glare. "Or that you're polluting a sacred wolf line that hasn't seen a mating outside the species in four centuries?"

Mari and Dayana smacked their brother—one in the chest and the other upside the head. "Shut up, Theo. Or I'll tell Nico and he can kick your ass from here to Atlanta. When was the last time you bested him in a fight again?"

I bit my lip so I didn't start laughing outright. Plus, I had a feeling if Nico cared about any of the "Alpha coming into power" bullshit, he probably wouldn't have mated me without explaining the details. But that was neither here nor there. And I sure as shit wasn't going to bring the whole "marriage without consent" issue up in this house. Nico and I needed to be a united front, and honestly, I was starting to care less and less.

Tilting my head, I studied Theo who seemed to be doing his level best to make me feel unwanted. Too bad for him I grew up a Bannister outcast. Sure, Theo could probably tear me limb from limb, but his intimidation game was weak.

I'm not stuck with you. Because I was already half in love with you before that mate call ever came.

It was tough to be mad at the man when he said shit like that, and Nico's words were the balm to my nerves that I so needed right that second.

Raising my eyebrows, I held in a snicker. "Sorry, my dude," I said, patting his shoulder. "I'm an outcast in my own family. If you're trying to intimidate me, you're going to need to step up your game. My aunt Judith is scarier than you without lifting a finger. Good try, though."

Truth be told, Aunt Judith could likely raise a single eyebrow and kill someone, so that wasn't as much of an insult as he probably thought it was.

Dayana and Mari both busted out laughing. Like, hanging off each other, almost spilling their wine, about to collapse from the sheer hilarity, laughing. Theo, to his credit, appeared to take it in stride, staring at his sisters like they were complete loons.

I loved them all already—even Theo, who seemed to like me just a little bit now that I'd dished some of his own back at him.

"Honestly, Theo," Catia said, handing me a glass of red wine as big as my head. "Already? At least let the girl get something in her belly before you start on your nonsense. Come on, Wren. Let me fix you a plate before these heathens eat it all."

Dutifully, I followed her, sitting where she told me, and placing the napkin on my lap like a good Southern woman. She dished up a mound of food on my plate, and I let her. Based on the heaps of food covering every available surface, this wasn't a family of dainty eaters.

"Are we waiting on Dad?" one of the brothers asked as the majority of the Acosta family began taking their seats.

See? Theo wasn't who I was scared of. *Theo* was barely a blip, even as he plopped onto his chair right across from me.

More than likely, he thought he was protecting his little brother. I was really scared of Nico's father—*and Alpha*. He could disown his son, or kill me on the spot, or... Really, the possibilities were endless, but all of them ended with bloodshed and despair.

And yes, every single scenario ran through my head so much I was cataloging the exits even as I eyed the lemon tarts across the table.

"No," Catia breathed, waving her hand as she rounded the table. "He had to take care of a few things, but he will be in shortly. Fix your plates and dig in, kids."

I hadn't noticed staff anywhere but there was no way Catia cooked this all herself—or if she did, she was *Wonder Woman*. Four baskets of biscuits dotted the impossibly long table in between platters of sliced tri-tip, mashed potatoes, mac and cheese, chicken fried steak, collard greens, and pretty much any other comfort food I could possibly imagine. On my plate was a sample of a little of everything—my personal favorite thing to do at any cookout ever—plus a little plate on the side with three rolls and my own little dish of butter.

Hesitating, I watched and waited, my shoulders only relaxing once Nico took the chair to my left in between me and the open seat at the head of the table. Across from me was Theo and beside him—and closest to the head seat—was Catia, finally sitting down now that all her children were settled.

Nico pressed a kiss to my temple, threading his fingers through mine as he sat, before picking up his fork with his left hand and digging in. For the first time since we got here, I took a full breath. Nico swallowed his bite and then leaned over.

Everyone was talking, bantering back and forth as they filled their plates, and somehow it felt like we were alone in this sea of people.

"Eat, little bird," he whispered. "You'll need your strength for later."

Nico's scalding gaze drifted to my lips before falling to my shoulder, his eyes glowing gold as they snagged on my mark.

A shiver worked its way up my spine. I'd need *a lot* of strength for later.

And that happy bubble lasted about forty-five minutes.

Less than an hour of banter and getting to know this crazy loud loving family.

Less than an hour to fall in love with every single one of them.

Less than an hour to get a glimpse of how families should be—how mine would have been if they would have loved me like they were supposed to.

That bubble lasted right up until a tall, raven-haired man shoved through the dining room doors with an elderly woman at his side, his decidedly unfriendly gaze trained right on me.

This was Nico's father—I knew it without a doubt. And he didn't like me one bit.

Yep. I was doomed.

CHAPTER 9

NICO

THE MASHED POTATOES IN MY MOUTH TURNED TO LEAD as my father strode into the room, his spine straight, his shoulders tight, his scent *off*. But it wasn't exactly my father that had my gut churning, it was the ancient woman trailing after him that did it.

Though she stood tall, Diana Silva was a thousand if she was a day, her silver hair cascading down her back in a waterfall. Her face was lined with the passing of time, her eyes a milky, sightless blue that had been that way as long as anyone could remember. And if the rumors were true, she was the last surviving non-wolf member of our pack. Sure, there had been some non-wolves mated after her, but most of them had died out in the vampire wars that made Savannah what it was today.

The conversations hushed, dying out once people

recognized the elder in the room, but Wren? She sat stock-still, not breaking eye contact with my father as she finished chewing her bite and swallowing. Then she dotted her lips with her napkin and gently laid the fabric on the table, ready to get up if necessary.

Ready to run.

She didn't freeze exactly, but she moved with a deliberate slowness that had me thinking she was trying not to look like prey.

To anyone else, Wren's expression and rigid posture might look like a challenge, but I saw it for the starch upbringing and Southern lady etiquette it was. Wren was giving him her unwavering attention, not backing down an inch. What she was also doing was looking an awful lot like an Alpha herself. Even though fear, alarm, and a fair bit of sorrow filled our connection, she didn't show it, I couldn't scent it.

Then again, displaying weakness in the Bannister house would likely get her in a world of hurt. Wren was used to not looking like prey. It was probably the only way she survived as long as she had.

Standing, I almost winced at the sound of my chair scraping against the hardwood floor. Almost. That sound had every eye on me and off Wren, allowing her to breathe a little.

"Dad, Diana, I would like you to meet my mate, Wren Bannister. Wren, this is my father, Tomás and my great-grandmother, Diana."

Wren inclined her head, not breaking eye contact with my father, even long enough to blink. "I'm pleased to meet you both."

My father lifted a single eyebrow, one of his signature stoic expressions that could mean anything from pleased, to enraged, to ready to rip someone limb from limb.

He tipped up his chin in acknowledgment. "It's time we had a conversation, son. Bring your bride."

Rage slammed through the connection, Wren's eyes glowing with my wolf. "Is this a last meal kind of a situation? Because Catia made these gorgeous lemon tarts, and if this is going to be my last meal, I'd like to sample them before I go."

The sheer amount of sass in Wren's voice had me aching to spank her ass and buy her a damn pony all at the same time. The only person on Earth who talked to my father that way was my mom. Most people got their throats torn out for far less.

The room froze—myself included—as I prayed that this would not be the day I'd have to challenge my dad. The place was so silent, you could hear a pin drop. Hell, no one even breathed until Theo, of all people, burst out laughing. I didn't think I'd heard my brother laugh in years—decades even—and Wren had not only sassed him and my dad on the same day but made his perpetually grumpy ass laugh.

There were reasons Theo didn't smile often. Hell, if I'd been searching for my mate for going on a century, only to have her die mere weeks from me finding her, I'd be a solid pain in the ass, too.

Both my parents, all my siblings, and their spouses stared from Wren to Theo as my eldest brother wiped tears from his eyes. Hell, if he had fallen out of his chair I wouldn't have been surprised.

"Lemon tarts," Theo wheezed. "Okay, she can stay. If anything, it'll up the entertainment value of this place."

The corner of my father's lips turned up ever so slightly as he squeezed Theo's shoulder. No one had Theo's approval. Not Zola, Gustavo's wife, or Logan, Lara's husband. Theo didn't think they were good enough, didn't care enough, didn't love our siblings enough.

But Wren did.

"Leave the tart. You'll come back for it."

I hadn't expected Wren to get Theo's approval—in fact, I assumed she wouldn't. Especially with her being a witch. I just hoped my father followed Theo just this once.

Wren nodded, standing with me and we marched behind my dad and Diana toward one of three soundproof meeting rooms. Of all the places to take us, I sort of wished he'd have picked something a little more open. I trusted my father. I did, but if he'd decided on doing something, he wouldn't always listen to reason. And if he decided Wren and I couldn't be, well, it was going to be a challenge.

I hadn't lied to Wren when I said everyone would love her. But my father could love someone and know in his whole heart and soul that they had to go all at the same time. He made the hard decisions—the ones no one wanted to make.

I just wouldn't let him make this one.

My father's downstairs study boasted a large library and hidden bar behind a speakeasy-type sliding bookshelf.

"Would either of you like a drink?" he asked, leading Diana to one of the leather wingbacks situated in front of his sprawling desk before heading for the hidden bar.

But his chivalrous air didn't fool me one bit. If Dad brought Diana here, there was something wrong, and him easing into it wouldn't help a damn thing.

"None for me, thank you," Wren replied from behind me when I'd let the silence stretch on for far too long.

"Tomás tells me you are a witch like me," Diana said, holding out her wrinkled hand for Wren to take. "Come here, child. Let me look at you."

Diana didn't mean "look" like anyone else would—tough to do considering she was blind—she meant *look*. She wanted to see into Wren and advise my father like she'd done so many times before.

Wren made to move, but I caught her by the waist and tucked her behind me. My wolf was screaming at me that this place was not safe, his voice so loud after being absent for so long. But why had he been gone? Was Wren drawing on me *and* him? Was my power fading with the mate bond?

"You can see her just fine from here."

Don't you touch her. No one touches her.

Diana's milky blue eyes landed on me, making me feel about five years old and about four feet shorter. "You shield her too much, boy. Can't you see how powerful she is? How strong? What do you have to fear from family, Nicholas?"

Her words tasted like dirt in my mouth, like lies and danger and more. "That depends on what your intentions are. I could have a lot to fear if you plan on hurting her."

My father stalked to his desk, his cut crystal glass hitting the desktop hard enough to make me flinch. I backed us up a step, ready to run if I had to. It wouldn't be fast enough—I had never been faster than my father—but damn if I wouldn't try.

I might be the next Alpha, but I wasn't ready to take him on.

Not yet.

"No one is going to take your mate from you, Nicholas. Diana just needs to inspect your bond. Your mother told me about how she has been displaying some odd wolf behavior—especially for a witch—and we need to know if the bond was formed appropriately. Though, considering how protective you are, I'd say you have nothing to worry about."

Wren squeezed my arm reassuringly before sliding out of my hold and heading toward Diana. It took everything I had in me not to catch her by the middle and rip her out of this room. She took the seat next to the ancient witch and across from my father, offering Diana her hand.

"Pleasure to meet you, again," Wren said, before her fingers were snatched up in Diana's palm, the elder witch's eyes glowing with a power I'd hardly ever seen before.

"You have been through much, child," Diana began, her voice a breathy whisper. "A life of hardship. And your family has taken much from you, leeched your light and your power for their own gain. But you found a new family—one that saved you from despair. One that you fought for—both as a child and now."

Diana's head cocked to the side, those sightless, glowing eyes trained right on me as a look of solid disapproval flowed over her features. "Your mate found you before the calling—rare indeed—drawn to you as if guided by Fate, and the bond formed—unconventional as it is. But *Nicholas*. You did not ask? I'm disappointed in you."

That stung. "There was a misunderstanding. Questions were asked, but I wasn't clear. I incorrectly made an ass—"

"You know what assuming does, son," my father broke in. "How can you lead if you do not first require clarity?"

It wasn't like I could tell my father that I was too busy thinking with my dick at the time to gain any clarity whatsoever. I wanted to ask him how clear he felt once the moon hit him on his thirtieth birthday, how much say he had in what he did and said. I wanted to ask if at any point if he'd been presented with his mate—one he was already in love with—if he would have thought it through.

I didn't think anything through—nor had I been capable—but I wouldn't change anything. Especially if it meant not making Wren mine.

Smartly, all I said was a bland, "So noted."

Truth be told, the only person who could judge me right now was Wren, and if that ghost of a smile on her face told me anything, it was that she was thinking of the exact moment I mated her, the very second my teeth broke her skin and marked her for me.

"Your bond is strong—stronger than I've ever seen—but it draws on you both. Your family draws on you, child," Diana whispered, her eyes widening as she readjusted her grip on Wren. "They are stealing what is rightfully yours, leeching your power to amplify their spells. Burdening you to a half-life. A cursed life. There is a curse upon you, child, put there by your family."

Wren ripped her hand out of Diana's grasp, knocking over the chair as she scrambled away.

"You're lying. They may not like me, but they wouldn't curse me." She shook her head. "I'm their blood, their family. No one would do that to family—not even mine."

But she was wrong, wasn't she? Time and time again her family had put her down, called her names, or forgot she even existed. In a blink, Wren was in my arms, my feet carrying me to her without my brain ever telling them to.

"They wouldn't, Nico. No one could do that to family," she repeated, her eyes welling.

"They could, beautiful. Don't lie to yourself, painting them as something better than they are. There's something up, Wren, and we need to get to the bottom of it."

Who knew if we even could, but I wanted her to be free of them—free of their weight on her shoulders. Diana and my father could fix it. Couldn't they?

"But *cursed*? Why? What purpose does that serve, other than me being a pain in their assess for twenty-four years? It makes no sense."

Diana chuckled. "Many things that are done for power make no sense. Why harm a child? Why make a deal? Why trade with someone you shouldn't? Power, child. Power. And they steal from you even now. You can feel it, can't you? The doubt, the worry, the fatigue." Diana turned to my father. "The Bannister matriarch steals from not just Wren, but Nicholas as well. Stealing Acosta power, shifter power. Power she should. Not. Have."

If I had linked myself to Wren and Wren drew on me, then... *Fuck.*

"Son of a bitch," I growled, turning toward the door. The urge for blood was so strong, I almost couldn't think straight.

I really should have gutted that bitch when I had the chance. Fuck throwing her out on her ass, I should have sliced my claws into her flesh and tore her the fuck apart. I was nearly out of the room before Wren caught my clawed hand, her soft touch stopping me in my tracks.

"We have to break her curse, free her from her family's shackles," Diana advised my father, her eyes glowing bright as if she was seeing far into the future.

"Yes," Wren breathed, skirting around me. "*Please.*"

"That is if you want her to stay in the family," Diana mused, sitting back in her chair. "Killing her would be far simpler. The other two options spill far too much blood."

Wren stumbled back a step before she was behind me, the growl ripping up my throat a warning. My father steepled his fingers, surveying us with a calculating expression I had never seen on his face.

"I'm warning you both," I snarled, backing toward the door. "Either of you touch her, and I'll rip your throats out myself. I don't give a fuck if you are family. Understand?"

"Wren will need to bleed either way," Diana murmured, her eyes glowing once more as she stared off into the distance. "Whether Death herself comes for your bride or not is up to the Fates."

And then Wren's hand wasn't in mine anymore. No, she was ripped from me, and by the time I turned around, my brother Theo had a knife to her throat, the blade pressing into the tender skin.

I met Wren's gaze, her eyes wide with the fear that flooded our connection.

Wren was right.

We never should have come here.

CHAPTER 10

WREN

I WANTED TO ASK WHY—WHY PUT A KNIFE TO MY throat, why I would need to bleed, why I needed to die—but I knew enough about the arcane world to know that the answer would be murky at best. Especially coming from what had to be a seer. Some called them oracles or psychics, but many witches with the sight were batshit crazy at best and at worst?

They were instigators of more war and strife and drama than you could throw a stick at.

While half of me still wondered if any of this was true—if my family would really curse me—the other half recalled a faint niggle of a memory, tickling my brain from when I had to have been a small child.

Blurry faces surrounding me as I called for my mama. The light of the candles glinting off a knife. Something biting into my flesh as they chanted in a language I didn't know.

A bright orange light.

Pain, so much pain.

Maybe that memory was true, maybe it really happened, or maybe it was a dream. Maybe it was the fevered imaginings of my subconscious, begging for another family not to let me down—to not let the Acostas be anything like the family I was born into.

Whoever held me tightened their grip as they roughly yanked me to the side, the blade at my neck jostling with the motion. Diana's words swirled in my head as the knife's edge bit into my skin, a warm wetness of blood trickling down my neck.

Whether Death herself comes for your bride or not is up to the Fates.

They were going to slit my throat. They were going to kill me.

"Don't move, Wren," Nico warned, his face etched in lines of fear for maybe the first time ever. He didn't think we were going to make it, but damn if he wouldn't fight till the end. "Just stay still, and I'll handle this. Okay?"

As hopeful as I was that Nico could yank my ass out of these flames, I wanted to flick him. *Stay still.* Did he honestly believe I was going to start some shit with a shifter twice my size and four times my age while he held a knife to my throat?

I was impulsive, yes.

A complete moron? No.

Nodding was off the table, so I settled for a simple "Okay," threading as much strength into my voice as I could muster. Nico's gaze moved from me to the man at my back, a snarl erupting from his throat.

"I'm going to break every bone in your hand for touching her, and when I'm done, I'll rip the heart from your chest and eat it. And there's not a damn thing our father can do to save you from me."

The man clucked his tongue. "You know better than to make promises you can't keep, little brother," Theo rumbled, his grip on my middle tightening as he moved us farther into the room. "You might be an Alpha, but you're not *my* Alpha. There's no way you'd best me—not with your witch in the way."

Theo pressed the knife into my skin more, making me hiss.

"Plus, you've got bigger problems than me."

Before Nico could turn, a black wolf the size of a damn horse tackled him from behind. Instantly, Nico jumped to his animal, and then the two wolves rolled in a tornado of black and gray fur and fangs. But it didn't matter that Nico was the smaller of the two, he was faster, fiercer, and he was out for blood.

And Nico and his brother weren't the only ones causing a ruckus. The study seemed a hell of a lot smaller now filled with the Acosta clan—some in wolf form, some not.

"You can't do this," Dayana screeched at Tomás, slapping papers off her father's desk. "Pack law—"

Santiago yanked his sister away. "Pack law is for the pack. She's not a wol—"

But Dayana was having none of it, her hand morphing from human to wolf so fast Santiago never had a chance to react. Those claws raked across his face, splitting his cheek wide.

"She's his mate, Santi. Wolf or not." Then she pounced,

jumping to a beautiful salt-and-pepper wolf before the siblings erupted into a brawl, knocking each other into the bookcase and spilling the books to the ground as the blood sprayed.

The twins, Francisco and Ella were battling it out just outside the study in the hall as Mari and Catia barreled through the door. Mother and daughter split up, Mari coming to me while Nico's mom leapt to her wolf and on top of her husband's desk. The growl that came from her belly had Tomás scrambling backward, and all the while, Diana seemed to pretend she wasn't in the middle of the battle she caused.

Sighing, the ancient woman stood, opening a slouchy leather satchel I hadn't realized she was carrying before now. With a wave of her hand, she knocked Catia off the desk before digging into the bag. She pulled out a mortar and pestle, spell ingredients, and a book bigger than a damn atlas from the bag. Immediately, fear took hold.

No spells. A spell might kill us all.

Then again, I did have a knife to my throat, so I figured death was probably on the table either way. And I would have stayed glued to whatever it was that Diana was doing, except that my focus strayed to the petite woman staring at her brother like she'd never seen him before in her life.

"How could you?" Mari hissed, edging toward us. "After everything you lost, after everything you could have had? How could you take from another this way? How could you want to kill your brother's mate?"

I didn't know what Theo had been through, but a lot of people did a lot of shitty things for absolutely no reason whatsoever—no good ones, anyway.

Maybe Mari had more faith in people than I did, because

the shock seemed too much for her. Her eyes welled with rage-filled tears, and she violently slapped them away. I wanted to tell her to help Nico. I was fine-ish right then, and Nico needed more help than me.

"I'm doing what needs to be done, Mari. And sometimes mates die."

Theo tightened his grip on me, pulling us until our backs were to the far bookcase near Tomás' little bar. Oh, what I wouldn't give to have taken that drink five minutes ago. Maybe then I could relax while I shuffled off this mortal coil. Instead, I was worried more about whatever Diana was cooking up instead of my own skin.

"You should know that spell work backfires around me," I called over the din of snarling wolves and fighting siblings as I watched Diana mix ingredients into her mortar. "It burns buildings down, makes things explode. If you care about this family, I'm going to need you to stop."

The old woman spared me a beatific glance. "I know what I'm doing, child. If you survive, you'll thank me."

Sure I would, and she probably did know what she was doing. And Carmichael Jones knew exactly what he was doing, too. Right up until he blew up his own damn apothecary.

My gaze shifted to Mari. "Get everyone out of here," I ordered, trying to use some of Nico's Alpha tone in my voice so she knew I meant business. "If she's set on doing this, this whole house could burn down. Your family could get hurt."

She squinted, seeming to make a split-second decision and then didn't listen to a fucking word I said. Because instead of running for the hills herself, or oh, I don't know, getting her family away from the ancient timebomb mixing up probable death, she went for the witch herself.

Leaping to her wolf, Mari raced for the old woman, eating up the short distance between them in the blink of an eye. She jumped, dodging the witch's power and attacked from the side. But it didn't matter that Diana was older than Satan himself or that Mari was one of the fastest wolves I'd ever seen.

Mari never even got within an inch of Diana.

All it took was a single glare from the ancient woman, and Mari was tossed across the room as if she was pulled by an invisible string, sailing into a bookcase and landing with a whimper in a pile of books and broken bones.

"Please," I whispered. "You can't let her do that spell—not with everyone here. Theo, please."

Because if what Diana said was true, my family wasn't just drawing on me. With our bond, they were drawing on Nico. On his Alpha power. On the Acosta line. Drawing on me was bad enough, but Nico, too?

I wanted that curse gone.

I wanted to breathe without worrying if I'd hurt someone else.

I wanted the people around me safe.

I just didn't want everyone in this house to die because an old woman was too damn stubborn to listen to me.

"Shut up," Theo growled, jostling me so that the knife bit into my skin.

"You don't understand," I said, totally *not* shutting up. "Azalea Apothecary burned down because Carmichael did a spell with me in the room. *Please.* I don't care about me. Save your family, Theo."

The knife slipped just a little before it came back stronger, then Theo spun me, shoving me against the wall, the blade just under my chin as he wrapped the other one around my throat and studied my face.

"I can't tell if you're lying or not," he spat, his eyes glowing green with his wolf. "You smell too much like my brother for me to tell. But witches lie all the time. You're no different."

Was I different? Probably not, but I *was* telling the truth.

"Break my leg or something if you don't want me to run, just get Nico out of here," I hissed. "Keep him safe. Get your family out. *Please.*"

Theo's grip got tighter. "Tempting. Breaking your leg sounds fun and all, but I'll do as I'm told rather than take your suggestion. Good try, though."

"Bring her here, Theo," Diana called over the din, beckoning us over to her smoking mortar.

Shhhhhiiiiiitttttt.

I dug in my heels as much as possible, but Theo picked me up by my throat and hauled me to Diana like I weighed less than a freaking feather. At that point, I didn't give a shit that there was a knife at my throat, I kicked Theo as hard as I could in the knee, the bone and cartilage crunching underneath my foot.

His eyes widened as his grip slipped on both me and the knife. He started to fall, and I aimed another kick to his stomach, knocking him away from me as I tried to run. But I wasn't expecting Diana to move as fast as a wolf, or for her to use a taloned hand to pin me to the spot, wrapping around my throat in an unbreakable vise grip.

"You have such fire in you, girl. Such life. And while it

would be easier to simply kill you, it would tear this family apart. If you make it to my age, you'll look back on all the people you should have just snuffed out, wondering if you'd done it different, if the Fates would have smiled on you instead."

She leaned closer, eyeing me like she was trying to see inside my soul. "I may be wrong about you—I hope I am. I pray the Fates look kindly on you, that you survive this. Just know that this way—as barbaric as it is—was the least violent option."

My gaze found Nico, his arms pinned behind his back as his brothers and father held him down. His gold eyes glowed, his fangs and talons at the ready but restrained by so many hands, so much power. He wouldn't reach me, couldn't save me.

Then she slammed my back onto Tomás' desk, knocking the air out of me as what felt like invisible chains kept me immobile. Snapping her fingers, Theo's knife flew into her free hand, and in an instant, it raced for my throat. The blade sliced through the flesh so fast I could do nothing to stop her.

Hot blood poured from my neck as I choked, my now-free hands scrabbling for my throat to stop the flow.

And as my sight wavered, the howl of a wolf rang through my ears, its melancholy call breaking my heart as the organ slowed.

Sorry, Nico. I thought we had more time.

But we didn't.

Our time had run out.

CHAPTER 11

NICO

I'D NEVER FELT LIKE A BIGGER FAILURE IN MY LIFE than when I watched Theo put a knife to Wren's throat. Never felt weaker than when my family held me down and I met Wren's gaze across that destroyed study. Never more betrayed than when my father used his Alpha power against me, forcing me to bend to his will. Never felt more helpless than when I couldn't stop that woman before she sliced through my mate's throat.

And I had never felt more rage in my life than when I watched Wren try to stop the blood pouring from the wound, her fluttering hands shaking with the tremors of her impending death.

Wren's agony, her fear, her helplessness all combined with my own, forcing a howl from my throat, the sound claiming something I had yet to accept before now. Because there was no going back to the way things were. There was life before Wren and there was life after Wren, and I prayed to everything—every deity, every spirit, every demon and trickster, every single being with more power than I possessed that I could save her.

My howl sent a shockwave through the room, knocking my brothers back, shoving my father away, making my mother whimper as she stood guard over Mariella's still form. Dayana was around here somewhere, fighting alongside me to save Wren. My sisters were breathing, I knew that much, but I couldn't care about any of it.

Because Wren was dying.

Her heart slowed with the blood loss, her skin graying, her breaths shallow, and I wasted no time getting to her, holding her in my arms as our fingers mingled in the blood. Wren's mouth moved as she tried to speak, but Diana had cut so deep, there was no way Wren could talk—hell, it was a wonder she could fucking breathe. Her eyelids drooped, and she struggled to keep them open.

"Baby, please," I pleaded, trying to shake her awake. "Come on, Bird, stay with me. Please, Wren. Please just stay with me."

I'd thought I'd felt helpless before, but this... this was so much worse.

Heal her. Fuck the consequences. Just heal her.

"I'm gonna fix it, okay? Just stay, beautiful. *Please.*"

Before I could summon my wolf, Diana snatched my bloody hand from Wren's neck, the old woman's grip tighter than even my father's had been.

"No," she hissed, her sightless eyes burning a hole in me. "Not until the curse is broken, boy."

She was keeping me from saving Wren. All this to break a curse I wasn't even sure she had. I didn't feel like I'd been drawn on, and who gave a shit if the Bannisters did it if it meant Wren's death?

"Fuck your curse," I growled, trying to rip my hand from her grasp.

"Here." She slapped a glass bottle filled with black dust in my hand and yanked the stopper from the top.

I recognized the substance right away by the smell. *Black salt.* But black salt was a low-powered way to cross witch circles. It wasn't going to break a curse, and it wasn't going to heal her, and it sure as *shit* wasn't going to put *Humpty Dumpty* back together again.

"Fuck you," I growled, not caring one bit who she was. She wasn't anything to me—not anymore. None of them were.

Diana rolled her eyes before guiding my hand to Wren's wound. "Pour it on the cut and hold on."

Cut? I'd seen near beheadings that were less brutal.

I didn't know why I followed her advice or why I felt a spark of hope in it, but I dumped the whole bottle on Wren's wound and held on just like she told me to. It had two seconds to work before I did whatever it was I had to do to fix this. If it meant giving her what she wanted to get Wren healed, well, then, so fucking be it.

As soon as the granules hit, the blood hissed, bubbling like a goddamn science experiment. On instinct, I pressed my hand against the mounded salt, letting it burn us both with a heat that seared my flesh much like it was Wren's. A convulsion rocked her whole body, Wren's fluttering eyelids flashing open as her mouth widened with a silent scream.

Irises glowing, Wren's chest heaved, trying to suck in a breath that just wasn't hers to have.

"Hold her, boy," Diana insisted, but I didn't understand.

I *was* holding her. I was holding on with all I had. Then as the charge of magic hit the air, I finally understood.

A shockwave of a spell breaking rocked the entire room, cracking the walls and shaking the earth beneath. What books were still left on the shelves rattled to the ground, the chandelier snapped from its fastenings and shattered on the floor. My family shouted in alarm, but I didn't care about them —not anymore.

And I held on as if Death was coming for Wren and I could fight her off myself.

Hell, I *would* fight her off. She wasn't taking her, not without me.

Wren's body seemed to fold in on itself as her irises dimmed, her breath stuttered along with her heart. Too late. I was going to be too late.

"Now, Nicholas," Diana whispered as the tremors finally quieted. "*Now.* Save your bride."

Sucking in a full breath, I called for my wolf, him coming to me far faster than he had been just moments before. And he gave, he gave all he had to give to Wren.

Because he could.

Because he was now free, the curse's weight no longer pulling at either of us. I hadn't realized it was there until it was gone.

Because she was ours.

Because he loved her as much as I did. And I did love her. More than life and breath and the fucking sun in the goddamn sky. I loved her before the mate call and before the bar. I loved her the moment I dragged her sexy ass out of the burning building, I just hadn't known it.

So he and I gave everything we had. I'd told Wren what seemed like a lifetime ago that she owned all of me, and she did. So if it meant that I'd paste a target on my back, if it meant that my pack might disown me, if it meant she'd live instead of me, well, then I was taking that chance.

The pulse of blood at her throat slowed as her heart picked up speed, thundering in her chest as her breaths restarted. Gently, I pulled my hand away, watching as the skin knitted itself back together. But Wren had been so close to death that the sheer power needed to heal her had taken its toll.

My nose began to bleed, and the coppery tang filled my mouth as darkness crowded the edges of my vision. *Just a little more...*

Wren's eyes flashed open, the glowing green-gold a sight I thought I would never get again. Her gaze finally met mine and she reached up, cupping my jaw like it was precious as she wiped the blood from my upper lip. Frowning, she didn't seem to understand, but still, she gave me my power back and then some. The spark of life—of her power—bloomed between us, flooding our connection, filling me up, letting me breathe again.

It was as if she plugged me into a fucking outlet with as much power as she gave me. And still, I just couldn't let her go, couldn't think about anything but her breathing, her living.

"Nico?" she croaked, trying to sit up, but I held her tighter, cradling her to my chest like someone was going to rip her from me. Hell, they damn near did. "Can we go home now? I don't want to be here anymore."

Staring at my family over her shoulder, I could say without a doubt in my mind that we agreed on that sentiment wholeheartedly.

A hand slapped my arm, and I fought off the urge to snap those fingers off with my teeth. "Get up, son," Diana scolded. "Let me look at her."

A snarl worked its way up my throat as my fangs and claws extended in an instant. "You're not fucking touching her again."

"Let me up," Wren whispered, and I reluctantly let her push herself out of my arms and climb to standing.

She wasn't steady on her feet—who would be after damn near dying?—but she still approached Diana, assessing her with a calculating gleam in her eye. It was the same look she gave Ames in the practical exam right before she shot him until she'd emptied her mag. In a flash, Wren's hand cracked across Diana's face, a red handprint blooming bright on the crone's cheek.

The old woman stumbled, shock written all over her expression as she staggered to the lone upright piece of furniture in the room and half fell into it.

"I appreciate you breaking my curse, but fuck you. Fuck you and everyone who went along with nearly taking me away from him. Fuck you for damn near killing me. Fuck. You. There was another way, and you know it. You just chose not to see it."

Wren's legs wobbled, and I swept her up in my arms, ready and willing to leave this place and never come back. Because how could I call this place a home if she could never feel safe here? How could I be a member of this pack when I couldn't trust the Alpha?

And how could I be a member of this family when so many of my brothers betrayed me?

My father stood in my way, his face bloody, his suit torn to shreds. I'd done a good amount of damage, but it hadn't been enough.

"Son—"

My glare cut him off. "You will give reparations for this. I told my wife that this place was safe—that she could find a family in us—and you made me a liar. You could have trusted us—trusted me—but instead you caused us harm."

My father advanced, but I'd be damned if anyone got to Wren again. "You don't understand. Our options were limited. We had to do something today or else it could have killed you. Sometimes Alphas have to make decisions for the greater good. Please, so—"

"I am not your son. After what you pulled, you don't get to placate me with 'son' ever again." I held Wren closer, tempted to bury my nose in her hair. The problem was, all I could smell was the blood and it just pissed me off. "And as an Alpha, you should have foreseen the ripple this would cause. Instead of talking to me, instead of telling me what needed to be done and allowing me to do it, you had your seer slit my wife's throat while I watched. Fuck you and your greater good."

My gaze drifted to a bloody Theo, a healing Mateo, and the rest of my brothers. They had followed my father without question, and each one of them bending to his will. "This is the Alpha you follow? A man who would have you betray your own brother?"

Slowly, I returned my attention to my father. "You have injured an Alpha's mate, and according to pack law, you *will* make reparations. My mate will decide how much you owe. And you will pay. In blood."

"Tell me—what could I have done different? The only other way to break the curse was to kill every last Bannister witch. Would you have had me do that instead? Or would you prefer I just have killed your mate outright?"

I didn't know the right answer—though, that Bannister murder spree sounded fucking awesome right about now—but it wasn't this.

"Look around you," I growled, the Alpha order strong enough that the man actually did it. "Your mate fought you against this. Your daughters. You caused a rift, ripping your whole family apart. And you still claim that this was the best option. *Look* at what you've done."

My father's face seemed to age before my eyes as it fell. "I just wanted to save you."

"No, you wanted to save the power in our line." That statement didn't feel quite true, but then again, maybe it did. "It wasn't about me. Because had it been about me, you would have treated me like a son and not a subordinate."

"That's not tru—"

I couldn't hear another word—not with Wren's fear and the scent of blood in my nose and the sorrow building up in my chest at what I had just lost. Because it wasn't just almost losing the woman I loved.

It was the betrayal of my brothers—that they wouldn't go

against Dad. It was the way they fought our sisters, our mother, all because Dad said so. It was the loss of safety—of family—that hurt the worst.

"I hope you like that Alpha seat. I hope you enjoy that crown. Maybe it'll help you sleep at night, old man."

Dad's eyes widened. "Please, so—*Nicholas*—just listen to me."

But he didn't have his Alpha sway over me anymore, and he knew it.

Wren's grip tightened on my shoulders. It was time to go.

"Almost done, Bird. Almost done," I said, rubbing her back.

Without another word, I went to Mariella who was still whimpering in pain. I set Wren down behind my mother who was still in full wolf form and on red alert. Mom curled around her, guarding my mate with her body. Then I knelt at my sister's side, gripped her ankle, and met my father's eyes as I let my wolf heal my sister.

"How?" Dad breathed, taking a stuttering step toward us until Mom's growl stopped him in his tracks. "This whole time? Why keep it a secret? Wh—"

"It wasn't for you to know."

When Mari was breathing easier, I moved to Mom, easing the cuts in her flesh that her wolf hadn't healed yet. Then while Mom and Mari were protecting Wren, I walked right past my father and went to Dayana, giving him my back in the ultimate sign of disregard.

Still in human form, Dayana was cradling her face to stem the flow of blood from her destroyed eye and cheek. Pulling on my wolf—on the power Wren was lending me—I helped my sister. Instantly, her cuts knitted themselves back together, her eye regenerating and shining with her wolf.

A cold nose bumped me in the cheek, and I turned to find my sister, Ella. Her white pelt stained red, though it wasn't her blood. She whined, nearly begging me to follow her, but I wouldn't. Even though he was her twin, Francisco had sided with Dad.

"No, Ell—"

Ella's wolf dissolved into the mist of her change, revealing my sister's teary eyes. "He changed his mind. Frankie told me to tell you he was sorry, but... I hurt him. Badly. *Please*."

If there was a fighter that I wanted on my side, it was Ella. My big sister was one of the fiercest wolves I'd ever met. Had the Alpha gene passed to her, she'd be running her own pack by now, of that I had no doubt.

Gritting my teeth, I shoved out of the study to find Frankie on the stairs, half his guts sitting on the riser beside him.

"Jesus fucking Christ, Ella."

Dad was so worried about losing me, he didn't bother to think how hard some of us would fight to not hurt an innocent—to not lose that bit of humanity that tied us to honor. In doing what he thought he had to, he had now almost killed a son and broken his whole family.

"Heya, Frankie," I whispered, putting a hand on his chest. Shallow breaths and pants of pain pulled at my brother as his dark-brown eyes focused on me. It was bleary, but he did it. No wolf in the world could heal from this—not without help.

"I'm sorry, Nic. Dad said she was hurting you. I-I thought I was helpin—"

His words were cut off by a hiss of pain as I gave him all I could. But this wasn't a shattered leg or a destroyed eyeball. This was major organ damage. The sheer fact that he was still breathing was a miracle. I didn't know if I could put Frankie to rights, and that made me burn up inside.

"Let me help," Wren said, her arm slung over my mother's shoulder. Her face was finally getting its color back, but her jaw was firm, and I knew she wouldn't let me do this on my own.

A moment later, Wren's hand was on my shoulder as she shoved power into me, helping me heal Frankie, when before, I could not.

He'd be scarred, but my big brother wouldn't die, and that was about all I could hope for.

And once he was out of the woods, I stood, grabbing Wren's hand, and directed my feet to the door. If I knew my mother, she would pack up my things and have them sent to me.

Because I wouldn't be coming back here—not until my father was willing to pay the price.

CHAPTER 12

WREN

I'D NEVER BEEN LESS HAPPY TO BE RIGHT IN MY ENTIRE life. Every few seconds, my fingers found my neck to make sure the wound was no longer there. It got to the point on our twenty-minute drive back to Fiona's house that Nico grabbed my hand, lacing his fingers with mine so I wouldn't keep doing it.

Stuck parking on the street, Nico and I trudged in the front door, looking like we'd just come from battle. Well, we kind of had, but that's beside the point. I'd sort of hoped that no one would notice, but my luck had been shit today, so of course everyone was not only home, but staring at the front door like they were waiting on me.

"What in the high holy hell happened to you?" Fiona damn near screeched as she practically flew down the stairs to Hannah's street-level apartment. "I swear to the Fates, Wolf-boy, you better have a damn good explanation for why my friend is walking in here like she just made it through a goddess-be-damned bloodbath."

Wolf-boy? "What happened to Instructor Smexy Pants? 'Cause I could have sworn he was Instructor Smexy Pants yesterday."

Fiona speared me with a look that could peel paint. "Don't you sass me, Wren Acosta. I'm your de facto witchy BFF—not to be confused with your human BFF who is sitting on Hannah's couch right now—and I will not be deterred. I don't know if you've strolled past a mirror in the last five minutes, but you could pass for a fucking zombie."

"Ellie's here?" Sure, I'd given her a call when we'd finally gotten off that stupid mountain, but all I'd been able to do was leave a voicemail.

"Yes, and so is her mama, but before you go in there, I'm going to need some answers," Fiona said, fitting a fist on her hip. "And if you don't cough them up, Malia will have no problem gleaning them herself."

To her credit, Malia raised a single eyebrow and peeled off a glove.

My gaze drifted to Hannah who was resting her shoulder on the doorframe. She wasn't looking at me, either. No, she was staring at an equally bloody Nico like she'd really enjoy eating him for dinner.

But it wasn't me who answered. It was Nico. "My family made me choose between them and Wren. I chose Wren."

That hadn't exactly been what happened, but if that was how he saw it, I wouldn't be the one to change his mind. I was still trying to figure out what the fuck had just transpired myself, and why I felt light for maybe the first time in my life.

I mean, sure, there was a light show and everything, and the world kind of rocked, but I didn't know if what Diana said was true or not.

"What?" Hannah barked, standing straight. "They made you choose?"

"There was more to it than that," I said. *More like they slit my throat while he watched, but sure, we'll go with that.*

"Speaking of," Nico continued, "I need a place to stay. Would it be okay with everyone if I moved in with Wren downstairs?"

Normally, I'd hate that he hadn't asked me first, but this one time, I didn't give that first shit. I wanted Nico with me—more than I could possibly put into words. Squeezing his fingers, I held on tight, praying no one had an issue.

If they did, well, then we'd just have to find somewhere else to stay. But we were sticking together.

"Of course," Fiona replied, wide-eyed. "We all sort of figured that if Wren was staying so were you."

It was a good assumption. I didn't think I wanted Nico out of my sight for a good long while, and I sure as hell wouldn't ever be going against his instincts ever again. Nico hadn't wanted me anywhere near Diana, and damn if his ass hadn't been right about that.

Then again, he thought meeting his family was a good idea, so maybe meeting people was just a bad idea for a while.

"Wren?" Ellie said before turning the corner, her eyes going wide as soon as she saw me. "Sweet mother of Mary, what happened to you?"

Ellie shouldered around Hannah and Fiona, gripping my arms harder than any human had a right to. "Please tell me this isn't your parents doing."

I had no idea why she jumped to that conclusion. My mother's tongue might be sharp, but it hadn't literally cut me before.

"As treacherous as they are, surprisingly no."

And considering that other than the PTSD from nearly getting my head lopped off, I was feeling positively awesome. Maybe that curse shit had merit. Maybe my parents were far more deceitful than I'd originally thought.

"Why do you think that?" Nico asked. It sounded a fuck of a lot like a demand, but after the day we'd had, I couldn't exactly blame him. He didn't need to put so much Alpha sauce on it, though.

Ellie's honey-brown eyes shifted from me to Nico and back again before falling to our entwined fingers. Eyebrows practically touching her forehead, she answered me instead of him. "Because they broke into our house looking for you. Or rather, your father came calling asking for you, and when we said we hadn't seen you, your mother blew up our door and walked in like she owned the place. They ripped our house apart searching for you."

Perfect. This was exactly what I wanted to deal with after damn near dying. Twice.

Sighing, I stared right at Malia without so much as a blink. "Please tell me you have alcohol."

A smile bloomed on Malia's face. "Vodka, tequila, whiskey, or gin?"

"Vodka," I replied, and Malia leapt off the stair she was

sitting on and raced to her apartment. Hopefully, she'd just give me the bottle because I was going to need it. I shifted my attention to Ellie. "Let me guess. This happened about forty-five minutes ago?"

Alice rounded the corner of Hannah's living room, her eyes the size of dinner plates before she shook herself. Alice was a nurse, she'd seen more shit than any human had a right to, and she'd already gotten the arcane crash course with me almost two decades ago.

"How did you know that?"

Nodding, I prayed Malia got me the vodka pronto. "Because forty-five minutes ago I was bleeding out on the floor and evidently breaking a twenty-year-old curse."

Malia tromped down the stairs, a vodka on the rocks in one hand and an iced, nearly full bottle in the other. She handed both over and I passed the glass to Nico. I flicked the top off the bottle and took a very long swig.

It meant that Diana was right. It meant that they *had* been cursing me, draining me, using me. And somehow, they didn't know where I was—at least for now.

Fabulous.

"Well, now I need to go tell a thousand-year-old crazy woman that she was right and probably buy her a fucking fruit basket." I took another swig, swallowing down the welcomed burn. I wiped my mouth with the back of my hand. "But that's tomorrow's problem."

"That's never going to be your problem. You aren't telling that woman shit," Nico said into his glass right before he tilted his head back and drained it. Then he hooked a finger under my chin, leveling me with his gold stare. "Especially not 'thank you.' Not after what she did."

"Fair," I said on a sigh. One more round of introductions, and then I was taking a shower and drinking this bottle until it was empty. "Alice, Ellie, this is Nico. Nico, this is Ellie and Alice. Nico and I are... married."

Ellie chuckled. "Yeah, Fiona filled us in. Wren Acosta, huh? I like that a hell of a lot more than Bannister."

Funny, I did, too.

"It's a pleasure to meet you both," Nico said, nodding to each of them. "I've heard a lot of wonderful things about your family, and I'm grateful you were there for Wren growing up."

Alice waved at her tearing eyes. "Oh, stop. She was a dream child. She and Ellie both were. The gruesome twosome." She stepped closer, cupping both our cheeks like she was prone to do. "Couldn't have asked for better girls."

"If I wasn't covered in blood right now, I'd hug the shit out of both of you." Sucking in a deep breath, a pain in my heart eased. Meeting the parents hadn't gone so well for either of us, but having Nico meet Ellie and Alice? That was the best feeling in the world.

"Well, if there's anything my mama taught me it was how to get blood out of the wash," Fiona said, making me bust up laughing. Considering who Fiona's dad was, that did not surprise me one bit. "You need help, you let me know."

Somehow through the laughing, tears welled up in my eyes. "I love you guys. I really, really do. If the last few days have taught me anything, it's that blood relations can really let you down. Thanks for being here, for backing me up. For being my family."

Nico curled his arm around me, tucking me into his front as he pressed a kiss to my hair. "I'll always hug you, Bird. I don't care if you're bloody."

"My heart," Alice swooned, with both her hands pressed to her chest, like she was practically bursting with happiness. "He calls her 'Bird.' It's so freaking cute I can't stand it."

It wasn't a stretch to go from Wren to little bird. A wren was, in fact, a tiny bird, but I loved it when Nico called me that. My belly did a dip, and my heart lurched every single time. I'd never had a nickname, and even though it was a small gesture of affection, it meant the world to me.

My eyes met Nico's and held. I was safe in this space. With family. I was safe in his arms. Nothing could hurt me here. And his scent filled my nose, reminding me that we were alive.

An emotion that felt like mine and *didn't* all at the same time, slammed into me. Yes, I felt that heaviness to my middle, that need, but now it seemed like there was gasoline poured on it. As if I wasn't just receiving my own emotions, but Nico's as well. Swallowing hard, I tried to focus on not jumping him in front of everyone. As much as I loved that Ellie was here and adored Alice, I had business to attend to.

"Well, that's our cue," Fiona said breezily. "They're doing the glowy-eyed stare thing."

"Glowy-eyed stare thing?" Alice asked. "Since when do Wren's eyes glow? Oh, dear, sweet baby Jesus, they *are* glowing."

Yeah, yeah, I was more of a weirdo now. I just couldn't muster the "give a fuck" for that one.

"Okay, we're going to bed. Love you guys." I yanked Nico by the hand toward the back staircase and glanced back at

Ellie. "Call me tomorrow? We'll go get lunch, okay?" I got an excited, "Sure" before we rounded the corner and plodded down the stairs to my apartment.

As soon as the door closed, Nico shoved me against a wall, his arms bracketing my head as he leaned into my space. My blood was all over him—all over the both of us—but right then I didn't care. I didn't care that he'd somehow gotten my vodka bottle away from me. I didn't care that the scent of fear still clung to us or that we'd almost died.

Hell, maybe it was because we'd almost died. His lips devoured my own, his fingers tearing at my bloody shirt. My belly dipped as he ripped the fabric right down the middle, exposing my bra and stomach. A taloned finger trailed down my neck, in between my breasts, cutting through my bra with the efficiency of a razor.

Then his lips were on my skin, closing over my nipple, making me writhe. The rough stone walls scraped against my back, but I just couldn't make myself give a shit. A moment later, Nico had ripped my leggings off, somehow managing to get my shoes and socks, too. A part of me loved that he was dressed, and I was naked—loved that he needed to see all of me.

But I needed him, too. I needed him so much, I almost couldn't breathe. I grabbed the shoulder of his shirt and ripped, tearing the fabric as if it were tissue paper. I never wanted to see this shirt on him again. Because it wouldn't matter if we could get the stain out, I'd still know it was the shirt he'd been wearing when everything changed.

Nico stood, capturing my lips with his again, yanking me up his body by my thighs. And then we were moving. At that point, I didn't give a shit where we were going. I just wanted his lips on mine and his breath against my skin. I wanted him moving inside me, fucking every bad thought out of my head.

Because we were alive and safe and together, and that was all that mattered.

My fingers found his belt. That thing needed to go. And then I reached my prize, circling Nico's length, stroking him with my hand and wishing it was something else. I didn't really care if he was in my mouth or my pussy or my ass. I needed him inside me any way I could get him.

I needed it.

Then I wasn't holding him anymore. I was standing with my chest pressed against the wall and Nico's hand circling both my wrists above my head.

"So fucking impatient, aren't you?" he whispered in my ear, causing gooseflesh to rise all over my body. "You need me, beautiful? Is that it?"

I tried pressing back just to get a little contact, but he held me still.

"Answer me," he growled, sending a shot of lust through me so hard, my knees nearly buckled. Those were his emotions, his need. It seemed to double my own, making me almost mindless.

"Yes. I need you. Please, Nico. I need you."

His grip on my hands got tighter, making my sex clench. "What do you need? Tell me."

His hand cracked against my ass, sending a bolt of heat through me.

"I need you to fuck me. I need you inside me. I don't care where. I don't care how."

Nico's free hand found my hair, pulling my head back as he gripped my wrists tighter. "And what if I need to fuck you right here against this wall, huh? What if I need you bound and helpless while I fuck you every way I can think of?"

That sounded like the best idea.

"Yessssss," I hissed, trying to move, trying to get any contact whatsoever. But Nico held me still. So still, I fucking ached.

"Tie you up and fuck your mouth until you can't breathe. Take your ass. Make you beg."

I wanted every bit of that. "Yes. *Please*, Nico."

The hand in my hair moved to my throat, gripping my jaw in a hold that would be bruising, but I just couldn't care. "You going to let me bite you, fuck you, make you mine?"

"*Yes*," I insisted, even though I was his already. I'd been his since he'd hauled me from the flames, I just hadn't known it yet.

He fit the tip of his cock against my opening, the combination of his words, his need, and my own, making me so fucking wet as he slid inside me to the hilt with very little resistance. I was so full, so full of him I could barely breathe, but it was so good I just didn't care.

Yes, we were still bloody. Yes, I was pressed against a rough stone wall. Yes, he was fucking me like a man possessed, fucking me so hard I almost couldn't breathe.

And I loved every minute of it.

My orgasm raced for me, cresting so fast I wasn't prepared, but Nico was. Right before it hit, he pulled out, making me whimper at the loss. A second later, we moved, and I found myself draped over a low-backed velvet armchair, the air kissing my ass and the slick wetness between my thighs.

I shifted, trying to find Nico, but his hand found my hair again, guiding my head down to his cock. Parting my lips, I took him in, tasting myself on his skin as I let him fuck my mouth. He wasn't gentle, and I didn't need him to be. I needed him rough, I needed him to make me, to make it hurt. To make me know he was mine and I was his and we were alive.

"Look at my beautiful little bird," he murmured, the praise in his voice making me wetter as his length filled my mouth. "Look at you, taking my cock so well. I love it when you moan around me."

As if on cue, I hummed out a moan. Maybe it was his command, or maybe it was his expert fucking fingers massaging oil in between my ass cheeks. Fuck it. I didn't care if I suffocated to death, I wanted him to keep doing whatever it was he was doing. And when had he gotten oil?

"You want me in your ass, don't you, Bird? You want me to fuck you everywhere, don't you?"

I moaned again, begging the only way I knew how.

Nico pulled himself from my mouth and circled me, his palm cracking against my ass when I tried moving against the chair. I needed relief. It was too much and too little, and every bit of his desire flooding our connection was making me crazy for him.

"Please fuck me. Please, Nico."

"Gods, you're so fucking sexy when you beg," he growled in my ear, the hint of his wolf coming out and making me shiver.

Then I felt him at the tight ring of muscle, the head of his cock pressing against me, breaching me, filling me so full. He eased in slowly, letting me adjust to him, taking care not to hurt me, even though I almost wanted the pain. Soon he was flush with my skin, and I was clawing at the chair, aching to move, needing something—anything.

I shoved back, making him move against me, making him thrust, and gods, it was so fucking good, I thought I was going to die. The moan that came out of me could have shattered the windows it was so loud. His hands found my wrists, pinning them behind my back as his thrusts got rougher, faster.

"Fuck, Wren. Fuck, you feel so fucking good."

His desire, his growls, his groans, his breath in my ear. I was so gone for him that every cell in my body was on fire. He could breathe on me, and I would be ready to go off. Nico's other hand skated down my body to my clit, and everything in me tightened. His thumb spread through my wetness before circling that bundle of nerves as his thrusts picked up the pace.

"You gonna come for me, little bird?"

It was as if my body was waiting for him to ask. Nico circled my clit one more time, and my orgasm slammed into me so hard I couldn't breathe, couldn't scream, couldn't move. Pleasure flooded my limbs, making me weak, but Nico held me up. He released my wrists and wrapped his arm across my chest, holding me to him like I was precious.

Then Nico struck, his bite searing into my skin, and his orgasm stole through us both so close after mine. It decimated me in a one-two punch. The noise that came out of my mouth sounded like I was being possessed.

Hell, maybe I was. Because Nico fucking owned me. He owned every cell in my body, every hair on my head. His heavy breaths in my ear, the way he held me so close, his praise all just made it that much more true.

I'd never in my life felt like this. Not for anyone. Like my heart was being ripped from my chest when they were gone, and it was put back to rights when they looked at me. Like their smile could change the course of an entire day. I'd never given myself over, never let someone be in charge, never wanted someone else to take what they needed.

And never in my life had I cared about someone—body and soul. Not like this.

A moment later, Nico slipped from me, coming back with a warm washcloth to clean me up.

My heart was so full, I thought I was going to cry.

Then I was in his arms, Nico cradling me like I was precious, like I was special, like he had his whole world in his embrace.

"I think it's time for that shower, don't you?"

I loved him.

"Okay," I whispered, unsure of what to do next. I'd never loved anyone before—not like this.

I love him.

It seemed too big, too much. It scared me, how big it was.

Nico set me on the closed toilet lid and turned on the tap to the giant shower. We'd been just like this before in a cabin—him knowing what he was doing and me freaking out completely because I wholeheartedly did not.

He knelt at my feet, closing the distance between us, hooking his fingers under my chin so I had to look at him.

"I love you, Wren."

No one—no boyfriend—had ever told me that before. I'd

never made it to the full relationship, "fall in love" stage. It took a minute for my brain to compute.

"Good. That's good." The relief I felt, the joy. It felt like my heart was going to beat out of my chest.

"Because you love me, too?" He said it with such confidence, it made me wonder if he could read my mind.

Nodding, I whispered, "Yes. So much."

Nico's expression softened, and it was as if the sun was shining on me. "Then tell me, Bird. Tell me you love me."

So, I did.

CHAPTER 13

NICO

The last time I woke up to Wren not in my bed, I panicked. I raced to find her and acted like a grade-A jackass in the process. This time was no different. My heart beat out of my chest at the feel of the cool sheets against my skin, sending alarm bells through me.

Where is she?

Did I dream it?

Is she even alive?

The memory of the blood pouring from her neck, of her gasping breaths, burned through my brain. Of not being able to get to her, of hearing her heart slow, watching her eyelids flutter closed. Begging her to stay with me.

It was as if I was still in my father's study holding on to Wren for dear life, praying if she went, someone would do me the favor of killing me, too.

My gut twisted, sweat beaded on my forehead, and I knifed out of bed, ready to tear the world apart to find her. My wolf howled at me, but I couldn't focus on him or what he was saying. I couldn't do anything but scan the room and know she wasn't there.

That was until I heard the sizzle and pop of bacon cooking on the stove, the scent finally hitting my nose through the panic.

She's alive. It wasn't a dream. She's alive.

But I needed to see it for myself. Snatching my jeans from the bedside chair, I shoved my legs into them and stalked to find Wren, not bothering to button or really zip them up.

Around the stone wall was a fully equipped galley kitchen with all the bells and whistles. And right at the stove in one of my T-shirts was Wren. Her red hair was piled on her head, a thick tendril escaping the bun and trailing down her neck.

Gods, she was fucking beautiful.

Headphones in her ears, she bounced to loud rock music as she transferred the bacon to a paper-towel-covered plate, my shirt riding up to give the best view of her naked ass. I could have watched her forever, but my dick had many, many other plans.

I stalked closer, wrapped an arm around her waist, and turned off the burner. She didn't seem surprised at my approach, rather that she'd known I'd been there the whole time. Wren popped her earbuds out, paused her music, and looked up at me. The now-paused song had been blasting at eardrum-shattering levels. How had she known I was there?

"About time you woke up. I was about to start the eggs. How many do you want and how do you like them?"

So innocent, so pure. I could have bathed in it if it were possible to have this much goodness. I just prayed I didn't ruin it.

Turning her in my arms, I hooked my hands under her thighs and yanked her up my body. Instantly, she wrapped her legs around my hips, and I got delicious handfuls of her luscious ass.

"We'll get to the eggs later," I growled, prowling out of the kitchen and back to bed. I put a knee in the mattress, returning Wren exactly where she should have stayed. Settling in between her thighs, I bunched the fabric of her shirt in my hands, tearing it off in one big rip.

There.

That was better.

Wren's eyes rounded even as her scent grew sweeter. "Nico, I—"

"How about when I'm sleeping, you don't leave this bed without waking me up?" It was an order, yes, but I hoped it had come out softer than it sounded in my head. "I know I'm being unreasonable. I know, Bird. I just... I need this. I don't care if it's to go to the bathroom or to make breakfast. I swear to you that I don't need the sleep. Waking up without you next to me..."

I shook my head, unable to properly articulate just how bad it was. "Every time I close my eyes, I see you bleeding. I wake up without you there, and it's as if saving you was the dream and I'm waking up to realize that you're really gone."

Wren's expression softened as she softly cupped my cheeks. "If that's what you need, then that's what you need." She drew me down, pressing her lips against my own, the heat of her skin against mine making my eyes roll up into my head. "I won't leave without waking you." She nipped at my bottom lip. "Promise."

Her feet unwrapped from around my back, and she started trying to shove my jeans down my legs—not too hard a task since I hadn't bothered to button the damn things. Still, I helped, guiding my cock to her opening and sliding in with a single long stroke.

Wren gasped into my mouth, her glowing green-gold eyes shining as her perfect legs wrapped me up like a fucking present. Our bodies pressed together, her eyes on mine, her gasps in my ears, it reminded me that she was really here.

She's alive. It wasn't a dream. She's alive.

My hands in her hair, her lips on mine, we moved together slowly, leisurely savoring every touch, every kiss, every moan.

She's alive.

Her eyes fluttered closed as she tilted her head back in the bed, but even that—

"Look at me," I demanded, sitting back on my knees and taking her with me. I needed to know it was real. That she was safe. I focused on the way her eyes flashed open, warming with a new heat as I took her harder, faster. "Watch what you do to me."

But she didn't obey me this time. Instead, she cupped my face and kissed my lips. "I'm really here, Nico. I'm with you. I'm alive."

Wrapping her in my arms, I hugged her to me, breathing her in, letting that jasmine and honey scent fill my nose as proof. Her heart pounded against mine as I thrust harder, swallowing her moans as we moved together.

When she was close, her eyes lit up, brighter than I'd ever seen, and when she smiled, a double set of upper and lower fangs lengthened her canines.

Holy shit.

She wasn't a wolf, and yet somehow, she drew on mine just enough to—

In a flash, Wren struck, her fangs breaking my skin like I had done so many times to her. Heat raced up my spine, tightening my balls, sending gooseflesh breaking out all over my skin. My release raced for me, barreling toward me like a freight train.

She released my shoulder, her mouth bloody and so fucking sexy I thought I was going to explode. Naturally, I did the only thing that I knew would send her over the edge. My own fangs sliced into her flesh, cementing her mark—our marks—in a way that could never be broken.

Wren's moan was guttural as she came, her nails clawing into my skin. I couldn't hold myself back anymore. Releasing her shoulder, I brought her face to mine, kissing her with everything I had, mingling our blood together as our tongues twined.

She's alive.

And I'd have proof that Wren was mine for the rest of my life.

OVER THE NEXT COUPLE OF DAYS, WREN AND I ORDERED takeout, purchased an inordinate number of things for our new apartment, filled out her wardrobe, and hung out with Fiona, Hannah, Malia, and Ellie. I refused to think about my family, Wren refused to hear a word about hers, and we adjusted to living together. Most disagreements were solved via orgasms, and I folded far more than I thought possible to a woman half a foot shorter than me.

The six of us were piled in my and Wren's apartment while Wren and Ellie finished up dinner—the pair shooing me out of the kitchen after I kept eating the tomatoes from Wren's sauce. Hannah and I were discussing the merits of certain hunting techniques at the dining table we'd moved into the courtyard, while Fiona and Malia were playing a witchy sort of game reminiscent of bocce ball that involved alcohol and floating orbs.

"Okay, people. Soup's on," Wren said as she laid a platter the size of a trough filled with pasta and fish and a creamy tomato sauce on the table. Her green sundress clung to her curves while the thin straps tried to fall down her shoulders.

As soon as the food was safe, I yanked her onto my lap, half-irritated that she hadn't asked me to help her carry it and half-amazed at this woman's cooking. Because Wren could *cook*. She'd made every single Portuguese recipe she could get her hands on because she wanted me to feel like home, and when she found out that my mom always switched up the traditional ones to include Southern flavor, Wren went off.

I couldn't get her ass out of the kitchen. At this rate, I was going to eat my weight in glorious food every night, and I just could not bring myself to think that was a bad thing.

"Thank you for the food, Bird. But if you try to do the dishes, I'm spanking your ass."

Wren turned, planted a quick kiss to my lips and slid into her own seat. "Don't you threaten me with a good time. But if you want to do the dishes, I won't stop you. That kitchen is a mess."

Wren was a good cook but a messy cook. She had some sort of chef magic that made every ounce of food she prepared end up a goddamn miracle, but she'd use every dish in the house to do it.

Ellie sighed, propping her head on her fist. "Wren said you've got brothers. You got any single ones that aren't murderous douche bags and don't mind human graduate students with time-management issues?"

I'd learned that now that Alice wasn't deathly ill, Ellie was now planning on going back to school for her master's in social work. But she had an essay to turn in on what she'd been doing for the last two years. She'd been hemming and hawing over it for three days.

"You'll meet the deadline, El. You can do this," Fiona said with a wink as she took her seat. "And if you don't, I know a guy who can help you out if you know what I'm saying."

I chose to ignore both statements—both the brother talk and the "knowing a guy" business. We only had a few more days before we'd have to report to the ABI—I was on leave, thankfully—and I had managed to not think about my family while Wren and I stayed wrapped in our little bubble.

I'd ignored calls from Wyatt and my brothers, only taking the ones from my mom, but even those ended after she tried to convince me to come home. I understood where she was coming from. No mother wanted strife between her children, and no Alpha's wife wanted a feud in her own home. But the Acosta house wasn't home anymore, and after what they had done, it never would be again.

"I didn't hear that," I grumbled, taking a swig of my beer.

Fiona stuck out her tongue. "I meant on the college admissions board, you weirdo."

Wren pointed the tongs at her. "You've lived in Savannah less than a week and you already know someone on the college admissions board?"

Fiona shrugged, sniffing as she held out her plate. "I'm personable. People like me."

That part was true. Fiona was a good egg, even being from a notorious family.

Malia snorted into her drink. "More like she makes it her business to know important people all around town so when she needs to question them later, she has all the dirt."

Fiona smacked her shoulder. "You stinker. You weren't supposed to tell anyone."

"Oh, please," Hannah said, dishing up her own plate. Funnily enough, ghouls only ate the *other, other* white meat about every six months or so. "You are not as subtle as you think you are. It's just those boys see your blonde hair and tiny waist and they're complete goners. You don't even need to prime them. It's just sad."

Fiona was nothing if not proactive. And the way she'd warded this house? It was a work of art. No one who didn't already know our address would be able to find it. Their eyes would pass right over it as if it wasn't there.

We laughed through dinner, filling our bellies with fabulous food and wine, and at the end of the night, Wren sat on the counter while I did the dishes. We made love and got to know each other and breathed. It was the happiest time in my life.

So, when Serreno showed up at our door at four thirty in the morning, it was more than a surprise. And when she told us what was at stake, it was a wonder we didn't hear from her before now.

I should have known. And if I had, there would have been no way Wren and I would have stayed a single day in Savannah.

But it was already too late.

CHAPTER 14

WREN

THE DOORBELL WOKE ME UP BEFORE DAWN TWO DAYS before Nico and I were supposed to report in at the ABI field office. I'd been oscillating between dreading it and being so excited I couldn't sit still in equal measure. It would be my very first arcane job, and considering I wasn't being drained or cursed anymore—not that I quite knew what that meant yet—I was hopeful.

We had a stash of Ames' null amulets on standby, but I wondered if I'd even need them now. Fiona hadn't had much trouble casting around me since the throat-slitting debacle, but I wasn't sure if that was just because she adjusted her spells to account for the added magic in the air or if I wasn't a magical time bomb anymore.

Personally, I was scared to find out.

And since Fiona had locked down our property so tight it

was a wonder air got in, the ringing of the doorbell was a bit of a shock. Given that no one could find our house without already knowing where it was, whoever was on the other side of that door had to be very powerful, very smart, very patient, or a friend.

But anyone coming to call at four thirty in the damn morning had to be bringing bad tidings.

Nico and I dressed in a hurry, tossing on whatever we'd peeled off each other the night before. Nico pulled on his jeans and a T-shirt while I struggled with my dress for about three seconds before giving up and going for yoga pants and a tank with a built-in bra.

Barefoot and freaked, I followed Nico up the stairs—much to his chagrin.

"I told you—"

"Look here, Wolf Man. You can be assured that I'm safe with you, or you can freak the fuck out because you can't see me and be off your game. You remember the Italian restaurant?"

Nico had damn near lost it because I was in the bathroom too long at this little place down on the River Walk. The place was packed, and the line took an age. By the time I got out, Nico was outside the bathroom waiting on me and damn near sweating through his shirt, he'd been panicking so bad.

I didn't want to bring it up, but not being at his side freaked me the fuck out, too. Call it codependent if you wanted to, but our shit was trauma bonded to the nth degree and that wouldn't be breaking anytime soon.

His glowing eyes flashed in the dim stairwell. "Fine."

Yeah, I was going to pay for that later, probably with some spankings or getting tied up or—

"Would you quit it? Gods, woman, I cannot deal with you thinking about how I'm going to punish you later. I can't concentrate with my dick hard as granite."

Sticking out my tongue, I followed him up the stairs, the mirth leaving me as soon as our boss came into view. Erica Serreno was resplendent in a rust-colored suit and cream silk blouse, her dark twists piled on her head in a complicated style. She held a steaming coffee cup in one hand and a paper shopping bag in the other.

There was something rotten in the bag, too, and I had a feeling I didn't want to know what it was.

"Wren, Nico, sorry to interrupt the last of your vacation, but—"

"You have a severed body part in that bag," Hannah finished for her, emerging from the kitchen holding her own steaming mug.

How either of them could be drinking coffee at a time like this was fucking astounding. And who needed coffee? The sheer fact that my boss was in my house, holding a severed body part was enough to wake me all the way the fuck up.

"I'm sorry. You what?" I asked, whipping my head back in Serreno's direction, really, really hoping I heard Hannah wrong.

Before Serreno could answer me, two sets of footsteps clomped down the stairs. Fiona came first, her blonde hair in a messy bun on top of her head, silk eye mask pulled up on her forehead, a fuzzy purple robe sinched tight on her waist with matching slippers on said feet, so her clomps were more of a shushing sound, but whatever.

Malia, however, had let her hair free of its usual sleek bun, the curls fanning up and out in a lion's mane of black coils. Normally so buttoned up, it was especially weird to see her in a holey sweatshirt with a collar stretched so wide it fell off one shoulder and a pair of oversized men's pajama bottoms. Barefoot, her stomps were hard enough they hurt my own feet by proxy. She yawned wide as she rubbed her eyes with her gloved hand, not bothering to open them as she trundled down to Hannah's level.

"There better be a good gods-damned reason you're waking me up at four thirty in the fucking morning. Someone better be dead."

Eyebrows raised, I shared a grave look with Nico, and he tightened his hold on my hand. He hadn't said a word since coming up the stairs, and I had a feeling he was thinking the same damn thing.

"Funny you should say that," Serreno replied, her smooth voice the picture of calm. "I need you to find out."

Malia's lids popped open, spearing Serreno with a glare fit to peel paint. "Excuse me? I'm not even on the job yet, and you want me to do what, exactly?"

Serreno's shoulders took on a steely set, solidifying into pure determination as she firmed her jaw. "As Agent Dumond so dutifully pointed out, I have human remains in this bag. I need you to tell me if the person belonging to them is alive, and if possible, where they are."

Malia stopped six stairs from the bottom, getting no closer to the bag or Serreno. "The fuck you do. I did not sign up to touch dead things, ma'am. It is written specifically in my contract. Give me one good reason I shouldn't go back to bed right now."

Serreno narrowed her eyes and took a sip of coffee, seeming to gather her strength.

"I second this," Nico said, his tone pure malice. "You don't announce yourself—you don't talk to the senior agent on the premises, you just show up at the ass crack of dawn with a severed body part in tow and expect us to jump to? In my den? With people under my protection? What the fuck, Erica?"

Serreno drained her cup before setting it on the entryway table. "Look, I would love to follow social norms and all, but I have an agent missing her foot, and said foot was hand delivered by a spelled human, high on that new Fae drug we've been trying to keep out of the college dorms since last August. The damn kid handed over a box and a note and then proceeded to OD in the middle of the lobby and skip on over to the afterlife before we could get him the antidote."

"Shiiiit," I said, parking my ass on the bench right beside the stair landing.

"Oh, it gets worse," Serreno bit out. "That note? It offers the agent belonging to this foot in exchange for Wren. Signed and everything. The name Desmond ring any bells with you?"

I was glad I was already sitting down because the world started spinning. I'd done my best to try and forget—just for a little while—that Desmond even existed. Girard's warnings about his dark Fae buyer seemed so fantastical, they felt more like whimsical bullshit to save his own ass than anything else. But faced with the reality of him made me physically ill.

"Now, all told, I have thirty agents and fourteen students

missing based off my calculations, and those calculations are a fucking wag because Girard's penchant for keeping off the radar surpasses known heights. It calls into question every single person that did not make it out of Blue Ridge for the last thirty years. Every single agent who left to go on assignment, every single one who decided to leave the Bureau for good. Every single one who got transferred."

I wasn't looking at the director, but I felt her stare. Forty-four people. That they knew of. Just gone. Forty-four women taken. Sweat broke out all over my skin as the lights in the room flickered. My tongue felt heavy in my mouth as saliva pooled, the scent of rotten meat filling my nose.

Nico's hand felt like knives on my skin as he rubbed my back, his words garbled in my ears as panic set in.

Forty-four women. And I had almost been one of them. And she was right. Girard had covered his tracks. When Fiona had gone missing, it was almost as if she'd never been to Blue Ridge at all. Even her scent had been wiped away. According to Nico, her records were clean, and if he hadn't already known something was up and I hadn't kept pushing...

A bucket appeared right in front of my face, and I latched onto it before losing what little I had in my stomach. I'd sort of shoved everything that had happened with Girard down somewhere deep, and now it was coming up vomit-style.

Forty-four women.

I heaved until there was nothing left, but still, my stomach wanted to revolt. Forty-four women. And Fiona and I had almost been among them. Forty-four women never searched for. Forty-four women never missed. People with no families or on the outs with them, I'd bet. People who wouldn't have someone looking for them.

Forty-four women stolen. Sold. Used. Like property. Like chattel. All to line Girard's pockets. If I had anything left in my stomach, I would have thrown up more.

A cold washcloth appeared as if by magic in front of my face, and I wiped my skin as if it would wash away how fucking dirty I felt. Nico took it from me and handed me a cup of mouthwash. Blissfully, I took that, too, rinsing my mouth and spitting into the bucket.

My gaze found Fiona's, and just like me, she looked ill. Like me, she was probably wondering if things had gone different if she'd be reduced to a severed foot in a bag. A lonely clue in a case so big it was a wonder how it had ever been a secret. Fiona's knuckles were white as she gripped the railing, her skin so pale it was a wonder she was standing.

"So, I need to know if this particular agent is still alive, and if this foot actually fucking belongs to her." Serreno's shoulders fell. "You know, six months ago, I told another agent that something like this could never happen here. That we could never have corruption go on under our noses to the degree of the Knoxville branch. Kenzari told me I'd eat my words one day, that I'd need her help and she wouldn't be able to give it to me. And damn if that fucking oracle wasn't right."

I didn't know who this Kenzari person was, but damn if she hadn't been right on this one. Because even I'd heard of the Knoxville dust-up—everyone had. Werewolf wars, death mages on a power trip, European vampires trying to take over. It had me wondering how they were keeping all of this under wraps.

"Look, I'm sorry you seem to have an internal problem, but I specifically said no dead things." Malia descended the last six steps, crossing her arms over her chest. "As I recall, you agreed. Personally. So you're telling me you're reneging on our deal?"

Serreno's eyes flashed, not with magic but with challenge. "Technically speaking, I don't know if the person that belongs to this is dead or not. One could make a case against a breach of contract."

Malia narrowed her eyes, her jaw firming to granite. "One year's worth of wages as a bonus for every body part read."

"Six months," Serreno haggled, eyeing the small psychometry witch like she was a particularly sharp thorn in her shoe.

Malia's unhinged laugh was a thing of nightmares. "A year. Mostly to pay for the fucking therapy I'll need after this."

Serreno growled as she gnashed her teeth. "Fine. A year. But this better be good. I want everything you can give me."

Malia's lip curled as she skirted around the director and headed for Hannah's kitchen, disappearing around the corner. "You'll get what you get, and I expect that money to be in my bank account by noon, or I'm ripping up our contract and going to work for Fiona's dad," she threatened, likely pouring herself a cup of coffee from Hannah's probably nearly empty pot. "Which side of the line do you want me on, boss?"

CHAPTER 15

WREN

I had a feeling that working for Fiona's dad wouldn't exactly put Malia in the driver's seat of her own life, but that was just me.

"I'll call accounting as soon as you give me what I need," Serreno bit out. "Will that make you happy, Agent Nadir?"

Malia emerged from Hannah's kitchen, sipping on a mug of steaming brew. "Not a gods-damned thing about this morning has made me happy, but sure. I'm peachy fucking keen."

Serreno reached into the bag, removing a pale-gray foot encased in a plastic Zip-lock.

"Whoa, no," Nico barked. "Don't you dare open that thing in here. It's bad enough you're bringing this here. You open that inside and we'll never get the smell out. Courtyard, Erica. Now."

Nico dropped a kiss to my forehead as he rested his palms on my shoulders. "Give us a minute, would you?" Shakily, I nodded, hanging back, and he shifted his eyes to Hannah. "Don't let her out of your sight, you got me?"

Hannah gave him the middle finger salute, but stayed right by my side as he moved to Erica, roughly grabbing his boss' arm and dragging her downstairs.

"I swear I'm going to need to bleach my nose after this," Malia grumbled before draining her mug.

But I couldn't look at her or Hannah who was absolutely watching me like a hawk. I'd slipped my leash once and I'd probably never live that shit down. No, my gaze found Fiona's again. It was one thing to be kidnapped by Girard. It was a whole other to have body parts of agents just floating around.

Fi descended the rest of the way down the stairs, reaching for my hand. I took it, praying that we found the poor woman, but also... I sort of hoped when we found her, she was at rest. It was a terrible thing to almost wish for someone's death, but sometimes, it was better to be dead.

Because despite what the world wanted you to believe, sometimes death wasn't the worst thing.

"That poor agent," Fiona whispered, shaking her head. "You don't think she's still breathing, do you? Stuck wherever that guy Desmond is?"

I had a sinking feeling in my belly that was exactly where she'd been for however long she'd been gone.

"Okay, let's get this shit over with. Hannah?" Malia asked as she directed her feet to my staircase. "Bring the vodka and the bleach, will you? I'll watch these two bozos until then, yeah?"

Hannah brought two fingers to her eyes and then pointed them at me.

Yeah, yeah. I was the problem child in this scenario. "I got it."

Following Malia down the stairs, I nearly gagged at the scent of rotten flesh coming from the courtyard. I had half a mind to run away screaming if I was being honest.

"You aren't trading her," Nico hissed, his voice as clear to me as if he were right next to my ear. "It's bad enough you still don't know why there was a termination entered onto her sentence when we both know Wren's crime didn't deserve that. Now this? I don't know what you think you're doing—"

"Of course not," Serreno said, cutting him off. "Agent Lewis might have been a powerful illusion mage, but there is no way I'm trading one woman for another. Not only is that completely unethical, but there is no way to know what the ramifications are with Wren's abilities. It would be like giving a dark Fae a fucking nuke. No, thank you. And I'm pretty sure the order was Girard's backup plan. If he couldn't get her one way, he was going to fail her, pretend to execute her, and hand her over. But that's just a guess since I can't find any records where that was her actual sentence."

Nico shot me a look over Serreno's shoulder, his gold eyes flashing in the dark. "And Wren's family?"

"Still causing problems, but since their wardings and spells are literally crumbling, half of Savannah has been scrambling to fill the void. Wren should be glad she got out of that family when she had the chance. I have a feeling the witch community is going to cannibalize them soon enough."

For once, I didn't feel even a little guilty at leaving the lot of my family behind. Not a single one of them ever came to my aid, never gave a kind word, never tried to help me. Would I feel different if they had? If it were Ellie or Alice instead?

Probably.

But if they happened to get their comeuppance after years of abuse? Well, I wouldn't be stepping in to save them.

"Come on," Malia urged, skirting around Fi and I as we dawdled in my bedroom. "Let's get this shit over with."

I moved to follow, but Fiona tightened her grip on my hand. "You don't have to stay here—neither of us do. I'll call my dad. He can get us out of Savannah in an hour if we need to. Go to Tennessee where the Fae are sparse. Just until the heat's off."

But all the while, I kept my gaze locked on Nico's. "If you think you need to go, I want you to be safe. But the only way I'm leaving is if it's with Nico."

The glow of Nico's irises built as if his wolf was looking out of Nico's eyes, staring right at me.

I'm not leaving. I'm not going anywhere. I won't go looking for trouble. Not by myself. Not ever again.

Knowing what I knew now, I wouldn't leave him without a damn good explanation and I sure as shit wouldn't go off half-cocked.

Nico deserved better than that.

Fiona sighed, loosening her grip on my fingers. "That's what I figured you'd say. And if he tells you to leave?"

"Then he needs to toss me over his shoulder and move me himself." I was completely serious, but the wide smile that pulled at Nico's lips made my heart race and my belly do a somersault.

"Okay," Malia said, settling onto one of the patio chairs. "Give me the damn thing."

If I thought the stench was bad inside the bag, it was nothing compared to when Serreno opened it. Both Fiona and I gagged, and we were barely within fifty feet. Hannah came up from behind us, and even she looked a little ill.

"Jesus, fuck. That is rancid," she groaned.

Another fun fact I learned about ghouls? They preferred fresh meat, not long-dead meat. Sure, they'd eat it if they had to, but it was a lot like me eating liver and onions. Like, sure, it was food, but no one thought it was a high-quality meal.

Personally, I'd take the liver over this.

Serreno and Nico must have ironclad stomachs because they appeared completely unfazed. Like this was just another Tuesday. Braving a glance, I forced myself to not avert my gaze. Whoever this woman was, she deserved me to at least witness what I could.

The flesh was grayer outside of the bag than in, the severed edge rough like it had been torn off rather than cut. And if I had a guess, this was what gangrene looked like before it was excised for life-saving purposes.

Malia held out a single finger, bare now that she'd stripped off her glove, and touched it to the exposed mottled flesh. As soon as she made contact, it was as if she'd been hit by a bolt of lightning. She jolted, her entire body going rigid as her eyes rolled into the back of her head.

"A-agent Penelope Lewis, i-illusion ma-mage, taken from Blue Ridge twenty-five years ago." She sucked in a breath, her brow furrowing like she was in pain. "R-rah-reported as deep undercover with only t-top-level access to her file. But she n-never made it."

Malia's body seized, her nose bloody and dripping down her front. I shoved past Fiona and Hannah and yanked Nico's shirt from his back, ripping the fabric to cover my hands. Only then did I touch her. Malia had to know she didn't have to do this alone. As soon as my hands landed on her shoulders, her breath eased, her shoulders relaxed. But she was hurt. I could smell the blood, so I pushed, giving over a little bit of power like I'd done with Nico.

Malia sighed as if I helped, and I hoped I did, but I couldn't be too sure.

"G-girard nearly caved in her skull before delivering her to a man. She never saw his face. He told her to make him see, but Penelope was too scared, too new. As powerful as she was, she was too green, too new and hadn't figured out how to tune her magic to Fae eyes. He was so mad that she couldn't make pretty pictures for him, so he told her to dance. S-she did. She d-danced until her feet were bloody and her body gave out. He'd wait for her to be rested, and she'd do it all over again."

A Fae could see through most magics, and illusions were the easiest for them to spot. It made no sense that a Fae would want an illusionist to keep. Not unless he enjoyed torturing young women.

Malia grabbed my covered hand with her own, squeezing it tight as she came out of her trance. Her whole body shook, faint tremors of whatever it was she'd seen. She started to sit up, but I gently pushed her back down. She was still bleeding from her nose and ears, and her body was sipping at my power, trying to revive itself.

"I don't know if she's alive, but if you were wondering if that foot belongs to a Penelope Lewis, you have the right agent. And if you want to look for her, I suggest you start in the Fae realm."

Nico grabbed my shoulder, spinning me around, so that I was staring right at his glowing golden eyes. "Don't even think about it, Bird. You hear me. This is one area where you can't help."

Is he high? Malia just described my worst nightmare, and he thinks I'm going to what, just hand myself over?

"I made a deal with Carmichael Jones instead of going to the River Walk to talk to the Fae on purpose. I'm sorry about the agent, I really am, but hell no." I shifted my attention to Serreno. "I don't know what you think of me, but I am not, in fact, a martyr. That shit with Girard was a fluke. No offense, Fi, but I did not get kidnapped on purpose. The only reason I went into his cabin at all was because I thought I knew where he was. I'll sacrifice for my friends, sure. Nico? Absolutely. But this agent? I'm so sorry, but there is no way on this earth or any other I'm giving myself up to save a stranger. Especially to a dark Fae. This is one area where you do not have to worry about me."

Serreno bit her lip as she tried to hold in a snicker.

"Plus, did you see that foot? That was not severed with a sharp knife. That shit was torn the fuck off. That woman is more than likely dead as a doornail. I am not skipping off to get kidnapped anytime soon to save a dead girl. No. *No.*" My eyes speared Serreno. "And if you think you're about to offer me a bonus, you can keep it. There isn't a payment big enough to make me hand myself over to my worst nightmare. No, thank you."

Nico wrapped me up in his arms, his laugh wildly inappropriate but welcome all the same. "I fucking love you, Bird. You know that?"

At that moment, I really, really did.

But I met Malia's gaze over his shoulder, and as much as I loved the way he was holding me right now, her haunted expression told me she hadn't quite shared everything with us. Twenty-five years of pain. Twenty-five years of torture and fear. I squeezed Nico and gently pushed him away. Malia and Fiona and Hannah needed me right now.

I knelt by her chair. "How about a scalding-hot bath followed by some mind bleach? I know I have some tequila around here somewhere, yeah? When you're ready, I'll even make you some soup or something. Some bread from scratch? I have a loaf rising in the fridge already."

Malia's expression was grateful, but the horrors she'd seen were still playing behind her eyes.

Yeah, she'd need all the therapy in the world and then some.

And maybe even that wasn't enough.

CHAPTER 16

NICO

I'd never been so pissed at my boss in my fucking life. It made no sense for her to come here, none whatsoever. Did I hate that Lewis was missing? Yes, but she'd been gone for twenty-five fucking years and *now* they were pressed about looking for her?

If it hadn't been for Wyatt sticking his nose into this shit, no one would have even known what was going on. His curiosity had started a domino effect, changing both Wren's and my life mostly for the better. But that didn't mean we owed the Bureau our souls for it, and it sure as shit didn't mean that we needed to sacrifice for their oversight.

Wren's copper hair was piled on her head as she paced our apartment. She had that look about her like she was about to ask me something, and if I couldn't feel her gut burning with anxiety, I would have made her quit already. We'd spent the better part of yesterday apart, my presence not necessarily all too welcome in a sea of estrogen and chocolate and tacos.

Malia was a far sight closer to crazy than she had been the night before, and whatever she saw from Lewis' flesh, I was very happy to not know. But Wren needed to help her friend, and I had to be a good mate.

Even though I hated to be apart from her.

Even though I wanted her to myself.

Even though I feared what she might do next.

Sure, Wren had said she wouldn't give herself up, but she'd also told me she wasn't going to give Dumond a hard time or leave the safety of numbers or go investigate Girard. I didn't know how much I trusted that my little bird's hero streak wouldn't rear its ugly head.

"Okay, Bird," I said, picking her up mid-pace and depositing her onto the bed before covering her with my body. "What has you in a twist? Is it Malia? The missing agents or—"

"I'm scared to go to work," she blurted, her lips screwing up into a grimace. "I know the curse is gone, but what does that mean? Can people do magic around me or not? Fiona seems to have figured it out, but... What happens if I go into the ABI building and shit starts blowing up? I mean, Ames' null wards work, sure, but not for very long, and—"

I dropped a kiss to her still-moving lips, nipping at the bottom one just to ease a little of her fear. "So you aren't thinking about the other shit? Just first-day jitters?"

"Well," Wren said, blinking like my question was a little odd, "yeah. I mean I'm worried about Malia, but other than being her friend, I can't do much about that. And the missing agent shit is being handled by people well above my pay grade.

Do I want to help? Of course I do. But other than getting coffee, doing scut work, and burying myself in paperwork, there isn't much else I have to offer. I wouldn't even know where to start."

I had a feeling she totally would know where to start and probably direct a few agents to look in the right direction, but that was just me.

"I'm more worried about what happens when they find out I wouldn't... wouldn't... hand myself over for her. And what if they find out I'm an amplifier? And... are they going to look at me funny for marrying my instructor? Even though I totally maintain that I require a pretty dress and a ring and all the bells and whistles to be fully considered married, but whatever."

Oh, she was getting the dress and the ring and a big dinner with all the people we cared about. I just hadn't had the time to give any of it to her. Though, I had picked up the ring yesterday while she was making tacos. It was a brilliant oval-cut sapphire—the color of the same moonlit night when I'd made her mine.

Though the glowing crescent mark on her shoulder was proof enough, she'd get her ring. She'd get anything she wanted, anything I could give her, anything in my power.

"So let me see if I have this straight. You're worried about work, how people will think of you, and whether or not you'll hurt someone while you're there?"

Wren gave me a little shrug, her perfect white teeth nibbling on her bottom lip.

"Well, I can help with a few of those things. Why don't we get dressed and go down to Factors Walk? You can see how magic reacts around you in the open. We'll bring some of Ames' null wards just in case, and then you'll know how everything will work."

Wren seemed a little skeptical, but hopeful, too. Maybe it would work, and if it didn't, well, we'd figure something out.

"I can't predict how other people see you, but wolf matings are pretty commonplace. No one will think twice about me being your instructor, and once they know you're mated to an Acosta, no one in their right mind would assume you'd give yourself up. Or that I would just sit idly by while my wife skipped off to the Fae realm."

"I just keep thinking that everyone is going to be staring at me the second I walk in there. I'm a Bannister for fuck's sake."

I fit a hand under her neck, squeezing just a little so she'd pay attention.

"No, you aren't. They never inducted you into their coven, they never treated you like family. You share their blood and that's it, Bird. You're an Acosta. It's on your badge and everything. And Acostas don't give a fuck what other people think. You're just as much an Alpha as I am. A fierce protector, a strong, capable leader. Plus," I said, turning us both so she was on top, "if anyone says shit to you, I'll be right there to rip their hearts from their chest."

And I was only half-kidding about that one. Okay, I wasn't kidding. I was so on edge if someone looked at her funny, death was a definite possibility.

"So, let's get dressed and take a walk. Then we can worry about something else. Deal?"

Wren dropped a smoldering kiss to my lips, and it was a struggle to remember that we were supposed to be doing something. Oh, that was right. Leaving the apartment. Somehow, we made it outside, laughing at silly, stupid shit as we tromped down to Factors Walk. It was a hike, but parking down there was a nightmare.

We held hands and stopped at food vendors and shared our finds. It was only when we'd traversed the treacherous stairs down to The Walk that Wren's good mood seemed to dissipate.

"You know, the last time I walked down these steps, I almost face-planted," she said, holding onto my hand so tight it was a wonder blood was making it to the tips of my fingers. "I was so nervous thinking Alice was going to die that I almost broke my neck on these stupid cobblestones."

"I remember," I murmured, pulling her under my arm. "I was trailing a spike in dark magic, and it led me straight to you. I remember seeing you, so nervous, so determined. You were going to that apothecary, and you were getting what you needed."

"Then the fire," she whispered, resting her head on my shoulder.

Her gaze drifted in the direction of where Azalea Apothecary used to stand. In its place was a brand-new apothecary owned by the Horne twins after they bought the land right out from under Carmichael Jones. In a little over two weeks, they'd completely rebuilt the place, and the witch and warlock community was in an uproar about it. Considering the Horne twins had bought out every other apothecary in town except for Jones' place, it was a big fucking deal.

The ABI was just waiting for shit to pop off before stepping in. If there was one thing the arcane community hated, it was a monopoly.

"I don't know why I thought it was still going to be a shell, but..." She shook her head. "I almost wanted proof it happened. Everything was such a whirlwind, I barely had time to grasp it, you know?"

And I did know. Wren would have died had I not pulled her from that building. And then I would have been just like Theo. Bitter, mean, stupid. All because I missed out on the woman I could have spent forever with.

Knowing what I did now, I couldn't imagine missing this—couldn't imagine losing Wren, losing what we had.

But I had found her, and I had pulled her from those flames, and I mated her, and nothing and no one was going to touch her. Not while I still had breath in my lungs.

I just had to remember that every second of every day, and then that panic that seemed to be camping out in my gut would ease.

Right?

We walked on, weaving through arcaners and tourists alike. So far, nothing had blown up, but that didn't mean that we weren't both on edge. Maybe it was my wolf so restless in my head, maybe it was Wren, or maybe it was real danger, but there was something wrong and I couldn't figure out what it was.

No one was looking at us. Nothing bad had happened. Nothing caught fire or exploded, and I knew there was magic about. So what the fuck was it?

"Nico?" Wren breathed, her hand tightening in mine. "I think we need to head back."

Were we just afraid of the world now? Were we so traumatized that we couldn't imagine even leaving the house anymore?

Wren's fingers tightened on mine, and instead of waiting, she pulled me back down the way we'd come. Everything in me screamed danger, but I could not find the source. Was it everywhere? Was it everything?

The sunshine faded away as storm clouds rolled in, sending a chill up my spine as I moved faster. The wind picked up and so did Wren's steps. Hell, we were practically jogging to get out of The Walk, a sea of tourists and arcaners standing in our way as we threaded through the crowd.

Then the first scent of a Bannister witch reached my nose. It was so different from Wren's jasmine and honey perfume. It was broken promises and lies. It was filth and stench and spent magic. And it filled my senses as if Eloise Bannister herself was right in front of me.

"We have to get out of here," Wren hissed, her grip so tight in mine that my bones rubbed together. "I smell them. My family. They're here."

"I do, too."

"Do you think they'll do something here? Out in the open?" she whispered, her gaze darting everywhere to try and find what we both smelled.

Danger had come calling and I'd been so stupid to have us walk here, so stupid to have her out in the open. I should have protected her better.

Because yes, I did think Wren's family would start some shit out in the open. I did think they would attack us in full view of humans. I believed with everything in me that they would hurt her to try and steal some of her power back.

Lightning flashed in the sky as a rolling crack of thunder shook the earth. Wind whipped through the trees and my wolf was screaming at me to run, to get Wren to safety, to get the fuck out of there before they struck us down.

Gripping Wren's hand tight in mine, I tucked her behind me, bowling through the crowd to the staircase. But more and more people piled onto The Walk, flooding it like they were trying to keep us there. Bodies packed into the crooked narrow lane, swarming us, suffocating us until I felt Wren shove them all back.

Humans squawked in protest at being physically moved, but the arcaners seemed unfazed by the small display of magic. She cleared a path, and we sped up the stairs only to stop dead at the top.

A redheaded woman blocked our way, her palm cracking with an orb of electricity. Humans scattered, screaming, but Wren and I stood stock-still. Dressed in a stained white blouse and wrinkled black slacks, Margot Bannister seemed like she'd seen better days. Her hair was a wild curly mess of snarls and mats, her makeup smeared under her eyes. All the glamour magic she'd done to hide her wrinkles had fizzled and died, aging her face thirty years.

"You did this," she hissed, her gaze locked on Wren. "You spoiled little brat. We gave you everything, and this is how you repay us?"

It was a struggle to keep Wren behind me because she really wanted to get a piece of her mother.

"You gave me shit. You stole from me. You took what

wasn't yours to have and then washed your hands of me. Fuck you, Mother. Your time is over."

The laugh that came out of Margot was hysterical enough to haunt my dreams. "Fuck me? Fuck me? Oh, no, daughter. My time is just beginning. You think I won't take everything you have? You think any of it is yours? You think I won't rip everything from you?"

I didn't wait for the blow that was inevitably coming or for Margot to finish whatever bullshit villain monologue she'd worked herself up for. I just ran.

Dragging Wren behind me, I raced for the house. So many blocks, so far, but Wren could keep up now. She let my hand go and we ran together.

But as fast as we ran, we just weren't fast enough.

CHAPTER 17

NICO

THE SHORT TREK TO OUR APARTMENT TOOK FAR TOO long. Probably because the little more than a mile distance turned into a hike all over the damn city as we attempted to avoid the Bannister clan. It seemed every vehicle was out to hit us, every person on the street came to stand in our way. Shop doors opened to slam into us, and cars jumped curbs to try and mow us down.

Obviously, it was magic, had to be, but that didn't mean it wasn't scary as hell.

"Come on, Wren," a woman cackled. "Come out and play." It wasn't Wren's mother, but it sounded enough like her that it could be an aunt or a cousin maybe?

Not that it mattered who it was exactly. The entire Bannister clan was out in force, ready to steal Wren's power for themselves. The Alpha in me wanted to fight, to stand our ground, but the man in me knew better. Just Wren and I could not go against an entire coven of witches—especially not a coven losing every single bit of sway, clout, and power they'd had for three centuries.

That made them far more dangerous than any pack, any nest, anyone. Because losing power made consequences matter a fuck of a lot less.

Covering Wren with my body, I yanked her out of the way as an orb of electricity sailed past us, detonating against the brick wall. The stone exploded, showering us with shrapnel. Humans yelled, cars honked. It was so loud. My senses were in overdrive, bombarded with everything, but especially the fear—both Wren's and mine.

Honestly, if I didn't know better, I'd think we were getting herded, but I did know better, and I knew this city far better than any Bannister could.

Breathing heavy, I guided us through an alleyway behind Price Hall and around another brand-new brewery I'd already forgotten the name of. Lightning slashed the air overhead as rain pelted us, slowing our steps, making the way more treacherous, but I picked up the pace.

"You can't run, Wren. You can't hide. We'll find you. We'll get what we're owed."

"Judith," Wren whispered, her eyes going wide as a shiver worked its way through her.

Wren had told me about her unhinged aunt who had far too much power harnessed under her skin. My mate's shoulders climbed up to her ears as she pulled ahead of me, running faster, her strides lengthening as she sailed down the street. Like she was drawn to it, she headed straight for home, trying to outrun her family, trying to get under the safety of Fiona's wards.

But the Bannisters seemed to be everywhere. On every corner, in every alley, their magic too much, too powerful, too many.

We needed backup.

Yanking the phone from my pocket, I dialed Wyatt. He was just about the only wolf I still trusted to back me up with no questions asked. He didn't answer, but his voicemail did.

"This is Wyatt. You know what to do."

"I'm sorry for not picking up when you called, but I'm fucked, man," I said on a gasping breath, ducking under an awning as hail pelted the ground around us. "Wren's family is gunning for us, and I need backup." I rattled off the address over the roar of ice smacking the street—just about the only way he'd find the place if he weren't following us. "I'll take all the help I can get, brother."

Meaning, if he wanted to bring my family he could, but I wasn't forcing him to choose me over them. The Acostas had been his only home for so long...

Right before we reached Jones Street, a lightning bolt struck one of the giant oaks, knocking the tree down right in front of us. Cars slammed into the thick trunk, and we crossed the slick road, trying not to get hit.

"Come on," Wren yelled, leading me to a slim alley next to our house. It was only about three feet wide, but it was enough to get us under Fiona's wards and to some backup. I gave her a hand up and followed her over, never so glad in my life that we had a Jacobs witch on our side.

Wren collapsed on the stone pavers, her breaths wheezing in and out of her lungs. "I can't... run... anymore."

She couldn't either. As much as she pulled on my wolf, Wren was losing steam. Her limbs were jelly, her emotions and adrenaline a ball of chaos. We'd have to hole up here and fucking pray the wards held.

But I knew damn well Wren's family were about to give us the fight of our life. I texted Erica, calling for her help as well, but I knew it was a stretch to get the ABI here in time. This was happening now.

"Get inside. Bar the doors."

Wren and I barricaded the glass French doors leading to the courtyard before running up the stairs to Hannah's level. She searched, and I went farther upstairs looking for Fiona and Malia. Both were gone, and by the time I made it back to Wren, I knew Hannah was gone, too.

We were going to have to do this on our own.

Thumps on the roof told me Fiona's wards had shredded like tissue paper, not keeping out a coven of that size. And why would it? The Bannister coven was at least fifty witches deep, and even with waning power, they had enough numbers to rip even the most powerful of wards to shreds.

It was already too late to leave, too late to call anyone, too late to get Wren somewhere safe.

As pissed as I was with my family, we should have gone there. Even if my dad was a bastard, even if he betrayed us, they would have helped us against the Bannisters. I knew that much.

Swallowing hard, I held Wren's hand as we crept back

down to our apartment. If the Bannisters knew where we were, we needed stealth to get out of this one.

Stealth and weapons.

In a cabinet under the stairs, I started a small collection with Fiona's help. Potion bombs, handguns, sleeping potions, and enough ammo to start a small war. Usually, I didn't use man-made means to make a kill, but when dealing with witches and as cornered as we were, we'd need it.

"Here," I said, offering Wren her service weapon and a paintball gun filled with sleeping rounds. "And leave off the null wards. We want these to be as effective as they can be."

Wren shivered, but took both guns, fitting the Glock into the belt of her jeans and priming the paintball gun. The echo of a door caving in upstairs rocked through the house, and our eyes met. Wren's were filled with tears she had no intention of shedding, and mine was with the knowledge of what was really about to go down.

Both of us wouldn't make it out of here.

Both of us weren't going to see tomorrow.

Both of us wouldn't stay breathing.

But she would. Wren would live. She would breathe. She would carry on without me.

My gaze tracked to the courtyard. It was still clear. Wren could leave out the back and run while I held them off. She could get to safety. Go to the ABI building where we should have gone in the first fucking place. Erica would protect her.

"I need you to go, Wren," I whispered, staring at those French doors like they were the key to everything. Because I couldn't look at her—not and tell her to leave. "You need to get out of here."

"No." Wren didn't look at me, either. No, she was staring at the door to upstairs like it had done her wrong and she'd really enjoy shooting whoever it was on the other side of it.

Grabbing her shoulder, I made her face me. "I *need* you to go. I can hold them off. You can get safe."

She shrugged me off, planting a hand in my chest. Her fingers fisted in my shirt like she never wanted to let me go. "I'm not going anywhere. You heard me yesterday. The only way I'm leaving is if it's with you. You want to go? Fine. Lead the way. I'll follow you."

Another crash sounded, closer this time. They were on Hannah's level, her aunt's voice calling for Wren with a sing-song tone that had the hairs on the back of my neck standing on end.

We were out of time.

I cupped her face in my hands. "We both aren't going to make it out. I can distract them so you can get somewhere safe. Wren, please. Please, Bird. I need you to be safe."

Wren's tears finally fell, her shuddering breaths heaving in her chest.

"No," she sobbed. "Not without you. I'll never be safe—never be happy—without you. Please just let me stay. I'd rather die by your side than live a thousand years without you in them."

Pressing a fevered kiss to her lips, I prayed there was a way out for us. Because she wasn't going to die in this fucking house at the hands of her family. No way, no how.

Wren's tongue met mine, tasting me like she was saying goodbye.

Like this was our last kiss.

Like the world was ending.

Maybe it was.

When I pulled away, a faint smile touched her lips. A smile that died as magic slammed into the door I was holding shut. The wood splintered, cracked, and Wren's fear flooded our connection. Glass breaking drew my attention, but I'd never been so happy to see who was on the other side of it.

Wyatt shoved through the furniture we used as a barricade, his shoulder landing right next to mine as I struggled to keep the door closed. "You called, boss?"

Nodding, I jerked my head to Wren. "Get her out of here for me, will you? Get her safe. Don't let her out of your sight. You got me?" I swallowed hard, knowing this would be the last time I'd see either of them. "That's an order."

Wyatt straightened, the mirth in his blue eyes dying as he studied my face. He knew exactly what was happening, exactly what I was saying. "Okay, Nic."

Without missing a beat, he latched onto Wren's wrist and tossed her over his shoulder.

"What? No," Wren shouted, kicking and scratching, trying to get out of Wyatt's hold. "Don't do this, Nico. Please."

But Wyatt was fast, so fast Wren didn't have time to get away from him. She didn't have time to say goodbye. But I had all the time in the world to watch her go, her red hair streaming over her teary face—a face that would haunt me in the afterlife.

They sailed up the wall and over it, racing to the safety I could not provide for her.

"I love you, Bird," I whispered, knowing she was far enough away that she couldn't hear me.

The door bulged, the magic on the other side of it shoving me forward.

I'd hold that damn door as long as I could, and when they killed me, I'd die smiling because I knew Wren was free.

She was free and she was safe, and she was somewhere they wouldn't get her.

But first, I'd take a few of them down with me.

CHAPTER 18

WREN

"Put me down," I ordered, praying I was pulling on just enough of Nico's power that the Alpha would leak out of my voice.

I needed Wyatt to let me go.

I needed him to let me go back.

I needed to get to Nico before my family did.

Please. I'll do anything. I'll pay anything. Just let me keep him safe. Please.

The sound of a car's brakes screeching had Wyatt pausing, his steps faltering enough for me to struggle out of his hold. And yes, I might have kneed him in the stomach on the way down, but that didn't stop him from grabbing my wrist and keeping me from Nico.

"Wren," Ellie yelled from the passenger side of her

mother's shit box of a car. "Get in the car. We have to get you out of here."

But I couldn't. I had to go back for Nico. I wasn't hamstrung by that stupid curse they put on me anymore. I could do... *something*. I'd only ever given power away, sure, but I could do something. Anything. I had to try. It was better than just letting him die.

I'd seen the look on my grandmother's face back in Blue Ridge. Even if I wasn't with him, they'd kill Nico out of spite. They'd kill him to hurt me. They'd kill him because they could.

"Get in the car, Wren," Wyatt growled, his wolf so close to the surface, his blue eyes glowed in the low light. The storm was still brewing overhead, ready to rain down from the heavens at any moment. "Don't make me shove you in that gods-damned trunk. Nico wanted you safe, and I'm making that so, even if I have to knock your ass out to do it."

"We don't have much time," Ellie insisted. "Your family is coming, Wren."

Orbs of magic bombarded the house, shaking the very ground we were standing on. My aunt Judith's cackle made all the hairs on my arms stand on end. She was in there with Nico. She'd do awful things to him. I couldn't leave him.

All of this felt wrong. It felt wrong to leave Nico. It felt wrong to get in a car and speed away. It felt wrong that it was Wyatt here and not my husband. It was wrong that after all we'd survived already that we'd be pulled apart this way.

It wasn't fair.

"I'll fight them. I can do it," I insisted. "Please don't make me leave him."

Wyatt gave me a sympathetic expression as his hands

landed on my shoulders, the weight of them too much, too little, too...

"It was his last wish to make you safe. Please let me give him that much."

Tears stung my nose as an ache grew in my chest, in my heart. My gaze fell on the wall that secluded the courtyard.

It was his last wish.

Sobs ripped up my throat as I spun, marching to Ellie's car and opening the door. But as soon as I did, the car itself melted away. Ellie melted away. As if spun by a dream, she dissolved in a puff of smoke.

The door, however, did not, and as much as I tried, I could not let go of it. It transformed before my eyes, morphing from the beat-up tan sedan door with the primer spot into an intricate one made of wood and crystal and vines. It was bigger than I was and nearly three times as wide with an arched top and a rough crystal handle.

Oh. Oh, no. Oh, fuck.

"I don't— What's going on?" I turned to Wyatt, but his face was the picture of regret.

"I didn't want to do this, you know. Sacrificing one for another seemed so wrong. Pen would have hated me for it. But I have to get her back. I have to get my little girl back."

Wyatt's face lost some of its fullness as his skin lightened from the golden tan to a sickly pale. His hair went from a dark blond to a lank brown and he shortened about six inches, his width withering before my eyes.

Wyatt hadn't pulled me from the building.

Wyatt wasn't here.

I didn't know this man, and I didn't know if he was wearing a glamour or—

Pen. Penelope Lewis. An illusion mage missing for twenty-five years.

"Pen is your daughter?" Of all the ways to make a liar out of myself, I chose to go this route. I swore to Nico I wouldn't sacrifice myself for Agent Lewis. I'd sworn I would stay safe, stay with him, and in my one test, I failed.

He nodded. "It was the only way to get her back. You had to open the door. It had to be your choice."

Of course it had to be my choice. It had been a forced one, but mine, nonetheless. I tried to let go of the crystal handle, but vines from the edges curled around my wrist, making that impossible. Damn if I didn't try, though.

"He swore he'd get her back for me. Swore that she would come home. The Fae have to honor the deals they make."

I didn't have the heart to tell this man that a Fae could twist every single aspect of a deal to suit their needs. He already knew. His eyes said it all. He didn't care if she returned alive or dead, as long as she came back to him.

"Is my family even attacking the house?" I hissed, still trying to yank my hand free as a weight settled in my gut.

Every sleepless night trying not to think about Desmond. Every single nightmare, worrying about the dark Fae out there like the fucking boogeyman, and this asshole just up and made me open the gods-damned Fae door myself. If it weren't so damn smart, I'd start screaming.

The man shook his head. "No. I needed you at this gate in particular. It was the easiest way I could think of to get you here."

My gaze went back to the wall. At least Nico was safe. No one would hurt him. No one would kill him. I chose not to think about what would befall me, regardless of however long it took to deliver me to Desmond. Or how Nico would feel with me gone. I'd seen his eyes at that damn Italian place. He'd been crazed, panicked.

The illusion bombarding the house died as well, dissolving in a puff of smoke as my aunt Judith's laugh faded away on the wind. The wind itself died, as did the storm, the rain drying up as if it had never been here at all.

I wanted to yell for Nico—I really did—but something made me stop. Yes, he'd be crazed with worry, but he'd be alive. I had no idea what was coming out of that door, and I didn't want Nico to meet that head-on. He'd sacrificed himself to save me.

I'd gladly do the same for him.

So I kept my mouth shut and prayed Nico didn't come out here.

"Do you care that she might not be alive? That he could twist that deal until you end up owing him? You'd sacrifice someone who has never done you wrong for a maybe?"

He tilted his head to the side. "Would you not do the same? I can see inside your head—it's how I create what you most fear. You would sacrifice the world to save your husband. And he would do the same for you. How is it wrong that I would do that for my daughter?"

I couldn't say exactly. Probably because it affected me. Maybe because it hurt Nico, and anyone else who would look for me.

But before I could say any of that, a dark-haired man dressed all in black strode from the open door.

"Where is she?" the illusion mage demanded, a long sword forming in his hand.

"Your tricks don't work on me, mage, just like your daughter's never worked on my father."

The mage ground his teeth, straightening like he knew something the man in black did not. "Do you know what illusion mages can do when they get to be my age? They make dream reality. Don't test me. Where is Penelope? Where is my daughter?"

The man in black firmed his mouth, raising a single eyebrow as he gestured to the open door. Two people walked out of it. One was a lanky man with a hunched back and ripped clothes, and the other was a woman who looked no older than I did. She struggled with her cane, favoring the wrong side of it like she'd never used one before. And that was likely due to the prosthetic she was using, which appeared to be made of a living wood carved into the shape of a foot.

"Penelope," he breathed, reaching for the woman and snatching her off her feet, his sword gone in a puff of smoke.

"Papa?"

And while this was touching and all, I was still trying to get the fucking door to let me go. Because I knew damn well what happened after this. If the deal was complete, then I was the price paid, and I had no intention of going through that damn door.

Force wasn't working, so I tried a little magic, shoving power into the vines in the hopes that it shocked them somehow. But shoving power into them only tightened them on my skin, the damn things growing stronger.

Perfect.

"I suggest you make your way, mage," the man in black advised, tucking his hair behind a very pointed ear. "The wolf will follow your scent soon enough."

The mage nodded, tucking his daughter under his arm and disappearing into another puff of fucking smoke. If I made it out of this, I would wrap a null ward around his neck and kick him in the junk.

Then the Fae's gaze moved to me. "And you. For someone so powerful, you seem to fuck up a whole lot. Who falls for an illusion mage's tricks?"

With nothing else for it, I flipped the asshole off. "People who can't see through them, dipshit. Got any more probing questions?"

A faint smile tipped up his lips. "My father is going to hate you. Personally, I love it. His plaything is a mouthy youngling with magic she can't control. It serves him right."

Oh, goodie, just what I always wanted. To be a plaything for a fucking tyrant.

"You seem to dislike dear old dad. Why don't you make this door let me go and I'll skip off into the sunset. No muss, no fuss."

Was I trying to strike a Fae deal? Had I sniffed glue in the last thirty seconds, and no one told me?

"You see, I would. You seem nice enough. A little rough around the edges, but nothing too bad. You don't deserve what's about to happen. But I need him occupied and contained while I seal these bloody doors shut, and you're just the proper distraction. Sorry, love, them's the breaks."

He lifted his chin to the squirrely looking dude who I could break in half with a good poke to the ribs. "I'll see to it your family is taken care of."

"Wait," I pleaded, realizing a little late what was going on. "Don't do this. I have to get out. I have to get the rest of them out." Because if Penelope was alive after twenty-five years, the other women could be, too. I'd sort of made peace with the fact that I was going in there. I hadn't with the fact that I might not come back out.

Dark eyes speared me with regret. "There is no getting out. Not for you, Wren Bannister, and not for anyone else left in the Fae realm. We've done enough damage. It's time for these doors to die."

The skinny guy wrapped his spindly hand around my bicep, his grip far stronger than I'd thought it was going to be. "Come on, witch."

At his words, the vines unwrapped from my wrist, and I was free—or rather free-ish. I tried yanking my arm from his grip, but I couldn't move him an inch.

"Let me go," I screeched, planting my feet as he tried pulling me toward the door.

"Wren," Nico shouted, his voice so welcome and so not all at the same time. I met his gaze, finding it instantly as if my eyes were drawn to him. He was coming over the wall, somehow knowing exactly where I was. In an instant, Nico jumped to his wolf, the animal racing for us, trying to get to me before I was dragged into oblivion.

The Fae in black sighed as he shot darkness from his hand,

the oily blackness so thick it was like a wall separating Nico from the rest of us.

"I am sorry for this, Wren. Maybe one day you'll understand why I had to do this. Maybe you'll know it was the right decision."

But I wasn't listening to the Fae. I was still trying to rip my arm from the iron grip of the spindly man and get to my mate.

"Nico," I pleaded, but before I could get away, I was through the door, and it was closing on us. "Nico!"

The door sealed shut, cutting off all light, all warmth. The air in this blackness was cold, cold and wet and smelled of death. And I wanted no part of going wherever this dude wanted me to.

"Let me go," I yelled, my voice echoing off what sounded like stone.

Instantly, the man let me go. "If that's what you want," he said as I stumbled and fell, landing hard on my ass on the rough, cold ground. "But I can see in the dark. Can you?"

A few days ago, I could, but... That was with me drawing on Nico's wolf. That was with a shifter's eyes, a shifter's power. I had a feeling that as far away as Nico was, there was no way I could use what he'd given me. Now, I was stuck with what I'd been born with and that wasn't the greatest night vision.

"No, I can't," I admitted, slowly getting to my feet. After having Nico's wolf for just a few days, the lack of light and sound and smell made me feel like my head was under water.

"Then, I'll guide you," he said, latching onto my hand. "Try not to talk to Desmond too much. He'll twist your words until you've agreed to something you had no intention of agreeing to. That's how Pen lost her foot."

No talking. Got it.

"My name is Cyrus, by the way, and we are sorry for this. Tristan never wanted to entrap you, but it was the only way. He couldn't take another woman being sold—another life wasted. I'll try to keep you out of the thick of it."

Those were the last words Cyrus spoke for a very long while. We walked down that dark corridor for what seemed like hours, our steps echoing off the stone enough to rattle my brain.

And by the time we made it to anything resembling light, I began to wish I would have stayed in that damned hallway forever.

CHAPTER 19

WREN

The light in the Fae realm was a dim, weak illumination from a muted sun and too much hazy cloud cover. The large windows of the throne room—or what I assumed was a throne room—let what passed for sunshine through, painting the scene of what I figured Hell might look like if it were trying too hard.

The floors were blood-red and black—either from actual blood or a design choice from some macabre stylist's nightmare. The walls seemed to bleed a dark-red sap that could have been actual blood or something else entirely. The throne itself was black, high-backed, and tufted with a material that could have been velvet or something more sinister like skin or hair. Cages were suspended from the ceiling, some all the way up to impossible heights and some almost touching the floor. Each of them held a person or an animal, each of them smelled like literal death, and each one ticked my anger up about a zillion notches.

It was incredibly difficult to be scared when I wanted to commit murder.

The man on the throne seemed bored, like a spoiled child looking for his next plaything. But that wasn't to say he wasn't beautiful. Just like his son, Desmond was dark-haired and dressed in all black. His jaw was sharp, his cheekbones prominent, and his lips full. His hair fell in a sleek waterfall, only interrupted by what might be a bone crown filled with sparkling stones. But where his son's eyes were a rich brown, Desmond's were the palest blue, the irises glowing in the low light like glittering diamonds.

He sat casually, one ankle resting on the other knee but exuded a manic sort of calm, as if everything from his posture to his crown was fake. As if everything I saw was affected rather than natural. Even the foliage outside was a pale representation of spooky trees, their limbs like fingers reaching to the sky.

Honestly, I was having trouble not rolling my eyes.

Okay, sure, in theory all this was scary. Of course in a normal person's brain, bleeding walls and prisoners strung up in cages would be the height of fear. But at a certain point, it was like, "Okay, we get it already." It reminded me of those haunted houses Ellie and I used to go to when we were teenagers that were so over the top, they were hilarious. This whole thing—from the realm to the king to the castle itself— was just trying too hard.

Cyrus let go of my hand as we approached the raised

platform, moving ahead of me as if to announce the fact that we were here. Fair enough.

"Sire, I have procured Wren Bannister as requested," Cyrus said, bowing so low it was a wonder he didn't melt into the floor.

Desmond's smile could have been alluring if it wasn't so joyless. His eyes were dead, the upturn to his lips fake, his whole posture just...

This was the man I'd been too scared to think about?

This was the guy I was supposed to be afraid of?

He was a fucking joke.

And procured? Was that a fancy way of saying he kidnapped me and dragged my ass down here? Because the euphemism was lacking.

"Very good, Cyrus," Desmond said on a sigh, but not one of pleasure. It was as if he was bored with himself, too. "You may leave us. Take your pet Elizabeth with you as a reward."

Cyrus shot me a repentant expression before opening the cage closest to my left. From it, he lifted a small woman from the confines and cradled her to his chest. Cyrus had said he'd try to help me, but he was more worried about the woman in his arms than me at the moment.

I couldn't say I blamed him. And I wasn't sure I needed his help, anyway.

"Well, on with it," Desmond ordered, peeling something rancid from the wooden platter to his right and slurping it into his mouth. "Show me your power."

Frowning, I just stood there. Unless he planned on using magic of his own, I was sort of at a loss. I knew I had power, but using it? Well, that was the rub, wasn't it?

"Do you speak, girl? Or are you a mute?"

Tilting my head to the side, I examined the dark Fae. I should have really saved all my worry for my family. Aunt Judith had this guy beat on her worst day and Eloise? Eloise would eat him for breakfast and shit him out by lunch. Hell, even the illusion mage's nightmare was scarier than this.

"Desmond, I take it. Hmm." I hummed my disapproval just like old Eloise would. Normally, I would hate the lessons my grandmother had taught me, but ripping someone's psyche apart with just my tone and words was a skill I'd picked up from her. And damn if I wasn't taught by a fucking master. "I thought you'd be taller."

If there is one thing I excelled at, it was annoying the fuck out of people—*just ask Grandma*. Might as well figure out where this asshole's buttons were, and the only way to do that was by pressing all of them. At once.

"And cuter." I tapped on my bottom lip, letting my gaze roam his body. He enjoyed imprisoning people? He enjoyed making people suffer? Well, he was going to know what it was like to be treated like a thing. "I suppose movies really have surpassed reality—even Fae reality. Pity."

Desmond's eyes flashed a darker blue as his smile faded. His relaxed posture tightened as he sat up straighter, his feet finding the floor.

"You would do well to watch your tongue before I cut it from your head."

First blood. A complete poser and vain to boot? Oh, this was going to be sweet.

"Big talk from a guy who had to send a runner to fetch me. Did I hurt your feelings?" I faked a pout. "Do you need a hug?"

If I was going to be here a while—and I sort of figured I would be, considering Desmond's son planned on closing the Fae gates forever and all—then I wanted to make this guy's life a living fucking hell. If everyone and everything I loved was lost to me? Well, he was going to really regret asking me to talk.

"I mean this is a hell of a lot of posturing you've got going on here," I said, gesturing to well, everything. "This is the Unseelie Court and not Hell, right? I mean, I'm not hating the whole torture and pain thing you've got going on, I just think you might need a little help with the execution is all. It has the air of trying too hard, don't you think? Plus, you might need to fire your decorator. Pronto."

Desmond leaned forward in his chair, practically vibrating with rage. *Oh, touchy, touchy.* Maybe he was the designer here.

"Maybe I'll cut out your eyes since you hate the place so much. See how you like it in the dark."

My smile had to be simpering, but that was what I was going for. "Just jumping in with all the clichés right off the bat, huh? Not going to space them out, or anything? Talk about blowing your wad too early."

Desmond flew from his chair, a blade in hand, seemingly conjured from nothing. He was on me before I could even blink. But even as I felt the breeze of the knife slide through me, the pain never came.

Opening both my eyes, I stared in shock as the cold weight in my middle seemed to intensify just a smidge. And that was because Desmond's hand—knife and all—was indeed in the general vicinity of my stomach. The problem for him was the blade, hand, and the wrist attached to it all sort of just passed on through.

Like I was a ghost or an apparition or... I didn't know what. What I did know was that Desmond seemed rather put out that his blade did exactly fuck all. He moved to backhand me, but his hand slid through my head like I was made of smoke.

I had no idea what was going on. I had definitely been hit before. Girard had done it not even a week ago, and I distinctly remembered Diana's knife slicing through my throat. That didn't mean I wasn't going to run with it, though.

"Wow. This must be really embarrassing for you. Big, bad dark Fae and you can't even hurt me. I've heard impotency is a real self-esteem killer." I sucked in a breath through my teeth as I let my gaze drift in the direction of his crotch. "Ouch."

Desmond reached for my face, his fingertips passing through my flesh. "What are you?"

Shrugging, I skirted around the arguably tall Fae, wondering if I could touch things or if things just couldn't touch me.

"I don't know. I suppose you could call me a witch, but that's not quite right, now, is it? Your guess is as good as mine. You're the one who wanted me here. You tell me, Tinkerbell."

Stopping at the first cage I could reach, I swept my hand over the lock. If I could touch it, I could pick it—in theory. If I could pick it, then I could get these people out of here. Again, in theory. Who knew if Tristan was successful in closing the Fae portals?

Who knew if Nico had broken through his magic and ripped him limb from limb?

One could only hope.

The cold stone-like metal brushed against my skin without passing through, the first win of the day. But it still didn't tell me why I could touch things, but Desmond couldn't touch me—a fact that became clearer and clearer since his Fae ass was currently trying to punch me in the head.

"This must be a huge bummer, right. I mean first you try to nab me yourself, but that backfires," I said, ticking off his failures on my fingers, completely ignoring his attempts to hurt me. "Then you try to get Girard to do it, but he shits the bed—not once, but three times. Now your son handles your little fuck-up, but you can't touch me. Which Fate did you piss off, buddy?"

Yeah, I was getting out of here, and I was taking every single prisoner with me. I just needed a plan that did not involve me stumbling around in the dark like an idiot.

"The Fates have no dominion here," he growled, his body right in my bubble.

My smile was simpering as I let my gaze travel down his body and up to his face. "Clearly. If they did, maybe they'd hire you a decent decorator."

I turned my back to him, exploring the throne room. Based on the coppery smell, it was indeed blood running down the walls, but I wasn't sure if it was arcaner blood, Fae blood, or some kind of animal. The throne was also made of burned skin? And his crown—which I hadn't gotten a good look at before—was made from bones and pretty blue jewels that matched his eyes.

Again, the try-hard in this place was fucking pathetic, and I was already bored. I needed to get back to Nico before he lost his mind, and this whole thing was getting in the way of that.

"Well, hoss, I'm assuming you wanted me here for a reason, and I doubt it's to listen to the tale of how your supplier of arcaner playthings got his throat ripped out. So what is it? Why go to all this trouble?" I gave him my most pitying expression. "Were you bored? You look bored. Fuck, I'm bored, and I just got here."

That was it, wasn't it? I wasn't scared here because I had nothing to lose. Everything I wanted was back home. Every threat? It was far away where he couldn't reach. My happiness? Was with Nico, with my friends, with the small little family I made for myself.

And I wanted it back.

"You are supposed to be an amplifier, a way to tap into all the power I have been denied. You're supposed to bring me my throne," he hissed, wanting to smack me around but missing the mark over and over again.

My whole body pivoted to the skin chair and back. "You mean that tacky thing? Weren't you just sitting on it?"

Desmond skirted around me, heading for the chair. "Stupid girl. This is not my realm and not my throne. This is my prison and yours. The Seelie Queen stuck me here when our marriage deteriorated, the petty bitch."

"Of course, and I'm sure nothing at all predicated said alienation. You're clearly the saint in this whole situation."

Yes, and I was a purple alien named Blerp.

"You will hold your tongue, witch," he said, his voice taking on a sort of influence, kind of like when Nico did his Alpha thing, but far less effective.

"Sorry." I shrugged. "That's not really my style. Can I offer you a sarcastic comment?"

Desmond's eyes narrowed and he stroked his chin like a gods-damned vaudeville villain. "I can't touch you. I can't influence you. But I wonder if my other pets can. I've collected many pretty pets over the years, you know."

A tiny little trickle of fear threaded through the boredom. Cyrus could touch me, and if Cyrus could, it was completely possible Desmond's other prisoners could, too. And I really hoped the *what the fuck* I was thinking wasn't showing on my face.

Because the illusionist had been very thorough in his conjuring, and that gun I had stuffed into my belt? Well, it was nothing more than air. The paintball gun filled with sleeping potion? Never existed. The potion bombs I'd stuffed in my pocket?

Yep. You guessed it. Gone just like all his other delusions in a puff of fucking smoke.

That didn't mean I didn't have any weapons at my disposal. There were chains and rocks and…

Okay, unless I found a sword somewhere or a really fancy handgun, I was fucked.

And this is why we keep our mouths shut, Wren. So we don't anger Fae Kings into getting creative with their punishments.

"If that's what you want, hoss. But how is that getting you your throne again? I thought you wanted power. Power I seem to have and you don't. Personally, I think you're going about this all wrong—especially since all the power in the world isn't going to help you get out of here."

I was totally bullshitting, but throwing Desmond's son under the bus was about the only card I had.

"Because your son closed down the Fae gates all nice and

tight. I have a feeling you can't open them, either. He sent me here as a distraction, and just like a toddler with a brand-new toy, you fell right for it."

Desmond let out a little whistle, snapping his fingers as a real smile finally stretched across his face.

I didn't see the rock aimed for my temple until it was too late, but I sure as shit felt it. Light bloomed in my skull as the pain slammed into me.

And the last thing I saw was Desmond tossing his head back and laughing like a villain in a cartoon.

Prick.

CHAPTER 20

WREN

I was getting really tired of concussions. Like, was it me? Was I a head injury magnet of some kind? Or was I just usually in the wrong place at the wrong time with the wrong powers and a big fucking mouth.

Groaning, I tried peeling myself from the cold floor. After doing this once already this month, I remembered to sit up slowly and hope for no vomiting. The stench from the place was atrocious, so the "no vomiting" thing was tenuous at best, but I did what I could.

My cell was made of stone and a living sort of metal. And by living, the shit seemed to breathe, the cracks lit by an ominous green glow that brightened and dimmed with each breeze that flit through the space.

Cozy.

Other than a bucket and a set of bars, the cell was barren,

the light only from the bars themselves and the torch sconces dotting the corridor beyond. Moans echoed through the dungeon—and this was most definitely a dungeon—like I was stuck on a haunted house playlist on repeat.

"Of all the places you could have found yourself in, you made it all the way down here," a woman scolded, scaring the absolute shit out of me. My head whipped to the left and right, but no one—and I did mean no one—was there.

A moment later, a woman appeared at my bars, a golden light in the middle of this darkness as she surveyed my predicament. Her hair was the darkest of blacks while her skin was a warm bronze that reminded me of sunshine and springtime and long, lazy days by the pool. Sharp eyebrows and cheekbones were tempered by a dusting of freckles across her nose and her eyes resembled the greenest of grasses.

"Yes, because getting kidnapped is the height of fun for me," I muttered, trying to peel my ass off the floor. So far, I'd only managed my upper body, but I'd get there. Eventually. "*What do you want to do today, Wren? Get kidnapped? Sounds swell.* Circumstances are out of my control. Obviously."

Her face—as pretty as it was—got infinitely less pretty when she gave me a skeptical glance. "Who falls for an illusionist's magic? Not once, but enough they don't even think to bring a weapon—"

Okay, that was it. "Not all of us can see through them, you know. And I appreciate the visit and all, but who are you, and why are you interrupting my perfectly good nap with insults and *judgeyness*?"

The lady fit a hand to her hip. "You were much more

pleasant as a toddler. I remember you distinctly saying I was the most beautiful woman you'd ever seen."

That... was new information. "Still true, but that doesn't tell me who you are."

"Call me Áine. To others I'm known as the Seelie Queen. To my ex-husband I'm the definition of Hell itself. Really, it depends on who you ask."

"And we've met before?"

She leaned closer. "You caught that, did you? I wondered, with the head injury and all. I suppose I'll have to fill you in now that Eloise has wiped me from your brain." She studied my face like I was particularly interesting.

Then a tremor shook through the place, the torches flared as the bar began to glow brighter. "Quick and dirty version, then?"

"Uh... sure?"

She smiled as if she was remembering a fond memory. "At four years old, you went on an adventure during... I believe a field trip with your school. Instead of the safe outing to a park with small children, it turned into you falling through a Fae door right into my throne room."

That... was not the story I got, and trying to think about it made my head hurt. I rubbed my temple, suppressing a gag when the world shook again.

"You walked right up to me and called me beautiful and asked for me to take you home. But when I tried to touch you, to take your hand, it passed right through."

"Sounds familiar," I groaned, the spike in my head doubling in strength.

The ground shook a little more, harder this time, and it took everything in me to not vomit all over the floor.

"Yes, well, we might not be able to touch you, but you, my dear, can touch us. You grabbed my hand and ordered me to take you home. That your mother would be worried. And so, I did."

I tried remembering anything about this but all I got was one big blank.

"You'd been gone so long, people had stopped looking for you. But I still honored the promise I made and brought you to your mother. I had no idea when I did, or just what they'd do to you, or how much power they would steal. Honestly, I am a much better judge of character."

"This is an awesome story of my childhood that I had no idea existed and all, but mind telling me why the earth is shaking like a damn maraca?"

"Okay, I see it now. You were just as precocious as a child." She studied me a little longer. "The reason the earth is shaking is because you are not supposed to be here. And the sooner I get you home, the better. But first, you need to get yourself out of that cell."

The world rattled again, harder this time, nearly knocking me off my feet. "Love to, lady. You got a manual in your pocket on how to do that or…"

"I really ought to turn your grandmother into a slug or something. She taught you nothing? After all the instruction I gave her? Honestly." Áine rolled her eyes and fit both hands on her hips. "You can give power, sure, but you can take it as well. Not just from others, but from the very universe itself. You draw on the energy of the ether no matter where you are. As a child born under particularly auspicious stars, it is all at your disposal. It is up to you to use it."

Super. That just cleared everything right up.

"If I wanted to open a door in a place like this, I might draw on the magic that held the door shut. Rendering it inert."

Maybe it was the head injury, maybe it was the pretty lady in the gold gown, but I figured it couldn't hurt to try. A careful step later, and I was hanging onto the bars for dear life as the world rocked again. This time, the stone ceiling cracked, hissing like a snake as it settled.

Okay, it was time to move this shit along. But I'd only ever given magic, I didn't know how to take it.

"Remember the feeling of Nico healing you, taking away your pain, siphoning it into himself. Try it that way."

Swallowing hard, I did what she said, trying to pull the magic into myself like Nico would have done to my wounds. This magic was dark, not putrid, but not good, either. It was almost a living, breathing thing, and it hissed in pain as I took from it. But the light in the bars died, the lock clanking open with a welcome thud.

"Very good. Now let's get out of here." Áine held out her hand.

I didn't take it—too wary of too much help. Especially in this place. "Lead the way."

Smiling, she turned, leading me down the hallway at a fast clip I could barely keep up with. And I followed her until I got to the next cell. The smell was awful, but the girl on the ground was barely older than I was. Dressed in tattered rags, she was curled in on herself, shivering.

"Wait. Can't we bring them?" I grabbed onto her bars,

pulling with the same sort of energy I'd used on my own.

"Stop," Áine hissed as another tremor rocked the entire foundation to its core. "We don't have time. This world is eating itself with you here. We have to go. Now. If we don't, there will be nothing and no one left for you to save." She reached for me again, her palm upturned. "Take my hand, Wren. I'll bring you back—to your world, to your Nico. That's what you want, isn't it?"

Shaking my head, I dropped my hold on the bars. "Prove you can't touch me, and I'll follow you."

Maybe it was my general distrust of literally anything in this place, but I didn't think taking Áine's hand was such a good idea. Sighing, she placated me, her fingers passing through my body like vapor.

"See. No Fae can harm you here. Please. I just want to take you home before this world implodes and takes mine with it."

She forcefully shook her hand in front of my face, begging me to take the offered help. "Fine. But if shit goes sideways, I'm coming back here and watching this place turn to dust myself."

Áine huffed out a laugh. "I would expect nothing less."

Reluctantly, I put my hand in hers, and as soon as I did, we didn't just move. We moved. A moment later, we weren't in that dungeon anymore, we were at the base of a mountain, its dark spires reaching for the muted sky.

Áine gestured to a door, the crystal handle and vined detail very familiar. "My son closed many doors, but not all of them. This will take you back to your world, but you need to hurry. I fear once again, you've been gone too long."

Warily, I grabbed the handle, turning the crystal in my

palm as the world shook again. A fissure opened up in between Áine and I, the earth falling away as I threw the door open and jumped inside.

"Be careful, young Wren. And hurry," Áine called and then the door shut, sealing me in the same darkness that had enveloped me on the way here.

Shakily, I stood, running my fingers against the cool stone walls, pressing forward in the dark. I walked for what felt like hours, the tunnel getting warmer as I trudged home, hoping the next turn, the next step was the one to take me back.

After a while I got scared, a feeling I hadn't quite had in the Fae realm. Was it because it felt fake? Was it the realm itself that leeched my fear? Or was it too close to a childhood memory of getting shoved into a closet for my liking?

A question for the ages.

Faintly up ahead, an orange glow filtered into the hall, softly illuminating the rough bricks and unlit sconces. I couldn't help it, I raced for the light, praying this was it, this was home, this was...

The door itself was hot to the touch, almost burning, and if I hadn't been trapped in the fucking dark, I would have thought about what that might mean before I shoved it open. Fire raged beyond, consuming a large oak tree like it was dry kindling. The grass was burning embers and the roar of it all filled my ears.

But I couldn't go back, I could only go forward.

Stomach churning, I headed for the lone spot that seemed safe, a small patch of green in a sea of flames. My skin scalded as I ran, the smoke burning my lungs as I raced through the blaze. Shaking, I landed on the lone patch of green earth before scrambling farther into the street. A fire engine screamed down the road, nearly taking me out as I crossed to safety.

It took me a second to get my bearings. This was the earth realm, and this was Savannah, but the place was in chaos. People walked right by like there wasn't a huge blaze just taking out Chatham Square. Cars screeched as people crossed the street without warning. And no one seemed too concerned about the flames jumping from tree to tree or that they might take out the houses next.

Home. I needed to go home. Orienting myself, I headed north, cutting through an alley to the courtyard. Only, when I struggled over the wall, nothing seemed right. All the ivy was dead, and the house was dark. That ivy had been lush and green just hours ago. The French doors leading to my apartment were shattered to bits, hanging from the hinges in pieces. My apartment was empty, dust covered everything, my stuff gone.

"Nico," I yelled, the fear really coming in strong now. "I'm home."

But the house echoed with my calls. I raced up the stairs, the stale air hitting my nose as I forced open the door to Hannah's level. Dried blood smeared the hallway hardwood leading to the front door, and the alarm bells just would not stop ringing in my head.

"Fiona? Malia? Hannah? Nico? Somebody answer me."

But all I got was silence. Silence when I checked every room, every closet. Silence when I picked up the house phone, only to get nothing but static. Silence when I cried at the bottom of the steps, the fear clawing up my throat.

Was I dead? Did I die? Did they?

Swallowing hard, I pulled myself up. Someone had to have answers. Someone had to be breathing. Someone had to know something.

The only other place I could think of to go was the same place I'd gone when I'd skinned my knee as a kid and where I'd gone when I'd gotten stood up freshman year.

Ellie and Alice.

But the Savannah I'd left was not the same one I'd come back to. Stores were boarded up and restaurants closed. The streetlights were off or broken and the traffic ones were blinking red in all directions. Trash burned in barrels in the alley, even though it was sticky hot outside and the people surrounding them held their hands out for warmth.

I picked up the pace, running the last two miles to Ellie's as if someone or something was following me.

Ellie's house was different, too. The windows had bars on them, for one, and two? There were cameras pointed in every direction. Salt covered the entirety of her stoop, the granules crunching underfoot as I banged on the screen door.

"Ellie," I called, practically shivering in fear.

She had to be home. Had to be. She was home and alive and so was I and things were fine. They were fine.

Far too many moments later, the door opened, a double-barreled shotgun leading the way with Ellie right behind it. I backed up a step, tossing my hands in the air as I got off her front porch.

"Ellie?"

"Wren?" she breathed, her eyes wide as saucers. Shakily, she unloaded the shotgun and unchained the bars, wrapping her arms around me in a hug so tight it healed a part of my soul.

I was alive. I was really here, and I wasn't dead in the Fae realm somewhere. I made it.

"Where have you been? It's been so long. We all thought you were dead." She rocked back and forth, not letting me go for an instant.

"I don't understand. What happened? I was gone for a day—tops—and I come back and it's like *Mad Max* and the fucking *Thunderdome*. What is going on? Where is everyone? Where is Nico and Alice and my friends?"

Ellie pulled away and met my gaze, gripping my shoulders like she'd fall down if she let me go.

"What do you mean you were gone for a day?" She shook her head like she was trying to make it make sense. "Do you think all this happened in a single day?"

By the look on my face, she seemed to realize a very bad thing, something that I was beginning to arrive at myself.

"It hasn't been a day, has it?"

Ellie shook her head again, her grip getting stronger as my legs threatened to give out.

"It's been three years, Wren. The Savannah you knew—the life you knew? It's gone."

Bile churned in my belly. Three years? Three?

"And Nico? Where is he?"

Tears filled Ellie's eyes as she held me up. "I don't know."

Heat flashed over my skin, like I was right back in those flames. Ellie might not know where Nico was, but I would. I'd find him.

Even if I had to burn the rest of this city down to do it.

ERRORS AND EXORCISMS

ARCANE SOULS WORLD: THE WRONG WITCH BOOK 3

ANNIE ANDERSON

The Moon will guide you through the night with her brightness, but she will always dwell in the darkness in order to be seen.

— SHANNON L. ALDER

CHAPTER 1

NICO—THREE YEARS AGO

IN-LAWS REALLY WERE THE WORST.

Sure, most people had clashes in personality, the odd conflict here and there, but me? I got the raw end of the deal when it came to my wife's family. Then again, Wren could have probably said the same shit about mine—and she'd have been right, considering the throat-slitting event at our first family dinner.

But at present, she wasn't dealing with homicidal witches hell-bent on eviscerating her from the inside out, and I was, so...

When I woke up this morning with Wren in my arms, I never thought my day would end like this. We were supposed to make sure she was ready to go to the ABI. We were supposed to laugh and joke and make love and go to bed and wake up tomorrow and do it all over again.

I wasn't supposed to run all over Savannah, trying not to get us both killed.

I wasn't supposed to realize we both wouldn't make it out of here.

I wasn't supposed to tell my best friend to take her away from me.

I wasn't supposed to tell her goodbye.

I wouldn't trade it now. Because Wren was safe, and these women would never touch her again—as long as I could hold them back.

Dodging the blade, I nearly ran into Wren's cracked-out mother, who was doing her level best to electrocute me to death. All things considered, I was pegging Wren's family as the raw end of the deal. Especially since they were the reason I was never going to see her again.

"What's the matter, Fido?" Margot simpered as she clutched a crackling ball of power in her palm. "You afraid of a little shock?"

A shock? No.

Getting roasted from the inside out? Absolutely.

Several decades my senior, the Bannister witches could make me a stain on the floor if I gave them the chance. It wasn't like our families had ever gotten along, but ever since Eloise Bannister found out I was married to her granddaughter, I'd known my days were numbered.

I just didn't think it would be this soon.

I thought I had more time—I thought *we* had more time.

Wren's Aunt Judith—who could definitely pass for a ginger Bellatrix Lestrange—slashed at me with a knife that reeked of poison. The wicked blade missed my skin by millimeters, stealing all my attention as a ball of electricity slammed into my shoulder.

I'd never been tased before, but if I had a guess, it felt just like this. The jolt surged through my body, frying neurons as it locked my muscles, nearly making me stumble.

Judith's blade slashed again, biting into my feeble forearm, still weak from the shock.

Fuck.

Acid-like poison snaked up my arm, its toxic fingers blackening the skin as I made a cut of my own.

I wouldn't let these women go after Wren. I'd made my peace with the fact that I wouldn't get forever with the woman I loved. Decided as soon as I let Wyatt take Wren out of here, that I wasn't going to make it. So this poison being my undoing? Well, it was expected.

But I'd be taking both of them with me.

My claws made a home in Judith's belly, and I ripped upward, tearing her middle wide. Shock colored her pale features that were so close to Wren's. But Judith was sadistic and cold—her sister no better—and I wasn't sorry she was going to die in this room right alongside me.

Margot howled, firing off more orbs of magic, but I used Judith as a shield, letting her take the brunt of the hits. The scent of ozone, spent magic, and burning flesh ran rank through the room, singeing my nostrils in the process. I was lucky I was dying or else I'd never get that smell out of my nose.

And I *was* dying. The poison had made my left arm useless, and standing was becoming a real problem.

But over the scent of Judith's burning flesh and the

poison rotting me from the inside out, and over Margot screams, and the strobing lights of the magic, there was something else. Flashes hit my brain, but unlike the first time they'd knocked me for a loop, I knew exactly what they were. I was seeing through Wren's eyes, the mate bond giving me this small glimpse of her before I wouldn't see anything else ever again.

But then the scent of mage filled my nose and the woman in my arms flickered out and disappeared. Margot faded to nothing, and the black fingers of death cleared from my veins.

Lies. All lies.

My wolf howled in my brain as more visions of Wren filled my head. Her heart raced in my chest, her fear. She was looking at Wyatt, but his face was melting away, another man standing in his place.

Illusion mage. It was all fake.

My gut bottomed out as my feet finally got with the program. I was out the French doors and over the wall before I even realized I was moving, following the scent of Wren and the mage.

How could I have been so stupid? They had never been here. Wyatt had never been here. I let some asshole take my wife right out from under my nose. It had all been a fucking ploy to get Wren away from me—get her to a Fae gate. That poor agent had family, probably. Family far stronger than she was.

The square across the street held several Fae gates. All it would take was opening a door.

I burst from the trees, only to see Wren struggling against the hold of an impossibly tall man, his hunched frame doing nothing to hide his size. He was thin as a rail, and he had hands on my woman.

"Let me go," Wren screeched, planting her feet as he tried pulling her toward the door.

But as much as I wanted to look at her, my gaze was locked on the man watching the tableau as if he were bored out of his mind. Blackness coated his fingers, the oily darkness like a death mage, but not all at the same time. Plus, he didn't smell right—not mage, not witch, not warlock.

No, he was a Fae.

A dark one, my wolf supplied, knowing far more about the liminal spaces than I did. I had to get her free.

Had to.

"Wren," I roared, and those gorgeous green-gold eyes met mine.

And then I knew.

There was nothing I wouldn't do to get to her.

No blood I wouldn't spill.

No one I wouldn't kill.

My wolf took over, jumping free of my skin, pumping my legs faster. We had to get to her, we had to move, we had to fight.

The Fae in black sighed, his boredom getting the better of him as he shot putrid darkness from his hand, the blackness so thick it was like a wall separating me from Wren. I lunged, trying to get through, but it was like ramming into stone.

I could barely see through the murky smoke, but I could still make out Wren's struggle.

"Nico," she pleaded, right before the lanky man wrenched her through the door and it slammed closed.

The dark one fisted his hand, and the door disappeared, almost as if the portal itself had been erased. Then, it felt as if my heart had been ripped from my chest. I couldn't feel Wren's mind, her emotions were just gone. I'd never been able to explain just what feeling her all the time was like, but it was as if everything about the woman I loved was cold and dead, stolen from my very being as if someone had sucked out my soul.

Tossing my head back, I howled, my wolf calling for a moon that was not there—for a pack that was not mine, for a love lost to me. But a wolf's howl did more than just call for aid, it was a magic all on its own. The blackness shivered, rippling into spikes as my wolf bade the whole of Savannah for help.

"Stop that," the pompous fuck of a Fae shouted, one hand covering his ear as he tried to hold me back.

My wolf completed its call before snapping at the Fae, ready and willing to take a chunk out of him the first chance we got.

The Fae fisted his hands as he threw his arms wide, his dark eyes alighting with his magic as they turned a very odd shade of blue. Black magic grew, the pressure of it nearly bringing me to my knees as it pressed on the very air around me.

It stole the breath from my lungs, leaving me gasping on the grass, praying for help.

"Look," the Fae bit out, his British accent thick. "I don't want to do this, but my father has left me no choice. The only way to stop him is to keep him from crossing into this plane. If

I have to sacrifice one girl to do it, so fucking be it. I know she's your sweetheart and all, but letting that girl stay will be the end of us all. At least this way she'll take care of a real problem before she wipes us all out."

The darkness faded, but the pressure squeezing the life out of me didn't let up for a second as he knelt by my shoulder.

"If we're lucky, you'll never see that girl again." He cocked his head to the side as if he were studying me. "I doubt you'll see it my way, but trust me on this one, mate. That girl will be the end of us all. But, since I can't have you following me—"

The pressure eased for half a second—just long enough for me to catch a breath—before his fist knocked right into my temple.

And my last thought before the light dimmed was of Wren.

"Are you going to tell him, or am I?" my mother hissed, her voice as quiet as a whisper but still felt louder than a fucking drum knocking against my skull.

Maybe it wasn't a drum. Maybe it was a jackhammer. If I didn't know better, I'd think someone had taken a baseball bat to my head.

I cracked a single eyelid and instantly regretted it. I hadn't had a hangover this bad since that one time Theo had taken me to spring break in Miami when I was seventeen. My hold on my wolf had been very new, and I hadn't figured out the healing bit yet. Healing myself from the alcohol poisoning had been a treat.

"What happened?" I croaked, trying to sit up. The only way to do this was to just get it done. I needed carbs, grease, and enough red meat to choke a goat. Then I'd be right as rain.

But something felt off. I was in my bed at the pack house. I shouldn't be at the pack house. Why would I when I hadn't slept here in weeks. Why...

Then it all came flooding back. The running, the fighting, the beautiful woman stolen from me.

Wren.

I shot off the bed, staggering as my head swam and my stomach pitched. My legs nearly folded beneath me, but I held onto one of the bedposts like my life depended on it. It didn't, but hers did.

"What. Happened," I ordered, the Alpha emerging from my voice in such a way that had Dayana shivering and Mari's gaze hitting the floor. It didn't matter if I was hurt. That Alpha power was enough to back me up.

But neither of them answered me. No, it was my mother who looked me in the eye and filled me in. "We heard your call and came to find you. You were in Chatham Square. Bloody, unconscious, barely breathing. Smelling of Fae. The bastard nearly caved in your skull. The boys helped me bring you here."

I'd get into the fact that my mother had my brothers bring me here of all places later. What I wanted to know is what she didn't want to tell me.

If she wouldn't cough it up, I'd start. "Wren's gone—taken—to the Fae realm. The one you smell, kept me from her. Anyone catch his trail?"

And there was no way they couldn't smell him. The scent

of his magic was all over me, nearly making me puke.

Mom nodded, but Mari spoke. "Theo and Mateo are out scouting—" At my censuring glare, she held up a hand. "They wanted to make amends for what they did. Santi and Frankie are rounding up Wren's friends. Making sure they're safe."

I had a very bad feeling about this. There was no way my brothers would be out scouting or helping me after what they had done—after my father's behavior—unless... Unless something was wrong with Dad. Unless there was another Acosta problem. No one would defy the Alpha unless they didn't have an Alpha anymore.

"What aren't you telling me?" Because they were leaving shit out, and if I wanted to find Wren—which I sure as fuck did—then I'd need their help.

My older sister Lara waltzed into the room, her pregnant belly leading the way as she munched on pita chips from a massive bag. Each crunch rattled my skull.

"A lot, little brother. First off, Mom challenged Dad and won." *Crunch.* "He's in the dungeon pacing like a caged animal right now, and honestly, I love this for him. Then she reprimanded Theo for putting a blade to your mate's throat—dick move by the way—and forced him to give up his pack second status, took his house, and made him pay two million in restitution. You should really check your bank account more." *Crunch.* "After that, Mom excommunicated Diana, stripped her of Acosta protection, and let the Savannah Arcane Council have her for attempted murder of a packmate." She turned to Mom, nibbling on another chip. "Did I forget anything?"

Mom rolled her eyes as she straightened the already-perfect

duvet. "Now is not the time for this, Lara. Nico needs to rest and—"

"*Mom.*"

But she wouldn't meet my gaze, instead her lip trembled. "It's bad, sweetheart. There's a lot going on and you're still not in fighting shape. I've done what I can, but I'm not the Alpha. Your father was, and even though I won the challenge... We need you, okay?"

But did they? I couldn't even keep my mate safe, and they wanted me to take my father's place? What good was I going to do?

Mom shook her head as she began wringing her hands—a bad sign if there ever was one. Mom's wringing of hands was the equivalent to the Joint Chiefs calling Defcon One. "The witches are in an uproar demanding Wren be returned to them. There's been disturbances within the pack, and some wolves are miss—"

My body went on red alert when Fiona strode into the room like she'd been here a thousand times before. If her light-blonde hair weren't a complete mess or her lip split, she'd be the picture of composure. But she didn't give me a second to ask why she was bleeding or why my brother Santi was walking in behind her with a black eye, a busted nose, and a limp.

"What your mama is skirting around is all the Fae portals in the city are locked up tighter than a duck's asshole, the River Walk is in a tizzy, the ABI is breathing down our necks trying to recall us all, and they need you to sack up an—"

Wren. If the Fae portals were closed, how was I supposed to get her back? How was I going to breathe? A sharp pain knifed through my chest as I struggled to suck in air.

"What I need to do is find my fucking wife."

CHAPTER 2

NICO

THE BLOOD ON MY FATHER'S OFFICE FLOOR WAS BROWN with age. No one had bothered to clean it up since I'd held Wren in my arms, her throat pouring scarlet lifeblood as her heart fluttered and stopped. His desk was in shambles, the bookcases torn apart with books and papers scattered over the floor as if there had been a war.

Maybe because there had been.

I'd faced down not only my family, but Death herself in this room, and luckily, she'd been kind—giving Wren back to me, allowing me to bring the woman I loved back from the brink.

But how lucky had I really been?

I rubbed at the ache in my chest, the stitch there wasn't getting any better, each breath no easier than the last. It was as if I was missing a limb. A huge chunk of me was just... gone. I'd gotten so used to feeling Wren in every single cell of my body, inured to her emotions, her heartbeat, her breaths, that to have them absent felt like I had lost myself in that gods-damned gate.

But I'd get her back—even if I had to tear this world and the next apart in the trying.

"Nic?"

The absolute last person I wanted to talk to was my eldest brother.

Not now.

Not in this room.

Not with Wren gone.

Not ever.

If I were steady on my feet—if this ache in my chest wasn't ripping me apart with every fucking breath—I would have honored the promise I made him. But ripping Theo limb from limb wasn't a possibility now. I would just ignore him, and if the fucker was smart, he would turn his ass around and never talk to me again.

But my brother wasn't smart. Never had been.

Theo's hand on my shoulder had me whipping around, my fist slamming into his jaw without my brain ever telling it to move. All I could think about was that gods-damned knife to Wren's perfect throat. His hands on her. His will to do her harm.

Theo fell to the floor, hands up, mouth bloody, his pleading expression doing nothing but making my teeth grind. But though I expected him to move, he did not. He didn't say a word. All he did was stay right there on that filthy floor and look at me like if I killed him, I'd be doing him a favor.

"What do you want?" I seethed through gritted teeth,

aching to take this pain out on someone—anyone else. Someone had to feel as bad as I did. Someone had to have this ache. Someone had to have every single breath in their lungs feel like acid.

His huff of laughter was completely mirthless. "To keep you from feeling like I bet you are right now. That's what I want. It's enough to make you crazy, isn't it? That ache in your chest that just won't go away? The feeling like something is missing? Like you're dying but the universe is just too cruel to actually do you that favor?"

But if anyone knew how I felt, it was Theo, wasn't it? His mate had died before he'd been able to find her—killed before her time, before *their* time. A pit of dread yawned wide in my gut, threatening to swallow me whole.

"Please tell me it always felt like this, and not..."

Please tell me you felt this ache always.

Please don't tell me you only felt it after your mate died.

Wren can't be dead. Please, Fates, don't tell me she's...

The ache in my chest intensified, biting through me as if the claws of the devil himself were reaching inside and ripping my soul from my body. I'd never understood Theo. Never understood why he was such a dick, why he hated everyone, why he refused to be around us if he could help it. Pack houses were meant to be filled to the brim, bursting with mates and children and life. But ours wasn't. So many of our pack lived without mates, outside of the pack house, away from the bustle of children and happy couples and reminders of what they didn't have.

Theo's expression did not waver. He held that pleading look like he was trying to hide the pity. Either that or he just didn't want to die. "It's always felt like I was being ripped in two. I haven't known a day of peace since she graced this planet and not a single one since she left it."

My brother was over a century old. A century of days filled with agony. Maybe him not wanting to die was a stretch. The thought of centuries without Wren was getting harder and harder to swallow.

"She's not dead, brother," Theo urged, his tone soft even though his face was not. "Your woman has far too much fight in her to let some pissant Fae take her down. She's an Alpha. Like you. Wolf or not."

My lip curled at his patronizing. Leave it to Theo to try and stroke my ego while he was bloody and flat on his back. "Pretty words won't save you from me. Not after what you did."

Again, Theo's chuckle was mirthless. "Do you think I had a choice, brother? Unlike you, the rest of us aren't Alphas. We *can't* say no."

He shook his head as he rolled, getting to his knees as he stared at me with an expression of disgust so powerful it made me wonder if I'd ever known Theo at all. If I'd ever known my father.

"I knew how wrong it was—how wrong we all were—the second she begged for your life. The moment Wren begged me to protect you, I knew Dad was wrong. That what we were doing wasn't the right path. But he'd been so blinded by Diana's premonition that he couldn't see just how much Wren loves you. But when she pleaded with me, I knew." Helpless tears filled his eyes before they found the floor. "But the order had been given, and I couldn't say no. Then again, wrong or right, I wasn't planning on leaving the room alive, so the consequences didn't matter, now, did they?"

That had me stumbling back a step. "You thought I'd kill you."

Had I considered it? Absolutely. But the reality of actually murdering my brother was far too big a pill to swallow.

Theo's gaze never left the floor as his shoulders rounded forward, his body sagging just a little. "I was hoping for it, actually. Too bad your honor's better than mine, isn't it?"

The truth was, had Wren died that day, my honor would have evaporated. There wouldn't have been anything good left in me. She would have taken it all with her.

Funny, I'd gotten a reprieve, but now I knew that the ugly side of myself was closer to the surface than it had ever been. Because she was gone and all I wanted to do was rip this world apart to get her back.

"Is it?" I growled, my wolf so close to the surface it was as if he were the one clawing to get out. "Tell me, brother—do you still want to die?"

Theo's shoulders straightened, his eyes finally meeting mine, his expression more of the brother I knew from my childhood before life decided to kill his soul. "Maybe later. I have things to attend to. Like helping you find your woman."

Theo and Matteo had been on the trail of the Fae who'd kept me from Wren. A dark one. A Dark Fae, maybe? My wolf had been a little sketchy on the details, and even as close to the surface as he was, the damn animal was still mum on the subject.

"You didn't find the Fae, did you?"

My brother clenched his jaw as his gaze slid back to the

ground. "We were close, but *he* called us back. Used the pack bond and..." Theo shook his head, his whole body vibrating with rage. "Mom might have won the challenge, but you and I both know Dad let her win because his wolf wouldn't let him kill his own mate and any other outcome would demand it. He's still Alpha. Unless someone takes him down, he's going to undermine everything he can so he can steal his seat back. Matteo and I were in fucking Kentucky when he—"

Theo swallowed hard, bending forward so his head was damn near on the ground. "I failed you, brother. I accept whatever fate you wish to dole out."

The bond I had to this pack had been severed days ago, but I still knew what my father had done. Taking someone's will away was not a favorite tool of mine, but for some, it was commonplace. Dad hadn't used that Alpha power much—at least not with me—but something inside me told me that this wasn't the first time he'd bent Theo to his will. No, my father might never have been who I thought he was.

And now he'd let Wren's trail go cold. On purpose.

That fucking bastard.

The stoked embers of all the pain and rage and loss in my gut burned bright as my wolf clawed at my mind.

"Look at me and tell me the truth," I ordered, threading every bit of Alpha into my voice as I knelt to stare my brother in the eye. "Did he take your will the night Wren almost died?"

I knew the answer already, but I needed to hear it from his lips. I needed to know if my father was unfit for leadership. I needed it unquestioned and concrete.

And I needed to know now.

"In what world would I steal another's mate from them

otherwise? He fed us lies and stole our will—believing Diana's prophecy rather than his own son." Theo's gaze fell to the floor. "I'm sorry for the part I played and the damage I caused. I don't have the strength to leave on my own like you do. But if you'll have me, I will fight for you until my last breath."

We'd have to circle back to Diana's prophecy, but I had a sinking feeling it had something to do with what the dark one had said after closing the gates to the Fae realm.

I doubt you'll see it my way, but trust me on this one, mate. That girl will be the end of us all.

Did I give a fuck what Diana saw or what that bastard said?

Absolutely fucking not.

Because whatever she saw, it had nothing to do with my Wren. Wren couldn't be the end of anyone or anything. Not unless they crossed her, and then it wouldn't be her bringing their end.

It would be me.

I stood, grabbing my brother's hand and yanking him to his feet. Pulling him close, I whispered nothing but the truth in his ear.

"When I get Wren back, you so much as look at her sideways and I'll gut you like a fish for the entire pack to see. Understand?"

Relief relaxed my brother's shoulders as he brought me in for a hug. "I would expect nothing less. And I'll expect her punishment when she returns as well. I know we aren't square, but I'll do my best to make it up to you both."

Squeezing him tight, I felt a minor hint of relief until the reality of what I'd have to do hit me like a ton of bricks. Theo wanted to be in my pack if I ever made one. He wanted help leaving. Well, he wouldn't have to go far.

If I wanted every resource to find Wren, if I wanted to keep my father from undermining every move, every effort, if I wanted my brothers to never have their will taken away again, I'd have to do the thing I'd been dreading for decades.

Because there was only room for one Acosta Alpha.

I released Theo, slapping him on the back so he knew I heard him. "Keep Mom busy, will you? I have to go handle some business."

Theo's face went gray for a second before he nodded. "I'll stay with her until... until the end."

Gritting my teeth, I directed my feet to the door, following them to the one place I did not want to go. That was the thing about being Alpha that my father forgot. Sometimes it wasn't about what you wanted to do.

Sometimes it was about what you *had* to do.

Savannah should not have dungeons of any kind. Being on the coast, the water table was obnoxiously high. Luckily, the arcane world was sometimes kind. A few centuries before I was born, this home had been retrofitted with tunnels and a cave system, and of course, the dungeon.

I never understood why anyone would build a dungeon in a shifter den. We didn't keep prisoners. Wolves were known to cut out the middleman and just take our enemies out altogether. If someone would have asked me a month ago if my father would ever be on my list of enemies, I'd have called them crazy.

Now? Not so much.

What else could the man be? He'd tried to have Wren

killed. He'd called Theo and Matteo back from Wren's trail. He'd intervened, took my brothers' will away, and destroyed our pack. If any other Alpha had done what my father had, the question as to whether or not they'd live to see tomorrow would be an easy one to answer.

"Finally come to see your old man, huh?" my father asked from the floor of the damp dungeon cell. A putrid bucket filled with something foul sat in the corner and Dad appeared to not have eaten in several days. The eyes of his wolf burned in the darkness, his sunken cheeks and eviscerated frame leaning listlessly against the bars. The magic in the metal smoldered bright, searing his flesh through his shirt, but still my father never flinched.

Maybe it was because of the arm hanging half-gone at his side, or maybe it was the still-wide-open- and bleeding wounds at his middle. Wounds that smelled worse than the bucket. Jesus fuck, what had Mom done to him?

"Was that your goal?" I swallowed down bile, my gut churning with all that I didn't want to do. "To make me come down here and deal with you?"

Because there was no way my mother would have the strength to kill Dad. They'd been together for centuries. Killing him had never been an option. But she wanted me to be Alpha, and there was only one way to do it.

"Come on, son. You and I both know how this is going to go. All I have to do is make you mad enough, and you'll handle the situation. You've always been a hothead."

But it was tough to find my rage, especially as the scent of death filled the air.

"Your wolf won't heal you," I murmured, guessing the

situation almost immediately. "Because you went against your mate—against your pack—and now you're facing the consequences."

I'd heard of our animals doing this, but I'd only ever seen it in the lore, not in practice.

And never to an Alpha.

"She's going to bring the end to us all, Nicholas. I was protecting my family. What else would you have me do?"

This was the second time I'd heard this supposed "end of the world" claim, and honestly, I was getting sick of it.

"Wren will do no such thing. She is my wife, which makes her your fucking family, too. Where was her protection? Where was your care for your son? Where was the fucking proof, other than the word of one old woman?"

"Diana has prevented more war and more bloodshed than your small mind can even comprehend, boy."

Weak. My father was weak and small and...

"At what cost? Sometimes, blood needs to be spilled. Sometimes wars need to be fought. And sometimes the word of your son is more important than that of an old seer aching for death. You tore your family apart at her word, took your sons' will away. You broke us. The Acosta bond is weaker because of you."

My father's wolf burned bright in his eyes once again, but something was different this time. Dad wasn't in control of his animal anymore. No, it was separate, other, his wolf aching—clawing—to come out. It called to me, beckoned me to use just a little bit of the power Wren had shared with me—that same power that made me almost positive she was still alive, still breathing, still able to come back to me.

"I was going to wait for Wren to decide your punishment, but we both know you won't last that long. This is only going to go down one of two ways. One, I let your wolf do what he wanted and let you fester and die in this fucking cell. Two, I rip your wolf right out of your skin and snap your insidious neck with a mercy you don't deserve."

I tried to reconcile the man before me with the one who helped me during my first shift. The same man that taught me to drive and be a man and an Alpha. How could he be the same person?

How could he do all that and be the man who took his sons' will away?

Dad—*Tomás*—tried and failed to sit up, his eyes wide. "There's no way you can do that. Only Spirit Alphas can even attempt something li—" He hissed in pain, clutching his middle. "Nicholas, this changes everything. Diana doesn't know what you are. Her prophecy is wro—"

But he hadn't put it together. Diana knew I could heal Wren before she ever sliced that blade. She'd just hoped I wasn't up to the task. And Spirit Alphas were a fucking myth—dreamed up by some seer ages ago. It was why my being able to heal others was so dicey. There were enough prophecies about Spirit Alphas to fill a gods-damned library, and any one of them could get me killed if the wrong person knew about me.

"She knows," I growled, cutting him off. "The problem you aren't seeming to grasp is that Diana is not serving anyone but Diana—a fact you should have caught onto as soon as she suggested killing my wife."

Bile rose in my throat. The only reason he was still alive

was because no one wanted to be the one to kill him. Mom didn't want to kill her mate. Theo didn't have the strength, Ella wasn't an Alpha, and Mariella was too young.

But me?

The only reason Tomás was still alive was all due to the woman he wanted dead. I couldn't kill my father in front of Wren.

But Wren wasn't here, now, was she?

"I won't have you interfering again, old man. No more controlling your pack. No more taking their will away."

"No, son. You don't understand—"

But I didn't let him finish. There wasn't anything he could say to me that would change his fate any more than it would change mine. Drawing on the power Wren had once shared with me, I closed my fist on the air itself and pulled, yanking my father's wolf from his skin. Blindingly white just like Theo, the animal jumped from the liminal space under my father's skin, severing the tie between the two.

Spirit Alphas were a myth, but then again, so was what I had just done. It had been said that they could heal or destroy, and as much as I hated it, destroying felt really fucking good right about then.

My father gasped as his skin grayed out, losing far more blood now that his wolf was no longer connected to him. He choked, trying to talk, and it reminded me so much of Wren dying in my arms that I fought back a snarl.

Without anything blocking my way, I opened the cell door to stand over him.

"See that feeling you have right now? That's the same one my wife felt when Diana slit her fucking throat." Tilting my head, I knelt at his side, realizing that this man wasn't anything to me—not anymore. "Lucky for you, I'm kinder than you were."

Tomás' eyes widened just a little, but his expression was resolute as my claws dug into the flesh of his throat and ripped it wide. Ten seconds later, my father took his last breath. Two seconds after that, the full weight of the Acosta line fell on my shoulders, the power hitting me like a ton of bricks.

Staggering to my feet, I let it fill me, let it heal the last of the aches... all except that one in my heart.

That was here to stay.

Turning my attention to the very large, very wild animal in the cage with me, I met its gaze, staring it down like I would any other potential threat.

Thank you for my freedom. How may I serve you, Alpha?

The sound of another wolf's voice in my head was something I would have to get used to, but it helped that this wolf did not sound anything like my father's voice. I didn't think I'd have been able to deal with that.

But that was before my mother's scream sounded through the house, ripping my heart in two. I'd taken her mate from her. And as much as it hurt—and it really fucking did—it also gave me hope.

Wren was alive—had to be. Because that ache in my chest was nothing like the pain my mother was feeling.

"Go comfort your mate. Stay with her, protect her, and when I need you, allow me to call on you."

As you wish, Alpha.

I rubbed at the ache in my chest and followed the wolf out of the cell where my father's body moldered. A part of me mourned the man from my childhood. The one who tied my shoelaces and taught me how to fight.

But that man was gone now.

And if anyone else stood in my way of finding Wren, they would be following him into the grave.

CHAPTER 3

NICO—TWO YEARS, SIX MONTHS AGO

"Please tell me you're joking."

I leveled my brother with a glare powerful enough to knock the paint off a car, and he snapped his mouth shut. Theo was getting smarter over these last few months, but he should know that I hadn't joked in a long fucking time.

"Six. Months," I growled, my voice as low as I could make it. "I have been hunting for this asshole for six months, Theo. What part of this plan makes you think I'm joking?"

It was bad enough that it had taken this long to find the illusion mage that had taken Wren from me, but it was worse that the Fae that locked all the gods-forsaken Fae doors seemed to have dropped off the fucking map. After all this time, this was the only lead I had, and I was going to make sure he didn't fall through the cracks.

Again.

But acting now was our only option.

"Maybe because the only protection either of us have is this silly little necklace," he hissed, dangling the charm Fiona made him in front of my face. "Or that the ABI refused to back us up, Mom is against this, and we still can't find Wyatt. Really, the options seem to be endless at this point. Not to mention..."

Theo gestured to the white wolf that hadn't left my side since we'd started this mission. Ghost was a good companion, diligent, and loyal to a fault. The wolf also got under Theo's skin, refusing to heed any command he gave him, tearing up his expensive Italian loafers, and pissing on his seat at the dinner table more times than I could count.

"Oh, get over it," Hannah growled, looking up from her book. It was one of those bodice-rippers from the '80s with the dude with the open shirt and flowing hair. Hannah loved those books, and all it had taken was one single, solitary body slam to teach my brothers not to make fun of her for them. "I've heard you bitch about that damn wolf more than should be allowable by law. And Fi's charms are top-notch, which you would know if you'd actually shut up for five seconds and listen to anyone else in your family. You're lucky you even got one at all."

That was true. Theo was lucky he got a charm. Considering Fiona had managed to avoid meeting my asshole big brother, making a charm to protect his mind was a little dicey, but she'd done it. Not that Theo would trust anything made for him by a witch, ever, but that was his emotional baggage to deal with and not mine.

"I'm not going to try and convince you again. You're either

going with us or you're going home. I won't take your will away, but you aren't fucking with my plan, either." I leveled him with a glare. "So, are you in, or are you out?"

Theo met my glare with one of his own before peeling his gaze away to stare at the cabin nestled in the valley below. It was a small cottage-style home surrounded by trees and a babbling brook for fuck's sake. Smoke bloomed from the chimney, bold as you please, and if neither of us were wearing the amulets Fiona made us, all we'd see is a cove of trees and that damn water.

Theo sighed long and low before nodding his head. "I'm in. If anything, just so you stay breathing long enough to get your woman back."

But the plan was going to work. It would because it had to. I'd spent the last six months telling the ABI to fuck off, turning in my resignation the millisecond the higher-ups refused to look for my wife. I'd never been more disillusioned in my fucking life before the day Erica told me she wasn't allowed to look for Wren.

Or worse?

When she told me that the ABI wouldn't lift a fucking finger to open the Fae portals. We were on our own, and that was that.

That didn't mean that Erica wasn't helping me on the side or that Fiona, Malia, and Hannah weren't playing both sides of the ABI fence. They were. It just wasn't enough.

"Gee, thanks. Your confidence really is inspiring. Now, before I keel over from your outpouring of faith in me, can you get into position?"

Hannah snickered from behind her bodice-ripper while

Theo flipped me off. I'd have smacked him in the temple for that, but he sauntered over to his assigned position, adjusting his cufflinks like he was going into a boardroom. Why Theo needed to wear a suit everywhere was beyond me. He always said it was because a century ago, that was how everyone dressed, but I called bullshit.

Theo just liked looking important. Or he had a clothing fetish. Dealer's choice.

"You ready, boss?" Hannah murmured, shooting me a look over the top of her book. She and I had come to an agreement these last few months. I wouldn't stop looking for Wren and she wouldn't give me shit about losing my own mate on my watch. I considered it a good enough trade. Plus, she respected me a little bit more since I'd given the ABI the finger and taken over my pack.

That was the thing about ghouls. They appreciated family more than anything, and kin killers were dealt with swiftly, sure, but mates? To harm a ghoul's mate was tantamount to starting a war. It was half the reason the Dumond nest was nearly extinct.

I tipped my chin in a nearly imperceptible nod and Hannah slipped a frilly bookmark in between the pages of her book and stuffed the worn paperback in the back pocket of her jeans.

"You planning on doing anything stupid in there?" she asked under her breath so Theo or anyone else couldn't hear.

My gaze locked on the sweet cabin down the slope. "I plan on doing whatever I have to. If you've got a problem with that, you can stay here. But if you go down there with us, your badge better not be an issue."

Hannah's chuckle was damn near silent as she shook her head. "There's a reason Fiona and Malia stayed behind, and I didn't. I don't have a problem getting my hands dirty."

That was good to know. Because I was getting the information I needed.

One way or another.

Mom was against this course of action, but, then again, she had an inkling of just how unstable I'd been over the last few months. She knew what I was capable of. Losing her mate had made her all too knowledgeable on that front.

So she elected to stay home with Fiona and Malia, protecting them as a good mother would just in case we were unsuccessful. The blowback on what we were about to do could be catastrophic, to be sure. But my brothers and sisters had chosen to come with me.

There had been a lot of changes since I'd taken my father's seat. One, I didn't make anyone do anything. And two? I asked my pack what they wanted to do, making a better environment for everyone.

In theory.

Taking a deep breath, I connected with my pack, giving them the signal to move down the hill to the cabin. Ghost and Hannah moved with me, melting into the shadows as we traversed the steep decline to the tiny cottage.

The scent of cooked meat and spices tumbled from the chimney as peals of laughter reached my ears. Irrationally, rage hit me at their joy. The mage was happy. He had ripped everything good from my life and he was just... happy. Content. Enjoying life to the fullest.

Yes, he had lost his daughter. I understood doing what one had to, to get someone they loved back, but...

My feet picked up speed as I raced for the home. I didn't bother to follow the fucking plan I'd put into place and decided at the last second to kick that door to smithereens just like he'd done to my life. The mage I'd seen in Wren's mind shot to his feet, his hands glowing with a power that wouldn't work on me one bit.

Peter Lewis was about five centuries my senior, but being as old as he was, he wasn't very smart. Peter thought I would go for him directly. Maybe the old me would go for him head-on, but the new me—the one he created—preferred the approach that would get his attention. Dodging a ball of magic, my claws found his daughter's throat before he could get another shot off.

As soon as I touched her, everything seemed to slow, her magic trying to find a way around Fiona's charm. She frowned, her whole body still as a statue, the magic rising on the air as she shoved her power into me. But Fi's spell held true.

"Sorry, sweetheart. We came prepared."

Agent Penelope Lewis hadn't aged much in the twenty-five years she'd been lost to the Fae realm. With her bright-hazel eyes and smooth skin, she didn't look a day over twenty, which was the age she'd taken her ABI identification photo.

But there was a hardness to her eyes, a calculated shell, and that made this so much worse.

"Get your hands *off* her," Peter snarled, fighting against Hannah and Theo's hold as I tightened my fingers around Penelope's throat.

I could sense my pack surrounding the cabin, waiting on standby just in case this turned sideways. Ghost didn't wait with them. No, against orders, he circled the tableau like he was waiting for something.

Ignoring the mage, I asked his daughter, "Do you know who I am?"

Grinding her teeth, she remained silent, a malice to her gaze that told me she was used to not saying a word. Luckily, it wasn't her I needed to talk.

"That's okay. I don't actually need information from you. I do, however, need information from your father. And your pops? He loves you a whole bunch. Why else would he sacrifice my wife to a filthy fucking Fae to get you back?"

Studying her, I wondered what the Fae saw when he picked women to steal. Was it the hair, the eyes? Or was it something else? A power he wished to have, an ability? Or was he just a collector of pretty women as if they were dolls to use at his disposal.

If I got her back, would she have this same hardness to her? Was she even alive? Was she safe?

Wren. My wolf practically howled her name, rattling my skull.

My nose burned, my chest ached, and I fought off the urge to dig my claws into Lewis' neck and rip it wide.

"See, judging by your leg, you're used to torture. But you know what? Your pops isn't used to seeing it."

Lewis blinked, her gaze finding her father's as her cheeks lost their color. She finally understood exactly why we were here.

"Now, I don't want to hurt you, but to get my wife back, I will. I'd do just about anything. All I need is a little information. Your dad coughs it up, we'll leave. No muss, no fuss. Everybody lives. But if he doesn't? I'll rip you apart inch by fucking inch while he watches until he gives me what I need."

It went against everything I was as a wolf—everything I was as a man—to even threaten something like this. Hell, I wasn't sure who I even was anymore with Wren gone. I didn't recognize the man who would threaten this damaged woman. But I also knew I'd do whatever it was I had to get my wife back.

Peter struggled against Hannah's hold, irrationally thinking the ghoul was the one to test. Just to prove him wrong, Hannah snapped his wrist, the bone crunching with barely a flick of her fingers.

"What do you want?" he howled, cradling his hand to his chest as Theo held him up so he faced his daughter.

"A name. Nothing more, nothing less. I need the name of the Fae you dealt with to get your daughter back. You give me his name, and I'll leave."

Lewis' lids closed like I was asking for a billion dollars or a piece of the moon or something. Maybe I was, but this was something they could give me. They just needed the right motivation.

"I-I can't give you that." Peter tried and failed to get out of Theo's hold, the poor bastard cutting himself on Theo's claws as he writhed.

Oh, but he could. He could and he would. Or else.

Meeting Lewis' eyes, I grabbed the hand that had closed around my wrist. "Take a deep breath."

Her lids widened right before I snapped the bone of her pinky finger, the sick crunch of the bone breaking nearly making me vomit. But she didn't so much as whimper. In fact, other than a sharp intake of breath, Lewis didn't so much as flinch.

Wren.

She had walked right out of the Fae realm, knowing Wren would have the same fate as her. *She knew.*

"Leave her alone. You want me. Torture me." But Peter was wrong. I didn't want to do any of this. I did, however, want that name.

"I need the name, Peter. Give it to me, and I'll leave her alone. Even send a healer your way to fix her hand and her foot. You won't have to run from me anymore. No looking over your shoulder. Give me the name and we'll be square."

That was a lie. We'd never be square after what he'd done, but I wouldn't hunt him until the ends of the earth, either.

"He'll kill us. Don't you get that? If I give you his name, we're dead." Peter thrashed some more, failing at an epic level to learn his lesson.

"You fucking idiot," Theo growled in his face. "What do you think we'll do to you if you don't? You'll watch your daughter die screaming, you prick. Hell, you'll beg for death before I'm done with you. You fucked with a wolf's mate. You should have hidden better."

Illusion mages were known for their control. It was hard to break them because they were so used to keeping calm, staying rational, keeping their illusions going so they didn't miss a beat. Breaking Lewis—father or daughter—wasn't going to be easy, but Theo wasn't wrong.

Honor didn't matter. Wren did.

"You left my wife to the same hell you lived through. To the same people who took your foot, who hurt you over and over. You think I don't know what you lived through? You think that was a secret? Saving yourself only goes so far. You damned another woman, and that makes you no better than scum in my book."

Lewis swallowed hard as she studied my face. She knew. She knew I wouldn't stop until I got what I wanted.

"T-tell them," she whispered, a single tear tracking down her cheek.

Peter struggled again in vain. "No. He'll kill you. Tr—" He cut himself off, nearly spilling the name I needed so desperately.

Okay, change of tactics.

"Take his eye, Theo," I ordered, a thread of command in my voice as I watched Lewis' expression.

Theo let out a dark chuckle. "You have a preference for which one?"

"Nope. You pick."

Peter's scream was piercing, but it had the desired effect.

"I'll tell you," Lewis pleaded, scratching at my wrist with her blunted nails. "Don't hurt him, I'll tell you. His name is Tristan."

My fingers squeezed her throat as I shook her. "His full name. Now."

"Sh-shadowfall. Tristan Shadowfall," she croaked, breath

barely passing the hold I had on her airway. "Crown Prince of the Dark Court."

Tricky. But she was leaving something out. "And what name did he use to bind your father in his deal? Because you and I both know I'm not leaving until I have *that* name."

Peter sniffed, swallowed, and whispered a name—the exact name I'd been waiting for. "Drystan. Drystan Haldrir Shadowfall. That is his given name."

Nodding, I pressed the comm button at my ear. Somehow, some way, Fiona had managed to stay quiet through infil and positioning. Hell, she'd probably put herself on mute.

"You get that, Fi?"

Her thick Southern drawl clanged down the line. "Sure did. Testing it now."

There was a slight pause and then a giddy "*whoop*" of excitement. "Good to go, hoss. It's going to take me some time to find him, but that name lit up like a damn firecracker."

At least one fucking thing went right today. "Good to know. Appreciate the assist."

Fiona huffed. "Like I wouldn't happily chop off my left chesticle for our girl. You going to rip those two assholes apart now? If so, I wanna hop off the call. Plausible deniability and all."

If ever there was a person who knew about plausible deniability, it was the daughter of the Jacobs Coven ringleader.

"I'm still thinking about it."

Fiona *tsked*, her judgment heavy. "Think faster. I'm gonna skedaddle regardless. The squelch of blood hitting the floor turns my stomach."

Then she clicked off the line, knowing the truth of it even before I did. Because right as she hung up, Ghost went apeshit.

The bark that came out of that wolf damn near made the hairs on the back of my neck stand on end. He threw himself at the wall, the wood breaking away to reveal a false panel. Then came the howl, a howl that broke into my brain, wrenching my gut.

"No," Penelope screamed. "You can't go in there. That has nothing to do with you."

When I absorbed my father's power, the whole of the Acosta pack made a home inside my brain. Unlike with Wren, I didn't feel their heartbeats or their emotions, but there was a link that gave me a certain bit of knowledge, a connection in cases of danger and the like.

But one packmate had been lost to me. It hadn't just been six months without Wren. I'd also missed someone who I considered a brother.

And as soon as Ghost broke down that door, I suddenly knew where Wyatt had been since before my wife had been taken from me.

"Sit still. Dayana, get in here and hold this bitch," I snarled, gladly handing Lewis off to my sister as soon as she came in the door. Penelope fought against her hold, but she was weak and tired, and my sister was ready to rip her apart.

"Santi, Frankie, help me." The order came without a choice attached—not that they'd need it. Wyatt's scent reached my nose as my brothers and I ripped the rest of the façade away.

I ducked through the opening, coughing at the stench of six months' worth of unwashed wolf, human waste, and who knew what else. Chained upright to a wall, Wyatt hung from a set of manacles, his body damn near skeletal. His long blond hair was plastered to his face, his body barely moving from his labored breathing.

But as soon as I touched him, he woke, his eyes wide as he flinched away from me.

"It's okay, brother," I whispered, threading all the calm I so did not feel into the pack bond. "We're getting you out of here. Promise."

"Ni-Nico?" Wyatt croaked, his eyes barely focusing on me as he shivered.

"Yeah, buddy. I gotcha. We're bringing you home, okay?"

Hesitantly, Wyatt nodded, and I yanked at the bonds, pulling the metal clear free of the stone walls as I caught my best friend. Frankie took his legs, helping me haul him out of that dank hovel and into the light while Santi stood there vibrating, trying not to lose his fucking mind.

Five minutes ago, Peter and Penelope Lewis would have walked out of this cabin.

Five minutes ago, I had every intention of letting them live.

But that was then, and this was now.

"Take him," I ordered, snapping Santi out of it as I passed Wyatt to my older brother.

I met Peter's eyes. He already knew that he wasn't making it out of here, and that was just as well. But I'd make him hurt first.

"Has nothing to do with me, huh? That is my packmate, my best friend, but you knew that already. What? Did you need him to make the illusion better? Is that it?"

"Sick fucks," Theo snarled, digging his claws into Peter's neck. "You get some kick out of hurting us? What the fuck?"

But I ignored my brother. I ignored everything but how I could possibly hurt this man as much as he had hurt me. The answer was easy enough. He had taken from me to get his daughter back. Now I would take it all from him.

"Peter Lewis, for your crimes against the Acosta pack, you will pay in pain and blood."

He nodded like all of it was expected, only becoming alarmed when I didn't walk straight to him but to Penelope instead.

"You took my heart from me," I whispered just loud enough for the both of them to hear. "Now I take yours from you."

Then my claws tore into Penelope's chest, ripping her heart out while her father watched. I let the organ fall from my fingers like the trash it was.

Peter screamed in agony, fighting against Hannah and Theo as the pair of them stared at me like I'd just done the unthinkable.

"I'll kill you," he railed. "You're dead, you piece of shit. You just don't know it yet."

Big talk from a man who couldn't wriggle his way out of a paper bag.

Tilting my head to the side, I had to study the mage who had upended my life. "Your death will not be so kind. You imprisoned my friend, you stole my wife, you conspired with a Fae to take from me—from us."

My gaze fell to the white wolf who was vibrating with the same rage that was thrumming from my every pore. "Ghost?"

Yes, my Alpha?

"Lunch."

Ghost's lips went wide, showing every single sharp canine in his large head. And when he was done, Peter was in ribbons and Ghost's fur was the red of freshly spilt blood.

And while I felt every eye in that cabin and the thrum of my pack's unease at my brutality, I just couldn't make myself give a fuck.

This was war.

And war was bloody.

CHAPTER 4

NICO—FOUR MONTHS AGO

SLEEP WAS FOR THE WEAK.

That was exactly what I told myself as I poured the last drops of the carafe into my mug, contemplating adding a little bourbon to it. But I knew the alcohol wouldn't do anything to help me sleep, just like it wouldn't numb the pain in my chest. That theory had been tested and discarded long ago. Even the thought of going to bed made me want to come out of my skin.

It didn't matter how comfortable the mattress was or if the room was the right temperature. It didn't matter if I was in wolf form or on two feet. None of it mattered.

I hadn't slept right in years, not since...

Rubbing at the ache that had made a permanent home in my chest, I gritted my teeth against the sting. Simply thinking her name wrenched at my heart. It had gotten to the point that

I snapped at anyone who said it—anytime I happened to see a redhead on the street, anytime I spoke to Ellie or Alice, or even so much as heard the whisper of the Bannister family.

Holding my shit together just wasn't going to happen. Which was why just the mere hint of a thought about her had me launching the cup—coffee and all—against the wall, splattering the hardwood floor and wall with the very thing that would keep the dreams of her at bay.

That was the real reason sleep evaded me—or rather, *I* evaded *it*.

As much as I tried to keep her out of my conscious thought, she invaded my dreams. Her smile, her laugh, her moans in my ear. The way she never stopped moving, never stopped thinking, never quit trying to be better. She was always reading or cooking or trying something new. And on the really hard nights, memories of the end would come—the ones of her pleading for me to come with her, to help, to not let her get taken. The ones where she screamed my name as she was ripped away from me.

The ones where my dreams turned to nightmares. Ones of her being tortured. Of her being hurt. Of her being killed. Would our bond know if she'd died? Would it know if she... if she... Those were the nights I'd wake up calling out for her. But she wouldn't come back to me. Couldn't. All because of the fucked-up Fae that was currently residing in my basement.

Letting out a primal growl, I swept the papers from my desk. With them, the glass paperweight flew, embedding into the wall. The lamp tipped on its side, the bulb breaking and winking out.

Ghost popped his head up from the floor, his whine letting

me know he could feel the turmoil doing my head in. That, and he didn't want to get caught in the crossfire.

Procuring Tristan—or rather, Drystan Haldrir Shadowfall, Crown Prince of the Dark Court hadn't been easy. It had taken Fiona months of storing her power, the right conditions, and a whole lot of help to even summon the bastard. And while she'd been preparing, I'd had the dungeon retrofitted to become the ultimate Fae cage. Because if the Lewis' taught me anything, it was that a good enough cage was all you really needed.

Well, that, and knowing where their weak spots were.

The problem with Tristan? As far as I knew, he didn't *have* any weak spots. No family, no friends, no allies, no nothing. There was no leverage to be had, and that had pissed me off for about a year now.

Another problem? Tristan did not react to torture. Not waterboarding, or burning, or removing limbs. Not that it mattered—the fuckers grew back almost instantly. Not a damn thing worked on him, and no matter what we did, he just. Wouldn't. Break.

He wouldn't break, he wouldn't talk, and he wouldn't so much as flinch. Not from isolation or starvation or any of the other thousand things we'd tried.

I'd lost hope a long time ago. Because hope? It was for suckers.

I wouldn't ever be getting her back. I wouldn't be opening those gates, and I wouldn't ever be happy again.

I'd thought about just killing him more times than I could count, but a part of me just couldn't do it. It was the "what ifs" that were killing me.

What if he changed his mind?

What if there was another way?

What if she found her way back to me?

With that tiny, infinitesimal grain of hope, I would always be looking, trying, praying that she made it home.

Somehow, I found myself in the basement dungeon, staring at my prisoner, my chest heaving, my heart racing. In the year Tristan had been in captivity, I had been in charge of his questioning, and while I was desperate, there were a few lines I would not cross.

But today it seemed my humanity, my compassion, my sense of right and wrong was long fucking gone. How I'd managed to hold onto it this long was a mystery.

"Come to play, Alpha? It's been weeks. I thought you'd forgotten about me."

How could I forget about this asshole? He was the key to everything.

The Fae tilted his head to the side, a winsome smile stretching his lips as his wrists hung from the manacles. "You seem to be a might bit worked up, though. I suppose that means I'm in for it, huh? Come on then. Do your worst."

But I had never done my worst. I had never shorn his hair, cut his ears. I had never plucked out his eyes or made him count grains of sand. I had never pumped the air with oxidized iron or cut his Achilles tendon with iron sheers. I never made wounds that would never, ever heal.

I had been kind.

Too kind.

Well, if drownings and burnings and amputations were considered kind. But I hadn't let Theo tear him apart or ask Ghost to eat him for lunch. I hadn't tried my hardest.

That ended today.

"My worst?"

Could I do my worst and stay sane?

Could I break him without breaking myself?

Did it matter?

Tristan's smile trembled a little before beaming wider. "That's what I asked for, wasn't it?"

"Indeed."

Did it matter that I would be broken if it meant she could come home?

Did it matter if it meant she would be in my arms?

No. I would take breaking myself over another day without her.

Slowly, I strode over to the cabinet and pulled out a set of iron sheers. They seemed ancient, the blackened metal heavy in my hand, but I knew they'd been forged with biting spells and the purest metals only a year ago.

Returning to the cell door, I met Tristan's gaze. "Tell me how to open the gates and I won't do this."

His eyes fell to the sheers, his body tightening bit by bit. "What fun would that be?"

Sniffing, I nodded, swallowing down the last of my reservations. A year. He'd been laughing at us for a fucking year. Faster than a striking snake, I slashed, raking the metal across his cheek.

With the silver blades, he hadn't so much as flinched. But with the iron? Tristan hissed as his whole body jolted, the sizzle of his flesh music to my fucking ears.

"You Fae like deals, right?" I ran the tip of the iron blade slowly down his other cheek, relishing every flinch, every howl of agony, every single bubble and pop of his burning flesh. "You open those gates, and I'll let you keep the skin you have left."

The Fae yanked at his bonds—something he hadn't done in the year he'd been down here—pure hate pouring from his eyes. But once he'd composed himself, the bastard was nothing but smiles and attitude.

"Someone woke up on the wrong side of the bed this morning. Finally decided to get serious, then? I was wondering when you'd gather the bollocks to really—"

The iron knife made a home against the vulnerable skin of his neck, the flat of the blade making his flesh sizzle.

"Open the fucking gates. Open one gate. Just give me back my wife."

The fucker had the gall to smile, his filthy, bloody face breaking into a wide grin. "No, I don't think I will. I fear my father and your wife far more than I fear you." He straightened, sitting up to take the next hit. "So do what you will, wolf. I will not break for you."

Oh, he'd break. The question was whether or not he'd live long enough to give me what I needed.

"So be it."

I trekked back to the cabinet and selected two sets of iron knuckles. This was going to be bloody. Bloody and brutal, and oh, so satisfying.

But... it *wasn't*.

It didn't matter how bloody the Fae's face was or how many times he yelped in pain. It didn't matter how I hit him. There was just no satisfaction to be had. He was hurt, but he wasn't suffering. He would eventually heal from his injuries and then what?

We would be exactly where we were.

All he had to do was be patient, and the Fae were nothing if not patient.

No, he needed something permanent. Something lasting.

Breathing heavy, I flung the iron knuckles off my hands and went back to the cabinet for the sheers. It was said that the Fae were revered by their hair. The longer it was, the more respect they had. It was also said that forcefully cutting a Fae's hair was tantamount to lopping off their balls.

As a child, I'd thought the act was barbaric. Who would hurt another being that way? But now I knew. Now I knew what this particular Fae was capable of—knew just what I would do to break him.

His hair in my fist, I sawed through the bundle with the iron sheers, cutting close enough to his scalp to draw blood, ignoring his feeble protests and weak, struggling jerks to get from my hold.

"Do my worst, huh?" I rumbled, cutting away every scrap of black hair. Even a year in this damn dungeon, it was still straight as an arrow, not a single tangle, and I relished the softness of it as it fell to the ground, mingling with the dirt and filth and blood.

But the Fae wasn't laughing anymore.

Gurgling breaths wheezed through his lungs as he hung listlessly from his bonds. So much like Wyatt had in the mage's cellar that it physically hurt to look at this man. Wyatt had recovered, but he wasn't the man he'd been before his captivity. Or maybe it was just me who had changed.

"Open the gate to my wife," I ordered, the Alpha power in my voice enough to break just about everyone. "Give her back to me, and this ends."

Slowly, the Fae's head rose, and he speared me with an expression so without hope it rang like a bell in my chest.

"If I have to die here alone and broken to see my family safe, there is nothing you can do to me to make me break. No crimes you could commit, no torture." His smile was despondently blank, the life, the spark that was once there, gone. "There is nothing, wolf."

And his blankness, his sadness made me rage. He was winning. And giving up meant he'd never give her back to me, never let me see her again, never...

My hand rose of its own accord.

"Stop," Mari screamed, racing down the basement steps and throwing herself against the bars. "This isn't you, Nico. Don't let him take you away from us."

But he had, hadn't he? Hadn't he taken away everything that I was? Hadn't he ripped everything good from me? Hadn't he stolen all that I was and all that I would be?

Hadn't he killed me already?

"Put the sheers down, brother. *Please.*"

Shaking my head, my fingers tightened around them. "He won't relent, Mari. He won't..."

"I know," she cooed, carefully opening the cell door and putting herself in between us. Trembling, she pulled the scissors from my bloody hand. "But Fiona found a way around him. Just... don't kill him."

But Fiona had been struggling for months to try and work something. She'd tried everything.

"You're lying. You just want me to have hope, but I can't have hope anymore. I can't do it."

Mari's gaze softened as she wrapped her arms around my middle. "She's found a way, big brother. We just need the Fae alive to do it."

Mari began pushing me toward the cell door, walking us both backward as she continued the hug. Could I have stopped her? Absolutely. But I needed this tiny sliver of hope more than I needed air.

"Please tell me that asshole is still breathing. I doubt I could do a damn thing with his ashes," Fiona called from the top of the steps.

Mari pulled back and shut the cell door, positioning herself in front of it like she was guarding the damn thing from me. "He is, thankfully. You really think you can pull this off?"

Fiona trudged down to our level, her thin frame so painfully gaunt it hurt my chest. She'd been struggling just as much as I had. Not sleeping, looking for something—anything—that would bring...

The poor girl would blow over with a stiff wind if she wasn't careful, but what she lacked in body mass, she made up for in power.

"Oh, yeah," Fiona practically growled, her teeth showing as she eyed the Fae in the cage. "That gate is going to open, dammit. I don't care if I have to use your fucking entrails to do it."

Tristan coughed out a weak chuckle. "You overestimate yourself, witch."

"Fuck you, Pixie Dust," she snarled, damn near throwing herself against the bars. "You're just mad because your last bargaining chip is gone. I don't need you to open anything. Not anymore."

That hope? It grew in my chest, a stoked fire that could go out at any minute.

"What do you need?"

CHATHAM SQUARE WAS A SMALL PATCH OF GREEN IN the middle of the city. So close to our old apartment, it hurt to be back at the place I'd lost her. The magic in this place was dead, the Fae portals stealing all of it when they closed, but someone, somewhere had been tending to the flowers. And that—as stupid as it was—gave me the confidence that this was going to work.

Fiona had needed an inordinate amount of shit to get this ball rolling. Specifically, she needed the door to the cabin where we'd sealed the mate bond. That was a big enough ask—especially since I wasn't an agent anymore—but then she gave me the rest of the list.

She needed my blood, the Fae's blood, and *her* blood.

The only place I could think of that had her blood on this plane of existence was my father's former office. It was either that or gut Margot Bannister and pray that was good enough. Personally, gutting Margot was still on the table even if the only purpose was to make me smile.

The laundry list of herbs and magical artifacts and salt—holy mother of the gods, the salt—was almost never-ending, but we'd gotten everything Fiona needed. What we didn't get her, was more witches.

The witch community of Savannah had dwindled significantly over the last year. Witches weren't disappearing exactly, just packing up and leaving without so much as a word. Covens with centuries of ancestral magic built up in the dozens of cemeteries, just skipping town. The rats were deserting a sinking ship, and I couldn't blame them. The place I called home wasn't what it used to be with all the Fae doors closed.

It was as if Savannah itself was mourning *her* loss right alongside me.

"Okay, we need to wait until the moon hits its peak, and then I can start," Fiona mumbled, staring at her watch as she fiddled with an iron blade.

Said iron blade was coated in... *Wren's* blood, the old, dried carpet of my father's study providing what we needed with a little bit of magic.

Wren.

Just thinking her name was a punch to the gut. But if we could get the door open, if we could just do something, it wouldn't feel like I'd lost her.

It wouldn't feel like she was gone forever.

It wouldn't feel like she was... *dead.*

Fiona approached with the knife coated in my wife's blood. "It's time. You ready?"

Holding out my forearm in answer, I nodded, more than ready to get this show on the road. Two years, eight months, four days, six hours, and twelve minutes. That's how long those doors had been closed. It had felt like decades.

Centuries.

Eons.

Fiona sliced through my arm, mingling my blood with Wren's. Then she moved to Tristan, not bothering to give him the same care. She brutally brought the blade down, nearly taking his whole hand with it. The Fae howled in agony, but Fiona paid him no mind. Instead, she positioned herself in the middle of her circle, the chants coming from her lips guttural and lilting all at the same time.

She was speaking Tristan's native tongue. Where she'd learned it, I wasn't sure, but she spoke with the fluid grace of someone who had studied the language for years. And with the blood and the chants and the ingredients, the world as a whole shook, the magic from Fiona spilling out into the night.

A door seemed to spring up from the ground, its edges framed in dark thorns with sharps spikes. A curl of blackened vines topped it, at their center a grim skull with glowing rubies for eyes. Fire kindled at its base, the embers catching on the grass, blackening it at the base.

This was wrong. Wren wouldn't come out of that door. No. No, I wanted the one from before. The one with flowers and green vines and no thorns.

I opened my mouth to say as much when an amber light lit the door as it opened. At the glimpse of red hair, my heart leapt, but I quickly realized that the person walking through wasn't Wren.

Not unless my wife had transformed into a tall, horned, bronze-skinned redheaded man in the last two years. Gold eyes scanned the square as the fire caught the grass, jumping from blade to blade, the iridescent scales on his bare arms shining in the light of the embers.

"You summoned a Prince of Hell by my blood. Where is my kin?" the man rumbled, but he wasn't a man, now, was he? Not if those scales and horns and title were anything to go by.

We'd wanted Wren, but we'd gotten a demon instead.

Fuck.

CHAPTER 5

WREN—PRESENT DAY

"What the fuck do you mean you don't know where Nico is?"

Exasperated, I stared at my best friend in the entire world like she had two heads. Was this the last straw in my already-crumbling psyche? Maybe. But I'd walked through a Fae door into what appeared to be a fucking apocalypse after being kidnapped and, and...

It was as if I had stepped right into *Bizarro World*. Savannah was on fire, and people were strolling down the street like nothing was wrong. Like this was normal. Like an entire city block being ablaze was just a regular Tuesday. Damn near every store was boarded up, there were burning trash barrels in the middle of the streets, and Ellie had just told me I'd been gone for three. Fucking. Years. And that was *after* she aimed a shotgun at my head.

Three years.

Granted, it made a sick sort of sense. The row house I'd called home for just a scant bit of time had been empty, barren, dust covering every surface. Dried blood had stained the hardwoods black, and I didn't know whose it was. I didn't know if my friends were even alive. And Ellie's house was fortified like she was prepping for a zombie apocalypse to descend on Savannah any second now.

But not knowing where my husband was, *was* the absolute last straw. I swear if she told me one more crazy thing, I would pass right on out. Maybe then I'd wake up in a place that wasn't on fucking fire.

Ellie's dark eyes softened with a little bit of pity, her grip getting tighter on my shoulder as she held me up. Why didn't she know where Nico was? How had everything gotten so fucked up? My chest wanted to cave in, and with the worry making a home for itself in my gut, I felt closer to Swiss cheese than an actual person.

"You were gone for so long, Nico couldn't even look at me without—" She shook her head, her throat sounding like she had a frog in it.

Meaning she'd seen him after Tristan had shoved him back with his power. He was alive—or at least he had been.

Three years.

I couldn't imagine losing Nico for three years. I'd been ripped away from him for a day—*tops*—and I was half out of my mind. Three years? I'd be a puddle on the floor.

Ellie stared at the front porch of the house she shared with her mother, tears pooling in her eyes. It was a small home, but once upon a time it was filled with laughter and love and so much warmth. Now it looked like it had seen better days. Three years of shit would do that to a house, I guessed.

And to a person.

"I couldn't look at him either. He'd come around every once in a while, making sure we were safe, but he's the Acosta Alpha now. Not that it means much nowadays."

Acosta Alpha? Did something happen to his dad? And why wouldn't that mean much? The Acostas were practically the kings of Savannah. How could three measly years change three hundred years' worth of power dynamics?

Nothing was making sense anymore.

Nothing.

"I'm so sorry, El," I murmured, latching onto her just as tight as she was to me. Maybe if I hugged her tight enough, she'd know just how glad I was to be back—even if being back meant the whole city was on fire. She was alive, Nico was alive. "Is Alice okay?"

Ellie gave me a wet sort of chuckle. "Of course. She's practically running the hospital. It's about the only place that's still running if you know what I mean. Hasn't gotten so much as a cold since you saved her."

I practically wilted to the pavement. Alice Whitlock needed to stay alive forever and a day if possible.

"We'd better get inside," she croaked, pulling out of reach. "It isn't safe being out too long anymore." Ellie gripped my wrist, dragging me closer to the front door.

But I didn't want to go inside. I didn't want to do anything but find Nico and Fiona and Malia and Hannah. I especially didn't want to be told to calm down and not to worry and to sip some tea.

I wanted answers—answers Ellie didn't seem to want to give me.

Plus, getting dragged places was how this mess got started in the first fucking place.

"Stop," I barked, ripping my arm out of her grip. If it wasn't arcane weirdos or Fae Kings or absolutely incomprehensible Seelie Queens, it was my best fucking friend.

But I didn't want to be touched by anyone, maybe ever again. Not without knowing all the facts about what I'd missed.

"I'm not going anywhere until someone somewhere tells me why Savannah is on fire and why shops are boarded up all over town and why—"

"Well, well, well," a male voice called, sending a bucket of ice water through my veins. It wasn't that his voice was particularly scary or mean. It was that he sounded just like the sinister Fae King that started this whole mess.

I half-expected Desmond to come walking out of the shadows when my gaze left Ellie. Instead, it found one of four Fae men slithering from the murky darkness. Okay, so they weren't slithering exactly, but the way they moved was... wrong. Just *wrong*. I'd never seen a Fae move like that.

With shorn hair and ears, covered in filth and rags and a fair amount of blood, they were unlike any other Fae I'd ever encountered outside of the Unseelie realm. Because the Unseelie realm had their kind in cages. Beaten and bloody, they appeared half-starved and crazed and...

Feral, my brain supplied, and the old noodle was one hundred percent right. Feral was the best word to describe them.

"You smell of the Dark Court," the talker growled, an

expression of hunger on his face as his purple eyes lit with his magic. "Fresh, too. You smell of home. Tell me, witch, how do you smell of our homeland? Tell us which gate you have opened." His smile was predatory, his canines filed to points. "Tell us and I may let you both live."

If his home was the Dark Court and they wanted to go back, these weren't the Fae to fuck around with. These were the Fae to run screaming down the street to get away from.

Awesome. Just what I wanted after my dramatic exit of the Dark Court only to be dragged back to it. *No, thank you.*

"Get in the house, Wren," Ellie hissed, reloading her shotgun and snapping the barrel closed. I could have sworn she'd set it down, but somehow it was back in her hands, and she was ready to fire.

And honestly? That seemed like the best idea anyone had ever had in the history of ever. Shooting first and asking questions later was absolutely the correct course of action. Unfortunately, I didn't make it three paces before the Fae were on us. Gritty hands yanked Ellie right off her feet, the men moving so fast they were a blur of speed. She managed to get a single shot off before her gun fell from her hands, managing not to go off again as it clattered to the concrete driveway.

One of the Fae staggered back, his middle a grizzly mess from the buckshot. But I was more focused on the hold the others had on my best friend. Heat flashed over my body as her screams ripped through the air. The scent of her fear spiced the air with a cloying perfume that made me want to gag.

I didn't even notice the hands on me—didn't even register them tearing me away from her. What I did notice was one of them striking my best friend across the face. Blood stained

Ellie's lips and I moved. The speed Nico had shared with me, the animalistic qualities that I'd garnered in just the short time I'd been mated to him, reared their very welcomed head.

It seemed like years ago when I'd sparred with Nico in the courtyard. In a way, it had been years, but that didn't mean I couldn't use every advantage I had against these fucks. Kicking my legs out, I twisted in their grip, tossing one away as I nailed the other right in the gut. But the one that touched Ellie had my full attention, a burning sort of fire churning in my belly as the rage settled in.

And then I wasn't the only one that was burning.

I swear, as soon as the mere thought of fire hit my brain, the Fae that was holding Ellie started screaming, his tattered shirt going up in smoke along with his shorn hair. The problem? My hand was also sort of on fire. On instinct, I flailed my fingers trying to extinguish the flames, but instead of them going out, they just spread, falling from my skin like raindrops onto the very dead grass.

What the fuck?

No, really, when in the blue fuck had fire become a problem I needed to deal with? Sure, once upon a time there had been fire issues when people had done spells around me, but not once in the history of ever had I made fire of my own outside of flicking a fucking lighter.

Ellie wrenched herself out of the burning Fae's hold while I proceeded to catch the grass, one of the other Fae's tattered pants, and my left shoe on fire. Stomping my foot, I managed to get that problem resolved, but the rest...

"You think a little fire is going to stop me from going home?"

The spokesman of the group latched onto my shirt, dragging me closer as he ignored the growing blaze in my palm. The back of his hand cracked against my cheek, sending a lightning bolt of pain through my whole head. When I could peel my eyes open again, the fire in my palm was out. Sure, his buddy was still writhing on the ground, catching every bit of Ellie's yard on fire, but that wasn't the problem at the moment.

No, the problem was that for the zillionth time in a handful of days—yes, the timeline was debatable—I was being carried somewhere I absolutely did not want to go.

"Get your hands off of her," a man growled, the animalistic cadence to his voice familiar and not, all at the same time.

Rough hands ripped me out of the Fae's grip, and somehow, I was on my feet behind the back of a hulking hooded figure holding a blade. His calloused and scarred hand held me behind him, almost as if he didn't want to let me go.

My heart tripped in my chest. The scent wasn't right, the voice was rougher, harder, but his touch? No one could fake the hold his touch had on my heart.

Nico.

I twisted my wrist out of his grip to put my hand in his and hold it tight. It had only been a day for me and that was too fucking long. It had been years for him.

Years.

But Nico didn't look at me. No, he was focused on the two Fae still standing.

"You're in my way, wolf. Stand aside and I'll let you live."

"You won't touch her again," Nico growled, his voice no smoother now than it was a few seconds ago. "And I remember you barely surviving the last time we did this dance."

"Come to finish what you started, then?" the Fae returned, flicking his shorn ear. The wound was months old, the pointed tip long gone. In stories, Fae would shear their own ears to fit into human society, but I'd never seen it done against a Fae's will.

But Nico didn't answer him.

Instead, he shot forward, taking me with him as he advanced. We moved together as his sword sliced through the air, the bloody squelch of it hitting home sending ice through my veins. By the time Nico stopped moving, the Fae were in pieces on the ground, the bloody limbs twitching as their nerves died. A severed head stared at me, eyes wide in the throes of its death mask.

I fought off the urge to puke.

"What the fuck, Nico?" Ellie griped, resting the stock of her shotgun over her shoulder. "You'd better call one of your brothers to clean this mess up. If Mom sees Fae innards on her front lawn, she's gonna shit a kitten."

Nico flicked blood off his sword before stowing it in the scabbard across his back. Then he gave a sharp whistle. "Ghost. *Lunch.*"

I about jumped out of my skin when a flash of white fur brushed against my hip, the giant wolf seemingly coming from nowhere. The behemoth of an animal made quick work of the Fae—even the charred one—leaving only the stain of blood on the ground.

"I suppose hosing the ground is necessary," Ellie grumbled, stomping off to the side of the house while I stared at the huge white wolf licking his chops, his fur stained red.

Shivering in the heat, I backed up a few steps until the leash of Nico's hold pulled taut.

Then he turned, finally meeting my gaze. His eyes were the same gold color, but that was about all that was familiar. They were harder—hell, his whole face was—with the faint trace of lines fanning out from the corners. A white scar bisected his right eyebrow, and another cut down his cheek toward his mouth. There might have been more, but the rest of his face was covered in a thick beard.

Nico's shoulders seemed to sit wider, his spine straighter. He knocked the hood of his coat off his head, revealing he hadn't cut his hair since I'd been gone, the strands reaching past his shoulders.

All of that came to me in the periphery, my focus on his eyes and how hopeful they seemed. He reached for me, his bloody hand trembling as it nearly made contact with my skin.

"*Wren*," he breathed. "Is it really you?"

CHAPTER 6

NICO

IT COULDN'T BE. COULD IT?

Years of searching—of spells, of all-out war—and she just shows up one day out of the blue? The wolf beneath my skin howled to get free, calling me to this very spot. Calling me to her.

"Nico?"

Just the sound of her sweet voice made my knees weak. My hands found her face, the Fae's blood staining her skin red, but I didn't care.

Wren.

There were so many questions I wanted to ask and none all at the same time. What questions mattered when she was here? There had been a time that I would gladly sell my soul to have her in my arms and here she was.

Healthy and whole.

Alive.

I ducked, pressing our foreheads together as I took her scent into my nose for the first time in three years. Other than the faint trace of Fae, she smelled exactly the same—that same honey and jasmine perfume that was all her.

And all I wanted to do was kiss her and hold her and make sure she never got hurt again.

"Missed you, Bird. Missed you so fucking much."

Then my lips were on hers, the warmth of them making me feel alive for the first time in years. That ache in my chest—the one that had me practically clawing my own heart out of my body? It had eased, my heart picking up speed as I drowned in her, our tongues tangling as I drank her down.

My arms found their way around her waist, clutching her to me with a roughness that scared me a little. My brain was screaming at me to be gentle, but my wolf was doing the exact opposite. He wanted our fangs in her neck and her heat surrounding us and her moans down our throat.

And he was getting harder and harder to ignore.

Lifting Wren off her feet, my palms found the swell of her ass, and the carnal moan that came out of her when the ridge of my erection brushed her center was fucking bliss. And she was wearing the same dress that she'd left me in—the odd dichotomy of frilly floral sundress and combat boots that had made my dick hard three years ago. I'd had plans for that dress, if I remembered right, and those plans were coming true just as soon as—

"Are you two planning on fucking on the front lawn or is finding someplace private on your to-do list? I'm sure the demons running around here would love a good show, but I'm going to need some eye bleach."

I loved Ellie Whitlock like one of my sisters, but now was not the time for her brand of humor.

Wren's lips broke from mine, her wide green-gold eyes lighting up with her magic. "Did she say demons? I could have sworn she said demons."

The sheer amount of shit we needed to discuss was vast, but my dick had other plans for the next twenty-four hours and talking about demons was not on that list. My grip tightened on Wren's ass, before I set her back on her feet and aimed a glare at her best friend.

"I'm taking her home. I'll make sure the boys patrol this area tonight. Make sure the Fae know to stay away."

Ellie rolled her eyes as she sprayed blood off the pavement. "Just let her come up for air sometime in the next week, will you?"

Her gaze shifted to Wren who seemed just as confused and alarmed at the demon talk as she was a minute ago. "And don't worry about the demons. They keep to themselves. Mostly."

Wren just blinked at her, her mouth agape. "I cannot begin to tell you just how not comforting that statement was."

But Ellie was right. The demons weren't the ones we needed to worry about. Wren peeled out of my grip, enveloping her best friend in a hug so tight it was a wonder Ellie could breathe. "I'm coming back tomorrow. You have to fill me in on all I missed, okay?"

Ellie squeezed her back, but smartly said, "You'll be back sometime next week when he finally lets you up for air. I'll be here when you're ready, babe. Now that you're back, there's no rush."

She was reluctant to let Wren go, but finally managed it with teary eyes and a pinched mouth. Wren was home. She was back. She was safe.

And she is ours.

My wolf had not quit his incessant howling, but he was right on that front.

Wren was ours. And she needed to come home where it was safe.

Without another word, I pulled Wren back, guiding her toward home. The warmth of her hand in mine was everything I'd wished for. In my wildest dreams, she came to me like this—showing up one day out of the blue. A sick part of me wondered if I was still dreaming, if none of this was true.

But my heart and my wolf did not give that first fuck.

Walking in Savannah was a necessary evil. With as many stalled, burned-out cars cluttering the road, there wasn't much use for driving, anyway. Still, it wasn't exactly safe. The demons that followed Zephyr out of the Hell gate were nice enough. The real deterioration to the city came when the Fae topside couldn't use them to go home.

That may have started a mini war between the species that pretty much fucked over the rest of the city. And with the ABI too busy making sure the world stayed none the wiser about our little predicament down here, the war raged on unchecked.

Well, sort of.

How Wren had made it here unscathed made my chest start hurting all over again. Just seeing those Fae with their hands on her made me want to rage. Tucking her under my arm, I guided us west toward home and buried my nose in her hair. Ducking into an alley between two burned-out buildings, we picked our way through trash and rubble.

Do you wish me to scout the way, Alpha? Ghost's voice rang in my head, yanking my focus back to the matter at hand. We needed to get three miles down the road without incident.

Sure. No problem.

Wren startled under my arm, staring at Ghost's retreating back like he was an actual ghost. "Did that wolf just talk to you. Like in your head?"

That gave me pause. "You heard him?"

No one else in the pack could hear Ghost—not even in their wolf form. Only me.

"Of course I heard him. He burrowed right into my brain and—" She stopped, resting her hands on her knees as she wobbled. "This is too much. Wolves just speaking inside my brain and Savannah is on literal fire and Ellie damn near blew my head off and evidently, it's been three fucking years, but to me it's only been a day, and the Fae could touch me here, but they couldn't touch me there and—"

Some things just never changed.

Cupping her cheeks, I pressed a kiss to her trembling lips, stopping her rant mid-sentence. I had never missed someone freaking out like I'd missed Wren's epic meltdowns. I had never wished to solve a problem or ached to listen to someone like this. Being Alpha I heard a lot about other people's issues, but Wren's was the only ones I wanted to solve.

She's here.
She's alive.

Her scent enveloped me, quelling that ache in my chest once more—the one I never thought would go away.

"Tell me, Bird," I murmured against her lips as I hauled her up into my arms, her legs wrapping around my waist like they were made to do it. "If I fuck you against this wall, will that make it all better, or—"

This time it was me that was cut off, her kiss searing a path all the way down to my dick. It had been so long since I'd had her touch, so long since her scent filled my nose and her softness in my arms. It had been so long since I'd had any sort of bliss—and having Wren's mouth on mine, her body close to mine, her ass in my hands was indeed bliss.

Two steps later, her back was against the rough brick wall and her hands were at my belt. Wren broke our kiss, moving to my jaw, my neck, the rake of her growing fangs at the tender skin sending chills down my spine.

Three years.

Three years without her touch. Without her kisses. Without her teeth at my neck, without her smile. Three years of searching.

Fuck.

I pressed the bulge in my jeans against her center, the heat of her calling my name. My whole body thrummed with her desire, her need, her emotions. I'd missed them so much, even though they nearly made me mindless. It took everything inside of me not to tear the fabric away and just plunge inside her.

Are we really doing this here?

For lack of a better term, this was indeed in public, and it wasn't safe with Fae crawling around, and...

The war raging in my brain died a swift death as her hand closed around my cock.

"Fuck me, Nico," Wren breathed, her voice hitching as my thumb raked across her tight nipple. "I need you."

Yes. We were doing this here and now.

"I fucking need you, too."

Hiking up her skirt, it took less than a second to rip her underwear out of the way and notch the head of my cock against her opening. My eyes practically rolled into the back of my head at her heat searing into me. And then I pushed inside, her gasping breath against my lips everything I wanted and more.

I paused a second, the need warring inside me almost too strong. My wolf was so close to the surface, I could hurt her and not mean to.

Wren's finger found my chin, jerking it so I had to meet her gaze. "I told you to fuck me, Nico." The walls of her pussy fluttered around my cock, nearly undoing me right there and then. "I didn't say be gentle. I didn't say be polite. We'll do polite later. Fuck me like you missed me. Now."

She even used a bit of my Alpha in her voice like she'd been the one who'd been crowned and not me. Fuck, she was so fucking sexy it almost hurt.

"Yes, my queen," I growled as I thrust into her, earning a gasp that quickly morphed into a moan.

I fucked her like a man possessed. I fucked her like I hated her, like I blamed her. Like she was the reason I'd spent the last three years alone. Like she was the guilty one and not me.

Her moans were loud enough to wake the dead, but I couldn't for the life of me silence them—I'd missed them too much. So instead, I swallowed them, kissing her as she whimpered into my mouth, her needy mewls sending fire straight down to my balls.

Fuck.

I was going to unman myself right here in this alley.

Breaking the kiss, I yanked at her dress, exposing one of her luscious breasts to my mouth. Her breath hitched, but she needed more. I didn't wait three fucking years to have our reunion ruined by my overeager dick.

"Open," I ordered, cupping her jaw. She did as told, and I thrust my thumb into her mouth. She eagerly sucked it, curling her tongue around the tip like she'd once done to my cock. Roughly, I pulled it free, finding her clit with the now-wet digit.

Circling the tight bud, I met her eyes, watching them glow with heat and magic and the wolf she didn't have.

"You're going to come for me, Bird. You hear me? You're going to come right the fuck now."

My thumb circled once, twice, three times and then she was coming apart, a silent scream showing me the flush of her perfect skin, her pleasure, the fangs that I ached to have in my own throat.

Without warning, she struck, burying those sharp teeth into my mating mark like it had a beacon guiding her there. My release slammed into me, pulling me under before I could even take a breath. My fangs ached with it, finding her skin and cutting through it without conscious thought on my part. A second release crashed through her, the bite's effect radiating through our bond.

Damn near boneless, I clutched her to me, relishing the

feeling of a satisfied woman in my arms as the breaths heaved in my chest. When both hers and mine slowed, I gently helped her get her clothes to rights. Her underwear was somehow not in complete tatters, but the strap of her dress was toast.

I slipped the sword off my back and out of my coat, placing it over her shoulders and zipping it all the way up. "Sorry. I didn't mean to—"

Guilt suffused me, twisting my gut until I was ready to beg her forgiveness. Wren deserved more than an alleyway fuck. More than me ripping her clothes. She—

"Stop." Soft hands reached for my face, cupping it like I was the most precious thing she'd ever seen. "Don't think for a second that I didn't love every minute of what we just did. I asked for rough and you gave it to me. Understand?"

Tipping my chin in a truncated nod, she raised a single eyebrow. *Fine.* "I understand, Bird."

"Good. Now, quit feeling like shit because you're harshing my mellow and I think I'm going to need it a lot before we get home." Her gaze panned over the alleyway. "Speaking of home, where is it? Also, I really like this." She reached up and gently pulled at a strand of my hair.

I hadn't cut my hair in three years. Now it was past my shoulders and an epic nuisance. Grumbling, I pulled it into a knot at the back of my head with an elastic band I'd had to steal from one of my sisters.

"Don't get too attached to it."

"Aww, come on," she pleaded, circling my middle in a hug. "Let me have it for just a little while longer? And the beard. I *really* like the beard."

Smiling, I pressed a kiss to her forehead. If she wanted me

to be a double for Rapunzel and keep a mountain man beard, I'd do it. I'd do damn near anything. If it meant she was staying here with me, if it meant she was really here, if it meant she was by my side for the rest of my life, I'd do any fucking thing she wanted me to.

"Come on, Bird. I'll show you the way home."

CHAPTER 7

WREN

THE HARRIED TREK TO NICO'S HOME WAS MARGINALLY uneventful. Other than sidestepping a burning car and ducking behind a building to avoid a roving group of listless Fae, the two-mile journey was peaches and fucking roses. I hadn't really taken it all in when I'd raced to find Ellie, but it was so much worse than I'd thought.

By the time we reached the Acosta pack house, the shock of it all had taken its toll. I'd lost three years. And in that time the world had literally gone to shit. Blinking away tears, I stared at a place I thought I'd never see again.

Nico's childhood home had changed significantly from the last time I'd stood in this very driveway. For one? It was shrouded so heavily by overgrown live oaks I barely recognized it, the Spanish moss and branch both going unchecked since

I'd seen it last. Two? It was cloaked in enough magic, even I had a hard time looking at the joint. Normally glamours weren't a problem for me, but this was just unreal.

"Come on, Bird. Let's get off the street."

Again, I wanted no part of this home, but for a very different reason this time. Last time I worried they wouldn't like me. This time I was just keen on keeping my head attached to my shoulders and my blood in my veins. But I kept my mouth shut, though, holding tight to Nico's hand as I followed him and Ghost inside.

My gaze immediately went to the closed door of Nico's father's office, and of its own accord, my hand reached for my neck. I wondered if that room was the same. Did they put it back to rights? Or was my blood still staining the carpet, blackened with age?

"Bird?"

Startled, I tore my eyes from the door and found Nico. "Yeah?"

His golden gaze centered on me just a little, making me suck in a breath to my frozen lungs.

"He's gone, you know. And Diana has been banished for years. And my brothers will never touch you again. I swear it. I know you think—" He shook his head, pulling me closer. "I actually don't know what you think, but there is so much to tell you, so much."

I probably should have felt relieved, but I didn't. There were demons walking the streets of Savannah, and somehow, something told me that I was the cause. There was no way I wasn't going to get blamed for that. There was no way that Diana wasn't right about me.

What had Áine said? That I was breaking the Fae realm? What if I did that here, too? Was anyone safe around me?

"It's fine. I'm fine." That was a total and complete lie. Three years? Three years. Just gone.

Nico squinted at me, his skepticism palpable. "You know that I can feel you, right? It's how I knew you were back, how I knew to find you. Knew you were in trouble." He tapped his chest over his heart three times. "You live here. Inside me. Your emotions, your heartbeat, the breath in your lungs. I missed it so much when you were gone. It was an ache that never went away. So, I know exactly what you're feeling, and I'm going to make sure you never feel this way again."

He let my hand go and cupped my jaw, pressing his forehead against mine.

"You will be safe and warm and loved, and I don't care if I have to move heaven or hell to do it, either."

The sheer determination on his face would be scary to anyone else. To me? It was a promise I knew he would die to keep.

And that was the problem.

"Like I said, I'm fine. It's just a lot, you know? I'll adjust."

Pressing a kiss to my lips, he eased some of the dread pooling in my belly, so I supposed that was a start.

"Holy fucking shit," a familiar voice called from the top of the stairs. I practically wilted in Nico's arms as Hannah and Malia sprinted down the staircase.

Hannah was just as stone-faced and stoic as ever, but she'd changed her hair quite a bit. It was now down to her waist, dyed a midnight-purple color that seemed to shimmer to cobalt in the right light. Malia was slightly less buttoned up, her hair hung loose around her shoulders, the curls only slightly tamed instead of her usual painfully tight bun. And instead of high-collared button-up shirts and wide slacks, she was in cargo pants and a fitted long-sleeve top with a deep scoop neck.

The biggest change? Her hands were free of gloves. And of all people, it was Malia who damn near tackled me in a hug.

"I can't believe it. Holy shit. Oh, my gods." She pulled away, staring at me like I couldn't be real. "I tried everything. I could never see you. Holy shit."

Tears filled her eyes before I was wrapped in another hug, her ironclad hold one I didn't want to break.

"Quit hogging her," Hannah griped before wrapping us both in her long arms. Being damn near six and a half feet tall, she had no problem squeezing the shit out of us both. "What happened? How did you get back?"

Shrugging, I opened my mouth only to close it again. How could I answer them? They had gone through so much—suffered so much—and for me it had only been a day.

A bad day, sure, but a single day, nonetheless.

"Is this for real?" Someone else said, accompanied by a thunder of several feet.

I was pulled out of Hannah and Malia's hold to get damn near squeezed to death by Nico's little sister Mari. "He told us through the pack bond, but holy shit. I swear half of us thought he was hallucinating or something. Holy fuck buckets, where have you been, girl?"

Someone pulled me from Mari, and I was patted on the back and hugged and squeezed by more people that I could shake a stick at. Lara gave me a one-armed hug with a toddler on her hip and Dayana picked me up right off my feet with happy tears in her eyes. Luckily, I was rescued once the love got overwhelming. Nico pulled me away from everyone with a gentle growl, fitting me under his arm like he'd shank them if they got too close.

"Let's get you some food and—" Nico began before I cut him off with a question that should have been on my lips from the get-go. There was a person missing from this massive huddle and the fact that she hadn't come down those stairs screaming her head off was the real concern here.

"Where's Fiona?"

I met Hannah's gaze as she stared down at me for a second before she turned to Nico. The look on her face said, "Your call, boss" and that was a very, very bad thing. A "no-good, very bad, oh, fuck" kind of a thing.

"She's fine," Nico said, but there was the teensiest bit of a lie there. "She's alive, she's conscious, she's—"

"She's under house arrest," Malia finished for him. "We'll tell you all about it, and you can see her for yourself in a minute. She'll be really happy to see you."

I was still stuck on that last bit. "House arrest?"

What the fuck had Fiona done to earn herself a punishment—especially with everything going on? Nico had filled me in a little on the way here. The ABI was in shambles trying to keep Savannah contained, but the Fae pretty much worldwide were losing their fucking minds. Luckily there weren't a ton of them on this side, so only the densely populated cities like Savannah, New York, New Orleans, and San Francisco were having instability.

Plus, Savannah was the only one with an active open Hell gate, so we were essentially ground zero for the fuckery. The ABI had cordoned off Savannah like it was a CDC black zone, quarantining us to the rest of the world. There was enough magic at the border to keep almost everyone in. Granted, some arcaners were leaving in droves—those with enough money and connections to grease the wheels of bureaucracy and cut through the red tape.

He had missed the part about how the Hell gate opened, though, and what they were doing to close the damn thing.

"I can eat later. I want to see her now."

"I don't think so," Catia said in a mom voice that had my shoulders reaching for my ears. "I can hear your stomach rumbling. When was the last time you ate?"

That was a hard question to answer. "Breakfast the day I left. But time is different there. I think it's only been a day or two for me."

Granted, I was unconscious for a little bit, so that timeline could get pushed a little left, but the truth of the matter was it hadn't nearly been as long for me as it had for them.

"Remind me never to go through a Fae door," Santiago muttered, eyes wide as he stared at me like I had spontaneously grown a second head.

Frankie smacked his little brother on the arm with the back of his hand. "There aren't any open Fae doors to go through, moron."

"One day or three years, doesn't matter." Catia grabbed my hand from Nico's and slung an arm over my shoulder. "You need food. I'm making you a plate and you're going to eat until you can't anymore, you hear me?"

"I'm fi—"

Catia's eyebrow should be against the Geneva Convention and classified as a war crime. "If you finish that word, so help me, I will force feed you until your stomach bursts. Then you can get a shower, and after that, you can go see Fiona. No offense, sweetheart, but you smell like a dungeon, and not a nice one."

I didn't want to tell her that was exactly where I'd been, so I kept my mouth shut, following her lead to the kitchen where far more people sat around the counter, spilling into the dining room. Every single person froze when we walked in—stopping mid-conversation and mid-bite.

Oh, good. Just what I always wanted. An audience to my awkwardness.

"Most of the pack lives here with us on the compound now." Catia grabbed a plate and started loading it down with more food than I could eat in a week. "With so many humans gone, we commandeered the surrounding properties for our use, but more often than not, we eat here. It's good to have a touchstone of family while everything is..." She trailed off, shaking her head as she dumped gravy on the mashed potatoes.

"At least there's many hands and all that. Makes it easier."

I had the hardest time wondering what I was supposed to be doing. Was I supposed to wave? Everyone was staring at me... But then I realized maybe they weren't staring at *me* but *us*. Studying Catia, I noticed the changes in her that I'd missed in all the hubbub. There was a sadness to her, found only in the lines of her shoulders and the tightness to her eyes. She was smiling at me, but I still saw the hurt and fear and pain behind the mask.

I didn't know what had happened to make Nico the Acosta Alpha, but I knew it had to have involved losing Tomás. And as much as he had hurt Nico, as much as he'd hurt me, I'd never wish her to lose her husband over it.

"Come on, sweetheart. I made lemon tarts just for you."

A sting hit my eyes making me blink hard, so I didn't start bawling in the middle of this kitchen surrounded by all these people.

"Thank you," I managed to choke out before a distinct growl made everyone more than freeze.

I looked up to an irritated Nico crowding into me, but his eyes were on his pack.

"Give us a minute, everyone."

Waving away his order, I shook my head. "No, no. I'm fine. Everything is fine. They are enjoying their meal. Let them be."

But my eyes did that stupid thing, like filling to the brim and spilling over, and Nico was having none of it. "Out."

I swear, that kitchen was cleared in two seconds, flat. Nico's whole family just up and left the room, no questions asked—even his mom—which made me feel like the biggest heel on the planet. Heat rose in my cheeks, and I forced myself not to duck my head—not that Nico would let me.

His rough hands cupped my face, making me look at him. "What is it, Bird?"

Sweet mother of the gods, can I not be a basket case for like three seconds?

"You're being overprotective," I grumbled, pulling out of his grip. "It's not a big deal. They were happy tears, anyway."

"You've been doing good so far with everything. It's oka—"

Oh, for fuck's sake.

"Your mom made me lemon tarts," I hissed, dashing away the tears that practically burned my skin. "She remembered that I loved them and didn't get to try one the last time I was here, and she made them just for me." I sniffed, praying a hole would just open up underneath me and swallow me up. "That's why I was upset. It has nothing to do with the pack or my trauma from the Fae realm or anything else. Your mom was kind, and it took me by surprise is all."

Gold lit in his eyes before he reached for me, folding me into a hug so warm and soft and safe, the tears threatened again.

Fuuuuucccck. Get it together, Wren.

"In case you weren't aware, the first chance I get, I'm ripping your mother's heart right out of her chest. That is if that craven bitch even has one."

I let out a watery chuckle. "You mean you haven't killed her yet? *Slacker.*"

"Yeah, well, I was more focused on finding you."

As far as excuses went, that was a good one. "Fine. I'll let it go just this once. Now can everyone come back and eat their freaking food?"

Nico was the Alpha and here he was married to Crybaby McGee and her merry band of sniffles. I swear, I needed a keeper.

And maybe a lobotomy.

Nico let out a piercing whistle and it was as if the floodgates opened. People streamed back into the kitchen, their conversations spilling through the door and over me in a wave of noise. It was so much better than the record-scratch event of earlier.

But the best was Catia's hand resting in the middle of my back as she put two of those lemon tarts on the edge of my plate.

CHAPTER 8

WREN

It took a damn age before I could get downstairs to see Fiona.

If it wasn't Catia's raised eyebrow making sure I ate every morsel on my plate, it was Nico ensuring no one in their right mind even so much as looked at me sideways. Considering what happened after the last dinner we had in this house, I couldn't say I blamed him.

He crowded me at the corner of the kitchen island, offering me a cushy barstool while he stood at my back, his hand never leaving me. If it wasn't threaded with my own, it rested on the small of my back or on my leg. It fiddled with the hem of my dress or played with the ends of my hair. It was as if he was reassuring himself that I was real—that he wasn't dreaming—and that made my heart hurt more than I could possibly say.

I wolfed down my food, my hunger getting the best of me.

As soon as the first bite hit my tongue, it was as if I hadn't eaten in a week. Granted, it was totally possible it had been more than a day or two in the Fae realm.

"At least she can eat," someone said under their breath, "even if she is a wi—"

Dayana and Mari both smacked a tall man upside the head, but that didn't stop Nico's growl sounding like a thing straight out of a nightmare as his chest vibrated against my back like my own personal guard dog.

Oh, shit, here we go.

This just wouldn't do. I couldn't have Nico threatening every asshole who called me a name, and Nico's pack hadn't even been introduced to me yet. I put a quelling hand on Nico's arm before hopping off my barstool to go meet the tall wolf who probably had a beef with witches.

The energy coming off of him meant he was probably in the seventy- to hundred-year-old range, and his shoulders were beefy and corded with muscle, meaning he could likely bend me like a pretzel. Plastering a beaming smile on my face, I held out my hand to the guy.

In for a penny and all that.

"Hi, I'm Wren. What's your name?"

The guy frowned at my outstretched hand like no one in the history of ever had offered one to him. They'd probably been too scared he'd crush it.

"Zaid," he rumbled, gently taking my fingers in his and shaking it like he could break me if he didn't concentrate. It was either that or touching me made him want to throw up. You know, dealer's choice.

"Now, I get it, like most of y'all, you probably have a

problem with the Bannister family. If you know anything about them, though, you'd know I am the black sheep and hate them probably—if not more—than you do. So in a way, we're on the same side, right?"

Zaid's face solidified like I was speaking in tongues, his jaw twitching as he geared up to be an asshole. "No. A witch can never be on the same side as a wolf." He looked past me to Nico, deciding to fuck up in a spectacular fashion. "They all deserve to d—"

"Enough," I growled, pulling on Nico's Alpha before this asshole said something he couldn't take back. "I have had it up to here with bullshit for one day. I went toe-to-toe with a Fae King and laughed in his fucking face. Do you honestly think I'm scared of you? You think you can *bully* me? You think you can hurt my *feelings*?"

I swear if it wasn't Diana, it was Desmond, or my mother, or fucking Ames. What was it about me that just pulled the assholes out of the woodwork?

"You might not like me, and that's fine. Based off your attitude, we probably won't be besties anytime soon. But you will respect my husband or so help me I will put you in the fucking ground. We clear?"

Zaid's gaze dropped when I didn't so much as flinch.

"I asked if we were clear. Are we?" I gestured to Dayana, Lara, and Mari, and a few of Nico's brothers who looked like they were ready and willing for this shit to pop off, crowding Zaid like they were all too eager to cut out a cancer. "Because if I don't put you in the ground, I have more than enough people at my back to do it for me. That is if your Alpha doesn't rip out your heart and fucking feed it to you."

Nico's warmth at my back was punctuated by a low growl that had heat thrumming through my veins and the hairs on my neck standing on end.

"My queen asked you a question," he rumbled, circling my middle with his arm and hugging me to his front. "Answer her."

Zaid's lips pursed like he had to fucking think about it, and that was right about when I lost it for the day. He wanted to call my bluff? *Fine.*

One second, Zaid was douching it up with his lip-purse, and the next, his big body was embedded in the kitchen drywall, blinking at me like I was a gods-damned wizard or something. Now, I would totally allow that I had surprise on my side. No one expected a five-foot-and-some-change, noodle-armed witch to put a seven-foot behemoth through a wall—not even said seven-foot behemoth.

Hell, especially the behemoth.

They also hadn't expected me to yank him out of the wall by the scruff of his neck, walk him outside, and dump his big ass on the back lawn, either.

Wide, dark eyes stared at me, but that stupid fucking look was off his face.

"You think about apologizing, you can come back inside, and we'll forget this bullshit ever happened. You act like an asshole one more time and I'll make you regret it." Raising a single eyebrow, I asked my question again: "Are we clear now?"

"Crystal, my queen," he croaked, back flat on the ground and hands up like a submissive little puppy.

I didn't know if I liked that whole "queen" business but if

it made assholes like Zaid shut up and sit down, I was all for it. If I was a queen, Nico would be their king, and he needed someone watching his back. A part of me wondered if I was good enough to do that job, but it wasn't like I could quit now.

Grumbling, I went back to my plate and my half-eaten mashed potatoes that were conspicuously warm, even though it had been a solid minute since I'd taken a bite. Didn't matter. Food was far more important and filling my belly was at the top of my to-do list.

"Holy shit, Wren. Why again did your husband have me watching your back?" Hannah let out a deep belly laugh when I flipped her off as I kept stuffing my face.

"That was hot as fuck, Bird," Nico whispered in my ear, and I had to fight off a shiver because his voice was doing ridiculously awesome things to my belly.

Ignoring him, I nabbed the first of two lemon tarts and popped it into my mouth. Flavor exploded across my tongue and my eyes rolled up into my head. I was pretty sure I moaned, too.

Before I knew it, I was off the barstool and being dragged by the hand up the stairs.

"Nico? What th—"

Then I was pressed against Nico's incredibly hard front, his golden eyes blazing as his warmth, his desire, his mindless craving filled our bond. It was enough to make my knees weak.

"Three years, Bird." His grip tightened on me, and the thick bulge in his pants pressed against my belly. "Three years of those moans I missed."

Dammit. I wanted him so much I ached. Ten seconds ago, I

was happy to get food in my belly, and now so much lust was pounding through my veins, I was damn near crazed with it.

Pressing up to my tiptoes, I nibbled on his bottom lip, the fangs that seemed to grow with my anger or desire nicking his lip. His eyes flared as a single drop of blood welled from the cut, but they went heavy-lidded when I darted out my tongue to steal the drop.

Then we weren't in the hallway anymore. One second, I was savoring the tangy flavor, and the next, I was over his shoulder with Nico's clawed hand holding my ass in place. Each point of those claws holding but not piercing my flesh made me slick between my legs.

Nico set me down in a large bathroom and flipped on the shower, his shirt gone before I had time to adjust to being vertical again. In the periphery I knew the bathroom was huge, with a ten-person shower and a large soaking tub. There were spa-like features but all I could focus on was him. His smooth golden skin was interrupted by long scars and a few burns. I refused to think about what he'd gone through to get them—what could cut him bad enough that even his wolf couldn't heal him. But damn if they didn't just add to everything that was Nico.

Another moment later and Nico was naked, his thick cock standing up and proud, making my mouth water. And while I would have loved to undress him myself, I couldn't help but enjoy the show as he stalked toward me. Nico's focus was so acute, it was as if I was the only woman on the planet, and that reverence—that almost worship—it was the most potent of drugs.

His hands found the zipper of his jacket and yanked,

pulling the heavy fabric off of me. I tried to help him with my dress, but he walked me backward to a wall, putting one of those claws to my lips. Then he ran the sharp blade-like talon down my neck, not cutting, but scratching, the danger there and not, all at the same time. When he got to my dress, he curved his finger—slicing through the fabric *and* my bra, in a single clean stroke.

Softly, he ran it down my belly before cutting through my underwear, too, baring all of me to his hungry gaze. His eyes roved over me like a caress, making me shiver with how visceral it felt. Steam clouded the room, fogging the mirror and the glass shower doors. The thick air made the giant bath seem smaller as it curled around us.

He knelt at my feet and worked the laces of my boots, removing the last vestiges of clothing as my heart tripped in my chest.

"You're so fucking beautiful, Bird."

Instead of responding, I reached for him, unable to wait for whatever he wanted to do next. I needed his touch on my skin—everywhere—but first…

Grabbing his hand, I dragged him to the shower, shoving him under the spray. Water spilled over his head and shoulders, darkening his hair to black.

Nico was wrong. He was the beautiful one, not me.

"Wha—"

"When was the last time someone took care of you?" I asked, pushing him to the stone bench, and forcing him to sit. "And I don't mean making you food or stuff like that."

While I waited for my answer, I found the shampoo and poured some into my hand. Then I fit myself between his thick thighs. His fingers caressed my skin, circling the top of my legs and pulling me closer.

"No one has ever taken care of me like you do. No one else ever will."

As awful as it was, I was so fucking happy that no one had touched him like this while I was gone.

"It makes me a horrible person that my first thought is 'good,' isn't it?" I massaged the shampoo into his hair and relished the near-silent groan that escaped him at my touch.

"No," he rumbled, his voice damn near a purr. "Because if you were in the same position as me and I was the one gone, I'd be just as happy no one touched you like this but me. Call it selfish or toxic or possessive, I don't give a fuck. But me turning to someone else was never going to be in the cards."

That made me both ridiculously smug and hurt deep in my chest all at the same time. If anyone needed to be taken care of, it was Nico. Working my nails over his scalp, I soaped his long hair, praying all the while that he found comfort.

Well, that, and that he'd never cut it.

Gently, I tipped his head back and rinsed his hair, enjoying the show as the soap raced down his body. His grip on my thighs got tighter, pressing our wet bodies together. His rough beard tickled my breasts before his lips closed around a nipple.

"This isn't about me," I gasped, squeezing my knees together to alleviate the ache in my sex. "I want…"

But I didn't get to finish that sentence before his lips were on mine and he was pulling me onto his lap. His hard cock rubbed against my clit in the most delicious way as I moaned into his mouth. Then his hands were in my hair, massaging my scalp, the scent of his shampoo filling my nose once again.

Not breaking the kiss, I reached for his body wash, pouring it in my hands before slipping it over his skin. It was a "two birds, one stone" kind of a deal. I wanted my hands all over him, and it had the added benefit of getting that awful Fae scent off his skin.

Growling, Nico gently pulled my hair, exposing my neck to his mouth as I rocked against him, my hips moving of their own volition. All it would take was the right twist of my hips and he'd be inside me, filling me so full. He rinsed the shampoo from my hair, running his hands all over me as the soap cascaded down my body.

"Fuck, I need to be inside you," he groaned against my skin. "I just had you, but I fucking crave you. Always. I'll always crave you." His fingers gripped my ass, stilling my movements as his other hand positioned his cock at my opening. "I'm never going to get enough of you, Wren. Never."

Oh, so slowly, I filled myself with him. At this angle he was so big, so thick, I almost couldn't move. That was until he moved me. One hand on my ass and the other threaded through my hair, he controlled every movement, every thrust, every circle of my hips, lighting a fire in me that made me damn near mindless.

"Look at me, Wren. Open your eyes."

That order was threaded through with so much heat, so much fire, so much power, I had no choice but to look at him. His irises were glowing the gold of his wolf, the animal so close to the surface I could almost see it. It was wild and primal, and the growl that came from him when I met his eyes only solidified that fact.

"Missed you, Bird. Missed you so fucking much."

"I'm not going anywhere," I whispered, the reassurance something he needed, even if he wouldn't say it.

His golden gaze bore a hole in me as I cupped his jaw, kissing his lips as if I'd die if I didn't get another taste. His hold tightened. "Say it again."

I swallowed hard. "I'm not going anywhere." Tears threatened to undo me, but I kissed him again before adding what he really needed to hear: "I'm here. I'm alive. I'm real. I made it back to you and I am never leaving. You hear me, Nico? I'm not leaving you. Not ever again."

And then I wasn't on top anymore. No, he turned us, putting my back on the stone bench, and then he was over me, in me, consuming me until there was nothing left but pleasure and his growls and my moans and his delicious weight on me.

"Again. Tell me again."

And I did. I said it over and over as he wrung my pleasure from me. He fucked me, made love to me, he bit me, and he made me come over and over until he had to hold me up as he helped me wash up and condition my hair.

I was boneless, well-fucked, and sleepy.

And before I ever got a chance to go down to the Acosta dungeon, I was curled against Nico in his bed, taking a well-deserved nap.

CHAPTER 9

WREN

Post shower, a nap, and some new clothes, we finally managed to traverse the wide staircase that led to the Acosta dungeon. And by "we," I meant me, Nico, and the giant wolf he called Ghost. The same wolf that had parked his ass in front of our room like a damn guard dog and apparently took a chunk out of Zaid's ass while Nico and I were busy showering.

The white wolf picked down the stairs ahead of us, sniffing the air like he was scenting for danger. But I didn't expect danger here. Truth be told, it was the nicest dungeon I'd ever seen—especially coming from the Dark Court one. Personally, I'd classify it more like an unfinished basement with dark stone walls and minimal windows. The area was wide open with a single cell at the center. The lighting was soft with pretty sconces dotting the walls to warm up the space. A few dehumidifiers had been set up in the corners to pull the ever-present Savannah moisture out of the air, reducing the dank coldness that should fill a room like this.

But no matter the lighting or the dehumidifiers or the throw pillows, the fact remained the same. It *was* a dungeon, and the woman inside the cell knew it.

Fiona sat on a pretty green velvet couch with rolled arms under a cute throw blanket with frogs on it, her gaze trained on a large TV playing *Legally Blonde* while she filed her nails. Sometime in the last three years, she'd dyed her hair a gorgeous shade of fuchsia, the brilliant color mixed with dark purples and a swath of blue. She had an entire manicure set in front of her, complete with every shade of green nail polish ever made. At her feet was a soft-looking shag carpet, and behind a privacy screen was where I hoped a shower and toilet would be. The room smelled of a little bit of ozone, spent magic, coffee, and one of those cute pumpkin spice candles.

The bars of her cell were a special metal, the power radiating from them practically stinging my skin as I got closer. Not that she heard me. Too engrossed in Elle Woods and the costume party debacle, she didn't even look away from the TV. Her prison guard, though, stared at me like I was a fucking ghost.

Theo Acosta sat in a hard metal folding chair, his jaw twitching as he set the old spy novel he'd been unsuccessfully reading on the ground. Considering the last time I'd seen this guy, he'd put a knife to my throat, I couldn't say I was filled with the warm and fuzzies. Then again, the last person to grab me got set on fire and then cut into ribbons, so I figured I was covered.

Plus, Ghost seemed to hate him, letting out a low growl before settling at Nico's side.

"So, you're what all the commotion was about?" Theo rose to his feet, his head bowed slightly. "I'm glad to see you made it home."

But there was resentment there, too. I could smell it. But Theo wasn't who I was here to see.

I tipped my chin up much like Nico had and turned to the bars. "Hey, Troublemaker, I brought you some food."

Fiona's pink braid whipped behind her back as she turned, but when she stood, she immediately plopped back down. I didn't notice at first since she was in a billowing sweater and baggy pants, but Fiona was gaunt. Like if she were anyone else, I'd make sure she was admitted to a hospital, gaunt.

She put a trembling hand to her forehead, even as a wide smile flitted across her face. "Did I fall off the deep end again, or am I finally dreaming in this gods-forsaken hellhole?"

Theo shot her a worried glance, his entire body tense before he seemed to consciously relax his shoulders and his jaw. "If you're hallucinating, Cupcake, then so am I."

Cupcake?

When had Theo started calling one of my best friends "cupcake"? And Fiona—save for a scalding glance in his general direction—didn't say a word about it.

Interesting.

Nico hadn't had a chance to fill me in on any supposed mental breaks or why exactly Fiona was in this cell under house arrest or why she was so damn skinny—all of which I really wished he would have at least primed me on. Walking in here blind was not a happy feeling at all.

"I leave for three measly years and the world falls apart," I joked, shaking my head, pasting a wide smile on my face. "Now, I know for a fact these mashed potatoes and gravy are the best I've ever tasted, so you really need to get them while they're hot."

Fiona's eyes misted up. "It's really you? You're really here?"

"In the flesh."

She sucked in a huge breath as tears spilled down her cheeks. "I'm not dreaming?"

Drawing nearer to the bars, the null warding grew more and more painful. "If you need me to pinch you, I can do that, but I'd rather you just take my word for it." I didn't like Fi under wards like this. She could barely handle the ABI school's wards—who knew what these were doing to her? "Now let me in there so I can hug the shit out of you."

I moved to open the door when Theo blocked my way. Smartly, he didn't touch me, but that didn't mean he still hadn't pissed me off.

"I can't let you do that."

My eye actually twitched even as Nico's growl erupted through the dungeon. This bastard had the gall to stand in my way? After he refused to see reason about what Diana was doing, after he put a knife to my throat, after he just sat there and watched Nico nearly lose me?

I don't fucking think so.

"How about you don't *let* me do a gods-damned thing, and you get the fuck out of my way, Theo?"

This close to null wards, who knew what my magic would do, but I had enough ill will to do damage regardless. Nico might have forgiven this piece of shit—which was the only way he would still be breathing—but I hadn't. And until I heard a damn good apology, Theo could tell me what to do around about never.

"Look, I get it," he said on a sigh. "I fucked up."

My eye twitched again. What was that, the Acosta family motto?

"I'm going to need more than an 'I fucked up.' I'm going to need a damn good reason to not put a knife to *your* throat, make *you* bleed, to make *your* family watch as some bitch damn near cuts your head off. I don't know what you said to Nico to make him forgive your sorry ass, but I'm not him. I'm going to need an actual apology, or so help me, I will rip your insides out and wear your hollowed-out carcass as a motherfucking party dress."

Theo's face drained of color before he took a huge step backward. "That was... graphic."

I leveled him with my most scalding glare. "And also, one hundred percent true."

His head bowed, a wolfy show of deference, but it just made me feel icky. "Look, I would love to say I'm sorry and explain and have everything be peaches and fucking cream, all right?" Theo rubbed at the back of his neck, his shoulders bunching up close to his ears. "But the truth is, until you have your will taken away from you, you can never understand. I didn't want to hurt you. I would never hurt someone's mate. I just co—"

"Stop," I ordered, the fight draining out of me. Because I had an inkling of what it was to be out of control of your own life, unable to sway the most basic path of your life. And if Theo was under an Alpha's order... "Your father?"

Theo nodded, bowing his head further, nearly bending in half. "I'm sorry, Wren. I didn't want to hurt you. None of us did. Well, maybe Santi, but he's come around since you saw him last."

Great. Now I had to forgive him, and I didn't even get to punch anyone. *Rude.* "Forgiven. Though, you still need to get out of my way."

Theo winced and remained immovable. "I—"

"I swear to everything holy, if the word 'let' comes out of your mouth, we're going to have a problem."

"Look," he growled as he moved closer, his voice dropping to a whisper, "you can't go in there. It took ages to get this set up going, and you being here will probably disrupt everything we've built. If you go in there, she's going to want to get out. And if Fiona leaves that cell, the ABI will be on her ass in a heartbeat."

Sure, she was on house arrest, but what had she done to warrant this? What could be so big that the ABI would risk their already-precarious situation to come find her?

Confused, I looked between Nico at my back and Theo practically bent in half at my front. "What? You planning on leaving her in there forever?"

Theo straightened, his jaw solidifying to granite. "No, I don't plan on imprisoning your friend until the end of time. Just until we figure out how to close the gate to Hell she accidentally opened trying to get your ass from the fucking Fae realm."

If Nico hadn't been at my back right then, I would have stumbled back a step. "I'm sorry, *what*? Someone needs to tell me what the fuck is going on, and someone needs to do it right now."

Nico's arm wrapped around my middle. "It's my fault. Fiona was just trying to—"

"Oh, for fuck's sake," Fiona shouted, drawing all our attention. "The only one to blame is me. It was me and my fool hubris and my need to be right. Had I listened to that Fae fucker just once, I wouldn't be in this mess, but here we are."

She approached the bars, her steps shaky and stilted. "But if what I did means that you're really here and I haven't gone off my nut again, well, I'll take it."

Theo snatched the plate out of my hands, fitting it into a little metal slot that I hadn't noticed in the door. "Eat something." At her raised eyebrow, he tacked on a "Please."

She took the foil-wrapped plate and the wrap of utensils and sat on the cold floor, not bothering to unwrap either. "I was the one who messed up. I thought your blood would make it a snap to open the Fae gates, and boy, did that come to bite me in the ass. Though, thinking it through, the one we should really be blaming is Margot. Had I known your origins, I would have crafted my spell a little better."

None of this made a bit of sense. "You mean my little jaunt to the Fae realm as a child, or the stars I was born under because the Seelie Queen talked about th—"

"Jaunt to the Fae realm?"

Rolling my eyes, I sat on the floor so I could see her better and Ghost parked his big ass right next to my hip, half-laying, half-sitting on me like a real dog. With nothing for it, I scratched him right behind his ears and he practically melted to the ground next to me, his giant head resting on my knee.

"Evidently, this last one was not my first visit. When I was a kid, my parents always talked about 'the incident' that had me transferring to human school. No one said dick about it being me opening a Fae door and just waltzing right through into the Seelie Queen's throne room. By the time I made it back they just assumed I was dead and moved on with their lives."

That bit still hurt—them forgetting about me—but it wasn't at all surprising. And it made sense that her spell went sideways on her. If I indeed was a Fae-realm-walking, door-busting freak, that was information everyone needed to have before a spell was cast to bring me home.

Variables and all that.

But the longer the silence stretched, the more I realized Fiona wasn't talking about that. No, she was talking about something else.

"Why do I get the feeling I'm not going to like what you're about to tell me?"

Fiona winced just like Theo had, fiddling with the napkin around her utensils. "After you were taken, that Fae fucker locked down all the doors to the realm. No one could get in or out, meaning you couldn't get out even if you tried."

This I knew. Tristan had told me before locking me in, leaving me to the whims of his father as a distraction.

"But he disappeared, and we had to find him. The first order of business was finding the illusion mage who made the deal with him to get his daughter back. And after we had his name, we could summon him. Unfortunately, I didn't have enough power to summon him on my own—not for months. We called in favors, made deals, did everything we could just to get him." She shook her head, her shoulder drooping. "But when we got him, he wouldn't talk. Wouldn't do anything but sit there and wait us out. So, I... got creative."

Fiona hugged her legs to her chest as if she were freezing, and I had the strongest urge to rip the door off its hinges and put a blanket around her shoulders.

"If I didn't have the power to open the door myself, and if Nico couldn't break him, and if that pixie dust motherfucker wouldn't do what was right, then I thought I could borrow his power and do it, anyway. And it worked. Sort of. I opened a door all right. I just opened the wrong fucking one."

"Okay, but the door you opened in Chatham Square?" I clarified to her reluctant nod. "Is the one I came through, so you didn't open the wrong one. You made it so I could come home. But I'm fuzzy on why my origins make a difference or why the city is on literal fire."

Granted, the Fae realm had damn near been breaking apart by the time I'd left, but still. And getting out meant I'd left everyone behind. The number still rang in my head. Forty-four. Well, forty-three now with Lewis free.

"Because she didn't open a door to the Fae realm," Nico answered, kneeling at my side. "She opened a door to Hell. That's why there are demons all over Savannah. It's why the ABI is trying their best to contain the city. Why if they ever figure out Fiona is the source of the power that opened it, she isn't just going to be on house arrest. She'll be dead."

Theo plopped back onto his folding chair. "You skipped the part about Zephyr. I really want to see her face when you tell her she's kin to a Prince of Hell."

I was glad I was sitting down because the world spun a

little and I held onto Ghosts fur like I'd spin off the planet at any second. "Excuse me?"

"Way to go, dipshit," Fiona grumbled, watching my face like a hawk.

Nico stood, smacked his brother upside the head and then continued his crouch by my side. "When Fiona opened the gate, a demon walked out of it. A Prince of Hell. He claims he is your kin, but in demon-speak that could mean anything. He's been reluctant to spill the details, only that when you came home, he would like to meet you."

There had been many a time in my life where I had avoided the truth to save my sanity. Where I would bury a problem so far down deep that it just didn't exist anymore. Unfortunately, this was one of the times that I had to face a problem head-on.

Because one moment, there were just the five of us in this dungeon, and the next, there was a giant, redheaded demon sitting on a leather wingback like he'd been there the whole time, his curled black horns reaching for the ceiling.

Aww, come on. I haven't even been back a full damn day.

"Hello, my kin," the demon said, his smile wide and his gaze calculating.

Nope. There was no getting out of this one.

CHAPTER 10

NICO

THE LAST TIME ZEPHYR ARRIVED UNEXPECTEDLY, THE majority of Savannah's historic district burned. If it weren't for a boatload of spells that kept the fire semi-contained to Chatham Square, there would be nothing left of my home or any other building in Savannah. A part of me felt responsible for the mess—especially considering I supplied the blood and the Fae asshole required for said spell—but the other part laid the blame at the feet of Desmond's fuckhead of a son.

The Prince of Hell seemed nice enough, but I knew better than to ever trust a demon. I had met many incorporeal demons in my days in the ABI and dealing with them had never been my favorite. Demon deals were more than frowned upon by not just the ABI, but all councils save the one in Flagstaff for some reason.

For one, demons were wildly mercurial, and twisting a

contract was their favorite pastime. Two, possessions were sticky business—exorcisms even more so. I'd only heard of one person surviving without serious mental damage, and word on the street was that she wasn't even wholly arcane but a demigod just walking amongst us.

I didn't know how Savannah was going to survive with the multitude of demons just walking around like it was an amusement park or how we could possibly exorcise that many people without killing them all.

But that was a problem for another day.

Finding my feet, I scooted Wren behind me—not that it would help. If Zephyr wanted to be somewhere, all he had to do was snap his fingers and he was there. There was no ward and no spell that could keep him out. At least none that could be created by anyone on this planet.

That didn't stop Ghost from growling at him or putting his enormous body in between us and the prince.

Shall I bite him, Alpha?

Rolling my eyes, I shook my head. *No, Ghost. He is not a threat.*

Lies. He is made of dark things. He is all threat.

"Hello, Zephyr. How can I help you?"

The giant demon tilted his head to the side, ignoring my pleasantries. His gaze was locked on Wren—the whole reason he had stayed in Savannah in the first place.

"You can stop hiding my kin, Alpha. She is in no danger from me. In fact, I aim to save her from those who would do her harm."

"Sweet Mary, please tell me this dude is not my dad," Wren griped, getting to her feet. She skirted around me and Ghost, closer to danger instead of running from it. "No offense to you, but my mother is already Satan's mistress. I do not need an actual demon as my sperm donor. And if you are actually my dad, I'm going to need you to lie to me on this one."

Zephyr's face split into a wide grin, his gaze soft as he stared at my wife. "I do not need to lie. I would never lay with a woman like Margot Bannister. No offense to you, but I have met Eldritch demons with more soul than that woman."

Wren tried to cover her mouth, but the laugh still echoed through the dungeon like the half-crazed witch cackle it was.

"So, you're acquainted." She schooled her features, refusing to back down an inch. I found it sexy as fuck and equally batshit crazy at the same time. She didn't know Zephyr from Adam, and still, she stood tall like an Alpha.

"Quite. And I will say the entire Bannister line is something of a case study in Hell. They use them to teach the young demons how to be petty."

I just fucking bet they do.

If there were ever a family with too much mean in them, it was the Bannisters.

"But the real question is why you have caged the witch? Did she do something she shouldn't?" He tilted his head to the side before snapping his fingers, the bars to Fiona's cell disappearing into thin air. "That's better."

"What the fuck do you think you're doing?" Theo growled, putting himself between Zephyr and Fiona. Hell, he did one better and picked her right up off the floor like she weighed nothing and herded her behind him like he was protecting something precious. "She needs that cage so the ABI doesn't cut her fucking head off, you asshole. Put it back."

Zephyr's form shimmered a little, the scales on his neck rippling as his jaw solidified. "You're the one who stuck her in a cage. Did you not realize you were killing her. Little by little every day, she was dying. And now she is not. Maybe now she can eat without vomiting it all back up five minutes later."

He directed his gaze back to Wren. "You were right to want her out from behind those bars. Your instincts will hone with time, but you need to listen to your gut more. Don't let that dreadful woman's voice ring in your head. Yes?"

Wren's lips pursed like she was trying not to cry. "Why don't *you* get out of my head?"

The big man shrugged, tapping at his temple. "Can't. I am aware of my kin at all times. Your voice is loud."

"It's still rude. If you can't shut it out at least don't comment on it."

She wasn't wrong.

"No, rude would have been to show up when you were indisposed. Rude would have been interrupting your *reunion*. You ate, you showered, you enjoyed your partner. I've waited long enough, and I will have your attention."

"Whoa," I growled, looping my finger into her belt loop and tugging her behind me. "Number one, it is creepy as fuck that you know that shit. And two, some things are inside thoughts."

Wren shuddered. "And here I thought my mother was intrusive."

"Speaking of your mother," Zephyr began before snapping his fingers once more.

A moment later it felt as if someone had taken a hook to my middle, yanking me through space and time and dumping us all in the parlor of a stuffy house that had seen better days.

Wren scrambled back, bumping into me, her breaths sawing in and out of her lungs in a panic.

"Why would you bring me here?" she hissed, her gaze darting to every corner of the room like she'd get attacked at any minute.

And that said nothing to the panic flooding our connection. On instinct, I stepped in front of her, pulling her behind me just like Theo had with Fiona. We needed to get them both out of here.

Because there was only one place on this earth that Wren would fear, and unfortunately, it was where she had spent the most time.

"Don't worry, youngling. There is nothing to fear from this place anymore," Zephyr practically cooed, standing from his makeshift throne like he was going to fix years' worth of psychological trauma with a single bullshit platitude.

Ghost didn't like it at all. He braced himself between our little huddle and the demon like he was seriously considering taking a chunk out of him.

"Yeah, right," she scoffed, her anger getting the better of her as she ignored the wolf and me and everything else. "You know nothing of what these people put me through."

His scales rippled again, a sign that the demon was not happy with the way this conversation was going. "I have an idea. And since it is my fault, I am here to make it right."

"Your fault?"

Zephyr sighed before turning, his giant hand gesturing to us to follow. "If you want the story, you're going to have to trust me just a little. Follow me."

I met Wren's eyes, uncertainty filling her more and more by

the second. Then all at once, her face blanked, she firmed her jaw, and she gave me a jerky nod. Only then did I take a single step forward.

Fiona made to follow us, but Theo pulled her back. "I don't think so, Cupcake. The ABI will be here any second. I—"

Another cracking snap, and Theo was following Zephyr like a mindless automaton. As funny as it was, I did not like one of my pack getting forced to do anything, and Prince of Hell or not, he wasn't going to hurt my brother.

My growl was long and low, making Wren, Fiona, and Zephyr freeze. "Let him go. No one takes his will away. Not *ever* on my watch."

Zephyr sighed. "This is not going how I planned at all." He snapped his fingers once more, giving Theo control of his body again. "The ABI isn't looking for you, Fiona. They believe the Bannister family were the ones to open the portal. There is no need to hide. You're *welcome*. Now"—He paused, eyeing Theo like he'd really enjoy squishing him underneath his big leather boot—"do you want answers, or do you want to stay in the dark?"

Fiona steeled her back, her gaunt frame hurting my very soul. "Oh, you bet your ass, I'm coming."

Wren held out her hand and Fiona took it, my wife funneling power into her friend so fast it was like watching a balloon inflate. Her cheeks filled out as her spine straightened. Fiona's color returned, and she took her first easy breath in years. I might have been able to heal someone, but Wren could restore power like I never could.

But I felt Wren's nose bleeding before she did. The scent of her blood filled my nostrils, and it took everything I had in me not to shift. My wolf was so close to the surface, it was physically painful to keep him locked down. Wren let Fi's hand go to wipe the red away and I felt myself lose it a little.

"You planning on teaching her how to combat that little hurdle?"

You asshole, I tacked on inside my head because it needed to be addressed. All this drama, and he was walking around like he was the king of the fucking universe.

Zephyr studied Wren for a moment. "You aren't drawing on the earth like you should, or the ether. You are breaking your own body down to give it away, and while I appreciate the sentiment, you need to stop."

Wren gnashed her teeth. "You and that damn Seelie Queen keep saying the same thing, but you don't explain it, you don't tell me what that means. Draw from nothing, from liminal spaces, draw from fucking what? It makes no sense."

The prince studied her a bit. "Did they teach you nothing?"

Wren's eyes started glowing. "Why would they teach me anything? I was their battery, not their equal. I was the fuel for their spells, not their family, not their blood. You call me your kin, but what exactly am I to you? I'm not your daughter, not your cousin, not your anything. I didn't see you waltzing in here when my mother locked me in a fucking closet for spilling a glass of chocolate milk. I was five. You know how long I was in that closet? Two days. Covered in vomit and piss and shit because I was so scared."

Her palm lit, that same fire she'd used on the Fae who wanted to kidnap her. She pointed to the closet in question, and I wanted to rip it apart plank by plank.

"Where the fuck were you when she didn't speak to me for

a month after I accidentally set the lawn on fire because she did a spell too close to me? Do you know what that does to a child? No one would speak to me—not my parents, not my aunts or cousins, not my grandmother. I was seven. No 'I love you,' no 'good night,' not one word. Eventually I stopped talking, too. I brought home straight A's, and it didn't matter. I broke things. I begged. Nothing mattered. She didn't talk until I was good enough for long enough. If it weren't for Ellie and Alice, I would have gone insane. If I'm your kin, where the fuck were you?"

I knew the day would come when I would rip every single member of Wren's family apart. It looked like today was the day. Without much thought to the flames building in my wife's palm, I wrapped an arm around her middle, and dropped a kiss to her shoulder.

"I'll be your family, Bird. I'll make sure you're safe and loved. That nothing like that ever touches you again."

But that was the thing about pain like that. It was always there, hiding, waiting. Ready and willing to lash out at any moment. I'd never be able to erase what her parents had done. It didn't matter if they were cold in the ground or alive and well. The scars on Wren's heart were here to stay. The only thing I could promise was that if we ever decided to have kids, nothing of the sort would ever touch them, either.

The pain and rage and hurt filled her heart as she swallowed hard. A moment later the flame in her palm went out.

Zephyr's face split into a smile. "Control. You've learned it so quickly. I'm impressed."

"I don't give a shit if you're impressed. I care about

knowing who and what I am and learning to master whatever power I've got. Can you do that or are you going to leave me to the wolves?"

He considered her, his black eyes calculating as they looked her over. "Fair enough. Follow me."

Zephyr led us through Wren's childhood home. At one time it must have been beautiful. The dark mahogany floors and expensive sconces and plush carpets had all seen better days. Dust coated everything along with a heavy layer of debris. Broken bottles and food wrappers and pages from grimoires littered the ground.

Someone was living here—had to be.

"They thought their wards were good enough, but hubris will get people like that every time." He snapped his fingers, revealing a hidden door in one of the beaten-up wooden panels. It exposed a staircase that led to a darkness that had the hair on the back of my neck standing up.

Something had died down there. Something or someone.

"Please tell me there is a point to this," I growled, clutching Wren to my back as I moved away from the door.

There were dungeons and then there were *dungeons*. No way was I subjecting Wren to whatever it was down there without a damn good reason.

"It is her revenge. Would you deny her that?"

Wren finally getting revenge? No, I wouldn't deny her.

I'd help her dig their fucking graves.

CHAPTER 11

WREN

There were plenty of things I wanted. A stable home life. A good place to live. Food on my plate and clothes on my back. Friends. People I could call family and mean it.

But revenge had never been on that list.

Of course, I loathed my family. I hated what they'd done to me—the way they'd made me feel. I hated their power and their complete disregard for people around them disguised as "just the way we do things." I hated the way they would step on anyone—even their own blood—to get what they wanted.

But all I'd ever wanted was to be free.

"I don't need revenge," I whispered, the truth of that statement questionable at best. It was the right answer, though—even if it wasn't honest. But making my family pay for their crimes was laughable. I'd already taken all my power back. I'd ripped their power source away from them, and by the looks of this place, I powered the whole fucking house.

What more could I do to them than that?

"The fuck you don't," Fiona hissed. "I showed you basic kindness and you acted like I was giving you the most precious gift. I treated you like a person, and it was as if you'd only gotten that round about never in your life. Day in and day out for how many years have you been alive now?"

I waggled my hand. "Twenty-four-ish years, but I don't know the date anymore. I could be twenty-eight by now."

Fiona planted her fists on her hips, giving me the full hip-jut and stomping foot. "Not the fucking point and you know it. Stop changing the subject. And if you won't do it for revenge, do it for me. Those bitches need to take the fall for the Hell gate fiasco, and dead bitches are much easier to pin shit on than live ones."

That was... fair. Not that I thought I could kill anyone. Plus, I still didn't want to go down to that rancid dungeon. Nico's little power boost made my sense of smell bulletproof, and I was paying for it now.

"There better be nose bleach after this," I grumbled, tipping my chin at Zephyr to lead the way.

Of all the places he could have brought me, here was the absolute dead last one I wanted to ever visit. In fact, I'd sort of made a promise to myself after they'd unceremoniously thrown me to the mercy of the council that I would never darken their door again in my life. Mentally, I'd cut them off, and after Eloise's tantrum up in Blue Ridge, I was more than done with my family. Had I known it was like cutting off a limb, I would have used a sharper knife.

Zephyr ducked, his horns nearly scraping the stone ceiling as he moved down the stairs. Reluctantly, Nico followed, his hand securely wrapped around mine as his thumb made a circuit over the inside of my wrist. If I didn't know better, I would believe he was trying to assess my pulse, but I did.

The beat of his heart thrummed in my chest just as much as mine did in his.

The stone steps were slick with condensation, proof no one had thought of a dehumidifier or even so much as a can of air freshener. And despite our less-than-stealth descent into this pit of darkness, no one attacked, spelled, or maimed us, but I had a feeling that was too good to be true.

There was no way this place shouldn't be warded out the ass. There should be sigils on every exposed surface of the stone—both hidden and exposed—but all I saw was a blank wall. This had a wonky feeling to it, the same as the circumstances that got me spirited away to the fucking Fae realm.

"I don't like this. This isn't right," I hissed at Nico's back. "No wards, no protection. This is fucked, man."

Illusion magic, my brain supplied, and that had my feet freezing to the spot. I'd already gotten fucked by illusion magic once and not in the good way. Fiona squeezed my hand, probably to agree, but I couldn't look at her. I was too busy keeping my head on a swivel, waiting for shit to go pear-shaped.

At the base of the stairs were three curved paths cut from a rough rock wall, the cave of a dungeon branching out into what seemed like nothingness. Now, I had lived in this house my whole life. Not once did I ever expect that we had a damn labyrinth underneath the floorboards. Again, not good. Three directions meant three chances to die.

I really didn't want to die right now. I had a hot husband, no one in the pack wanted to kill me at the moment, and I'd had roughly a zillion orgasms today, which was a solid improvement from Fae imprisonment from yesterday. Life was on an upswing.

It just figured shit would go straight to Hell in a hand basket.

But it wasn't until we reached the antechamber right before the paths, did shit really go sideways. Fiona—being the only one of us who couldn't see in the dark—snapped her fingers. And just as that pretty pink flame bloomed in her hand like a rose, spells came at us from all sides.

Theo grabbed Fiona, ducking back into the stairwell while Ghost and Nico stood in front of me like they could block every spell with their bodies alone, the pair of them growling like the sound would do something. And Zephyr practically giggled as he flicked orbs of electricity and fire away from him, batting them like a cat would a particularly interesting toy.

An orb of electricity hit Nico, knocking him sideways and slamming him into the stone wall, and I realized I was just about done with this shit.

Áine and Zephyr had both said that I could take energy into myself, that I could pull it from space and time and use it to fuel my magic. I'd been scolded twice in twenty-four hours about the same damn thing.

No time like the present to see if they were pulling my leg.

The magic called to me, damn near begging me to take it. Just like in the Fae dungeon, I used that sound to my advantage. Focusing on the ringing of the power itself, I pulled it to me, damn near plucking the magic out of thin air and consuming it.

An orb I missed hit Ghost, another hit Nico, burning them both. Nico let out a pained grunt and Ghost whined, and my rage got the better of me.

Roughly, I yanked at the power in the room, consuming it, eating it, sucking it dry until I reached the tipping point. Then a scream ripped from my lips as I gave it all back. Rivers of fire flew from my fingertips, snaking down the three paths like a damn tsunami, coating everything. No one—no spell, no witch was surviving that unless they were gods-damned fireproof.

By the time the flames petered out, I was a shaky mess on my knees, but no more spells materialized from the depths of those fucking paths, and that was a win in my book.

Zephyr's paw of a hand hauled me to my feet, but I didn't have the energy to deal with him.

Nico. I need Nico.

Bleary and unsteady on my feet, I ignored everything and stumbled to my husband.

"Jesus, fuck, Bird," he rumbled, his arms closing around me like I was something precious.

"Are you hurt? Is Ghost okay?" The room was getting darker, and I didn't know why. "I need a nap, I think. I'm tired."

Nico lifted me off my feet—probably before I fell—snarling at Zephyr when he tried to touch me. "This is your fucking fault. Bringing her here—letting them hurt her again—this is your doing and I swear if she—"

"I'm fine," I mumbled, patting his chest. Or at least I thought it was his chest. Shit was a little fuzzy right then.

"Sweet Pea, your ears are bleeding," Fiona sassed. "If you'd admit you're a little more than not fine that would be awesome. No offense, but this stoic, Alpha's wife bullshit is already getting old."

Tell me about it.

"I just need a nap."

"You need a fucking keeper," Theo grumbled. "You two never heard of ducking and letting the giant demon prince handle shit? I thought you were supposed to be her mate not her charge, little brother."

Nico hugged me to his chest. "Fuck you, Theo."

"Yeah, yeah. Fuck me and you're the one who let her stand there and—"

I peeled open an eyelid, not sure when I closed it. "Fuck you, Theo."

A cold nose poked my cheek at the same time a very sharp claw tapped my forehead. Somehow, I peeled both lids open to spot a very put-out Zephyr eyeing me like I was a test to his sanity.

"I stand corrected. You do not have even the smallest inkling of control. You do, however, have an anger problem and the power to strip an entire compound of magic, so, well done there. Here," he said on a sigh, pressing the pad of his finger against my forehead. "This should fix it."

And then a power unlike I'd ever felt filled me, fixing things I had no idea were even broken. Like with Nico, I actually felt wounds closing and blood drying. I felt organs repair themselves and blood replenish. It was fucking wild.

But then an awareness hit me, making me scramble to my feet and a wash of fire hit my palm.

Whatever I had done, it hadn't killed everyone down here. Hell, it likely hadn't killed anyone at all.

"Someone is down here. Two... no, three."

What I didn't say was how many dead bodies lined those three paths. People long since dead, and not by my hand, which wasn't quite the relief it should have been.

"Yes, well," Zephyr murmured, snapping his fingers.

As if pulled by a string, three women flew from their paths, colliding in a heap at Zephyr's feet. Another snap later, and a black ring encircled them before glowing red with an unspent fire.

"That's enough spells from you three. Wren, my dear, say hello to the last three Bannister witches on the planet."

I opened my mouth to correct him, but he held up a finger.

"You are not a Bannister witch. As someone who has never been inducted into their coven, any claim you have to that name ended when you married into the Acosta pack. Therefore, any curses, spells, or debts—soul or otherwise—of the Bannister name do not affect you."

Respecting this line of thinking, I snapped my fucking mouth closed and paid attention. My grandmother, Eloise, my aunt Judith, and my mother were sprawled in a tangle of limbs. It sort of made sense that they would be the last ones standing—or at least living, as it were.

Eloise shoved away from her daughters, climbing to her feet as if all three hundred years had finally caught up with her. The last time I'd seen her, she had looked no older than forty at a push. Now, she could pass for a grandmother to one of the *Golden Girls*. Hell, the only reason I even knew it was her was the stuffy, bitchy, insult that fell out of her mouth as soon as she saw me.

"Well, if it isn't the screw-up and her mongrel. What? You come to finish us off, you ungrateful little bitch?"

I should have expected something like that, but the insult still hurt. I wasn't the one who'd stolen power not meant for her. I wasn't the one who'd done everything to make me feel unwelcome. I wasn't the one who'd broken her family.

No, that was on them.

Nico's growl shivered down my spine as he yanked me behind him. "You'd better think up a spell to shut them up, demon, or else they won't live long enough to play out whatever bullshit scenario you brought us here for. They insult my wife again and I'm ripping their tongues from their heads. You understand me?"

Zephyr's smile was practically beatific. "I like you. You're a good husband and protector. I approve." His attention shifted to Eloise. "Your input is no longer needed. You may stay silent now."

Ghost circled the spelled ring, his growl growing louder by the second while the three women remained silent.

"Now, I brought you here so you could have your mother tell you how you came to be, but seeing how they treat you, I'm not sure this was a good idea," Zephyr mused, tapping his chin.

Theo threw up his hands. "Ya *think*? Perhaps you should ask people before you transport them places and make them relive childhood trauma, maybe?" Nico's brother was telling the complete truth. "Fuck, man, are you new or something?"

I couldn't help it: I snorted a laugh that was one-part

hysterical and one-part pure joy. Because Nico's brother was indeed scolding a likely ancient, most definitely god-level-powered Prince of Hell like he was a naughty puppy. I'd never met someone with a bigger death wish.

"I should have kept you mindless, wolf. Your mouth is going to get you into trouble one day."

"That's what they tell me." Theo's smile was as wide as it was patronizing. "And yet, I'm still here."

As funny as it was, this wouldn't get me the fuck out of this dungeon anytime soon. "Can we get back on task, please? How I came to be? The whole sordid tale—can we get back to that before I get the black plague from this dank-ass dungeon?"

Zephyr sniffed, his eyebrow raising in indignation before he snapped his fingers. "Margot, why don't you tell us all about the deal you made?"

He said it like a request, but I knew my mother had no choice in the matter.

Margot's eyes narrowed to slits as she stood like she was gearing up to spew enough emotional trauma to power the bank accounts of every therapist in Savannah—maybe even the great state of Georgia as a whole.

"Why else would I summon a demon? Power. Had I known what I do now, I would have never done it. You failed to hold up your end of the bargain."

If Theo had a death wish, Margot was actively courting Death herself to come rip her soul right out of her body—that was if she even had one.

Zephyr stood to his full height. "I fulfilled every aspect of our deal. It was you who failed to be clear. You asked for power, and I gave it to you. It's not my fault you lost it. You asked for wealth and influence, and had you actually fostered any kind of goodwill, you would have had it for the rest of your days. Instead, you ostracized the one person who could have given you everything you asked for and more."

But I had no idea what that meant.

But Margot was used to my confusion. I didn't have to say a word before she decided to drop a verbal bomb on my life.

"You, my *darling* daughter, are what happens when a demon deal goes south while pregnant."

CHAPTER 12

WREN

Margot Bannister was the worst mother on the planet.

"Who the fuck makes a demon deal while pregnant?" Fiona asked.

I had to give it to her, that question also blazed across my brain about fourteen times while I stood there gaping at my bitch of a mother.

No. "Bitch" was too nice for Margot. There had to be something worse than that.

I didn't even know what to say to her. Like how could she be so fucking stupid? How could she care about no one but herself?

Margot's gaze sliced to Fiona. "It wasn't like I knew, okay? I was only six weeks along. How was I supposed to know that her father's sperm were impervious to every birth control spell in the book?"

First, gross, and second, there are birth control spells?

Probably not a good idea for me.

I'd probably torch my whole uterus.

"That... actually makes me hate you a little less, and I didn't think that was possible. But a demon deal for power? Even I'm not that stupid and I've done some questionable shit in my day."

Judith stood, her calculating expression the one I needed to watch out for. Out of the three, Judith would kill without a second thought. "Yes, we all know about your penchant for missteps."

The disdain just dripped from her words, but I was on this side of a demon's circle and she wasn't, so...

Margot flipped her matted red curls from her shoulder. In the last three years she had gone from a twinset-wearing, pearl-clutching, Southern Belle to little better than a street urchin. Hell, street urchins were probably cleaner.

"There was no way around it. The Acosta pack was expanding, the Fae wanted payment, and there were some upstart covens trying to take what our family fought and died for. Power was the only way."

Judith snorted. "It should have been me. If we had gone with the plan as I laid it out, none of this would be happening and yo—"

Eloise's hand cracked against her youngest daughter's face. "It was your thirst for blood that got us in this situation in the first place. You killed that Fae child for spell ingredients. What did you think would happen?"

"Does anyone else have a hankering for popcorn?" Theo mused, his fingers massaging his temples. "Because I know telenovelas with less drama. *Shit*."

The man was not wrong.

"Does any of this have a point?" I asked Zephyr, trying not to run screaming from the dungeon. I thought my family was bad, but killing kids? Demon deals? Mysterious cave structures and dungeons? *The fuck?*

"It does. You see, Margot made a deal for power, but since her soul is just as black as her sister's, I couldn't in good conscience give it to her directly. Tell me—have you ever played Corrupt a Wish?"

I could honestly say I had not. Loopholes weren't exactly my cup of tea.

"Well, I gave her exactly what she asked for. I gave her power, and when she grew you in her womb, her power grew. But when you were born, she thought she lost it. It wasn't until you fell into the Fae realm, did they even consider that you were amplifying their magic. And when the Seelie Queen brought you back? And the blessings she gave you? Well, it was too late to stop them."

I would have gone my whole life without magic, put down, and cowering if it weren't for Nico's family breaking the curse. I didn't appreciate what they had done to break it or the steps they had taken in deceiving us, but...

"Stop them from what? Cursing me to drain the power you gave me? The power she was promised? Not for nothing, but do you happen to think about the consequences to your actions, or are you a 'fly by the seat of your pants' kind of demon?"

But that didn't mean my family was off the hook, either.

"And you three. All your scheming, all your talk of power, and what do you have? Dirty clothes and janky hair and a gods-damned dungeon in the middle of an apocalypse you probably had a hand in creating. I swear, for all the times you called me a fuck-up, I would like you to look around at your current circumstances and eat your fucking words."

Plus, the only reason I was considered a "fuck-up" at all was due to their bullshit curse.

"That's rich," Judith hissed. "You couldn't even break my wards with all your *power*, but sure, you're not a fuck-up. A waste is more like it."

Zephyr stepped in between us, staring down at Judith like he would really enjoy burning the flesh from her bones. "And how many sacrifices did you make to strengthen that ward, witch?"

One thing about Judith, she had a spine made of steel. "Evidently not enough since she's still alive, but don't you worry. I'll be sure to do better next time."

Next time? Did she really think that she was getting out of here?

"I thought we discussed this," Nico growled, pulling me away from the circle. "Either end them or I will."

But ending them wouldn't do a damn thing. All they wanted was power, and they didn't have it. What more punishment did they need?

Sighing, I squeezed Nico's hand, tugging it as I tried to head back for the stairs. "I'd like to leave. If you're done with this walk down memory lane, I have about a million places I would rather be."

"I am not done with you, child," Zephyr growled, snapping his fingers. "It is time for your revenge."

I would have screamed that I didn't need it, but that snapping sound was compounded by the ward surrounding the remains of my family breaking.

Oh, fuck.

Margot shot a spell across the now-open space, aiming right for me faster than a lightning strike. Smartly, both Nico and I ducked, but she wasn't alone. I supposed gunning for me was on brand and everything, but I was just so fucking tired of it all.

Tired of them using their limited power to get whatever they wanted. They didn't deserve what they had. They had *never* deserved what they had. They shouldn't have any of it.

Just like their spell from before, I drew from the magic on the air. Only this time? I took it directly from the source. Rage filled me once again as I yanked on their bullshit power—the same power they used to siphon mine from me. The same power that had stolen my happiness, my childhood, my self-worth. The same one that made me feel like a burden, like an idiot, like a touch-starved drain on the Bannister name.

Another scream ripped up my throat once again, only this time it came directly from my soul, unleashing years of pain, of tears, of fear.

And all at once, I drew from them everything that made them witches. Their magic, their knowledge, their potions, their books. I took away their years, their lifespan, their connection to the earth.

I took everything. But I didn't let it fill me. No, I sent it out, away, out of their reach.

"This is what you deserve," I snarled, drawing every single thing away. "To have human years and human lives and human protection—which is none in case you were wondering. You get human health and human fragility. And when you are old and decrepit and begging for death, I want you to remember me. You don't get to just shuffle off this mortal coil. No, death is too good for you. You get to *live*."

Granted, in the middle of the mess of Savannah, their lives might be short, but I wouldn't be the one to kill them. No, I wanted them to live nice long lives with nothing. *That* would be my revenge.

I watched as they remained crumpled at my feet, but the feeling was bittersweet. Even this was unsatisfying, just as all revenge always was. I just wanted to move on with my life.

"Are you sure, child?" Zephyr asked, assessing me with an inscrutable expression. Who knew how old he was or how many times he'd witnessed just the same thing? Who knew what he saw at all when he looked at me? He called me "child" and "kin" but that was only because he made the mistake of ever dealing with Margot at all. "Are you positive you want them to live?"

Rolling my eyes, I crossed my arms over my chest. "Are you asking me if I want their blood on my hands? Because if so, the answer is no. They cursed me so magic was lost to me. They took more than their fair share. What do you do to a bully who takes and takes and takes? You cut them off so they can't take more. This is enough."

It wasn't enough—it would probably never be enough—but it was all I was willing to do.

"And what if I told you that the reason they are the last

Bannisters is not because of outside power grabs and violence, but something else? What if I told you that they killed everyone else and took their power to fuel their spells—even your father, if you can call that man a father at all."

Swallowing, my gut roiled with that new knowledge. Eloise, Margot, and Judith probably all deserved to die. They likely deserved an eternity roasting over a spit. But I wasn't going to be the one to do it.

"Then, I'd say they have plenty of time to think about what they've done while they wait for their turn in Hell."

"Are you fucking kidding me?" Nico rumbled, his eyes glowing with the gold of his wolf. "No. You don't leave a threat free to come back and kill you. They need to die, Wren. Now."

"I took their knowledge, their spells, their books. They know magic exists but can't reach it. That is enough." I swallowed down a pit of dread that maybe I failed to do this right, too. "They don't get to take my soul away from me. They don't get to kill the last part of me that's good. They have taken *enough*."

My gaze cut to Zephyr. "You can't use me as your weapon, and you can't manipulate me into meting out your revenge. I wasn't the one who made the deal. If you want to punish someone, punish them."

Zephyr's smile was once again equally beautiful and the thing of nightmares. "You surprise me, child. I worried with Margot as your mother, you would be just as debased as she is. Then again, Áine did put an angel in your path, didn't she?" That made not one bit of sense, but Zephyr didn't deign to elaborate. "You, my dear, have passed the test."

With that, he pressed the pad of his index finger against my forehead, sending a searing rip of agony through me. My scream was silent, but I still fell to my knees all the same. If I thought his boost from earlier was good, this was that times a million.

Because everything I tore from my family, every bit of power that I refused to take into myself—the knowledge, the magic, everything—flooded my veins. That, and Zephyr gave me more.

So much more.

I couldn't see anything, but I felt every molecule of the world as it moved around me. Nico held me to his chest as he yanked me from the demon prince, his heartbeat erratic, the breaths in his lungs stilted and full of fear. I felt Theo change into his wolf as Ghost launched himself at the source of my agony.

"Stop it," Fiona screamed, a spell I couldn't see forming in her palm. "You're killing her."

A snap of his fingers later and the room was eerily silent, all except for the demon's voice in my head, soft as a baby's breath.

Soon, you will not feel this pain, and you will understand why I had to test you. I had to know if you deserved the full extent of your power. You may not be my child by blood, but I had a hand in creating you, and you have earned everything I am giving you.

This is protection, my child.

Protection and insurance.

And when you find yourself in need—and you will—please do not hesitate to call on me.

Then all at once, the bright, white-hot agony and Zephyr's voice was gone.

"Bird?" Nico called, gently shaking me. "Baby? Jesus Christ, Wren, are you okay?"

With a sheer force of will, I peeled one eyelid open and then the other to stare into Nico's eyes. The gold irises were filled with so much worry, so much pain, it was as if it touched my very soul. I put a hand to his cheek, the soft hairs of his beard tickling my palm.

With that one touch, it was as if I took years off of him. His brow relaxed as relief hit him, filtering through our bond in a shimmering wave.

"I'm okay. Let's get out of here, yeah?"

I didn't want to see my family ever again, and with the knowledge I'd just absorbed, I would never have to. Hell, if I wanted, I could make it so they couldn't find me even if they were looking right at me. And as pissed as I was at Zephyr for leading us here and then just ditching us, his gift and promise was a decent consolation prize.

Nico pulled me to my feet and pressed a kiss to my temple. "There are some things to button up here first. Go upstairs with Fiona. Theo and I will handle this." He shook his head, his jaw clenching as he surveyed what remained of my family. Eloise was on her knees, clutching her head while Judith was in a ball on the ground, sobbing. Margot kept snapping her fingers, trying to get her magic as silent tears poured down her face.

"What did you do to me? Why is nothing working?" she muttered to herself, shaking her head as she snapped her fingers over and over again.

Frowning, I pulled my hand out of his and backed away. "There is nothing to 'button up' down here. It's done."

Nico's eye twitched as he set his jaw. "Do you think as your husband, I will let a threat to your life live?"

A cold pit of dread filled me. "What threat? Three sobbing witches with no access to power?"

It was as if I pulled the pin on Nico's rage.

"No access?" he whispered. "No access?" This one was a whole hell of a lot louder. My ears rang as his body seemed to double in size. His wolf—which had been so close to the surface—shimmered behind the features of his face. "Do you honestly believe they can't get *access*? That they can't make a deal with one of the zillion demons running around Savannah or trade with a Fae or summon another coven here?"

I opened my mouth to counter, but he wouldn't let me.

"Never again, Bird. I swore to myself when they took you that I wouldn't let another threat to your life live, and those bitches are a fucking threat."

Without warning, he hauled Judith up by the throat, his fingers squeezing the life out of her. Her feet barely scraped the ground as her fingers clawed at his hand, but he didn't even spare her a glance.

"This one has knives filled with poison all over this house. Did you take all the magic out of those? Did you blank every grimoire and burn every bridge she has? Did you wipe her mind of you?"

Again, I opened my mouth, but I couldn't get a word out before Nico snapped her neck right in front of me. The shock that filled me stuttered the breath in my lungs, and I covered my mouth before a scream ripped from my lips.

Margot scrambled away, staring at her sister as she tried to save her own skin. "I'll stay away. As soon as I can I'll leave Savannah. Please don't kill me."

But Nico didn't so much as *seem* to consider her offer. One second, she was breathing, and the next, her heart was on the floor outside of her body, the squelch of it hitting the stone making my stomach turn.

A moment later Eloise stood, not bothering to look at her fallen children or the man who had every intention of taking her life. Instead, she turned her hateful glare onto me.

"Margot should have killed you the moment she lost her power. She should have snuffed you out like I told her to. Maybe then she wouldn't have had such a stupid, ungratef—"

And then Eloise joined her children on the floor of the dungeon, her head rolling to a stop as her body fell.

I met Nico's golden gaze, his expression not the least bit sorry as he wiped the blood from his sword.

Maybe those three years I'd been gone changed him far more than I knew.

CHAPTER 13

NICO

THE LOOK ON WREN'S FACE CUT ME TO THE QUICK. IT was as if she had never seen me before in her life. Funny, she hadn't cared at all when it was the Fae nearly killing her and I'd done the same.

"No one is getting to you again, Bird. Not on my watch."

Her hand fell from her mouth, the white imprint of her fingers against her skin blooming red as anger took the place of shock. But she didn't say a word. Instead, she turned her back on me and marched up the slick stone steps to the main level.

Fiona sighed and followed her, shaking her head. She knew. She knew exactly what it had been like and how brutal life had been. It was kill or be killed. In-fighting, grudges, and outright enemies had made mincemeat of the arcane population of this town. And that was before we fucked up and opened a fucking demon portal.

I couldn't have Wren in one more spec of danger.

Theo shot me an understanding expression as he followed Fiona up. Had his mate been in the same position, he would have done exactly as I had. Only this was Theo. He probably would have dismembered them from the toes up so they could watch as he hacked each bit of them away. I wouldn't call my brother sadistic exactly but hurting someone he loved meant he showed no mercy.

Not ever.

Lunch? Ghost's hopeful voice in my head set my teeth on edge. I had a feeling Wren wouldn't take too kindly to the resident untethered wolf just chowing down on what had once been her family—not that they'd ever treated her as such.

"Absolutely fucking not," Wren yelled down the stairs, the simmering rage in her gut getting the better of her. "You let them rot where they sit, Ghost. No lunch for you."

I couldn't see her face, but the disgust in her voice was enough.

Ghost ducked his head, his worried expression something I'd never seen on his wolfy face.

Yeah, buddy. We're both in trouble.

Sighing, I marched up the stairs behind them, just waiting for my wife to finally lose it. But she didn't. No, she stayed silent as she moved through the house, leading us to a room that had seen better days.

Unlike the rest of the house, this room had cheap furniture and sparse decorations. Covered in layers of dust, it was as if it hadn't been touched in some time. The walls were a dingy baby pink, the paint at least twenty years old, maybe older.

Wren moved to the closet, but instead of finding clothes or whatever it was she was looking for, all that remained was a pair of wire hangers and a fair amount of nothing. She moved to her dresser, only to come up empty, too. Same with the nightstands and under the mattress.

Whatever she was looking for was just... gone.

"Bird?"

Wren straightened, narrowing her eyes at me. "Don't you 'Bird' me, Nico Acosta. I don't want to hear a fucking word out of you for the foreseeable future, you understand me?"

Oh, she was *mad*, mad. *Perfect.*

Taking my life in my hands, I just could not shut my mouth. "I'm not sorry."

A spark of fire ignited in her palm, making my whole gut clench. "Oh, I know you aren't, and that's the fucking problem. I didn't want their deaths on my conscience, dammit. Now all I can do is feel sorry for women that I absolutely should not feel sorry for. Or maybe I *should* feel sorry for them. What if they could have been better? What if they could have changed? What if that punishment meant they... they..."

But she knew better. She knew it but didn't want to accept it. There was no redeeming those women. There were no redeeming people who would sacrifice their own family for power. There was no bringing them back from that. She'd known it three years ago when she kicked Eloise out of our cabin up in Blue Ridge.

Her family had never cared about her unless it was to use her for power.

Wren stamped her foot before sweeping out of the room. Down the hall, up a flight of stairs, and down another corridor, she entered a library. Filled to the brim with grimoires and photo albums and more leather-bound tomes than I could shake a stick at, she searched high and low for whatever it was she was looking for.

"Wren, honey," Fiona cooed, "if you told us what you needed—"

"Proof," Wren barked. "Proof that they gave a shit. Proof that at one time—maybe when I was a baby—they cared a little." She opened a photo album, slamming through each page before tossing it aside. She moved to the next. "I'm looking for anything. A picture, a memento, a letter, something that says it's not true. That the knowledge that Zephyr gave me is wrong, that…"

I decided right then and there that Wren needed letters. She needed little notes everywhere that told her how much I loved her. She needed a million pictures. She needed movie tickets and concert stubs and every little trinket in the world.

She'd have a library full of them.

I gave Theo a nod, telling him with a single look that he, Fiona, and Ghost should take a hike. Wren didn't need an audience to this anymore than she needed Zephyr to bring her here in the first place. And ignoring her ire, I got closer, wrapping an arm around her waist from behind as she tore through another fruitless book.

She stiffened as I settled around her but then she melted into me, the fight leaving her. "There's no one left and still this building is just another reminder that they never… they never... not once did they ever love me. It's stupid, but... I want to burn it all down."

I couldn't blame her. If I was in her shoes, I would, too. This huge stately mansion filled with no love, no kindness, no hope. If I had to, I'd hand her the fucking matches.

"Then do it, Bird. Is there a single book in this library you want? A single memory you need?"

She looked around, opening a grimoire only to find blank pages. "I took everything. All their knowledge, the magic out of their potions, I rendered every ingredient and every ward inert. I took it all." She swallowed hard. "I still don't quite know *how* I did it, but I know in my soul there was no magic left for them. I wanted them to suffer. I wanted them to know what it was like without magic. But I didn't want their blood on my hands."

"And it's not." It wasn't. The blood was on my hands, and I held zero remorse for it. "They dug their own graves. So burn it all down if you have to, but let that shit go."

Wren sighed before a flame bloomed over her palm once more. I was still getting used to that flame, but in a way, it made sense. If Zephyr had a hand in how Wren came to be, then the fires that seemed to follow her every move meant that her power had been aching to be one with her since the day she was born.

Hesitantly, she pressed her palm to the blank grimoire. The ancient pages caught fire like dried kindling, jumping from book to book as Wren played with the dancing flames. In what seemed like moments, the entire bookcase was engulfed.

"Time to go, Bird," I murmured in her ear, and when she turned, all the pain of her loss was stamped all over her face.

Silent tears fell down her cheeks, and it made me want to kill Margot all over again. Her and Eloise. It made me want to watch as their corpses burned to ash.

But Wren didn't need me to do that. She needed someone —anyone—to give a shit about her. And I'd make sure that every single member of our pack adored her almost as much as I did. She would have family—real family—for the rest of her days.

Wren let me lead her out of the Bannister prison, the fresh night air kissing our skin as the flames raged behind us. But she wouldn't let me lead her back to the pack house. She tugged her hand away as she watched the fire engulf her childhood home. And I had to say, I was glad we were doing this alone.

"We have to close the Hell gate," she murmured, her cheeks drying in the heat of the night and the flames.

If I could have figured out how to do that, it would have been done already. Sure, Zephyr wasn't too bad, and the demons had been the least of our problems, but the massive fire burning in the center of the city wasn't exactly good for tourism.

"I'm aware."

"I know how to do it."

I grabbed her shoulders, spinning her to look at me. "That's great. What do you need? How do we do this?"

Wren winced, her gaze landing anywhere but on me.

"Tell me what's going on, Wren."

Yes, I used every ounce of Alpha in that command, and no, it did not work on my wife one bit.

She spun on a heel, briskly heading to the pack house and

ignoring me completely. This was not good. If she didn't want to answer, shit was about to take a turn for the worse.

Silence stretched between us until she walked into the pack house, made a beeline for the kitchen, and finally unearthed a bottle of vodka from the freezer. She flicked off the cap and took a swig directly from the bottle.

When the thing was half-drained, I snatched it from her, my patience at its end.

"Talk. Now."

Her gut churned, making my own nearly cough up my dinner.

"I have to open the Fae gate," she mumbled behind her hand.

I didn't understand. "Okay. And why is that a problem? I don't know how you're going to do it, but—"

"It's a problem because I have a shitty-ass Fae King who would really enjoy squeezing the life out of me after he makes me dance for a million years, I only have a vague idea of how to open said gate, and then I have to close the Hell gate. All without dying. Plus..."

Plus? There was a plus in there?

"There are women to save in that fucking Fae prison and I can't go back there without ripping the whole realm apart. And I need Desmond's son to help."

Wren snatched the bottle back from my loose fingers and took it with her as she skirted around me and headed for our bedroom. Did she honestly think I was just going to let that shit go?

"You want me to just sit idly by while you seek out this kind of—"

We were only halfway up the staircase, so when she turned and speared me with a glare that was so incendiary, I was surprised it didn't have actual fire coming out of it.

"I don't want you to sit idly by, Nico. I want you to understand that this isn't the way. Hell gates and Fae gates and demented kings and spoiled princes. Don't you miss the way our home used to be? I've been home for less than a day, and even I know this isn't how it's supposed to work."

She took a swig of vodka.

"But somehow in all this mess, I am somehow the fucking chosen one. I've never been chosen for a damn thing my whole life or managed to not fuck shit up at any point, but sure."

Malia and Hannah peered down at us from the top landing while Fiona and Theo peeked around the corner. I could practically feel the rest of the house listening in while also trying to give us a modicum of privacy.

Wren sensed them, too, and weaved through the growing crowd to our room. On the other side of the door, she set the bottle down. Her back turned, she stared out the window, not even looking at me.

"You can't protect me from everything and everyone, Nico. I'm not a bird you can cage or a princess you can put on a pedestal. I'm just me—a little more than I was before, but I'm just Wren. I'm a clumsy, semi-witch with a job to do. And as much as I don't want to do it, it needs to get done."

I had a feeling I was not going to like this at all.

CHAPTER 14

WREN

Sleeping was not in the cards for me.

If it wasn't the totally insurmountable fact of what I was supposed to do, it was Zephyr's bevy of knowledge that he'd just decided to drop on my head. Every moment, more and more of it filtered through my brain. Ancient spells, a library full of grimoires' worth of information—all of it carved out space in my brain.

Before dawn, I finally said, "fuck it" and decided to do something about it. Only, I knew better than to just leave the bed without letting Nico know. Trying and failing to sleep beside him the night before, I got to see his face calm, his brow unfurrowed, and the years I had been gone leave his expression. Tristan's gate idiocy had damn near killed him.

He hadn't known if I was alive, or if I was hurt. He had spent years of waiting, of worrying, or slowly going mad. I saw it every few seconds—the way his gaze darted to me. It was almost as if he was reassuring himself that he hadn't dreamed it.

That I was real.

That I was home and safe—or as safe as he could make me.

But as much as I wanted him to have me safe—as much as I wanted to ease his worry—I had to actually *be* safe. Zephyr's knowledge provided more cautionary tales than I could shake a stick at, but the most important one was how unstable Hell gates were. How easily they can be overrun by souls trying to escape Hell.

How simple it was to tear apart the fabric of our reality.

I had already been doing it in the Fae realm. I wondered how soon it would be before that gate fucked everyone and everything over here.

By the nearly imperceptible tremors I'd been feeling since I set foot back in Savannah, the answer was soon.

I left a note on my pillow after kissing Nico's cheek.

Downstairs. Don't worry. I love you.
—W

And I did love him. I loved him so much, I could forgive a lot of shit. Watching him kill the last members of my family was a big pill to swallow, though. I kept putting myself in his shoes. If his family had done what mine had, would I let them live? Would I not do just as he had?

I probably would. Pretty sure I wouldn't have done it right in front of him, though.

Finding Ghost right outside our bedroom door, I clucked

my tongue for him to follow. At the very least, Nico *might* not shit a kitten if I had wolfy backup.

The house was quiet as I padded down the stairs. I needed books—blank ones—and I needed them now.

"Well, look who's back causing trouble," a smooth Southern voice said, stopping me in my tracks.

My gaze darted to the entryway chair at the base of the staircase. Nico's friend Wyatt sat with his hand around a mug of coffee, one ankle resting on his knee. His cowboy boots and western-style shirt seemed at odds with the blond hair obscuring the side of his face and the casual nature he was affecting.

No, this Wyatt was harder than the man I'd met before, his stare less jovial, his jaw tighter.

He tipped his chin at my hand, as he brushed the hair from his face, revealing a gnarled scar spanning the whole of his cheek and down his neck into the collar of his shirt. "That's new."

Looking down, I realized my hand was engulfed in flames. "Oops. It is. It seems to pop up when I'm startled. I'll... get the hang of it."

I hope.

Concentrating, I willed the fire away, and by some miracle, it actually listened to me. "See?"

"Your mate know you're galivanting about? I sorta figured he'd be surgically attached to you for the rest of forever." He sent me a censuring eyebrow raise as he sipped his coffee.

I waggled my now-fire-free hand. "I left him a note. I tried waking him up, but I don't think he's slept right in years.

Waking him when he was that peaceful just seemed wrong, you know?"

Plus, I had shit to do before the whole of the world went tits-up. *You know, priorities.*

"If you say so."

I raised my own eyebrow. "How patronizingly noncommittal of you, Wyatt."

At my ire, Ghost showed the big man his teeth. All of them. No growl, but the goal was achieved when Wyatt held his hands up in surrender.

Good puppy, I thought, chuckling to myself.

Ghost straightened and leveled me with a wolfy glare fit for instant death. *I am not a pup. Ghost is ancient.*

"Whoa, now, I didn't mean anyth—"

But I ignored Wyatt to respond to Ghost.

"All dogs are puppies. Old dogs are puppies, puppies are puppies, and even ancient, spirit-ripped wolves who do awesome things are good puppies. Take a compliment, Ghost."

Not a pup.

"*Fine.* I will never call you a puppy again, you temperamental beast."

Ghost's ears perked up. *Beast. I like beast. Call me a good beast.*

I snickered. "Beast it is."

"Ho-ly *shit*," Wyatt said, climbing to his feet. "You can talk to that thing? I thought only Nico could communicate with Ghost."

I shrugged, not understanding it in the least. "Yeah, well, it was a surprise for all of us." But back to the matter at hand.

"You got any books around here. Preferably blank ones. Journals? Something?"

I needed to get the information written down before it fell out of my brain, and I lost it all. Okay, that was the lie I was telling myself. Worry churned in my gut—had ever since I got back. At the beginning, it was because I was running through apocalypse world with an open Hell gate. Though, considering what had come out of it, it wasn't too bad.

Now it was because I knew what *could* come out of it if we left it open too long.

"Maybe in Tomás' old office, but no one has been in there in years. Not since..."

Wyatt hesitated, following us as I pivoted on a heel and headed for the absolute last place I ever thought I'd go. Tomás' office hadn't changed much since the last time I'd been here. Sure, the carpet was stained with my blood and every surface was covered in about three inches of dust, but it was the same.

And here, class, is where Diana tried to cut off my head. And here is where Nico fought his brothers, and here is...

Shuddering, I rubbed my arms. I couldn't believe they hadn't touched it. Not once. It was like the whole house was constantly reliving the same shame I felt right then, and I hated it.

"You might want to stand back," I ordered over my shoulder, using every bit of Nico's Alpha to my advantage. I didn't see so much as sense Wyatt take three healthy steps back, placing himself across the threshold and into the foyer.

Other than the dungeon—a place I did not care about in the slightest—or under duress, I had never done a spell at all. But this room needed me to change it. It needed me to make it right. Concentrating, I saw the room as it should be—expanding it, making it bigger, wider, filling it with tomes and spells and an apothecary's worth of ingredients. When I opened my eyes, I snapped my fingers.

At first, nothing happened. Not a single book moved, or cobweb vanished.

But two seconds later, it was as if the whole place got the *Fantasia* treatment. The chandelier that had sat shattered on the ground for years reassembled itself before reattaching to the ceiling. The desk mended, and the sullied papers arranged themselves in a stack at the corner. The chairs sucked all their fluff back in as the bloodstains disappeared and the fabric stitched back together.

Books flew from one side of the room to the other, stacking neatly on the shelves. The dust and cobwebs melted away as the wall expanded, making the room twice as tall and three times as wide. Tables sprung up out of nowhere with little green library lamps and comfy rolling chairs. Wide plush seats fell from the ether, landing in cute little groups.

And stacks and stacks of books filled the shelves, each one full to bursting with the knowledge I so feared would leave my head for good.

Because closing the Hell gate was going to be risky. Opening the Fae one even more so, and even as awful and unconscionable as my family was, the knowledge should not be lost. I couldn't be the only one who had it.

"Did I get slipped a roofie when I wasn't looking?" Wyatt muttered, daring to walk into the room now that the conjuring had settled down. "Or did you just *bibbity, bobbity, boo* your ass a whole new library?"

I leaned over and sniffed his coffee. "I'm pretty sure the second one, but I've thought I was dreaming since yesterday, so I wouldn't call myself an expert on reality at the moment."

It was as if I hadn't said a word.

"And where did all these books come from?"

I pulled the first one off the shelf, inspecting it. Indeed, it contained my great-grandmother Gertrude's account of the vampire wars of 1723 and the spells she used to drive the bloodsuckers back.

"My brain," I said on a sigh, the relief hitting me.

I performed a spell.

And it worked.

I didn't know exactly *how* it worked, but it had. And that was one less thing to worry about as we moved forward.

"Quick and dirty version? I stole every ounce of knowledge from the last remaining Bannister witches. Every spell, every memory of magic, every sordid tale. I had to put it somewhere. So..." I held out my hand gameshow-host-style. "Here we are."

But looking at the place now, I wondered if I may have overstepped. There had to be a reason no one touched this space. Sure, Nico's father was dead, but maybe they left it in memory of him.

"Do you think Nico is going to be mad I turned his father's office into my own personal library? Worse, do you think Cat—"

Wyatt shot me a sharp look. "No. Not even a little."

That was emphatic. "Okay. If you're sure. I just didn't want to—"

Wyatt's look only got darker.

"What?"

"Just a question, but have you talked at all about what happened when you left or how Nico became the Alpha?"

I nearly laughed but managed to hold it in at the last second. Between alley sex, dinner, shower sex, a nap, meeting Zephyr, and the Bannister family bonfire—no, I could say with certainty we had not discussed any of that.

"Not even a little."

Wyatt's chuckle was mirthless as his gaze darkened to one of loss and pain and a fair bit of rage. "Nico killed Tomás the day you were taken. I wasn't there to see it, but I heard the stories. Nic was hurt bad by that Fae fucker, the bastard nearly crushed his skull just to get away clean. Catia sent the boys out so they didn't lose the scent trail, but Tomás? Well, even though he was in a cell half-dead from a challenge, he was still able to call his sons back."

I could see where this was going, and Wyatt didn't disappoint.

"As soon as Nico woke up and found out, it was all she wrote for Tomás. He ripped his wolf from him." Wyatt tipped his chin to Ghost. "And then tore out his throat."

Ghost was Tomás' wolf? Nico killed his dad? What the fuck?

Not Tomás' wolf. Am own wolf. Never owned. And Tomás was not worthy of me as his animal. The Alpha freed me.

I gulped, staring at the white wolf with its golden eyes and regal features. Nico was able to take an Alpha's wolf from him. He could command the liminal spaces for himself if he wished. I wondered if that was something I gave him with our bond or if he had that all on his own. Or what if it was both?

Spirit Alpha, Ghost supplied. *A ruler of the in-between. Like you.*

Shit. Ghost had tapped into my thoughts, and that was not at all comforting.

"Six months later, Nico found me. I was chained to a wall in that illusion mage's home. Starving, beaten, bloody, half-dead."

I covered my mouth, the sheer awfulness filling me. "I knew the illusion was too good. They took you, picked your brain clean. Oh, gods. Are you..." This time it was my laugh that was mirthless. "I was about to ask if you were okay, but... Okay is an illusion, too, isn't it?"

His mouth tipped up on one side. "It sure is."

Guilt hit me then, hurting my heart in a way I had yet to feel when my own family was killed right in front of me. "I'm sorry, Wyatt," I whispered, the pain of it all ripping me wide open. "I'm sorry they took you. I'm sorry they hurt you. I'm sorry they used you to get to me."

Swallowing it down, I reached my hand out and caught his. I couldn't do much, but I could heal him like I had Fiona. I could take away the pain in his joints and the ache he had in his lungs every time he took a breath. I could help.

Even if it wasn't enough.

Because the shit I couldn't take away was the real problem. I couldn't strip the memories from him. I couldn't give him six months of his life back. I couldn't take away the feeling of being used.

But I could help on the revenge front. "I take it the illusion mage is dead?"

Wyatt's smile was pure malice. "*They* are."

I tried and failed to feel sorry for Penelope Lewis. Her life had been stolen from her. She'd lost years of it and came back a shell of herself. But if she helped her father hold Wyatt captive for six months, whatever she got was too nice.

"But the Fae Prince. He's still alive, I'd bet."

Wyatt jerked a rage-filled nod.

"What do you say we find him?" I asked, knowing full well that Nico would throw a monkey shit fit if he even thought I was planning this.

His eyes narrowed as his "good old boy" face morphed into the meanest, "Don't fuck with me" mask.

"I'm in."

CHAPTER 15

NICO

I KNEW MY DAY WOULD GO SIDEWAYS AS SOON AS I opened my eyes.

For one, I woke up to a cold mattress and a note instead of my wife when she damn well knew to wake me. And two, Wren wasn't downstairs like she said she would be.

No, downstairs would have been a luxury. Downstairs would have been the height of perfection. Downstairs would have kept my heart from beating out of my chest and the contents of my stomach firmly in my gut.

Because my wife was outside barefoot in the middle of a sigil burned into the back lawn, speaking a language I could only guess was a Fae dialect.

Not exactly the way I wanted to wake up, maybe ever.

I had half a mind to march through that circle and snatch her ass out of it. Just as I was about to do just that, two pairs of hands stopped me. Wyatt and Theo shook their heads and pointed upward.

Suspended midair was Tristan—or rather, Drystan Haldrir Shadowfall, Crown Prince of the Dark Court. A coating of blackness held his arms and legs immobile while another snake of black fire collared his neck. Tristan gulped for air like a fish out of water, and then all at once, he fell to the ground, his bonds pulling at his limbs as if he were being stretched by four invisible horses.

After four months, the Fae seemed a hell of a lot better than I'd have thought he'd be. There was no getting out of Savannah—not without a damn good ABI deal under his belt and I seriously doubted he'd get one of those. The ABI was notorious for not dealing with the Fae as a rule. Plus, I'd passed along his information to Erica. My old boss had disseminated his likeness to every boundary agent. There was no getting out of here.

Not for him.

Still, he was dressed in clean clothes, and though his cheeks were sharp and his scars bright, he seemed better off than he should.

"Now, Drystan—you don't mind if I call you by the name your mama gave you, now, do you?" At his stoic silence, Wren carried on. "Well, Áine and I go way back—all the way to my childhood when she helped me come home. Gave me blessings and everything. She's also the one who helped me out of the Dark Court this time."

Wren clucked her tongue, her voice carrying a thicker accent as she let him know just how much he'd fucked up.

"You see, me being there is not a good idea. If it isn't your daddy hating me, well, my mere presence seems to cause a problem with the fabric of reality as we know it. As in, me being in the Fae realm doesn't just destroy the Dark Court—like I suspect you knew it would—it breaks the Seelie Court as well."

Oh. Oh, shit.

That got Tristan's attention. "My mother. Is she all right?"

Rage boiled in my belly, and it took everything I had not to find an iron blade and cut his fucking head off. Wren would have died because of him. She would have just... just...

"You selfish fuck," I growled, nearly losing the hold on my animal. "Is that all you care about?"

The Fae's gaze met mine. "Is not your wife all you cared about? She is my family. Why is that any different?"

Heat washed over me, and if I hadn't known better, I would have thought a flame could bloom on my skin just as it had on Wren's. "Because my wife was helpless against you."

Tristan raised an eyebrow. "Well, she's not helpless now."

No. No, she wasn't. That didn't mean shit, though. Wren didn't deserve any of this. *We* didn't deserve any of this.

"No, sweet pea, I'm not. But I do need your help, so I'll offer you an exchange." Wren snapped her fingers, the bonds around Tristan's neck and wrists and ankles melting away. "You help me open the Fae gates worldwide, and I promise to never summon you again. No torture, no pain, no grudges."

"Speak for yourself," Wyatt and I said at the same time.

Wren raised an eyebrow. "Yeah, but he isn't scared of you, now, is he? He's scared of me. Because he knows I could rip him limb from limb and make it stick. Or I could call on a Prince of Hell to haul his dumb ass on down to have a chat.

Mr. Tristan thinks I am a destroyer of worlds, and while I can be, I have no interest in that particular pastime."

She focused on Tristan, her expression just a touch wrong as she leveled him with her sweetest smile. "Now do we have a deal, sugar plum, or am I going to have to get creative with my incentive? I guarantee I am meaner than my husband. I'll make what your daddy did to you look like fucking Disneyland."

Her eyes lit with twin flames, her green-gold irises changing to orange so fast it scared the shit out of me. She was bluffing. Or at least I hoped she was bluffing.

"Tik tock, Tinkerbell. I have problems to solve."

Tristan's gaze scanned the yard, which was full of my brothers and sisters and the majority of the pack. It stuttered on someone before moving away.

"Fine." He stepped closer to Wren, his voice going low, but I still heard: "I will help you open the gates, but you know what will happen. You know what he'll do."

Somehow between him taking his first step and his last word, I had his throat in my hand and his feet off the ground. I'd crossed Wren's circle and latched onto him so fast no one could have stopped me. And as much as I would have loved to squeeze the life out of him, I didn't.

Barely.

"You so much as look at her wrong and I will make sure whatever punishment she dreams up a reality. I know you don't care about pain, so I'll use my imagination."

Tristan's smug smile made me want to smash his face in with my boot. "You could try, wolf, but your bride is correct. I fear her a lot more than I fear you."

But he didn't know what hope could do to a man. How it could make someone like me more ruthless than I had ever been.

"Let him down, Nico. He needs his voice if he wants to open the gates, and it's not like I can substitute him for another Fae. Trust me—I checked."

I nearly ground my molars to dust, but I released that fuckwad and backed up a step. "Sure thing, Bird."

Did it matter that I was irrationally angry that she had started this shit without me? Probably not. After the discussion we'd had last night, I sort of thought this plan was not something she could do on her own. That just showed me, now, didn't it?

And when this was all over, I would put her ass over my knee and spank it until she begged me to fuck her. When this was all over, I would make her delirious with pleasure until she understood that we were in this shit together. And then... Then we would be us. She'd cook and I'd do the dishes, and we would lead this pack, and I would have her smiles and her laughs and one day—when things were calmer, and the world wasn't a complete dumpster fire—maybe we'd have kids.

We'd never talked about it. I knew she was covered as far as birth control, but we'd never discussed if she even wanted kids. With a family like hers, it was always a good possibility that she didn't. And as much as I wanted them, if she didn't, I knew we were enough.

But the thought of her round with my child did something to me.

Later, asshole. You have a Fae Prince to deal with.

Tristan looked at his feet. "I can't open the Fae doors."

Wren laughed—her giggle sweet as if she thought he was adorable. "Of course you can't. You borrowed your father's magic to do it, didn't you? I bet with all his playthings, he didn't even notice when you siphoned it off of him. It didn't matter how much they tortured you, you were never opening those gates. Right?"

Tristan took a healthy step away from Wren. "How in the blue bloody fuck do you know that?"

Wren pointed to the delicate skin beside her eye. "I can see better this time around. I bet you wished I was still the naïve little child falling for illusion mage's tricks, now, don't you?"

His lips twisted. "It would certainly help." His sigh sounded like he was trying to let his soul escape before Wren got ahold of it. "Fine. Do you have a plan, or are our asses just swinging in the wind?"

"Of course I do. But we need a change of venue."

A single snap of her fingers, and we weren't in the backyard anymore. No, we were in Chatham Square, its burning gate still going even four months later. But this time, the fire didn't so much as singe our skin. We were in the middle, sure, and the flames roared so loud I couldn't hear my own thoughts, but nothing touched us.

Our pack stayed on the edges of the Square, but Wren, Tristan, Ghost, and I were right next to the Hell gate as if she was waiting on something.

Wren sucked in a deep breath, and then it was as if all the fire in the entire square filled her lungs. The never-ending flames flickered and died, their heat melting away on the breeze. The Hell gate stood tall for all the world to see, but it wasn't on fire anymore.

ERRORS AND EXORCISMS 603

But Wren seemed to be made of it. Flames danced in her eyes as her red hair failed to follow the rules of gravity, floating in the air in a nimbus cloud around her head. And that didn't even touch the fact that she was floating at eye level with Tristan.

Tristan, smartly, was ghostly pale, his shock and fear stamped all over him. "I—I... I'm sorry—"

Wren's head tilted as she studied him, latching onto his wrist in a grip that made him wince. "The spell, Prince. Before I lose my temper. I will lend you the power you need while I can."

The Fae swallowed hard, trying to pull out of Wren's hold. "Trying" being the operative word. "You know what's coming. He'll cross over. There won't be anything I can do to stop him."

"You let us worry about your father," I growled. "Here she has a whole pack at her back and the whole of the ABI. There she had squat. We can handle it."

Tristan's fear reminded me of Theo—of him horrified at his will being taken away. At the pain and filthy feeling he had when he had to do things against every rule he ever made for himself.

Fuck.

I did not want to empathize with this shit stain—especially when gratitude seemed to be stamped all over his face.

With a nod of agreement, dark magic swirled up his arms and legs as his brown eyes went black. He spoke in a guttural language similar to what Wren and Fiona before her had used, but it had a different cadence, different rhythm.

And maybe that was the difference. Or maybe he had always been the key, and he knew he couldn't do it alone.

A vine-covered door shimmered into being amongst the still-smoking grass and ruined trees. Flowers bloomed on the vines, a bright spot of color in the midst of the blackness. But more than that, it was as if the world itself took a breath, as if someone had opened a window in a stuffy house and now the air flowed freely.

Tristan almost wilted as fear really hit him, the stink of it coating his skin like oil.

"You're not done," Wren snarled, her grip on him going from tight to crushing. "As payment for fixing your fuck-up and lending you my power, you will bring me the forty-three women that your father stole."

What? She was letting him go? After everything he'd done, Wren was going to trust that he would do what she asked and—

"What? No." Tristan yanked at his arm in her grip, but Wren didn't so much as budge. The smell of burning flesh hit my nose as Tristan fell to his knees, Wren's feet touching the ground for the first time in minutes.

"*Yes.* I can't go into the Fae realm without destroying it," she hissed, pulling Tristan to her in an iron grip I didn't even think I could break. "As much as I would love to watch your father get crushed beneath his absolute *cliché* of a castle, I need those women back more. You get them out, and we'll be square."

Tristan howled as a flame flickered over Wren's hand, only getting louder as her fire-like gaze grew brighter. "Fulfill this bargain, and no member of the Acosta pack will hunt you— even though you deserve it."

"That's a tall order, Bird."

Wren's fire eyes cut to me, the censure in them enough to make the words on my tongue dry up. Well, that and she decided to speak inside my head like Ghost sometimes did.

I have a plan. Just trust me, will ya?

Wren turned back to Tristan, pained tears filling his eyes as she continued to burn him. "Because you and I both know that you can't go back home. You were banished to the Dark Court with your father for a reason, and your father wants to secure his crown, so... Earth is the only realm that will accept you. Bring me my payment, and you will have nothing to worry about from our pack."

Her smile turned cold despite the flames that seemed at home in her skin.

"Don't? And I will make sure you never stop running. There will be no safe place to lay your head or rest. No one hiding you, no one making sure you stay alive, no one showing you an ounce of mercy. Understand?"

Tristan's gaze fell from Wren's to my pack and back to her.

"We will never stop hunting you—not until we take an iron blade to your neck, or worse, our pack brings you to me. Now, do we have a deal?"

The Fae Prince gritted his teeth but gave an emphatic nod.

"The words," I growled, knowing full well a Fae or a demon deal required consent. And I had a feeling my wife was a bit more demon than I'd originally thought.

"We have a deal," Tristan gasped. "I will bring back the forty-three women stolen from Earth by my father. If they live, I will bring them home or give you the bones of those that have passed. I will not kill them, deal with them, or cause any undue harm."

"Excellent."

Wren let go of his wrist, the skin not quite as charred as I'd thought it would be. Where her hand had been was a blackened brand of shapes and lines, forming an intricate sigil.

"What did you do to me?" he whispered as his trembling fingers reached for the burn.

Wren's lips tipped up. "Cemented our deal. The marks will go away once you have fulfilled our bargain, and they allow me to track you on any plane should you decide to break it. You will also have a chaperone."

At the snap of her fingers, Wyatt strode forward, cutting the distance with long purposeful strides that told me that he would take great pleasure in Tristan not even attempting to fulfill his deal.

But she was asking him to lose years of his life in the Fae realm. She was—

He wants this, she said in my mind, breaking me out of my hastily formed planning session to figure out how to get him out of this predicament. *It's how he can heal. There are things Wyatt needs to do for himself, and this is it.*

But I was his Alpha. I was supposed to protect him like my father never did. My father didn't so much as flinch when he got taken, didn't say a word, and he had to have known when he'd dropped off the map.

Wyatt slapped my shoulder. "Don't worry so much, Nic. You'll grow yourself an ulcer."

His smile was resolute but sad, that carefree calmness that he'd had all of our childhood long gone. I hadn't seen it since before he'd been taken, and I feared I'd never see it again.

"I'll get right on that."

Of course I would—right after he came back safe and sound and hopefully with that Fae's head on a spike.

Wyatt bent, giving Wren a hug and then petting Ghost. When he straightened, he was kitted out in armor and weapons, a little gift from my wife.

"Be right back," he said, striding for the door like a man on a mission. "Come on, Pixie Dust, we've got a job to do."

Tristan stared at his brand before meeting my wife's still-flaming gaze. "This will go away when I deliver them, yes? No tracking, no hidden spells, I'll just be free."

Wren tipped up her chin. "That's the deal, but I'll offer a word of warning. Should Wyatt not return, or return harmed in any way, we'll strike a brand-new deal—one that will leave your mother gutted in front of you after I cut your eyelids away so you can't even blink. Understand?"

Tristan's face went white as he shakily nodded. "Yes."

"Fabulous. Now, off you go."

And then I watched the Fae I hated—and my best friend—walk through the same fucking gate that had taken Wren from me for three years.

All before my first cup of coffee.

CHAPTER 16

WREN

I was in deep shit.

If Nico's face was anything to go by, I would be in said shit until the end of time. His emotions—which had a baseline of livid since I'd made it home—were dialed more to "burn the world down" levels. Add to that the trickle of a nosebleed coming from the power usage, and I figured I was fucked.

And not in a good way.

Before anyone could see it, I wiped my nose and ducked my face out of sight. Summoning Tristan had been a wild hair of an idea, sure. Lending him power to open the Fae gates, though. That had been really stupid.

Stupid and necessary.

But now that I had, I had no idea how I was supposed to exorcise every human in Savannah, close the Hell gate, *and* potentially rally against a Fae King who could be coming through those doors at any second.

Nico latched onto my bicep, pulling me into him so he could whisper in my ear: "You're bleeding. Why the fuck are you bleeding, Wren?"

It reminded me so much of that time up in Blue Ridge when he'd scented my blood for the first time. I'd been walking for hours, and the boots I'd worn had cut my feet up so much I could have been permanently deformed if he hadn't helped me.

I met his gaze, his gold eyes glowing in the morning sunlight. Gods, he was just as beautiful today as he had been that night up on the mountain. A little scarred, a little scruffy, but he was so fucking sexy it nearly killed me.

But I didn't answer him, and that pissed him off.

"Take us back home, Wren. Snap your fingers and bring my pack home, and then you and I can have a conversation."

I gulped. "Is conversation code for something, or do I need to write a Will?"

My smart mouth was going to get my ass killed one of these days. I had spent all the bravado I had making sure Tristan had no other recourse but to do what I wanted. Now, I was at Nico's mercy, and I couldn't decide if that was a good or bad thing.

"Do it. Now."

If I didn't do this, Nico would know just how weak I was now. If he knew that, he would never go for what I needed to do next.

This was going to suck.

Drawing in a deep breath, I snapped my fingers again,

shoving the lot of us through space and time back to the Acosta compound. Squawks of indignation sounded all around me as we landed, the complaints mixed with a healthy dose of fear.

I couldn't blame them. Who knew what I even was anymore? A witch? A demon? Something in between?

Zephyr had given me so much power, so much knowledge, it was as if the girl I used to be was gone. I knew too much, felt too much, saw too much.

And that little trickle from my nose? Well, now it was a full-on waterfall.

My only stroke of luck was that I'd made the smart decision to glamour myself before I yanked out of Nico's hold, marching through the house and straight to the library. If Nico was going to yell at me—and I had a feeling he most definitely would, then I needed a sound-proof room for him to do it in.

But as quickly as I was moving, Nico still caught up to me just as I reached the door.

"Where the fuck do you think you're going? This is—"

His words died a quick death when I turned the knob and pushed the door wide. "Someplace new. I needed a place to put all the Bannister knowledge. Now, no matter what happens, we have it."

No matter what. No matter if I don't make it. No matter if I fail. But I didn't share those thoughts, I managed to keep them to myself.

Growling, he yanked me through the door and slammed it shut behind us, rage and heat and awe filling his gut. "You're pouring blood, but I can't see it. Don't you dare glamour yourself against me, Bird."

Bird. If Nico was still calling me Bird, then there was hope to be had. It meant I hadn't destroyed everything we were by overstepping, by acting like the Alpha I most definitely was not.

Sighing, I dropped it, letting him see what I'd done to myself just getting those gods-forsaken gates open.

"Jesus, fuck, Bird. What did you do to yourself?"

My knees wobbled and I wilted to the floor to my ass, my hands holding onto the hardwood planks like I could fall off the world at any moment. Opening the gates had been in Zephyr's instructions, but the deal? That was all me. I had a feeling casting the repercussions was biting me in the ass right about now.

Savannah was broken because of me. Tristan, Diana, they thought I was a destroyer. Maybe I was. But I was also a fixer. Okay, so I caused more problems than I fixed, but I—

I could do this.

"There's a restroom right past the third shelf on the left. Can you get me a towel a—"

Nico cupped my face and pressed his forehead against mine. Instantly, warmth filled me as the blood dried in my nose and the worst of the aches eased. But even with as much power as we shared, he couldn't touch all of it.

"Thank you," I breathed, latching onto his wrists. The thrum of his pulse vibrated through my fingers all the way to my own heart.

"It's not enough."

No, it wasn't. But I didn't have enough time.

"Stay here, you understand me? Do not move from this spot."

Nodding, I didn't have the heart to tell him I couldn't stand on my own two feet if he'd paid me. I didn't know how I was supposed to exorcise anyone in this damn town let alone close the Hell gate. And the sheer thought of fighting Desmond on my home turf sounded exhausting.

Because I knew without a shadow of a doubt in my mind that he was coming. The way Tristan had felt about it, his father was worse than the devil himself. Granted, the pompous asshole hadn't been able to touch me in the Fae realm, but I had a feeling that ship sailed as soon as I made it back home.

A moment later, Nico returned with a hand towel and wiped away the blood that coated my face and neck. His hand trembled as he did it, the scene likely reminding him of that last time we'd been in this room. Well, not exactly this room, but still.

"You have to keep yourself safe. You have to live." Gently, he cleaned my skin, not letting himself look me in the eye. "I can't make it in a world where you don't exist, you hear me? I did it for three years and I... I... just can't do it anymore. Not without you."

"Nico," I breathed, but he cut me off with a violent shake to his head.

"Not without you, Bird. Before there was hope. Hope that you'd come back. Hope that you were out there somewhere safe. Hope that one day I'd see you again."

My heart was splintering into a million pieces in my chest at what he must have gone through. Because I knew exactly what too much hope could do to a person.

"It was the only thing that kept me moving, day in and day out for three years. It was the only thing that kept me breathing. If I lose you, I won't have that back. I'll never have anything close to it again."

I swallowed hard, the grief that he held in a tight little ball in his gut, the longing, the fear, it filled me in a way that I had never felt before. He was finally letting me in, finally letting me see just how much these last three years had scarred him.

"So you have to live, Bird. Whatever it is you have planned, I need you to remember that if you die, I die. If you fail, I fail. Because as much as I care about my pack, as much as I love them, I love you more."

What else could I say to that?

"I love you, Nico. I don't know what you survived to be here with me, but I'll thank every god if I have to." I ran my fingers through his long, wavy hair. It hung loose around his shoulders, the color mingling with his black shirt. "And I'll do everything I can to stay right here with you."

But I didn't promise I would stay alive—I couldn't—and he seemed to realize it.

Before I knew it, I was up and in his arms, my legs around his waist as he carried me to one of the tables. Knocking a stack of books to the floor, he set me on the edge. The way he looked at me, I might as well have been naked. It was as if he could see every inch of my skin, every freckle. Hell, he could probably see the way my nipples tightened and my sex clenched, both practically begging for his touch.

He hadn't even kissed me, and yet it was as if he'd marked every millimeter with his teeth.

Frozen, all I could do was let him look at me. All I could do was let him unbutton my top and spread it wide. There was nothing else but allowing him to peel the fabric from my skin, piece by piece until I was bare for him. I loved being exposed like this so he could feast on me with his eyes, that hungry gaze like a physical touch.

"As soon as I woke up this morning, I knew I was going to spank your ass today."

Fuck.

My sex clenched around nothing as I sat impatiently, squeezing my thighs together in an effort to control the ache. I remembered the first time Nico had spanked me. It was a lesson on who he belonged to—who I belonged to. I'd tried teasing him, and it had backfired in the absolute best way possible.

Without warning, Nico latched onto my hips and yanked me to the edge of the table before spinning me until my feet were on the floor and my ass was bare to him. The cool wood kissed my hard nipples as I scrabbled for purchase. But the first crack to my ass came before I was ready, the sharp sting so fucking good it had me rocking up on my toes.

"I told you to wake me if you left my bed, Little Bird."

The heat of him at my back, curling over me to whisper in my ear? Fucking marvelous.

Another crack against the opposite cheek had me moaning, and that was before his thick fingers played with the slick wetness between my thighs.

"You going to leave it again without me?"

I couldn't think of the right answer. On the one hand, I wanted his cock inside me, and if I answered in the affirmative, he'd most likely give it to me.

Oh, but if I hesitated, if I played stubborn, he'd play with me some more, spank me more, let the raw power that coursed through his very being wash over me. And *then* he'd fuck me until I couldn't walk.

Decisions, decisions.

"I don't hear an answer, Bird. Am I going to have to fuck it out of you?"

His hand cracked against my thigh right next to my pussy and the heat had me moaning again, which was the only answer he was going to get.

A second later, his cock was at my opening, the rough kiss of his jeans against the now-hot, over-sensitized skin a thing of beauty. And then he pushed inside, every single inch of him filling me so full I could hardly breathe. Nico's hand fisted in my hair, yanking me vertical as his other hand gently wrapped around my throat.

He didn't squeeze. It was more that he was reassuring himself in the space that I was breathing, I was alive, and he was, too.

"You're not leaving me," he growled against my lips. "Say it."

I wanted him to move—needed it—and I knew without a shadow of a doubt in my mind, he'd stay right there until I gave him exactly what he wanted.

He circled his hips, teasing me into near mindlessness.

"Say it, Bird, and I'll fuck you so good. I'll fill you so full. I'll make you scream. Tell me what I want to hear, and I'll do anything you want me to do."

His hand left my hair and encircled my wrists, damn near bending me in half as he continued to torment me—refusing to offer the friction I so desperately needed.

"Yes," I choked out, my greedy moan twisting my voice until it was almost unrecognizable.

Nico's grip tightened on my wrists as his one on my throat softened. He turned my chin with the softest touch, nipping at my bottom lip. "Yes, what?"

"I'll never leave your bed."

That earned me a delicious thrust of his hips that had me clenching to hold onto him. "What else?"

"I'll never leave you," I promised, and the truth of it was, I wouldn't. I couldn't. Death couldn't drag me away.

"That's my good girl." He let my wrists go as he kissed me until he had to hold me up. "Now hold onto something."

My hands scrabbled for purchase on the table, but just like the last time, I wasn't ready.

Nico fucked me like a man possessed. He fucked me so good I saw stars, whole universes, the heavens itself. He turned me, nearly bending me in half as he took out every ounce of his frustration, of his fear, on me, and I loved each and every minute of it. He kissed me until neither of us could breathe.

And when his fangs struck, I knew I'd keep my promise or die trying.

CHAPTER 17

NICO

"Are you sure about this, Bird?"

Wren was currently poring over a book in her brand-new library, her shirt unbuttoned and hanging open to reveal her bra and miles of smooth, pale skin. While I appreciated the view, there was something to the frantic way she skimmed the book that had me sitting up and taking notice.

And no, I was not talking about my dick.

Wren creating this library for herself was a stroke of genius, one that felt like a slap in the face to my father. She had never gotten her revenge for what had transpired here, but taking this place and making it hers? That was masterful.

She waffled her hand at me while she turned the pages. "Yes and no. I need power. I used almost everything Zephyr gave me fixing what Tinkerbell broke. If I want to exorcise a whole fucking city without killing everyone, I'm going to need more juice."

She swiped the pages until she let out a *whoop* of joy. "There it is. Liminal spaces. Ghost said something to me earlier that got me thinking. He called you a Spirit Alpha, a ruler of the in-between. He said I, too, ruled that space. Now, I don't quite know what that means outside of liminal spaces."

Funny, I had been with that asshole wolf for three fucking years and now he was spilling his guts? He hadn't said a fucking word about this shit to me. Not one.

"Liminal space includes but aren't limited to, pocket worlds, Fae dimensions, the In-Between, and ancestral wells."

I didn't know dick about pocket worlds or the In-Between, but ancestral wells I knew enough about. And more often than not, they ran dry quick. Witches used them—especially ones that practiced ancestral magic. When a witch died, the family would bury them using a sacred ritual, allowing their power to fill the well. The problem was, witches didn't die every day, and the amount of power needed to sustain ones like the Bannisters was probably too much to keep magic flowing.

"Now the problem is, I have no idea if my family knew about the well, or if that was why they were killing off coven witches to siphon from. But the only way to tell is to go to the family plot and start asking questions."

Had I not been sitting on the table beside her, I would have fallen on my ass. "And by asking questions, you mean?"

Wren piled her hair on top of her head and secured it into a messy bun. "Commune with the dead and pray they don't get handsy?"

Outside of grave talkers, there weren't many people who

could talk to the dead. A rare subset of arcaners, I only knew of one, and even she wasn't a full-on grave talker. "You got a grave talker in your pocket and forget to tell me?"

Wren sighed. "No, but I was empowered by a Prince of Hell, so it's possible I can use that to my advantage." She blew a raspberry as she stared at the book. "It's the best I've got."

"And what happens if the well is dry—if there are no more Bannister witches to siphon from?"

Frowning, she slammed the book shut. "Then we'll cross that bridge when we come to it."

While Bonaventure Cemetery was the most famous in Savannah, the Bannisters had never once been interred there. Too common for their tastes, maybe, or maybe they just didn't want tourists tramping all over their dead. Savannah had more cemeteries than anywhere else, but the arcane ones weren't on any tourist map.

Hidden in a forgotten corner of Forsyth Park, the Bannisters built a place that couldn't be accessed by anyone not of arcane blood. The only reason we knew about it at all was due to the information download, courtesy of Zephyr. Given that Wren was the last living person with Bannister blood, only she could give us access to the last spot on the planet she might draw from.

No, that wasn't true. There were other liminal spaces, but Wren worried that by drawing on them might destroy what was left. I mean, technically, she could open a Fae door and suck it dry, but then Wyatt and the women he was trying to bring home might be forfeit. She could call on Death herself for access to the In-Between, but that was a shade too risky—even for her.

No, the Bannister Forsyth Crypt was our best shot, even if it was a long one.

Hidden behind three thick oak trees that seemed to be twisted together into one, the entrance refused to reveal itself without a drop of blood from the pair of us. Only then did the trees untwist, unveiling a small meadow and a sprawling crypt with a spire that reached for the sky.

I had a bad feeling about crossing this boundary, but unless Wren wanted to burn herself out trying to exorcise all of Savannah, we were shit out of luck. Sacking up, I crossed first, making sure the place wasn't going to collapse on our heads or there wasn't a small pocket of rogue Bannisters waiting to kill us.

Only then did I beckon for Wren to follow me, my unease growing by the second.

Wren and Ghost crossed together, the damn wolf not leaving her side for a single moment since we left the library. He wouldn't say why, either, only that he was coming with us. Since Wren's return he had been stuck to her like glue, and while a modicum of jealousy hit me every time he wasn't at my side, it was replaced by the sheer relief that someone, somewhere, was always watching out for her.

As soon as Wren's foot touched down, the whole of the ground trembled, not easing my fears one bit. But then the air seemed to sigh as if it was happy someone was coming to visit.

Wren's gaze went wide as she whipped her head this way and that as if she could see shit I absolutely could not.

"What is it, Bird?"

She swallowed hard, putting her trembling hand in mine. "Either Zephyr scrambled my brain a bit when he worked his mojo, or I'm looking at a shit-ton of ghosts."

The trees shivered as a tinkling bell of a laugh shimmered on the breeze. *Oh, shit.*

Cold dread yanked at my stomach, and I tugged Wren behind me, backing up toward the entrance. Only... the trees moved of their own accord, twisting once more so that the entrance was just *gone.*

Fuck.

There was a small list of shit I was afraid of in this world. At the very top of that list was anything at all to do with ghosts. They were just a portion of the arcane that was outside of my wheelhouse. I couldn't see them, I couldn't fight them, and if they decided to be mean enough, they could rock your shit until you were a stain on the floor.

Ghosts were assholes.

And my wife could see them.

"Here," she said, forcing some of her power into me—power she absolutely could not afford to lose.

But then I saw. I saw and I wished I hadn't. Because it wasn't one or two or even a solid gaggle of five. No, that was a number I could work with. What fit into this small meadow was a gods-damned horde of ghosts.

And every single one of them was staring at Wren.

Did I say fuck? Because I meant fuuuuuuuccccccckkkkkk.

But it wasn't like I could rip a ghost's throat out so unless these people were friendly, we were on the losing end of the stick here.

Their voices thrummed through the air like a swarm of bees, the see-through people buzzing with whispers as they talked amongst themselves. Some of them nodded and then a woman older than time made her way to the front. Even dead, she walked with a limp. I kind of figured ghosts would glide or something, but see-through and grayed-out, she hobbled forward until she was so close to us, I could almost scent her.

"Why have you come to us, child? Do you seek the well?" The old woman tilted her head to the side.

Slowly, Wren nodded before bowing at the waist. "Yes, Great mother, I wish to seek the power of the well. If it pleases you."

Her cadence was off, as if she was remembering a script at the last second, but I was still stuck on how fucking full this place was. I'd never heard of a well this stocked—not that I'd dealt too much with this side of the arcane.

"And you bring non-witches with you? In our sacred space?" It wasn't a chastisement, only an observation—or at least it was phrased like one.

Wren straightened. "With me is my husband, the Spirit Alpha of the Acosta pack, as well as a soul-ripped wolf. They are here as my protection, and I will not cast them from this space. They are family, and they are granted all rights afforded as such."

"Very well, if you feel you need your *protection*, you may have it."

Wren's gaze narrowed, and I could tell this was about to get real disrespectful real quick. "I wasn't asking."

The old woman smiled as if she'd said something funny, but I knew that Wren could only handle so much bullshit before she lost her shit, and this woman was already on her last nerve.

"If you do not wish to ask for our protection, why is it that you come to us? And so young? Why not consult an elder for what it is you seek?"

Wren's smile was as rueful as it was cold. "There is no one else. And I do not need your counsel. I need your power. All of it."

The buzzing intensified as the souls gossiped like old biddies. The ancient one's gaze seemed to really focus on Wren, a touch of fear there.

"I am the last witch of Bannister blood. The last born of our name. I will not birth a witch of our name, nor will any witch from my loins call upon this well. If you do not wish to help me, you will stay here. You will have no one to call upon you. You will have no one to receive your blessings. And you will remain here until the world ends and Death finally comes for what's left of you."

The ghost squawked, straightening as if Wren just told her to go fuck herself.

"But," Wren said holding up a single finger, "if you help me now, I will release you from the well so you may move on. You will find peace."

Avarice flitted through the woman's expression as the buzzing only got louder. "And what makes you think, child, that *we* need *your* help?"

Yep, this had the potential to turn real shitty real fucking fast if Wren didn't get them on our side.

Flames lit Wren's eyes as she stepped closer to the ghost before she blinked, and her irises returned to their normal green-gold. And even though that ghost was deader than a doornail, she backed up as if Wren could kill her twice.

"As someone who has been used for my power, I know exactly what help you need. You may want to feel some sort of honor in this, but you and I both know that you're trapped. You and I both know that you're bored and restless and release is the kindest thing I can do for you."

"You... you..." the woman gasped, still backing up. "*Demon.*"

Wren waggled her hand. "Not exactly. My mother made a demon deal while I was in utero. The demon thought my mother would abuse the power, so I got it."

The woman gasped again, only this time it was in shame. "Your mother is Margot Bannister."

"*Was*, yes."

The woman sighed again, her expression gaining more and more understanding as time went on. "And Eloise is your grandmother, Rupert, your father."

Wren nodded. "You refused her request for power, I take it? And Eloise and Judith, and any other slimy, worthless asshole in the line. Is that why there are so many of you left? Because Eloise destroyed everything the Bannisters used to be?"

"We would not let her gain an ounce of the power she sought. She wished to drain us dry to make herself Queen of this city, to destroy any other arcaner who stood in her way. Margot was delusional and too full of herself. They were not under attack. There was no war. But she was just like her mother—my daughter. Too much for my liking."

So, this was Wren's great-grandmother. Definitely not the oldest ghost in this place, but not the youngest, either.

"Eloise was nothing like her sisters. Where my other daughters were kind and trustworthy, Eloise only wanted more. More power, more money, more influence. I would not let her come to the well, and eventually, I put a spell on it so that she could not gain access. In time, she killed us, one by one. Either it was accidents or in-fighting or other arcaners, but I knew it was her. Soon, her daughter petitioned the well."

And because Margot was Eloise-lite, they said no, tipping this whole thing into motion. It was hard to tell if she'd done the right thing. If she hadn't, Wren wouldn't be the woman she was today, but if she had, Margot would have run this city into the ground decades ago. Wren might not have been born. We might never have met.

If Margot hadn't needed her, Wren's mother might have killed her or cast her out or...

"I don't blame you for telling her no," Wren murmured, staring at her feet. "You did the right thing. But now I need your help, and I hope you see me without the stain of my parents."

"Tell us why you need the power, child," a man said, stepping forward. Dressed in turn-of-the-century garb—and by century, I meant the eighteenth—he seemed older than most here. "Tell us and we will decide."

"A Hell gate was opened in Savannah. I wish to exorcise the humans it has infected and close the gate. Also, a dark king from the Fae realm seeks to kill me and mine. I wish to protect them as best I can for as long as I can."

He studied Wren. "You do not seek status or money or fame?"

Wren looked at me and then back at them. "I don't need any of that. Hell, I don't even want any of that."

Too bad she already had most of those things. She had status as my wife and on her own as an ABI agent—if she still wanted to do the job. She had money because I had money. Plus, whatever was in the Bannister coffers was hers now. And fame? No one truly wanted fame. They only wanted the privileges fame afforded them.

"You only wish to help the city become one again?"

Wren raised an eyebrow. "That's what I said, isn't it? You want it written in blood or something?"

The man smiled before grasping the ancient woman's hand. "No need. We can see inside your soul, child. We see past the words and into the marrow. We will give it all to you, and we will be free."

I kind of figured the deliberation would have lasted longer, but...

The horde shimmered into a swath of gold, fading slightly on the wind before moving in a massive murmuration right at Wren. It faded into her skin, filling her full of magic before my very eyes.

It was only then that I felt the slightest bit of hope.

But if anyone knew what hope could do to a man, it was me.

CHAPTER 18

WREN

Being ready was an illusion.

Because there was no way to gauge just how ready one had to be to exorcise a whole city full of people. Or close a gate straight to Hell. Or not kill everyone while I did both.

Did I have enough power? Maybe. Was I prepared with spells and potions and odds and ends? Sure. Did I have that first clue of what I was actually doing?

Absolutely fucking not.

"Tell me again what Erica said when you called her?" I asked Nico as I stuffed a stasis potion bomb into my satchel. If I could, I'd wear a bandolier of them like an old-West gunslinger.

Fiona and I had been working on them all day. Those and black salt vials and iron ferrite bombs and blessed salt charges and anything else we could think of to cover our asses. Malia tried to help, too, but she said everything I touched was like grabbing onto a live wire even with gloves on.

A part of me hoped I'd go back to regular-powered Wren when this was all over. Because while I enjoyed being a badass, I missed just being able to hug my friends without zinging them into oblivion. The only person who didn't seem affected was Nico, which was a blessing all by itself.

Nico sighed before stilling my hand. "That the ABI couldn't get involved. While she wants to help, they are having a hard time securing the border. Too many months without news has made the rest of the region unstable. The ABI is dealing with a power-grab situation. It's not the first time and it won't be the last, but it looks like we're on our own."

Perfect.

The Acosta pack was large, but it was split almost in two after the Hell gate fiasco. The ABI cut off most of the city from the rest of the state, but a decent number of the pack was outside the limit. We had fifty fighters that were of age, not caring for an underage loved one, and capable of battle.

Fifty.

Against a city full of demons.

Like I said. Perfect.

I'd sort of hoped the ABI would *want* to back us up. I mean, we were solving a huge problem for them. Sure, it was a problem that we created—sort of—but a major one, nonetheless.

Nico's arm wrapped around my shoulders, and he pulled me into him. "Bird, don't you know that one wolf is worth at least ten fighters?"

Against demons?

Evidently the skepticism was stamped all over my face because Nico tipped his head back and let out a huge belly laugh. I would never get tired of that sound. His laugh lightened his features and took years off his shoulders.

"Don't worry, Bird. We'll handle this. Promise."

Yeah, we would. I just hoped we didn't get our asses handed to us before then.

BY THE TIME THE PACK WAS SETTLED IN CHATHAM Square, night had fallen in earnest. Without the constant flames, the din of the city was nearly gone, the silence almost peaceful if it weren't for the fact that we'd be calling roughly the entire city here in just a few minutes.

Okay, that was a complete exaggeration.

But incorporeal demons were the equivalent of fifty people. Each. And there were a fucking lot of them.

"Oh, come on," Hannah muttered, hip-checking me as she passed. "You faced down a death mage with no power at all. You can do this."

I finally broke my stare-down of the Hell gate to send her a skeptical side-eye. "That is an oversimplification, and you know it."

Fiona did the same on my other hip, only where Hannah was trying not to knock me over, Fiona put her whole ass into it. I stumbled a little before flicking her in the nose.

Before long I was giggling, which was likely the intended purpose.

"Oh, good," Malia said on a sigh. "Now I don't have to try

and trip you or some other such bullshit to get you to settle down. No offense, Wren, but your power makes nuclear reactors look weak."

I winced, shrugging. "Sorry. But never fear. I'll probably blow the whole wad on the exorcisms and then you can relax. Speaking of relaxing, I was under the impression you'd be doing that instead of this?" I shot Fiona a glare. "You, too. What are y'all doing here?"

Fiona flicked me in the tender meat of my arm. "You know better, and how come you didn't ask Hannah that?"

Because I indeed *did* know better than to ask Hannah that question. She'd likely punt me into next week, Alpha's wife-slash-demon spawn or not. She was still pissed she didn't get to rip my family apart limb from limb and would not speak to Nico because he left her behind—not that it was his fault.

"Because I choose life?" I muttered, flicking her back.

Yes, we were acting like children, but dammit, I'd missed them. I knew it wasn't the same—to them I'd been gone for years—but having them around made life... better.

"Damn right she does," Hannah said under her breath, adjusting her weapons. On top of the axes Hannah had strapped to her back, she also had a satchel filled with as many potions as she could carry. Every one of us did, but especially the few of us who couldn't shift.

The ones that could? Well, they had a small arsenal, but they'd be using claws and teeth more than potion bombs. Before we'd come out here, Nico had made a new rule—one I approved of more than I could say.

Both parents could not fight together if they had children underage. The families had to choose which parent to send—if any—so no child would be left orphaned. He also decreed that no one *had* to fight. He would not force them, and he would not take their will away.

He had more people fall to his feet in loyalty at that statement alone than Tomás had in nearly four hundred years. Wolves pushed back at the parent rule, asking to fight for him —for us.

But Nico wouldn't budge.

It made me proud of everyone who came to fight with us. Because this was family. This was loyalty. This was what I'd wanted my whole life. Now I had it and I prayed to every god, demon, and spirit that I could possibly think of that I didn't fuck it up.

Nico cut through the blackened square straight to me, his expression one of a determined Alpha. He was in his element, leading his people, and if I wasn't scared shitless I was about to accidentally napalm the entire city, I would have jumped his bones right then and there.

I mean, come the fuck on. How strong was I supposed to be against a full beard and his hair pulled back at the nape of his neck and that T-shirt stretched across his—

"You know I can feel that, right?" he whispered in my ear.

My eyes widened a little in faux surprise. "What? You're kidding. I had no idea."

His golden eyes melted me a little. They made me think I could do anything, and when he pressed a kiss to my lips, I almost believed it.

Almost.

Stuffing my fear down where emotions went to die, I managed a nod to signal I was ready. But before I could start the spell that would call the demons forth, I had one thing to say first.

"Thank you," I murmured, knowing every single one of them could hear me. "Thank you for being here with us, for being willing to fight. For showing up. I appreciate all of you." I cut a smile to Nico's older brother. "Even you, Theo."

He flipped me off and I blew him a kiss.

"You all embody what family means, and I will be forever grateful you accepted me into yours." Squeezing Nico's hand, I mouthed, "I love you" before walking into the biggest fucking witch circle I had ever made.

Only then did my chanting start.

I had to be careful with this part of the spell. If I used too much power, I wouldn't have enough left to exorcise the demons, but if I used too little, I wouldn't get them all. It was a delicate balance—a tight rope I was barely staying on.

One by one, possessed humans filtered through the carefully constructed wards at the perimeter of the square. It allowed the possessed in and no one out unless the wards were taken down from the inside. They wandered as if they were sleepwalking, bumping into each other, and stumbling over charred earth until they nearly reached the Hell gate.

There they waited, docile as a lamb, until I amassed almost more demons than the square could hold. Gulping, I quelled my chant, moving onto phase two of the plan.

Giving the signal, everyone readied their salt bombs while I did the completely asinine task of waking them up. There were too many to do the entire city at once, so batching them seemed like the best option.

Upset murmurings reminded me of talking to the ghosts of

the Bannister ancestral well. The buzz was damn near deafening. I shot a pleading glance to Nico, and he let out a whistle so loud, dogs on the fucking moon covered their ears.

"Hey, everybody," I began from the center of my circle. "I know you're confused, but I need you to pay attention."

Fiona, in all her purple-haired glory, gestured to the Hell gate while I continued my exit announcements like I was their damn cruise director or something. "This is the Hell gate. We are closing it tonight. If you wish to go home where it is warm, I need you to politely exit your host's body and pass through the gate immediately."

The demon closest to me practically clapped he was so happy. "Thank Deimos and all the torturers in Hell," he said, practically knocking me over with a feather. "Prince Zephyr told us we needed to stay here until you sent us home, and we cannot *wait* to get out of here. No offense, lady, but this place is freezing. I haven't been this cold since the Cubs won the World Series, and even then, Hell only froze over for twenty minutes, tops. I'm not allowed to kill anyone, I can't eat the animals, and the fresh meat selection is lacking."

Pressing my lips together, I tried not to lose it. This poor bastard had been stuck here just like I'd been stuck in the Fae realm, but his disposition was just...

"Umm... no offense taken?"

But reality set in quicker than lightning.

Why would Zephyr tell them to stay until I could send them home? Did that mean I didn't need to amass all this power? Did that mean I didn't have to fight?

As much as this was good news, I had a feeling it was pretty fucking bad.

Was this another test? Or was it something more?

My confusion rattled down to everyone else, and Nico tensed at my side, moving closer to me, crowding me, totally going off script as far as the plan. I couldn't make myself give a shit.

"Did Zephyr say anything else?" Nico asked, his voice low and commanding, making the demon stand up straight. "Give you any other instruction?"

The demon frowned at him before cutting his gaze to me as if he were waiting to see if I was okay with him spilling the beans. I nodded, urging him on.

"It's okay. This is my husband and our pack. You can tell us."

The demon screwed up his mouth and stepped closer. Almost everyone tensed, but I met him at the boundary of my circle because I knew. I knew it was bad and he was going to tell me the worst.

"Zephyr said we had to take care of our hosts. Keep them fit and fed and clean. We couldn't destroy their lives in any way—which is rude. These people accepted us of their own free will—putting 'Welcome' signs everywhere. It was as if they were just asking to be possessed, and we couldn't do *anything*. It was actually quite opportune because not all of us could find a host and had to go back home."

"That's not—" I shook my head. "The 'Welcome' signs are meant for humans. Those are not blanket consent. Did anyone express their consent where your host said that you could possess them and not just a 'Welcome' sign? Raise your hands."

A decent pocket of people raised their hands, including the

demon closest. Okay, so not a total takeover via cutsie welcome mats.

"But more, Prince Zephyr said that we must obey you. Protect you. He said a battle was coming and you would need the help."

It was as if the ground dropped under my feet. We needed to move this shit along, and fast.

I nodded, understanding hitting me square in the face. "Anyone who did not get express consent from your host or gained it using trickery, it is time to leave. Now. Go home to Hell, and thank you for caring for your hosts. Your job is done."

There was one such demon about ten feet away, and she gave me a grave nod before tilting her head back. Then she vomited an oily black smoke into the sky, her whole body shaking like she was being electrocuted. The black smoke headed for the gate, slipping into the seams of the door before winking out of sight.

One down...

The demon's host—a yoga-pants-wearing, mom-bun-having human crumpled to the ground on her hands and knees, coughing up what remained of the black sludge. Then one by one, the others followed suit, blotting out the full moon and all the stars with the incorporeal bodies of the demons on their way home. By the time it was all said and done, I had maybe thirty humans wondering how the fuck they'd gotten here.

That's where Fiona came in. With a wave of her hand, the bright-blue potion bottles surrounding the gathered demons exploded, their contents waving through the air as it sought out the non-possessed like heat-seeking missiles. The smoke collided with the humans, filling their noses, leaving them like mindless automatons.

"Go home, go to bed, remember nothing of this night. You will awake in the morning and go back to your life as you know it."

I'd heard of vampires being able to mind-control people, but vampires had been *persona non grata* in Savannah for centuries. When Fiona mentioned a potion that could replicate that same power, I knew it was the only way. Or at least, it was better than trying to mind-wipe them one by one with my untested magic.

The group moved in different directions, heading to wherever they called home.

This was good, so why did it feel like it was about to bite me in the ass?

CHAPTER 19

NICO

THIS WASN'T RIGHT.

Zephyr had set this up so we had an army at the gate. So, what did he think was about to come through that we'd need a whole pack and a gaggle of possessed humans at the ready?

And how did he know to send them through in the first place?

Everyone, move to the Fae gates. Be ready.

My command shimmered through the pack as many set down their salt bombs to shift to their animals. Wolves were better prepared for battle in their animal skins than in human form, anyway. And it looked like the salt bombs were probably the most unnecessary endeavor we'd done in the last twenty-four hours.

I had a feeling we'd need those iron ferrite ones a fuck of a lot more.

"I don't like this," Theo said, moving closer to our circle.

I didn't, either. "Fi, call the rest of the demons. Fuck the batching shit. Get them all here. Now."

"On it," she replied, nodding as if she was just about to do that very thing. "You might want to put out a call to our ABI buddies. Demon-possessed humans aren't exactly the top of the food chain."

Wren jerked her chin in the affirmative before waving her hands in an intricate dance. Cell phone towers had been down since the Hell gate opened, as well as most Internet access. Wren's little hand-waving was the only way to get a long-distance message out.

"She might get wigged out by the mental download," Wren said, shrugging, "but it got the job done."

I reached for her, wanting to pull her behind me, wanting to get her the fuck out of here, wanting just once for her to be safe and sound with no one and nothing trying to kill us. Her fingers found mine and then the whole world seemed to tilt.

The ground pitched, roiling beneath our feet as all those demons poured right back out of the Hell gate. Blacking out the sky, they screamed past us, shouting warnings that none of us could hear.

The door burst wide as the flames ignited once again, and out came scores of Fae, but none of us were paying attention to the smaller offerings from the Fae realm. They didn't seem to want to be here at all. No, we were looking at the tall man with the bone crown waltzing onto our plane like he had any right to be here.

Desmond.

Like most Fae, he had a long fall of hair, his the blackest of midnight with the same sharp features his son had. But while his son was tall, Desmond was taller, thinner, and power seemed to roll off him in waves.

Wren had said he hadn't been able to touch her in the Fae realm—that according to the Seelie Queen, no Fae could. But given that the Fae at Ellie's house had picked her up with no problem—that they struck her and tried to take what was mine—that reprieve was over.

Desmond scanned the crowd of shifters and demons and his amassed army of Fae before he landed on my wife. I had the strongest urge to fly across this circle. To put my sword in his gut and split him open.

His mouth stretched wide in what could have been a smile, delight hitting his eyes. He'd come for her, and he'd get her over my cold, dead corpse.

"Wren Bannister," the fucker simpered, his smile a touch too big for his face, his sharp white teeth too large for his mouth. "I've been looking for you."

"Funny," Wren shot back, "I was sort of hoping you'd have fallen off a cliff by now and drowned in your own blood." She pulled a sharp dagger from the sheath at her hip as she drew Fiona, Hannah, and Malia back with her magic, placing them inside the circle with us. "Looks like neither of us are getting what we want."

Wren stabbed the earth with her blade and a circle of golden magic drew up from the ground like a shield. "You couldn't touch me there and you sure as shit can't touch me here. So whatever throne you want, you're not getting it."

Desmond sauntered forward and put a single finger to Wren's ward. His finger sizzled but he didn't so much as flinch. "I was hoping for more power from you. What with your parentage and demon lineage and all. Pity. But the pack you provided and the demons just lying about? Well, they might just do the trick. I'll even take your husband this time. Had I known you were mated to a Spirit Alpha, I would have had my son steal you both."

Be ready to shift, Wren's voice screamed across my thoughts. *Make sure the pack is ready.*

But the pack was already shifting, jumping to their wolves as quick as a blink while Ghost was gearing up to eat his weight in Fae.

Three... two... one.

Wren ripped the blade out of the earth and threw it, hitting the Fae right next to Desmond in the neck. This close to the open Fae gates, she'd insisted on using iron blades. Now I could have kissed her for thinking of it because that Fae dropped like a stone, catching Desmond off guard.

My wolf took over before I ever told him to, jumping to his form and leaping forward as the world erupted into battle.

"Protect the daughter of Zephyr," the demon closest to Wren cried into the night, and the rest obeyed, surrounding my wife in a wall of bodies.

Possessed humans didn't have a ton of magic, but they were better than nothing, and the incorporeal ones? Well, they were already wreaking havoc with the Fae around Desmond, choking them, blinding them, doing anything and everything they could to give us an advantage. But as much as they were doing, and the spells that were coming from Fiona, and the brute force of Hannah, and the claws and fangs of my pack...

Nothing touched Desmond.

Not even me.

CHAPTER 20

WREN

I watched Nico jump before I could tell him to stop. Stuck behind more bodies than I cared to think about, there was no way I could have reached him in time.

No way I could have warned him.

Because I hadn't thrown that blade at just *any* Fae. I had thrown it directly at Desmond, and my aim had been true. But somehow nothing hit him, not one spell, not one blade. Nothing penetrated his defenses.

So when Nico jumped, all I could do was scream as Desmond's arm shot out, plucking Nico's wolf right out of the air like a flower in a garden. And just like with all his other playthings, he tossed my husband away from him like trash.

And even though I could feel Nico's heartbeat in my chest better than my own, even though I could feel the breath in his lungs, when he didn't get up, it still felt like I was dying. Like my soul was breaking apart piece by piece.

The scream that ripped from my throat had a power all on its own, casting demons and wolves and Fae alike away from me as if they had all been pulled by a string.

Zephyr. Please. Please come. Please help me. Help us. Please don't let me lose him.

The wealth of magic from the ancestral well roiled beneath my skin. I'd done a good job of cloaking it, but now was not the time to be modest. No, now was the time to rip that Fae fucker to shreds and dance on his innards while I bathed in his blood.

Or I could just kill him. Killing him would be good.

But it didn't matter what I threw, it just bounced off. Sure, those ricochets landed on the Fae surrounding him, but I didn't give a shit about those assholes.

I wanted the king.

The definition of insanity was doing the same thing over and over and expecting a different result. After tossing more power than I could afford to lose, wising up was my only option. If pushing didn't work, maybe pulling would.

So I drew him to me, reaching his ward and digging my fingers in it like I could bend the magic to my will. Desmond's smile—which had seemed so joyous before—trembled and fell.

"You think you can come here to my home and start wrecking shit? You think you can take and take and take and no one will put an end to your fuckery?" My fingers breached his ward, ripping it away like I wanted to do to his flesh. "You think you can hurt my family and I won't put your ass in the ground?"

"Stop, Wren," someone called but I couldn't focus on the fight around me.

Sure, I saw the demons ripping into the Fae, I knew the pack was taking their lickings and returning the favor. I felt Fiona using all she had to push against the horde Desmond had somehow called to us from all around Savannah.

I knew all this and still...

All I wanted was to know for certain that Nico was okay and to rip Desmond limb from fucking limb, and as long as I had those things, I would be happy as a clam.

But there was a flaw in my plan.

You see, when I ripped away Desmond's protection, I took away the barrier between us. Simple. Logical. But I wasn't logical right then. Because as soon as the magic floated away on the wind, the Fae King proved a theory.

He could most definitely touch me here.

And as the sharp slice of the blade cut through my belly, I knew for a fact what it was to lose. Because he wrapped his fingers around my throat, his icy skin making the dreaded knowledge worse. I had been so focused on revenge, so fixated on showing him that no one could hurt me, I'd let him far too close.

I'd handed him the winning ticket and he'd barely played the game.

"I knew hubris would do you in," Desmond murmured, his face too close to mine, his lips at my ear, his touch leeching the warmth from my very bones as the blood leaked from my belly.

"In my kingdom all you could do was taunt me. All you could do was insult my kingdom before stealing what I was promised. I think I'll make you beg me to kill you before I'm done."

"Fuck you. I'll never beg for you." Using what little strength I had left, I spat in his face, the blood-tinged saliva painting his skin red.

Then he dropped me just like he had all the others—just like he had Nico. Personally, I just figured the fuck wanted to stand over me, and if I could have moved my legs, I would have kicked him. But I was pretty sure he'd nicked my spinal cord with that fucking blade so moving said legs was out of the question.

So was breathing and walking and pretty much everything. I had been so stupid.

Nico. I'm so sorry.

A flash of red-stained white fur sailed over me headed straight for Desmond. Ghost bowled over the Fae King, his fangs tearing into his shoulder as the pair of them rolled. Desmond howled in pain as Ghost readjusted his grip, ripping the wound wide and damn near taking the whole arm off. Desmond's uninjured arm shot out, calling the blade that was still in my middle back to him.

Then that blade was in Ghost, tearing him open just like I was. The giant wolf yelped, staggering away as Desmond cradled his abused arm.

Ghost. My good beast. I'm so sorry.

I reached for him, only making contact with the blood that poured from his middle. Neither of us could move, and it wasn't enough. I hadn't done enough—I hadn't tried enough. I just wanted Savannah back the way it was, but maybe that was too much.

I should have played it smarter, should have consulted anyone else.

Am not good beast. Did not protect you. You're dying. We're dying.

Swallowing, tears ran into my hair as the pain bit into me. *You're the best beast. You kept him from taking all the power. You did so good.*

So tired. Don't want to leave you.

The reality of it was too much. Nico was alive out there. He could heal him, right? He could do something.

Nico, Nico, Nico. Please, someone help us. Please. Zephyr, someone, please!

Nico's face appeared over mine along with Zephyr's, two more men next to him—all four with this odd golden halo around their bodies like they were angels or something. One was blond, the other dark haired. Princes. Brothers. I returned my focus on Nico, and the wolf under his skin stared at me, his gaze sad.

Help Ghost. Somebody help him. I messed up. I'm sorry.

"Jesus fucking Christ, Bird. What happened to you?" Tears swam in Nico's eyes as he cradled me to his chest. "Not again. Please, no, I can't do this again. Stay with me."

Help him. Help Ghost.

"We're losing them," Zephyr warned, scraping his fingers through my open middle before mixing it with Ghost's blood. "I—we—can help."

"I don't care what it costs," Nico growled, "or what favor you need. Whatever it is, do it. I'm not losing her again."

The two men and Zephyr locked gazes and nodded. Each one dipped their fingers in our mingled blood, drawing a rune with it into the side of their cheeks. Zephyr latched onto Nico.

"Sorry about this. It's gonna hurt."

At once, all three brothers snapped their fingers, and Ghost, Nico, and I all convulsed.

Don't want to leave you. I want to stay. Please let me stay. Ghost was ripping my heart in two, and that said nothing to the tearing ache in my whole body at Nico's scream.

But Nico was a Spirit Alpha. Maybe... *Maybe...*

Then Ghost melted into a pool of golden light, his fur, flesh, and blood just gone. As much as it hurt, as much as I couldn't move, none of that stopped the sobs that ripped through me.

I want to stay. I want to stay. I want to stay, he pleaded and the pain of it damn near killed me.

That pool of light reached for me, and I reached for it. It settled on me, filling me, healing me, merging with my very soul as Ghost's light crowded my heart and settled there. I felt myself stitch back together, and I took my first real breath in minutes.

Ghost?

Something stirred in the back of my mind, growing larger with each passing second. A presence that hadn't been there before.

My queen?

It wasn't the same voice as Ghost had used before. It was lighter, younger, less masculine.

Ghost, is that you?

Ye-yes, my queen. I think so. I feel different but still me.

Trembling, I put a hand to my mouth, curling into Nico's warm embrace. "You saved him. You saved us."

Nico dropped kisses to my face in his relief. "Never again, you hear me? Don't you ever do that to me again."

Zephyr snorted. "Oh, I don't think you'll have to worry about that. Wren, my darling girl. You must shift. It's the only way to keep Ghost. You must cement the bond."

But I didn't know what that meant. Was Ghost part of me now? Was he my wolf? Was this what Nico felt when he said his wolf was speaking to him?

"I can help, but it must be your choice. Do you wish to keep Ghost with you?"

Of course I did. "Yes."

Zephyr smiled, breathing a sigh of relief. "Then you need to step back, Nico."

At his snap, it felt as if I was being squeezed through a soft portal, and then I wasn't on two feet but four.

"Holy shit," Nico breathed, his eyes wide. "That's not... She's a—"

Zephyr shushed him. Shaking myself, I stretched my shoulders, feeling an unfamiliar weight there. You know, it was probably better if I didn't see myself right away.

"What in the fucking dragon wolf is that?" Theo said, and I could only guess he was talking about me.

Ghost?

Zephyr and Aemon and Bael gave you pieces of themselves to save us. We look a bit different.

It seemed like I would be getting to a mirror soon enough, but first...

Desmond's Fae stink filled my nose and I found him trying

to get away from the battle. Hannah had him by the ankle, his bone crushed in her hand as Fiona bombarded him with her magic. Flesh burned and screaming, he tried to claw away, but not from either of them. Malia held onto his head, her hands glowing as she poured something into him as he tried to bat her away with his one good arm.

"You like pain?" she snarled in his face. "This is all the pain you caused. Fucking choke on it."

I'd have felt sorry for him, but I damn near died, so my pity was shot for the time being. Desmond had taken so much from so many people.

A growl filled my—our—belly.

Ghost?

Lunch, my queen?

Yeah.

With the moon overhead and the battle still raging, it was lunchtime.

CHAPTER 21

NICO—SIX MONTHS LATER

IT TOOK TIME TO GET USED TO THE NEW NORMAL AND even more time for Wren to get used to shifting. For one, she wasn't a wolf—or at least she wasn't all wolf. Zephyr, along with his brothers Aemon and Bael, and I used our essence to merge Wren with Ghost. In doing so, it put little pieces of us in her, too.

The only place Wren could shift was up in the mountains in secluded spots and a few pockets of Savannah. Wolves were sneaky and could blend in. The midnight-blue, winged, scaled, fire-breathing smoke monster of a wolf that was now Wren's other form?

Not so much.

There wasn't a place in Savannah she could hide, except for a small clearing hidden from prying eyes, being three braided oaks at the back of Forsyth Park.

There, she learned to fly, learned to shift, learned to be.

But tonight was special in more ways than one.

A flame hot enough to melt a car shot into the sky, heating the cool air up a bit. It was winter in Savannah, and though that didn't mean much being so far south, the nip in the air was noticeable. That was one of many bonuses to the fire power that Wren now had.

That and she was damn near indestructible. Nothing could get past those scales, and if it did, well, she'd turn into smoke or fly away or... honestly, she could be a little scary if she wanted to be.

I fucking loved it.

A moment later, Wren stood on two feet, her jeans and sweater no worse for wear in the change. It irked me a little bit that shifting came so easy to her. It took me years before I figured out how to take clothes with me and even longer to figure out how to stay clothed when I came back.

Shifter houses made for a lot of accidentally naked people sometimes.

"Is it almost time?" she asked, cutting through what had once been the Bannister ancestral well. There were no ghosts here anymore, but Wren still liked the place.

It still gave me the creeps.

"Yeah," I said, grabbing her hand in mine. "They'll be back in about an hour. You ready?"

Wyatt and Tristan were due back today, the information a gift from the Seelie Queen herself. She'd shown up about a week after the battle, quelling nerves and smoothing the rough edges of the aftermath.

Desmond was dead, and most of the Fae around town were

celebrating. It was possible that there was no other choice but for them to be happy, and at the moment, I just didn't care. The Fae were now someone else's problem, and unless they made it mine, I was staying out of it.

Áine seemed to have the lot well in hand, but she would be going home soon and leaving her bastard of a son in charge. That was if he followed through with the deal he made, and Wren didn't eat him first.

"Yep. I just needed to get my wiggles out. Ghost was getting restless."

Wren was restless a lot these days.

Her ABI contract was still "processing," and until they got their heads out of their asses, Wren was in limbo. I understood the problem from both sides. She was an Alpha's mate, a brand-new shifter, and the product of a demon deal. Just one of those things disqualified her from service, but all three?

She was an insurance nightmare.

Wren just wanted her books cleared and to move on. With all she'd done for Savannah, you'd think someone higher up on the food chain would have gotten the lead out. But I had a feeling she wished she could do something that was just hers.

"Come on. I want to show you something."

We strode together through Forsyth down to the parking lot, and I took her to the one place I'd been dying to all day. If today went as planned, I knew the ABI would allow Wren to cancel her contract. With returning that many missing agents, it was a no-brainer. But Wren needed something all on her own.

And maybe she would want friends with her.

"Keep them closed, Bird. If you ruin this surprise..."

"Yeah, yeah, yeah. You'll turn me over your knee. If I've told you once, I've told you a thousand times. Quit threatening me with a good time."

Truth be told, I'd turn her over my knee just because she liked it, but I didn't want to spoil the surprise. I parked on Broad Street and guided her down the treacherous stairs that led to our first meeting. But unlike then, she didn't so much as stumble on the cobblestones.

"Why in high holy hell are you taking me down to the Walk tonight of all nights?"

"It's a surprise, woman."

Grumbling, she kept her eyes closed until we stopped at the very building that was now in her name and her name alone.

"Open them."

Azalea Apothecary had once held this very spot. After it burned down, another apothecary took its place, but the people of Savannah didn't take to it, putting it out of business. Now it was a new building, one that would likely stand the test of time.

Wren's green-gold eyes focused on the blue building, her gaze zeroing in on the sign. The white "Midnight Investigations" sign was brilliant against the midnight-blue paint, highlighting the name for all the world to see.

"I'd originally thought of Bird Investigations, but Fiona and Ellie vetoed it."

Wren's mouth opened and closed as hope bloomed in her expression.

"The building is yours. Just yours. The business is yours. You can tear it down or build it up, but I think what you love about the ABI can still be in your life, even—"

Wren's smile was a touch evil. "Even if they fire me tomorrow?"

I wrapped my index finger around her pinky. "Yeah. Plus, I wanted you to have something that was just yours."

"I love it. Plus, the ABI in this town leaves a lot to be desired—especially without its best agents. This is..." She sighed like the relief was just hitting her. "Perfect."

"Want to see inside?"

Giggling, Wren dragged me by the hand, unlocking the door with a snap of her fingers. She studied every nook and cranny, loving the reception desk and offices, but when she turned back to look at me, she found me on one knee.

I wasn't nervous. I'd been married to Wren in my mind for years. But it always irked me that in the confusion of our mating, I'd never really asked her.

"Wren Adelaide Acosta, will you be my wife?"

Her irises flashed gold. "I'm already your wife."

"Is that a yes then?"

"Ask me like you did the first time. I know what it means now."

I pulled the velvet box from my pocket, opening it to reveal the sapphire that now matched the color of her animal.

"Tell me you want this. Tell me you're mine. Tell me you want me."

"I do," she whispered, and that was all I needed to hear.

WE WERE MORE THAN A LITTLE LATE TO THE GATE AT Chatham Square. Okay, we were fifteen minutes late, rumpled, and a teensy bit fuck drunk, but luckily Wyatt and the motley crew were also running behind. Áine stood beside the door opposite my mother, Theo, Erica, and a small assortment of pack and Fae alike.

I'd had feelings about Erica and Áine being here, but they'd both insisted.

"Oh, good, right on time," Áine cooed, her smile not the least bit sarcastic. "I knew you'd be a little late today, so I padded the timeline a bit."

Nope, not touching that.

Three minutes later, the door that we'd been waiting six months to open creaked wide. Wyatt's blond head came out first, followed by a sea of women in various states of injury. Some walked of their own accord, and some were carried on makeshift stretchers. Tristan was the last one out, carrying a small woman with no hair and as thin as a rail.

Erica whistled and a team of medics descended, escorting them away so they could be cared for, so they could regain their lives, so they could actually breathe. After the last woman was handed off, Tristan approached my wife, his forearm still burned.

"I've fulfilled your bargain," he snarled. "Take it off."

Wren's smile only served to piss him off. "To you it's been half a day. You wish to be free so soon? What if someone wanted to find you?"

Tristan waved his arm in front of her face. "Then they'd summon me themselves," he ground out. "Take it off."

She latched onto his arm, making Tristan's face pale. "You have brought me every missing woman?"

He gulped. "Yes."

Wyatt seemed no worse for wear, either. Considering Desmond was dead, the resistance at his castle had probably been nil.

"Very well." She let him go and snapped her fingers, the burn melting away instantly. "Talk to your mother. She misses you."

With that, the Fae contingent was dismissed. Erica met my eyes over the heads of my pack, her gaze landing on Wren and then flitting back to me. The ABI would let her go tomorrow with her years paid in full. Erica's gaze fell on Fiona as well. Erica knew all about who really opened the Hell gate, no matter what Zephyr passed it off as.

By the look on her face, someone else in the ABI might know as well.

But that was a problem for another day.

My pack was whole, Wren was safe, and soon things would finally calm down.

Eventually.

THE END

This concludes The Wrong Witch Series.
Thank you so much for reading. I can't express just how much I have adored writing Wren & Nico and their ragtag bunch of friends.

However, if you would love to see a special glimpse of Wren & Nico many years later, turn the page for an epic Wrong Witch Bonus Scene. I hope you enjoy it!

*If you loved Wren & Nico and would like to see more from the Acosta pack, stay tuned for **Curses & Chaos** and all the crazy, witchy shenanigans that is to come. I hope you're buckled in to see Fiona contend with the aftermath of her Hell gate snafu, life as a witchy mob princess, and her sinfully hot, totally clueless mate.*

Want the skinny on future releases without having to follow me absolutely everywhere on social media?
Text "LEGION" to (844) 311-5791

BONUS SCENE

Dear Reader,

I hope you enjoyed The Wrong Witch Series. Wren & Nico have a very special place in my heart, and I am absolutely ecstatic for you to read more about them.

I have an extra special bonus scene for you as a thank you for reading. All you have to do is click the link below, sign up for my newsletter, and you'll get an email giving you access!

SIGN UP HERE:
https://geni.us/ee-bonus

CURSES & CHAOS
The Lost Witch Book One

If the ABI finds me, I'm dead.

Agent or not, when your dad is the head of the most notorious arcane crime family in the country, no one believes you when you say you didn't open that gate to Hell on purpose.

Now, I'm practically glued under enough null wards to hide a god and stuck with a stupidly sexy shifter of a jailer who hates my guts.

When my former employer comes sniffing around, not only does he keep me alive, but we find out that our pasts are far more connected than either of us realize.

And the lies we've been told could kill us both.

Grab Curses & Chaos today!

Want more in the Arcane Souls World? Check out...

DEAD TO ME

Grave Talker Book One

Meet Darby. Coffee addict. Homicide detective. Oh, and she can see ghosts, too.

There are only three rules in Darby Adler's life.

One: Don't talk to the dead in front of the living.

Two: Stay off the Arcane Bureau of Investigation's radar.

Three: Don't forget rules one and two.

With a murderer desperate for Darby's attention and an ABI agent in town, things are about to get mighty interesting in Haunted Peak, TN.

Grab Dead to Me today!

Want more in the Arcane Souls World? Check out...

NIGHT WATCH
Soul Reader Book One

I'm a killer. He's a bounty hunter. A match made in Hell. Literally.

Waking up at the foot of your own grave is no picnic... *especially when you can't remember how you got there.*

A year ago, I was a college senior still living with my parents. Now? I'm the boogeyman of Ascension, TN, snapping up rogues and draining them dry.

That is until I'm ensnared by a mysterious bounty hunter whose blood and body I crave.

We'll likely kill each other once it's all said and done, but until then, he's bound to keep me on the straight and narrow.

Unless I can convince him to follow me to the dark side. *What? We have cookies over here.*

Grab *Night Watch* today!

THE ROGUE ETHEREAL SERIES

an adult urban fantasy series by Annie Anderson

Enjoy the The Wrong Witch Series?
Then you'll love Max!

Come meet Max. She's brash. She's inked. She has a bad habit of dying... *a lot.* She's also a Rogue with a demon on her tail and not much backup.
This witch has a serious bone to pick.

Check out the Rogue Ethereal Series today!

To stay up to date on all things Annie Anderson, get exclusive access to ARCs and giveaways, and be a member of a fun, positive, drama-free space, join The Legion!

facebook.com/groups/ThePhoenixLegion

ACKNOWLEDGMENTS

A huge, honking thank you to Shawn, Barb, Jade, Angela, Heather, Kelly, and Erin. Thanks for the late-night calls, the endurance of my whining, the incessant plotting sessions, the wine runs... (*looking at you, Shawn.*)

Basically, thanks for putting up with my bullshit while I recovered and clawed my way out of post-surgery brain fog.

Every single one of you rock and I couldn't have done it without you.

About the Author

Annie Anderson is the author of the international bestselling Rogue Ethereal series. A United States Air Force veteran, Annie pens fast-paced Urban Fantasy novels filled with strong, snarky heroines and a boatload of magic. When she takes a break from writing, she can be found binge-watching The Magicians, flirting with her husband, wrangling children, or bribing her cantankerous dogs to go on a walk.

To find out more about Annie and her books, visit www.annieande.com

- facebook.com/AuthorAnnieAnderson
- x.com/AnnieAnde
- instagram.com/AnnieAnde
- amazon.com/author/annieande
- bookbub.com/authors/annie-anderson
- goodreads.com/AnnieAnde
- pinterest.com/annieande
- tiktok.com/@authorannieanderson
- patreon.com/annieanderson

Made in the USA
Monee, IL
09 March 2025

13724421R00395